WHITE CLOUDS ON THE HORIZON

DEBORAH TADEMA

Published by Tate Publishing & Enterprises, LLC
127 E. Trade Center Terrace | Mustang, Oklahoma 73064 USA
1.888.361.9473 | www.tatepublishing.com

Tate Publishing is committed to excellence in the publishing industry. The company reflects the philosophy established by the founders, based on Psalm 68:11,
"The Lord gave the word and great was the company of those who published it."

Cover design by Gian Philipp Rufin
Interior design by Jomel Pepito

Published in the United States of America

ISBN: 978-1-63268-526-1
1. Fiction / General
2. History / General
14.09.10

1

1789. "Run! Winda run, hide!" Her mother pushed her toward the trees but Winda clung desperately onto her sleeve. "Hurry little one, before they see you." Winda's tiny hand was ripped from the security of her mother with a forcefulness that she had never known before. Her mother pushed her again. Winda ran across the clearing in her Cree village and into the woods as fast as her legs could go.

"Do not look back," her mother called to her.

Branches slapped at her face, roots tried to trip her, bushes grabbed at her ankles as she ran. Winda followed a woman who carried a baby in her arms. The woman tripped and dropped her baby which landed on a rock, its lifeless body draped over it face down. Winda heard the thud of the arrow as it pierced into the woman's neck and watched as her blood spurted out with every heartbeat. Winda forced herself to run.

She didn't stop until she reached the river and hid behind a big rock. Winda gasped for air and tried to ease the pain in her chest. It seemed a long time before she dared to look over the rock. Winda could see the flames through the trees as her beloved Cree village burned. She stifled a scream when her best friend was hit in the back with an arrow as she rushed toward her. Tears ran down Winda's face while she watched her friend struggle on the ground until there was no life left in her body.

Warriors came through the smoke toward her, one with his arrow aimed at her heart. An ugly sneer spread across his scarred face as he came within a few yards of her. He pulled back on his bow ready to strike.

A younger warrior walked confidently through the trees and held up his hand. "Stop," he said in Ojibwa. "I want this one."

Scar Face turned, his expression turning dark and deadly. "I will kill this one." He pulled back further on his bow. "They all die today."

"No!" The other man stepped in between Winda and certain death. He faced the other man. "I ask for this one," he said as he turned and looked Winda over then back at his friend. "She is to be my slave."

Scar Face grinned wickedly at Winda and then lowered his weapon. "That will be good. We need more slaves, women slaves." He nodded to the younger warrior and walked away.

The second man lifted her up and held her close to his chest. Winda could smell the sweat and felt his hard chest as she struggled to get free. He only laughed and squeezed her tighter. Winda held in a sob as his fingers dug deep into her arm. "You call me Pakwis," he told her before he set her on the ground and took her hand in a vice-like grip. As they walked back through the trees, other Ojibwa warriors greeted her captor and poked at her until he fended them off. Winda wanted to close her eyes but couldn't. She had never seen so many of her people dead like this before. Her uncle was speared to a tree, his scalp without his full head of grey hair. She could hear the screams of a woman as three men dragged her behind a bush. Valuable items and food were set in a pile in the clearing. Every wigwam was ablaze.

Pakwis stood her beside a nine summers old boy named Little Fox. He cried while he stood there and watched the warriors celebrate. *Be brave,* Winda wanted to tell him, *do not let them know you are afraid.* That was what her father had taught her. Winda wiped the tears out of her eyes and looked around for her parents. She held her breath when the warrior with the scar on his face approached. Little Fox wet his pants and watched as it ran down onto his moccasins. The warrior took out his knife and slashed the boy's throat.

1800. Late spring, eleven years later. A fierce wind blew across the lake and headed westward along the dunes. It followed the river as it wound through the hills covered with pine, spruce, maple and ash trees. Snow and sleet whipped around the small Ojibwa village that nestled in the valley. It was in a territory that the Hudson's Bay Company owned called Rupert's Land, a land that the Ojibwa still occupied as a free people.

Winda sat close to the fire and watched the lodge billow in and out. Behind her, sacks of food and clay pots swung on their hooks. Wind howled through the cracks in the walls. She pulled the buffalo robe tighter around her shoulders and watched the door, waiting for Pakwis to return, hoping that he wouldn't.

"Our husband will not return tonight," Lanick told her from across the fire. "He has gone hunting."

Winda put another log on the fire before she looked over at Pakwis's first wife. "He told you this but did not say anything to me?"

Lanick shrugged. "Surprising, is it not? You are his favourite"

Winda stirred the fire with a stick and watched the flames. "But I am still his slave."

Lanick let out a snort. "Not as far as he is concerned. He loves you, you know."

"He has never told me," Winda shot at her. "Just because he saved my life a long time ago..." she let that hang.

"I can tell. It is you he wants in his bed, not me. And that is my wish; then he leaves me alone."

"But, you are his true wife, I'm just the one," she lowered her head, "the one he shares his bed with." Winda looked back up at the other woman. "I did not have a say in it," she said with disdain. "All I want is to leave this hateful place and find my true people." The sharp sting on her face from Lanick's slap made her gasp. Winda put her hand on her cheek and fought back the tears.

"Do not make such talk again," Lanick hissed as she lowered her hand to her lap and glanced at the door, "he might hear."

"He is hunting." Winda inched away from the door just in case. "He cannot hear."

They both looked around when a gust of wind rocked the walls. One of the sacks burst open the grain poured out. Winda stood up, got a clay pot and held it underneath until the sack was empty. She set it on the ground and then sat back down by the fire.

"Your village does not exist anymore," Lanick continued, "and just because you did not have a wedding ceremony like I did, does not make you less a wife. Now, you need to go out and get us some more water and firewood."

Winda glowered at the older woman. "You send me out in this storm?"

Lanick's sneer widened as she crossed her arms under her chest. "I am first wife, you are just a slave. You will obey my order."

A hundred miles to the east in a town called York, a civilized land in Upper Canada, an oil lamp sat on a mahogany table between two friends in a two story, white house. Three candles placed around the room created shadows on the walls. A settee stood along the opposite wall from the women. A small fire flickered in the fireplace in front of them to take the chill out of the air. Statuettes adorned the mantle. Small scatter rugs covered the highly polished wood floor. Gertrude Paterson stretched out her legs to warm her toes. She glanced around the room with a satisfied smile at the paintings her husband, Anthony, collected.

Gert sat back in her dark green, wing-backed chair and admired the patchwork quilt she had just finished. It sported rich colours of blue, burgundy and grey. As far as she was concerned the effect was stunning. She set down her teacup and turned to her friend, Dorothy. "I think this is the best one I've done yet."

Dorothy nodded, a sad expression in her eyes. "It's too bad about your niece though. I can't imagine what she must be going through right now."

"Nor I, marrying a man you've never even met before." Gert sipped her tea and then sighed. "Anthony told me about the arrangement just a week ago and it still makes my stomach turn." She offered her friend a homemade blueberry tart. "So, now I'll give this quilt to Carrie instead of donating it to the church bazaar."

Dorothy nodded as she took a bite. "These are scrumptious, as usual." She chewed slowly then sipped on her tea. "That doesn't allow much time to prepare for a wedding." She leaned forward. "What does Mary say about it? Surely she could put a stop to it."

"Well, you know Mary; she has as much backbone as a mouse. I think she's afraid of Ivan." Gert popped a tart into her mouth.

"He does order her around like she's his servant, I've seen him." Dorothy patted Gert's arm. "I know you don't like your brother-in-law."

Gert nodded as she swallowed. "Don't get me wrong, Dorothy, I love my sister. I've tried to talk sense into both of them, but Ivan is quite adamant that this wedding will take place." She picked up her cup and sat back in her overstuffed chair. "I don't know why Mary would marry a man like that in the first place," she said with an exaggerated sigh.

Dorothy put down her empty cup and stood. "I must be going dear; before it gets too dark."

Gert walked her to the front door and handed Dorothy her coat and umbrella. "It's still raining. Shall I get Anthony to escort you home?"

"Oh no, it's not that far." Dorothy opened the door. "Look, it's slowing down."

Gert watched her splash across the muddy street and down the other side. The door shut with a soft click. She picked up the lantern and blew out the candles one at a time before she started up the stairs. With her free hand she pulled herself up by the rail and then stopped halfway to catch her breath. Gert knew she needed to lose some weight; she had gained it slowly throughout their marriage of twenty-nine years. Her husband had never said anything to her about it for which she was grateful. She did keep her dark brown hair up in a tight bun as was the fashion. Gert also made sure her dress apparel was up to date as well. Today, she wore a light blue dress with a lace collar and copper buttons. Even this dress was starting to get a bit too snug on her. On her feet were new black boots that hadn't been broken in yet and gave her blisters. She rubbed her tired brown eyes when she rested again at the top of the stairs.

Halfway down the hall she looked at a picture of her and Anthony just after their wedding. In it, he looked up at her with such love in his eyes. She let out a chuckle. The photographer had been upset with him. "Everybody looks right at the camera," Anthony had told him, "and nobody smiles."

She headed toward the light that filtered under the door at the end of the hall. It creaked when she opened it. "That late already?" Anthony asked when he looked up from his ledger. He smiled and pushed his reading glasses up with an ink stained finger.

"Dorothy just left." She set the lantern down on a small table by the window and noticed that the wind had picked up again. The wooden chair creaked when she sat down on it. Gert faced her husband's large oak desk. The usual clutter of papers, inkwells, pens and books were piled around a small clearing in front of

Anthony. She watched him bend over, deep in concentration, and felt a sense of admiration and pride for his dedication to his work.

Anthony was shorter than most men. His light coloured hair had started to turn grey at the temples. He squinted his hazel eyes at the book before him. Stubby fingers held the pen tight as he filled in columns of the ledger with numbers.

How he could work in such a mess, she didn't know. She allowed her eyes to travel up above his head to a large painting on the wall. It was a ship almost hidden in the large swells of the sea; the sails tattered from the gale force wind. It seemed cold and lonely to Gert, but it was Anthony's favourite painting.

The small room was crowded with furniture. A wall-to-wall bookcase stood behind her, stacked full of papers and books. A filing system was against the wall beside her, across from the window and beside the door. Gert noticed that the room had started to get chilly. The logs in the fireplace had burned down to coals.

Anthony closed the big, black ledger with a thump and looked up at his wife. "I found out something that disturbs me very much." He shook his head and frowned. "It doesn't feel right at all." He looked soberly at Gert, took off his glasses, and set them carefully on the desk. Gert sat up and gave him her full attention.

Anthony turned down his sleeves and undid the top two buttons on his shirt. "Ivan, it turns out, has deposited a large sum of money in my bank."

Gert's eyes widened in astonishment. "But, he doesn't have any money."

"Exactly!"

The next morning, Anthony watched through the front window as a small battalion dismounted in front of his bank. Some of the men went across the street into the hardware and grocery stores. A major he hadn't seen before walked into the bank and tipped his wide-brimmed black hat at the ladies. He then stood near the door, tall and straight. Sandy-coloured hair that matched his trim moustache stuck out from under his hat. He tugged down on his blue uniform coat. A smile spread across his tanned face when the bank owner stepped up to him with an outstretched hand.

"Major." Anthony shook the large calloused hand. "Come; let's go into my office, shall we?" He led the officer through the lobby and into a small room in the back. Anthony shut the door behind them and felt more nervous by the minute. He wondered if the major was there to investigate Ivan and the money that was now in the safe. Sweat beaded on his brow as he offered the man one of his finest cigars. His guest accepted one with a smile, took off his hat, and set it on a pile of papers. Anthony struck a wooden match to the side of his desk and held the flame out while the man puffed.

"Aren't you having one?" the major asked as he pulled out a chair and flopped down.

"Oh no." Anthony slid into his chair behind the desk. "They make me sick, truth be told." He looked at the officer straight in the eyes. If Ivan got this bank into trouble, he would personally put a bullet between his eyes, even though he had never handled a gun before.

"I'm Major Grant Sievers of the Twelfth Militia," the man said as he pulled a piece of paper out of his coat pocket. "I have a draft here so we can pick up supplies for my men."

Anthony let out his breath he didn't know he had been holding. Relieved, he studied the note. The signature on the bottom of the page said it came from General Brooks, a man that Anthony had dealt with before. It wasn't a large sum; his bank could handle it easily enough. "Yes, of course, Major." He rose on wobbly legs and walked over to the safe. His hands trembled as he took out a small pile of bills and handed them over. "I didn't know the militia was around these parts. Is there trouble?"

"Not here, yet anyway." Grant took a puff. "We're heading south. There's been some raiding and killing."

"I didn't know we were having problems with the Indians again?" Anthony wrote out a bill for the loan, adding interest and a service charge, then folded it into three.

"We're not, at least anything as serious as this. The Americans want to take over Upper Canada." Grant took a long drag from the cigar. "It seems that when one war ends, another one starts up with someone else."

Anthony sealed the letter with red sealing wax. He then imprinted the wax with the bank's stamp then handed the letter to the major. "I agree, Major. And we think the Indians are the savages. Now we have to tame the Americans as well." He pulled at his collar that threatened to suffocate him. "What about the Indians? Who do you think they will fight for?"

Grant took another inhale of tobacco and blew the smoke over Anthony's head. "I don't know. Guess we'll just have to wait and see." Anthony coughed and gave the major a wary look. Grant picked up his hat and stood.

Anthony walked the major to the door. "What about the British troops? Where are they?"

"As you know, the French will protect Lower Canada. The British troops are mostly guarding their forts. They're building new ones at both ends of Lake Erie." Grant put his hat back on. "Thank you, sir." The major patted the pocket where the money was and left the bank.

Anthony watched Major Sievers hand over some of the money to his sergeant then hop on his horse and ride off with the cigar in his mouth. The sergeant ran back into the stores presumably to pay for the supplies. Anthony thought for sure Ivan was in trouble some how. Blast him! He walked back into his office and shut the door.

But it wasn't just Ivan he was worried about. Anthony had become rich by swindling money out of people. He would wait until his clients were near death, too sick to investigate him. He'd counsel them, as their financial adviser, into giving large donations for charities that never saw it. And Gert thought he made his money by investing wisely.

After he let out a long breath of relief he went over to the sideboard and poured himself a stiff drink. He then flopped back into his chair. "I need this," he told the glass.

"I did not sleep well all night long," Lanick complained as she sat up with her buffalo robe wrapped around her. "I am hungry and cold. That constant wind out there and the dripping in here is enough to make me scream."

"No one will hear you, so why bother." Winda put more logs on the fire. "I have already been out and got more wood to keep you warm. Is it not enough?"

"That is the last of our meat," Lanick said while she pointed to two sacks near the wall. "Our husband is not a good provider."

"He is stuck someplace. Would you travel in this weather?" Winda poured hot water into two cups. She handed one to Lanick, picked up her own cup, and sipped the weak elderberry tea. "I hope this is the last storm of the season. I could not see the lodge next to us through all that blowing rain and snow this morning."

"A person could get lost in this," Lanick said as she watched Winda closely.

Winda ignored the undercurrent of that statement. Instead she looked up at the walls that billowed in and out and at the water that dripped all around them. She could see the shadow of the big rotting tree on the wall bend and twist in the wind. Soon, she thought, it could break. All she did was pray to her spirits, as she had done all night that it would not land on their wigwam.

The spirits were not kind this time. Suddenly Winda heard a huge cracking sound. She jumped up, grabbed her coat, and headed toward the door. "Get the meat," Lanick ordered as she picked up some of her belongings. "That old tree is coming down." Winda tried to push Lanick out the door but the older woman blocked her. "Get the sacks, I'm hungry."

Winda ran to the other side of the wigwam and reached down for the sacks. Another crack sounded from overhead. The branch ripped through the hide walls. Winda was knocked to her knees as it crashed down beside her with a loud thump. Snow and freezing rain rushed down on top of her. She grabbed her coat but it was stuck under the branch so she left it as she climbed out with the sacks.

"Lanick!" Winda tried to see through the branches but all she saw was that the fire had spread with the sudden gust. The wind blew it toward Lanick who lay on the ground under a large limb. "Lanick, watch out!"

The older woman did not move.

Winda climbed over a huge branch to go around the tree. She found a buffalo robe in the snow and wrapped it around her and still shivered as she tried to get to Lanick. A scream stuck in her throat when the wind spread the fire. Winda watched as the flames consumed the body.

Winda fought her way through the blizzard and dodged fires that had spread from campfires. She called for help but there was no answer. Tears were wiped away as she called again. She didn't see anyone as she made her way through the village. It was her time to escape, she decided. Once past the lodges she pushed her way along the bottom of the valley, dodged trees as they swayed viciously back and forth and debris that flashed by in a blur. Behind a large rock she ducked down and wrapped the buffalo robe around her to wait out the storm.

Five mornings after, sunlight in her eyes woke Winda. She blinked up at it and took out some dried meat from a sack and chewed on it slowly. When she finished, she wiped the grease from her hands on her deer skin dress. Shaky legs took her weight when she stood. A stitch ran up her back, but she was able to ignore it. She picked up her sacks and a spear she had found earlier.

Winda walked on melting snow, dead leaves, and pine needles from maple, pine, spruce, and many other trees that dripped on her as she walked under them. She stopped by a small stream, and then she sank to the ground and lifted hands full of cold water into her mouth. More was splashed onto her face and she felt alive and free for the first time in her life.

Winda checked behind her and didn't see any signs that anyone was following her. For several miles she picked her way along the fast stream. It would hide her footprints, just in case. On numb, soaked feet, she climbed onto the opposite bank. That evening two sticks stuck into the ground held her moccasins over a small fire to dry them out. A rice cake did for her evening meal.

2

A small band of Ojibwa trudged along the flat open grassland many days later. Men, women, and children led dogs that pulled travois beside a fast flowing river. Dirty faces watched their holey moccasins as they staggered through the tall grass and sandy soil. A small boy clutched at his empty stomach. They didn't know it but they had stumbled from Rupert's Land into Upper Canada.

Pakwis watched the survivors of the storm pass by him. He was Chief now. He was responsible for these people. Guilt plagued his soul. The signs of a bad storm had been there, he had seen the dark clouds. He felt the strong winds. He felt it in his bones! They had hunted during storms before. All they would do was find shelter and wait until it blew over, then continue on their way.

No one could remember such a wicked storm, and so late in the season. This one would definitely make a legend of its own. Overnight his band had turned from sixty-six to twenty-three people. He should have stayed home. He could have saved his family. Pakwis and three others had left that morning. The sun was over the horizon then. By the afternoon grey clouds had blown in from the north-west. He should have returned home then. Instead, they kept on. When the full blast swirled down on them, they took shelter behind a narrow ledge on the lee side of a cliff. One man slipped and fell into the icy river below. It took them a long time to find his body afterward and carry it home.

A child fell in front of him and didn't even cry. Probably too tired and hungry, poor thing didn't have the energy. One of the women stopped and helped the little girl up and gave him a somber look. Pakwis didn't know where he was leading his people yet. All he wanted to do was to have the Place-of-Sorrows behind them and start anew.

He remembered the first time he saw his village after the storm. Only five wigwams stood whole and untouched. Two others had gaping holes in the sides. The rest were gone. The wood frame, birch-bark, and hide structures never had a chance against such a force. All the other dwellings either burned down or blew away. Three were crushed under huge trees. Litter had covered the entire area. Precious belongings were scattered all over. Clothing, pots, sacred items and sacks of food that had been soaked through were now mouldy. Branches and tree trunks blocked access to the people that lay crushed to death in their homes. Everything was soaking wet.

The three hunters had looked for survivors, searched where each lodge should have been. Pakwis heard his friend Night Wind's howl when he found his pregnant wife's body. A branch stuck out of her chest, a look of surprise on her face. His daughter's lifeless body was underneath a pile of debris. Stealth Man had lost both of his parents. They still had their arms around each other locked in time from when their fire whooshed all over them in a sudden gust. Their wigwam burned down around them. Their bodies weren't recognizable but the beads, shells, and coloured stones they wore were.

Pakwis had stumbled over to where his own home should have been and found charred remains of one body. He couldn't identify the blackened corpse that had shrivelled up into a ball.

He had searched for his other wife with no results, not knowing which one was still alive. But as the days passed by, he came to the conclusion that Lanick would stay close, and Winda would run. He wiped a tear away before anyone saw it.

For a second, he thought he should track her down and bring her back home. Then he decided not to. His people needed him there, now that he was Chief. His responsibilities kept him with his band, at least until they were settled again. He had helped pull out the bodies, his own wife included. They had built platforms and put them in the trees because there were not enough men to dig so many graves. The ground was still frozen anyway, this way was quicker. They prayed for all the dead, then left.

A woman walked by and stumbled. He reached out and steadied her. "Thank you, Pakwis." She smiled at him with a dirt-smudged face.

"You are welcome, Little Blossom." He walked beside her, following the line of people. Her sad, brown eyes watched the back of the person in front of her. She was pretty under all that mud with high cheek bones and full lips, slender and shapely. A handsome woman, he decided. But not as exciting to look at as Winda! Lanick, he remembered had a straight, dull body that she denied him after he took Winda as a second wife. He had only married her out of obligation to his clan and soon regretted it. She complained and whined about everything. He just didn't have the patience for her anymore.

He watched the woman beside him. She had lost her husband and two young boys in the storm. Pakwis tried to comfort her as they walked. "We will start a new life, Little Blossom. You will see. Things will get better." He didn't sound believable, not even to himself. The spirits just weren't with them anymore.

Light fluffy clouds floated across the sky. The sun drifted in and out, playing hide-and-seek. Winda sat on top of a small hill and looked out over the valley below. She inhaled the musty scent after a spring shower. What a beautiful day! The snow was gone. The trees were in bud. Wild flowers poked up through the ground at her feet. A noisy flock of geese flew northward overhead. Low, ground fog spread out along the valley bottom below her like a misty buffalo robe.

Her stomach growled. Four days ago her food had run out. Fourteen days since the storm. Empty sacks hung on her belt. Yesterday, she had been lucky enough to catch a small fish. The sun poked out again as she scanned the valley below. A dark shape floated toward her in the mist. She squinted to see. Winda took her spear and crept along the ridge to get behind the strange being. A light breeze blew up from the valley bottom from the south, the fog slowly dissipating.

The ghostly shape emerged as a young doe. She watched it walk along as it ate at the new shoots of grass. Winda stopped and held her breath when it lifted its head up to check for predators. Her heart pounded, sounded loud in her own ears. Sweat dripped down into her eyes. The doe looked right at her and froze. They stared at each other. Winda felt it breathe, heard the doe's heart beat and knew its caution. They were as one. The doe lowered its head and continued to pull the shoots out of the ground. The spell broke.

Winda forced herself to take long deep breaths and crept closer. She thanked the spirits that took the wind and her scent up and over the hill behind her. The doe was in range. She lifted her spear. It looked up at her again. Winda stood still and admired the majestic animal in front of her. The weapon pushed down heavy on her arm from high above her head. She thought she saw forgiveness in the doe's eyes. Her arm started to shake, her palm started to sweat. The spear almost slipped from her grasp.

The doe moved. Winda put all of her strength into the thrust of her weapon. She heard the thump when it dug deep into the animal's side and knew when the heart pumped its last beat. And she felt the instant that the beautiful doe gave itself to her. Winda ran down to her kill and prayed to thank the spirits for the gift. She would eat from it, make clothing, and use the bones for tools and sinew to sew with.

Winda pulled her knife out of the sheaf. She split the animal up its stomach and then flipped it onto its side to let the guts fall out. The intestines were removed from the abdominal cavity and set aside. Winda hummed a childhood song to herself while she made a circular cut around the doe's neck. She cut the legs off at the knees. The hind quarters came off next.

After she had all the meat cut up into manageable pieces Winda cooked as much as she could so it wouldn't spoil on her travels. The hide was stretched out on the ground and scraped to remove the blood and fat. Then, she rolled it up and tied it with a string to make clothing from it later. She ate the hot meat as she worked then filled her sacks as full as she could. Afterward Winda walked down to a nearby stream, lifted her bloody dress over her head, washed it, and then laid it out on the ground to dry. She rewarded herself with a leisurely bath. Winda fell asleep on a grassy knoll as dusk fell.

Gert stopped her carriage in front of her sister's house the day before the wedding. Carefully, she retrieved a package from on the seat beside her and stepped down. The plain board house stood at the opposite end of York from where her house was. Here they were smaller and run-down. She noticed that Mary had planted a few flowers by the front step. Already they were wilting from lack of water.

Carrie answered the door and hugged her aunt. "Oh, Aunt Gert, come in. Please sit down." The young girl of sixteen fluttered around the room. "I'll make us some tea," she said as she disappeared into the kitchen.

Mary's home was simple with just enough room for the three of them. A fireplace, built in the middle of the house, separated the kitchen and parlour. Behind it, on the kitchen side, a row of shelves covered the wall. Jars and boxes of food stood beside plates and cups. Tucked up under the slanted roof upstairs were two bedrooms.

Gert set herself down on an old brown chair that needed to be re-upholstered. She looked at the sideboard beside the fireplace. Mary's good dishes were in it, the type that Gert would use for every day. The room was plain and simple with only a few ornaments. One picture hung on the opposite wall that was of a wolf as it stalked an elk in the snow. She likened the wolf to Ivan who she thought of more like the predator.

The items on the tray clinked and rattled as Carrie brought it in and set it down on the table. "It's good of you to come, Aunt Gert. I was hoping you would."

"You know I'm here for you, Carrie." Gert patted the young girl's hand.

Carrie handed Gert her cup then poured one for herself. "I'm so nervous about tomorrow." She sat down next to the front window. "I don't know if I can stand it." Carrie's frightened eyes stared at Gert as she leaned close to her. "What if he's mean?"

"I'm sure your father has your best interest at heart, Carrie." But, she didn't feel that he really did. She was afraid too, for her niece. "Where is your mother now, dear?"

"Oh, she's at Mrs. Candon's place. It's her day to do the cleaning there."

"Oh yes, I forgot." Gert took a sip of her tea. "Are you all set for tomorrow?"

"I guess so. I have my dress. I'm borrowing it from a friend." Carrie's hand shook as she took a sip of tea. "I'm just nervous is all."

Gert handed her niece the package. Carrie squealed in delight and began to tear at the plain brown wrapping paper. "Oh!" She stopped and took a breath. "I better slow down and act all grown up now, shouldn't I?" Delicately she peeled the rest of the paper off and unfolded the quilt. "My, Aunt Gert, this is the best gift I have ever gotten." She bent over and kissed Gert on the cheek. "This is so beautiful. I'll treasure it always." Carrie laid it out across an empty chair and admired the blue, burgundy, and grey pattern that Gert had carefully sewed. "Just for me," she said as she ran a hand over it.

"You're quite welcome, my dear." Gert stood up after she finished her tea. "I'd better get back now. Anthony will be home from work soon."

A sense of foreboding stuck with her for the rest of the day.

Anthony dabbed the sweat from his brow with a handkerchief. He sat beside his wife in the Anglican Church and looked nervously at Gert. "This has got to be the hottest day of the year so far," he complained as he pulled at his collar.

Gert sat on the hard pew and stared at her sister's back as she sucked on her bottom lip and fanned herself. "Yes it is. But I think it's because you are also boiling mad." She adjusted her light blue hat on her head. Even the long feather looked droopy from the heat. It matched perfectly with her new summer dress that she had made for this occasion. She had to pay the seamstress extra to get it done in time. It was a light silk with a row of buttons of the same colour that ran all the way up the front. A small bustle had crunched when she sat in the pew. It wasn't elegant but expensive to her taste and pocket book. She'd paid for it out of the household budget that Anthony gave her every month. He was generous enough that she could afford such luxuries. And as a banker's wife she had to keep up appearances. Gert's lace collar that also matched her cuffs had started to get itchy and she had complained to her husband. She fingered her pearls around her neck in contemplation and frowned at her sister.

Mary sat stiffly in the front row by herself and watched the piano player in the corner. She hadn't moved a muscle in twenty minutes. She wore no hat, only a piece of ribbon tied into a bow over her left ear. Her dress was pale pink with a plain white collar and cuffs. No bustle (as was the fashion).

Anthony checked his pocket watch. "They're late."

Gert nodded slightly and didn't take her eyes off her sister. Mary was very thin with light brown eyes that never seemed to look right at you. She was the nervous sort and jumped and twitched all the time except now. It was like she had forgotten to breathe.

Gert was five years older than Mary and felt that she never really knew her. After she married Anthony they settled in York. They had built up their modest wealth and status through the bank. Mary and Ivan had just moved there four years ago. Ivan had yet to find steady employment. A door to their left opened and the reverend walked in. Gert and Anthony looked at each other in surprise.

"That isn't Reverend Bates. Where is he?" Anthony looked around. "I talked to him yesterday about this wedding. Who is this one?"

Gert watched the man look around nervously. "He looks too rough to be a reverend." This reverend had stubble on his face, dirt in his fingernails and mud on his boots that he tried to hide under his robe.

A big, half-bald man with a scar over his right eye followed the reverend out. He wore new black pants and a grey shirt, no tie, no jacket, only a black waist coat. When he turned to survey the congregation Gert saw that he had a crooked nose. His mean grey eyes passed over the few people in the room with a smug look. He stood beside the reverend, hands clasped in front of him, feet apart. He looked too calm for a groom.

Gert watched the reverend fidget with the sleeves of his robe, who seemed to be at odds with himself. This made her more nervous than she had been earlier. The white robe he wore was elegant satin with gold patterns up both sides and long puffy sleeves. A long scarf sat around the man's neck and hung down in front. It was white and gold with scalloped ends. He adjusted it several times and stopped only when the bald man glared at him. The reverend glanced nervously at the groom and swallowed hard.

Everyone turned to the back of the church to watch Ivan lead his daughter up the steps and down the aisle. Gert looked at him in disgust. He wore his old tattered blue suit that she had seen him in countless times before. Ivan was only slightly taller than she was with medium brown hair that curled around his ears. His blue eyes bore into her when he looked their way. His waxed moustache twitched as he grinned nervously.

"Poor girl," Anthony shook his head as Ivan forced Carrie to the front of the church. "This isn't right at all."

Ivan stopped in front of the reverend and puffed, red faced and out of breath. He gripped his daughter's arm tightly. Carrie stood beside him and trembled in a white dress that was miles too big for her petite frame. She had tripped on it several times when her father dragged her toward the two big men at the front of the church. Her shoulder strap continuously slipped off her left side.

The reverend looked over the congregation. "Reverend Bates is sick. I will perform the ceremony today."

Anthony nodded. "That makes sense."

The reverend bowed his head and led them in a prayer that he read from the Bible.

Gert leaned toward her husband after it was done. "Mary told me just this morning that Ivan and this man have some kind of deal going on."

Anthony looked back at her. His mouth opened then closed. "What do you mean?" he asked a minute later.

"I guess Carrie is part of a payment or security or something. Mary isn't sure just what is going on."

Anthony scowled. "And she couldn't stop this?"

"When she tried, Ivan told her to mind her own business." Gert put her fan down beside her on the bench. "Can you imagine, her own daughter?"

Anthony twisted in his seat and then turned back to his wife. "There's no one on the groom's side."

Gert checked. "That's odd." She looked behind her. "There's only about ten people here."

"Small wedding, isn't it?"

"You are now man and wife!" the reverend pronounced in a loud squeaky voice.

"What?" Gert and Anthony responded at the same time and looked at each other dumbfounded.

"That was fast, wasn't it?" Gert asked.

"Yes, too fast," Anthony said as he stood up to protest. Mary in turn fainted. She landed on the floor in a heap. Ivan strolled over and fanned her with a bible and tapped her cheeks.

The few people that were in the church muttered their disapproval. The reverend wiped the sweat from his face with the scarf from around his neck. Then he used the other end to wipe the back of his neck. Gert watched him in horror. How could he do that? A man of God.

Ivan helped Mary sit back up on the pew. Then he straightened, his harsh gaze sweeping over the congregation. "It's over now," he yelled at the crowd. "Go home."

People glared at the reverend as they filed out of the church. Gert watched the groom back Carrie away with what looked like a painful grip on her arm. Carrie squealed, but he didn't loosen up. His deadly glare stopped anyone who dared approach them.

The church had finally emptied. Ivan lifted Mary from her seat and guided her outside, followed by Carrie still in the vice-like grip of her new husband. Gert and Anthony stood in a daze on the front sidewalk as they watched the four of them walk down the street toward Mary's house.

Anthony put his arm around his wife. "It's too bad," he whispered. "This should have been the happiest day of her life."

Winda clutched the heavy sacks slung over her shoulders as she headed toward a thicket. Purple vetch, windflower, and columbine waved their colourful heads in the light breeze. She hummed a cheerful tune as she walked across a flat meadow in a light rain.

She wanted to head north and try to find her own people, but she feared the Cree were too far away. Just two days ago she had turned eastward to avoid a group of voyagers. Before that she took a wide berth around settlers heading west into Ojibwa land. She wondered where all those white people were coming from. It seemed that more and more crept into their lands.

A pair of bear cubs wandered out of the trees in front of her. She looked at them nervously because she knew the mother would not be far away. The growl behind her told Winda where it was. Slowly, she set her sacks on the ground and turned around. She did not look directly into its beady, brown eyes but just off to the side. It stood up on its hind legs and growled at her with big, pointy, yellow-stained teeth. Its huge paws with long, knife-like claws waved in front of it. She turned slightly to see that the cubs were coming up behind her. There was only one avenue of escape, however slim. She backed up slowly toward a big maple tree and hoped that the bear would stop at her sacks.

Winda grabbed a limb, pulled herself up, and skirted out onto a narrow branch. The bear charged, and then stopped at the base of the tree. A squeal caught in her throat as it stood up. Winda hoped that she was high enough that it wouldn't be able to reach her. She was wrong. It took an angry swipe at her and tore a gash in her leg before she had a chance to lift it higher. She pulled her leg up with her hands just before it took another swing at her with its huge claws.

Unbelievable pain ripped through her leg as it dripped blood onto the ground beneath her. The bear dropped back down on all four paws and sniffed around the tree. The cubs ran up to their mother and it seemed that they played for a bit. Then the bear found her sacks and clawed at them, sat down on its rump and devoured most of the contents. Winda clung to the branches and fought to stay conscious.

As the cubs finished the meat in her sacks the mother returned and took another swipe at her, thankfully it missed this time. Winda's world spun as she tried to climb even higher, out of the bear's reach. It followed. Winda's world went blank.

3

Carrie held in her tears as she rode on the back of a horse behind her new husband, Dusty Blackman. Her honeymoon hadn't been at all what she expected, what she had dreamed it would be like. She had envisioned her husband's loving gaze and soft kisses as they made love. He'd take his time and be gentle with her. Not Dusty. He had ravished her every night since their wedding five days ago.

He pulled on the rope that led the packhorse. Only one of the sacks on it was filled with her belongings. They had followed the east road and then turned north onto a near invisible trail. Carrie's back ached and her bottom was sore from bouncing in the saddle. She wasn't used to riding on a horse all day. Her husband seemed unaffected by their fast pace and wouldn't let her stop and rest in the middle of the afternoon. All she needed was to stretch her legs and get circulation back into them.

Finally, a small cabin came into view through the trees in the middle of the wilderness. It looked dark, lonely and deserted. Except for the wild flowers that had taken over the clearing around the cabin. The golden yellow heads of black-eyed Susan contrasted brightly against the darkened woods behind them.

"Here's your new home, my love," Dusty laughed as they pulled up to the cabin and dismounted. He didn't help Carrie. Her back cracked when she got down off the horse by herself.

He ordered Carrie to help him unpack the supplies. They took a couple of sacks into the cabin and dropped them on the dirt floor. She scurried back out after him and was handed a heavy bag, which she nearly dropped. He frowned at her but turned back to unload more packages.

"You cook up something for supper, I'll tend to the horses," he snapped at her as he gave her the last sack. He grabbed the reins and led the horses into a small coral at the back of the building.

Carrie stepped inside her new home and looked around. It was a one room place with one door and a window, which actually had glass in it. For some reason she was surprised by this. A few dishes and cooking utensils lined the shelves near the door. Spiders and cobwebs were everywhere. A mouse scurried along the wall and disappeared through a hole. The bed sat by the rear wall with one thin blanket on it. In the corner was a pile of rusty and broken trapping gear. A small table with three mismatched chairs around it sat in the middle of the room. A cold and empty stone fireplace took up the remaining wall.

Dusty returned with a bucket of water. Carrie hadn't moved. "Haven't you started cooking yet?" he spat at her. "I'm starved." She looked up at him wide-eyed with fear. He grabbed her by the arm and led her to the stove. "Get moving if you know what's good for you, woman."

She wiped the tears from her cheeks as they spilled from her eyes. Dusty went outside as Carrie slowly turned and searched through the sacks for something, anything to cook for him. She wiped the dust off the dishes then set the table. While the biscuits baked in the big pot, she stirred the beans and then checked out the glass window. Dusty was rubbing down one of the horses, his mouth moved as if talking to it. His hands seemed gentle as he ran it along the horse's flank. She turned back to the stove.

By the time Dusty came back in the table was set. "Smells good," was all he said while he plunked himself down on the nearest chair. He reached over and helped himself to a biscuit, plopped it into his mouth with his filthy hand. Carrie dished out a generous helping of beans onto his plate. He took it from her without comment. After several mouthfuls he looked up at her. "Aren't you eating, darling?"

"Yes," she told him timidly and took a small spoonful of beans. She had a hard time swallowing and almost choked but managed to keep it down. When she reached for a biscuit, his free hand snapped up and grabbed her wrist. Carrie jumped and squealed. Dusty threw back his head and laughed then let go of his grip. He gobbled down the rest of his supper while Carrie ate slowly.

When her husband had finished, he wiped his mouth on his dirty sleeve, pushed back his chair and lit up his pipe. He sat there smoking while she cleared the table and washed the dishes. As she finished up she dried off her hands on a rag. Dusty tapped out his pipe and laid it on the table. Then he patted his lap. "Come here, sweetheart."

The time had come that she dreaded. Carrie forced herself to sit on his lap and put her arms around his neck. He pawed at her breasts; his mouth came down on hers hard. She pushed away and stood up. "Please, Dusty. You're hurting me."

"I'm not."

"You're too rough."

He narrowed his eyes at her. "You want rough. I'll show you rough." He stood up, grabbed her arm, and dragged her over to the bed. "Strip," he told her. Carrie did and then laid back and waited for him to pounce on her. He stood there and looked down into her eyes. In a lighter tone he said, "you're too soft, Carrie."

He undressed before he joined her. She cringed as he pawed her breasts again. When she squirmed under him he hit her. Dusty forced her legs apart and took her, panting like an animal.

He just satisfied himself, rolled off, and went to sleep. Carrie cried silently through most of the night.

Before the sun rose the next morning Dusty pushed her legs open and crawled in between. Carrie tried to push him off and got slapped, again. He entered her sore and bruised body anyway. She lay there stiff and still until he finished. Without a word, he walked out, saddled his horse and rode away.

He didn't tell her where he was going or for how long he planned to be away. Carrie felt like a mule had kicked her. She stayed on the bed and shook, and listened for him for a long time afterward. When she was sure he was truly gone Carrie rolled over and finally slept.

It was dark when Winda opened her eyes to the flames that seem to dance on the rock walls that surrounded her. The only sound she heard was the crackle of dry wood from a nearby fire pit as it sent whiffs of smoke into the air. Panic set in when she realized that she couldn't move. She tried to push up onto her elbows but pain shot through her whole body. Her left leg was the worse. She flopped back down on the bed and groaned.

"Easy there girl," a strange voice told her. She knew some of his language. Pakwis had traded with the English and spoke their language well. The British soldiers had given them blankets and pretty beads, for furs and knowledge about the land and their enemies. "You finally woke up, eh? Well good, good."

A hairy beast walked up to her. Her mind screamed, *bear*! She pushed back and tried to meld into the hard rock behind her, eyes wide in fear.

"Easy; easy there." It held up its hands in surrender, human hands. Slowly Winda started to relax.

A white man stood over her and smiled through a bushy face. "You had me worried, little lady. You slept a long time." He reached down and gently felt her forehead. "Yep, fever's down."

The man stepped back and returned with a cup of water which he held for her so she could drink.

"Are you hungry? I'll get you something to eat." The stranger turned back toward the fire and dished out food from a pot.

"Here, have some rabbit stew. It'll help get your strength back." He helped her to sit up enough so he could spoon feed her from the steaming bowl.

While she ate, Winda studied this strange man. He was tall and thin with long brown hair that also covered his face and hung down to his chest. Bright green eyes sparkled as he watched her eat. He wore a red plaid shirt and grey pants. He carried no weapons on him. She came to the conclusion that he must be a trapper.

His voice was soft and soothing to her which made her relax even more. After she ate, sleep came easily. She felt the man adjust the blanket around her shoulders before she nodded off. When she woke the next morning she vaguely remembered that he said, "Sleep little one, then you won't feel the pain."

Winda drifted in and out for the next few days. When she became fully aware of her surroundings, she was alone. Sunlight filtered through the cave's entrance. Slowly the memory of the strange hairy man surfaced. She smiled, remembering his kind ways and soothing voice. She tried to remember how long had it been since someone had been kind to her. Winda thought hard but couldn't recall. She lifted her head with some effort. Her back ached because she'd laid on it for so long.

She lifted the blanket and widened her eyes. She was naked. Winda's face flushed. *How dare he!* Her eyes travelled down further. More scratches and bruises covered her whole body. He had completely wrapped her left leg in bandages, right down to her ankle. All of the scratches and bruises she had sustained didn't compare to the pain she experienced from this leg. Weakly, she settled back down and pulled the blanket up around her chin. Dizziness set in as she closed her eyes and slept.

Gert and Anthony sat in the parlour after their evening meal and drank tea. "Ivan deposited another fifteen hundred in the bank again today."

Gert looked at her husband, her cup stopped in mid air. "Again, what is he doing?"

"I don't know. He deposits it, then after a few weeks, he withdraws it again."

"Very strange, isn't it? Mary says she doesn't know what he's up to and I believe her." Gert finally sipped her tea. "I don't think she wants to know."

Anthony agreed. "Well, one thing's for sure, it can't be good." He fumbled with his collar, finally released his tie, and threw it on the table. Then he took off his glasses and rubbed his tired eyes. "I think that maybe I should tell the authorities about it. What do you think?"

Gert mulled this over in her mind. "I don't know. We have no proof of any wrongdoing. But at the same time, we know something is going on. I, for one, don't like it. Mary hasn't seen any of this money either. She still has to count her pennies." Gert refilled their cups. "She doesn't even know where Carrie is. She hasn't seen nor heard from her since the wedding." She set her cup down on her lap. "She's positive she saw Carrie's husband talking to Ivan the other day."

Anthony lifted his eyebrows. "If he was here, then why didn't he bring Carrie with him? Surely, he'd let her visit her own mother." He shook his head. "Something definitely is not right. Those two are in it together, I'm sure."

They sat silently for a few minutes. "I was talking to Dorothy this morning. She ran into Reverend Bates earlier. He still doesn't know what happened when Carrie got married. He was in his office reading scripture when someone hit him from behind. When he came to, everything was over with. One of his parishioners found him on the floor and untied him. No one seems to know who the other reverend was. If he's a reverend at all."

"If that's the case, then Carrie isn't even married."

Gert blinked several times.

"I'll see if I can find out about that," Anthony said as he downed the cold tea. He grimaced at the cup. "Right now, I'm tired." He stood. "I'm going to bed. Coming?"

"Yes, just let me clean up the dishes. I'll be right up." Gert picked up the cups and teapot and headed into the kitchen. Anthony made his way up the stairs.

Winda kept her eyes tightly closed until she felt better. After she let out a long slow breath of air, she opened them again. Slow and easy she reminded herself. Blood crept back into her head easing her headache. She had just tried to sit up in a rush; it didn't work.

Carefully, she turned her head and surveyed her surroundings. The cave she found herself in was small. Most of it consisted of dirt and rock. A person would have to watch where they walked or they'd trip on the uneven surface. The man had used some of the rocks that stuck out of the walls as shelves to store food. The coals in the fire pit were glowing with red, orange, and yellow hues. Piles of deer, rabbit, beaver, bear, and other furs hugged the wall to her right. Next to them was an assortment of traps and other gear. Along the other wall was the man's bedding. She could walk across the whole cave in twenty steps.

By the other wall were her two pouches she had tied to a belt around her waist. One had a long tear in it. This pouch carried smaller sacks of roots, dried berries, and herbs. Some of her herbs had spilled onto the floor. The pouch was still full enough that she didn't think she lost much of its contents. The other pouch had her personal things in it, like a hair clip and comb, a cake of soap, a bone needle, sinew for sewing, and other various items she needed for survival.

Winda turned her head toward the cave entrance when she heard whistling. The hairy man came in with an armful of wood and set it down to the left of the doorway. He turned and faced Winda. "You're awake."

After he threw some wood on the fire and made sure it ignited, he walked over to her and squatted down. Winda cringed when he lifted the blanket. He didn't seem to notice her nudity but checked each of her scratches, bumps, and bruises. Lastly, he checked the bandage on her leg. The man grunted, his face had flushed red or what she could see of it through his beard. Her own face had heated up. She tried not to look at that area of his pants when he knelt down in front of her again.

"Looks good," the man told her in a raspy voice. He watched her for several seconds before he pointed to himself, "Lucas." She squinted at him and shook her head slowly. He repeated the gesture, "Lucas."

After several attempts, she realized what he was trying to tell her.

"Lookas," she repeated and pointed at his chest. She smiled when he nodded.

She pointed to herself and told him, "Winda."

"Winda," rolled easily off his tongue.

Lucas pointed to the pile of wood and went around the room until she was able to remember and pronounce each word in English. She knew the word for fire, rain, and the different animal pelts he held up. He smiled at her when she was able to remember and pronounce each word in English. She, in turn, tried to teach the man her names for the same items he pointed at. He couldn't pronounce some of the words and soon gave up.

There were no curtains on the window of the small cabin. All of the spiders and cobwebs had been illuminated. Carrie had scrubbed clean all the dirt and grime that had accumulated over years of neglect. Her new quilt covered the narrow bed even though most nights it was far too hot for it. A glass of wild flowers gave off a fresh sweet fragrance from the middle of the table. The blue, yellow, and white gave a small splash of brightness to the otherwise dull room. Even though she didn't know what the flowers were she still liked to have them in her home. "Weeds," Dusty had called them but she continued to pick them anyway.

Dusty was gone again for the second time this summer. He left her stranded out in the wilderness all alone. A small knife was her only means of protection. There could be strangers, Indians, or wild life, or any other unforeseen intrusion. She had no means to hunt but he did show her how to fish and laughed at her when she caught a trout. A squeal of delight escaped her lips when she pulled in her line. She was afraid to take it off the hook as it flopped around at her feet. Dusty showed her how to clean it. But what other food she had was left by Dusty and she had to make due until his return. "Stay close to the cabin," he had warned her. "I'll be back as soon as I can. It'll be quicker this way."

It had been hot, sticky, and humid. For the last two days she felt uneasy, like someone was watching her. When she went to bed at night she would prop a chair under the doorknob to stop any intruder. It gave her some sense of security.

Dusty always took a different route, never approaching the cabin from the same direction. Carrie figured this was his way of making sure she would never know which way to go. She did try to follow him though, once, and got lost. If only she knew how to get back home, or turn back time to when she wasn't married to such a brute. Gratefully, she found her way back. From then on, she didn't leave the area around her little home. The only place she went was down a small hill beside the cabin to a clearing, and a small pond where she got her water and fished.

One day in late summer, she stood in the middle of this clearing listening to the birds. A flock of crows made a horrendous noise and she could hear a cardinal sing a high note, then a low one several times. Carrie envied their freedom and wished she could fly away when the desire arose. But she just turned and hung the laundry on the rope she had installed herself between two birch trees. She wiped the sweat from her brow and noticed the faint bruises still on her arm. Tears were held inside as she hoped someone would rescue her from this lonely place, someone other than her husband.

When Carrie had all her laundry hung she sat at her favourite spot in the shade against the side of the cabin. She picked up one of her two books but watched as a butterfly fluttered from one flower to another. Her eyelids got heavy and her head dropped to her chest.

The cardinal no longer sang and the crows stopped their noise. The woods went silent. Carrie jumped up her heart pounding. The crunching of heavy feet on dried fallen pine cones came from the other side of the cabin. She froze where she was. The creaking of leather and a horse's neigh told her the intruder was on horseback. She watched the far corner of the cabin and pulled her knife out of her pocket in her dress. Carrie's body tensed in anticipation of what was to come.

Dusty rode around the corner, leading the other horse on a short rope. He dismounted, grabbed her and kissed her hard on the mouth and slapped her behind. "Ain't you glad to see your husband?"

She nodded, grateful he came back for her, and fearful because he did. Carrie wondered how much damage her little knife would do to this big man. He released her and unloaded the horses. Carrie pocketed her knife and led them into the coral where she fed and watered them. She needed him to get her out of there. As soon as she could, she'd escape.

He had her help him drag two long crates into the cabin and stack them against the wall. "Tomorrow," he grinned at her, "we'll be leaving."

A lone rider in army uniform raced across the grassland and into the woods. He slowed his lathering horse and jumped off when he approached the makeshift camp. A corporal grabbed the horse's reins and led it away. The man was directed to the major's tent which he promptly marched up to. After he saluted he reached into his pocket and handed over a piece of paper.

Major Grant Sievers read the urgent dispatch the messenger handed him. He had just finished his morning coffee as he sat on a crude bench outside his tent. He set his cup down on the makeshift table, two boards on top of four barrels.

"Sergeant," he bellowed.

"Yes, sir!"

"Pack up, we have to hurry."

"Yes, sir," the sergeant replied, then under his breath mumbled, "Finally, some action." He strode off to alert the men.

Grant's stomach became queasy. He wanted to avoid "any action," as much as possible.

The men gathered up their belongings. Most of them slept out in the open in ratty blankets. Besides their guns and ammunition, they packed up their cups and dishes into sacks and threw them into a wagon. Then they stood in two straight lines and waited for their orders.

Grant picked up the papers and loaded his horse while two of his men emptied and struck down his tent. They dismantled the table and bench and re-packed them into the same wagon. Grant pulled himself up on his horse and felt glum. He turned toward his men and stopped a few feet in front of them. They were mostly farmers or drifters or men down on their luck who needed the meager pay. Young, too young. Some of them had questionable characters, but the militia was desperate for men and signed them up anyway. He couldn't be choosy right now and took whatever he could get.

Grant was the recruiting officer for his unit and travelled all over to promise men a steady pay check and three squares a day. This was more than what most of these men had seen in a long time. Jobs were scarce. Many of their crops had failed due to overly wet weather. Now they needed the money to feed their families.

"We have orders to head to Greenstown and meet up with General Brooks. Some Americans have been raiding settlements along the Lake Erie shoreline for a while now. They have been making their way north. When we get to Greenstown, we will get further orders as to how we will deal with this problem. I expect to be there in about eighteen days." Some of his men fidgeted with their muskets. Others waved their rifles in the air and cheered. One young man looked like he was ready to run. "Sergeant," Grant bellowed again.

"Right face," the sergeant yelled. The march was on.

The sergeant rode up beside him. "A lot can happen in eighteen days, sir."

"Yes it can, so we need to keep an eye out, always."

A light rain spattered on their heads. Some reached for their rain slickers and threw them on without missing a step. Most of them, however, had nothing but their hats or bare heads to take the rain. It came down harder but they continued to walk through puddles, splashing themselves in the process.

By the end of the day, the men were soaked through and miserable. Many nursed blisters on their feet. A few who had worn socks were only slightly better off. They camped under a grove of maples, birch, and cedars then huddled around three fires to dry out as best they could. Major Sievers sat under a tarp and drank hot coffee. No tent was set up tonight. Water dripped from the trees onto the men curled up inside their bedrolls, too exhausted to care.

Travel was slow through the dense colourful trees as the end of summer grew near. A heavy dew from the night before had left the ground damp and slippery. Dusty led the saddled horse down a steep, gravelly grade, carefully placing each step so he wouldn't slip. To do so would send him over the edge and onto rocks. He tried to keep his balance and at the same time keep the horse quiet and calm. Carrie followed gingerly.

The horse skirted sideways and reared. Its foot had slipped and sent dirt and gravel raining down the side of the cliff. Its eyes widened in fear as Dusty pulled it back onto the trail. He stood there, talking to it and stroking it until it settled down again. He looked over the edge and swore. Carrie held her breath, she shook until Dusty continued on slowly. Finally, they made it to the bottom.

Carrie took the horse and tied it to a nearby tree while Dusty climbed back up for the pack animal. He was almost back down when the horse bolted and ran, knocking Dusty to the ground. Carrie ran over to help him up. He cursed at her when she pulled on his arm. Then he cursed the horse, picked up his hat, and flopped it back on his head.

"Get the horse," he ordered. Carrie ran over, untied it, and led it to her husband. Dusty jumped on and raced after the runaway.

Carrie stood there, suddenly alone and lost. She walked over to a large rock and pulled her jacket up around her neck while she sat down and shivered. The sun hid behind a cloud and made her feel cold. Tall grasses and thistles mixed in with columbine along the edge of the woods. Bees buzzed from one flower to the next collecting nectar. She watched a rabbit eating stubby leaves a few yards away. A hawk flew down and picked up a small animal from the bushes, then flew away with it in its powerful claws.

She jumped out of her trance when Dusty rode up leading the pack horse. He slid off and tied the horses securely to a bush. Dusty took biscuits and jerky from the saddlebag, handing some to her. He sat beside her and tore angrily at his food. She remained silent so as to not set him off, again.

Four days later, they walked the horses through an open wood. Clear, blue sky greeted them when the sun came up. It was still hot and humid. Carrie watched grasshoppers jump out of their way when they waded through a clearing of wildflowers. To their left goldenrod waved in the slight breeze.

They walked up to a small house. It was a one storey board and batten with a wood-shingle roof. A small garden plot to its left had corn, squash, potatoes, beans, most of them harvested. A small barn behind the plot leaned to the right. Its door hung open on one hinge.

As they approached, a man walked out of the house with rifle in hand. When he recognized Dusty he lowered it and ran up to greet them. "Dusty. You made it." They shook hands smiling at each other.

"How ya doing, Jack?" Dusty laughed. "It's been a long time."

"Fine, just fine, the knee pains me some but I'm not complaining."

Carrie walked up beside them. Dusty grabbed her arm. "Jack, this here's Carrie."

"Ah, ya?" Jack looked her up and down. "So this is Iv-, ah, her is it?" It was more of a statement than a question.

Dusty gave his friend an irritated look but said nothing. Carrie wondered what that was about. Jack almost said her father's name, she was sure. The men unloaded the crates from the pack horse and took them inside. She unsaddled the other one and took both horses to the water trough for a drink. She could hear the men laughing inside. When she opened the door, both men stopped and watched her. As she sat at the table with them the conversation turned to the weather.

4

War whoops, gunfire, and screams startled Major Grant Sievers early one misty morning. Still half asleep, he jumped out of his bedroll and grabbed his rifle. From around the dying campfire the rest of his men did the same in what seemed like slow motion to him. A spear hit the man next to him in the chest with a thud. The man grabbed at it, eyes wide in fear before he stumbled to the ground.

Men ran everywhere and shot blindly into the trees. One Indian ran toward Grant with his war club raised high above his head. Grant aimed and fired. He hit the Indian in the stomach, who dropped his club and sank to the muddy ground. The dampness of the morning made Grant's clothing stick to his skin, grabbing at him to make movement slow and difficult. Gunpowder and the smell of blood assailed his senses as he ran up the slope to kneel beside one of his men.

A lead ball hit the sergeant in the face and took his eye out. Grant turned and shot the Indian that killed his sergeant. The sergeant had been with him for four years. He bent down on one knee and tried to stave off the grief until later. Grant started to reload his musket when he felt, rather than heard, someone behind him. Just in time, he turned and swung his rifle hitting the man with the butt end. The man grabbed his knees and withered on the ground. Another blow to the back of the head sent him face first into the mud.

To his left, Grant saw a couple of his own men overtake three enemies in a fist fight. To his right, four of his men were hunkered down behind trees firing into the distance. In front of him, Indians ran from tree to tree between volleys of gunfire. He levelled his musket and waited.

Suddenly, an Indian jumped out and charged toward him, yelling. Grant waited until the man was only a few feet away then fired. The impact of the lead ball sent the body backward into the underbrush. Another enemy charged at him while he tried to reload. He wouldn't be ready this time. His hand slid on the barrel. His foot slipped in the mud in his haste.

After a loud bang of a musket discharging, the Indian flew sideways into a tree before he slid to the ground. One of Grant's men ran up. "You all right, sir?"

Grant fought back the bile that percolated in his stomach and gave the young man a pat on the back. "Thanks," his voice quivered. The youth nodded then ran off. Grant tried to calm himself while he finished loading his musket.

A sudden silence filled the woods and made them more eerie than before. Men eyed the trees nervously. Slowly, they backed into camp. There was a loud explosion at close range and a bullet smashed into a nearby tree trunk. The man whose gun went off, accidentally, looked over at Major Sievers as if waiting to get shot. After a few minutes when nothing else happened Grant motioned the men back to the centre of their camp.

Two of the horses were gone, but all three wagons were unharmed. They brought in the wounded. Grant watched one of the older men set a broken arm. The youngster screamed. Several men turned and aimed their rifles, then lowered them again when they realized there was no threat. Others were gathering up the dead. He ordered his men to leave the Indians where they had fallen. Grant surveyed the damage done to his men. A young boy lay dead on the ground close to him. His arm was twisted in an unusual pose; his head had been smashed in. The kid only looked to be about twelve years old. Grant saw that several of the men had tears in their eyes. He pointed to the youngest man's body. "What's this boy's name?"

A man stepped forward who didn't look twenty yet. "That's my brother, Raymond." As he looked at the corpse tears ran down his cheeks unchecked, his lower lip quivering. "I was supposed to watch over him." He looked at Grant as if asking for forgiveness for letting his brother die.

As some of his men began to dig a pit to lay the bodies in, he wondered why men weren't supposed to cry. When all the dead had been piled into the mass grave Grant stood over it and quietly said a prayer, hat in hand. Someone sang a heartfelt song, albeit in a low voice.

As sunlight filtered through the tree tops Grant located the man who saved his life and pulled him aside. "What's your name, son?"

"Bill, Bill Egelton, sir!"

"Well, Mr. Egelton, you are now my new sergeant."

The young man looked at him with a surprised expression on his face. His blond hair stuck out from under his hat in all directions. He was a head shorter than Grant but the young man was stockier. His big brown eyes stared up at the major in admiration.

"Where are you from, sergeant?"

Egelton squirmed, as if he was not used to his new title yet. "Up by Kingston, sir. Worked on ships."

"How come you're down here?"

"Got tired of working on ships," he said with a shy grin.

"Lucky for us, eh?" Grant smiled. "Go get you're gear, sergeant."

The major looked over at his men. Not a bad job for being so green. Most of these men had never been in battle before.

Vibrant autumn colours of yellows, oranges, reds, and greens gave the promise of winter soon. The days grew shorter. Lucas smiled at Winda as she sat in front of the fire with her injured leg stretched out in front of her. She had made herself a new dress from the hides he had given her. Her other one had been torn up when she fell out of the tree which rendered it beyond repair. Now she worked on a pair of leggings for the winter season. Next, she planned to make herself a coat, and perhaps something special for him, she had told him. He was glad because she was able to sew longer each day before she became tired, or her leg would begin to ache. Then he'd lift her up and tuck her into her bed where she'd sleep for a few hours.

The gentle man watched her sew the leggings with her new needle and cotton thread he had given her from his pack for emergency repairs. He thought she needed them more than he did. The sinew from her pouch had run out and she was delighted with the gift. She had smiled shyly at him, and had been working on some kind of garment ever since. His new jacket was folded nicely on his bed and looked to be warmer than the one he had worn for the last five years. The old one was ruined after he'd wrapped Winda's leg in it while he carried her to the cave.

Lucas cut off a chunk of rabbit meat that had been cooking on a spit. Winda set her sewing aside when he handed it to her. After he cut a piece for himself, Lucas leaned back against a sack of supplies. Juice dripped down her chin. He picked up a rag and handed it to her and motioned for her to wipe her face. She did and laughed. They listened to the rustling of autumn leaves blowing around outside the cave entrance. A grinding in the pit of his stomach was bothering him, though. He wondered if he should tell her that she might never walk again.

He remembered as he carried her back to the cave, her left leg dangling and dripping blood along the trail. He was surprised she had lived at all, there was so much blood. She sat across from him now and smiled at him with her soft, brown eyes that drew him in like a deep pool of... *Stop it!* he admonished himself. He shook his head to clear his thoughts.

After the meal, Lucas carried Winda back to her bed. He saw her grit her teeth as if pain had shot through her leg when he eased her down. It seemed to heal too slowly for him, but the gouges were long and deep. Give it time. He was surprised there were no broken bones. His sewing job on her leg wasn't the best either, the stitches uneven. He did it while she was still unconscious and with only the aid of the campfire to light the inside of the dark cave.

He had wrapped her torn leg with his jacket, which he burned later on. When he took out his supplies his hands had been shaky. It took him all afternoon to get the bleeding to stop. She had so many cuts and bruises, most of which he left unattended, to heal on their own. When he had her all stitched up, he cut the thread with his knife and fell asleep right where he was. His eyes were sore afterward from the strain.

He had lain awake last night while Winda had tossed and turned. She screamed and bolted upright, hitting her head on the low ceiling. Lucas jumped up and took her into his arms to comfort her. "Shh, it's only a dream Winda, only a dream." He kissed her lightly on the top of her head and held her close to his chest.

"Lanick was chasing me," Winda said with a quivering voice. "She had a long neck and sharp green eyes like that of a bird of prey, and her body was like a bear's. She gained on me and clawed at me with her huge claws." Slowly her eyes focused, her breathing eased. Lucas held her in his arms until she stopped shaking.

"You're safe now, Winda. It was only a dream."

"I am sorry, Lookas," she told him sleepily.

"There is nothing to be sorry about, Winda. I'm just glad I was here for you." He laid her back down on the bed. She closed her eyes and instantly fell back to sleep.

"Any time Winda, any time at all," he whispered to her.

The raid had gone badly. Pakwis had lost five of his best men. Not that he had many to start with. Why did he let Stealth Man talk him into this?

"We will sneak up in the middle of the night and steal the horses and maybe one of their wagons," Stealth Man had told him. "They must have food and blankets in them. If we are quiet, we can be in and out before anybody wakes up."

"They have three men to our one. It will not work."

"That is why we have to sneak in while they are asleep. And if something does go wrong, we have surprise on our side." Stealth Man had smiled at him. "They will be drowsy. I have prayed. We will have the spirits with us."

"The spirits with us," Pakwis almost laughed at his friend. "When was the last time we had the spirits with us?"

"Yes, I have prayed and sent offerings. The spirits will help us in this," Stealth Man had said.

Pakwis had wondered if the man could predict the outcome of the raid, or if he only looked for glory. Stealth Man faced him with squinted eyes. He looked determined. He would do this with or without the Chief's blessing.

"We do need the food and supplies for our village, desperately," Stealth Man had said.

Pakwis bit his bottom lip. How he wished he could take back his answer. Seventeen men raided the army camp. Only nine returned. Stealth Man was dead, shot in the chest. Pakwis saw him look at his killer in surprise. He had grabbed the blood-soaked jacket and dropped to his knees. Blood squirted from his mouth while he pitched forward into the mud. Pakwis shook his head to clear it. The raid had gone wrong from the start. They hadn't counted on so much rain and had to backtrack around a swollen river which took up precious time. They hadn't counted on being discovered so quickly, either. All they managed to get away with was two horses. One of them had been eaten already by the people whose stomachs still ached from lack of food. It wasn't enough.

Those who survived had to scramble back to safety so fast that some of them lost their weapons in the confusion. They only had four guns amongst them in the first place, now two of them were lost. How did they expect to fight against an army with what they had?

Three days after the raid Pakwis folded his arms across his chest and faced the hills in the distance. He watched an eagle silently soar across the sunny sky. Light footsteps behind him told Pakwis that his favourite warrior was heading his way.

Night Wind walked up and stood beside him. "Come my Chief, you need to eat." When Pakwis didn't move he said, "You are not to blame for the death of our people, Pakwis. Stealth Man had a good idea. The idea did not work. You had to try something."

"I should have just gone fishing or hunting."

"Maybe, but game has been scarce. You needed to feed many people, and we were starving. Remember that."

Pakwis just nodded his head as he left Night Wind and walked up to Little Blossom's fire. She smiled as he approached her and handed him a strip of horse meat. He stood by the fire and ate. It tasted good but he had to force it down. She cut off a small chunk of meat for herself and stayed beside him. When he was done, Pakwis wiped his mouth on his sleeve.

She flipped her waist long hair to her back after she swallowed her last bite. Her hair looked like a long black wave of fine cloth. Her pouting lips drew in Pakwis who leaned over and kissed her. Her soft lips kissed him back. His arms went around her neck, pulling her in closer. He stepped into her and felt her lean toward him. Suddenly, she let go and fled.

Pakwis stood there, stunned, his manhood swollen and aching with need. What was he thinking? Even if she did look upon him, it was too soon. She had just lost a husband. He kicked at the ground, sending mud and stones in all directions. Or maybe she thought he was too old for her. He guessed he was at least twelve summers older than Little Blossom. But that didn't stop the way she affected him. He stomped off in the opposite direction. If Winda was here, he could take his yearnings out on her.

Dusty had traded his horses for two canoes. Each one carried one of the crates along with other supplies. Jack led the way up stream. Carrie paddled from the front of the second one, Dusty sat behind her and steered.

The narrow river was slow this time of year which made travel easy. Carrie enjoyed the scenery as they glided along. She saw a flock of geese fly south for the winter, honking loudly as they went. A blue jay startled her when it suddenly flew up from the shore next to her, scolding her because they'd disturbed it. She watched a red squirrel chase another one up a tree. A deer taking a drink ahead of them, eyed them closely before it disappeared into the bushes.

As they drifted along in the idyllic setting she wondered how Dusty knew Jack. They seemed to be good friends. Neither one would tell her where they were headed or what their plan was. They also kept the contents of the crates a secret too.

"You don't need to worry your pretty little head about that," Dusty told her.

Jack twisted his paddle in the water to steer his canoe around a bend. Dusty followed. The river bank rose higher on both sides which gave Carrie little to look at. She turned her attention to Jack. He was shorter than Dusty by a head, and slimmer. He looked to be in his mid-thirties while her husband looked older. Dusty wouldn't reveal his age either. Jack's hair was dark brown, short, and neatly trimmed. He was clean-shaven with light blue eyes that seemed to sparkle when he smiled, which he did often. Yet there was a sneakiness to Jack which kept Carrie wary of him. She had to fend off his advancements whenever Dusty's back was turned.

Jack slowed his canoe and pulled his collar up on his brown jacket. A cool breeze showered them with colourful fall leaves from the trees above them. Dusty pulled up beside him and set his paddle across the gunwales of the canoe. Jack flipped his leg over into Dusty's canoe to hold the canoes together as they talked. Carrie turned around just as he pointed upstream.

"We can save a lot of time if we take the left fork up ahead."

"It's too shallow, I think." Dusty shook his head. "We'll run aground."

"Well I don't think so. I say we try it."

"I say we go right." Dusty narrowed his hard grey eyes at the man.

Carrie faced the front of the canoe with her back to both men. She looked down at her dirty torn skirt and brushed a couple of leaves from her lap. And she prayed that Dusty would control his temper.

"There are two portages that way," yelled Jack.

"At least we'll get there," Dusty yelled louder.

Carrie huddled into her jacket and tried to disappear.

"Look! We are scaring your wife," Jack chuckled, as if unconcerned of her welfare. Carry wondered if he acted this way to impress Dusty.

Dusty also calmed himself. "All right. We'll try it your way. But as soon as we hit bottom we're turning back, got it?"

"Got it."

Carrie relaxed and helped paddle as tears trickled down her face.

An hour later they steered the canoes between two huge rocks. Carrie pretended that her paddle slipped and splashed Dusty.

"Hey! Watch it," he hollered.

Carrie turned around. "Sorry, almost lost my paddle." He just fixed his grey eyes on her and wiped his face off with his coat sleeve. She turned back around and smiled.

"Hold on tight," Lucas whispered into Winda's ear, "one step at a time. Easy does it. Good."

Winda took another tentative step and put all her weight on her left foot. Lucas held her with one arm around her waist. Winda had her arm around his neck. They walked around the fire pit inside the cave. Cold rain kept them inside the whole day, splashing just inside the entrance. Both of them wore their new jackets that Winda had made.

Lucas smiled to himself and leaned in closer to smell her lavender-scented hair. It was one of the herbs she had in her pouch. She had just washed it that morning with the water he had heated up and poured into a wooden bowl. He combed it out for her afterward while she sat between his legs on the dirt floor with her back to him. His hand glided the comb down from the top of her head right down to her waist. She squirmed when he touched a certain spot on her back, a ticklish place where he went over several times. Winda had scolded him after she caught on to what he was doing. He laughed then set the comb aside and just held her while she laid her head back against his shoulder.

"Lookas!" Wanda scolded, "You hold too tight!"

"Oh, sorry." He loved the way she pronounced his name, "Look-as." He loosened his grip. "How does your leg feel now?"

"Still hurt, but is better."

Carefully, he eased her down by the fire. "You want something to eat, it's ready?"

"Yes, thank you, Lookas."

He pulled out their bowls and dished out wild turkey stew for both of them. It was a tom that he had snared yesterday. She had kept all the feathers.

Winda brought her spoon up to her mouth and tasted it. "Is good."

Lucas smiled back at her and ate hungrily. After the meal, he cleaned the dishes while Winda watched. She lifted her bandaged leg and shifted it over to get comfortable. "Lookas, what happen? You find me."

He watched the way the firelight shimmered on her long, blue-black hair. It had swung forward when she settled herself. Now the light danced through it. He longed to run his fingers through the soft silky strands. Instead, he blinked and took a drink of bee balm tea. Would she let him touch her? It was probably too soon. Or, worse yet, she wouldn't want him as he did her. He cleared his throat and watched her reach down for her hair clip and insert it into her hair. "I shot the bear just after you blacked out. He was dead before you hit the ground."

"I fell out of tree?"

"Yes, that's why you had so many cuts and bruises."

Winda sat there for a few minutes before she spoke. "I see me falling, laying there like dead. And you carried me a long way to this cave. " She shivered. Her hand reached up and stroked his beard. "You sewed up my leg."

Lucas gasped. "Winda. I..."

"Shh," her hand travelled down his arm then came to rest on her lap. She studied every inch of his face.

He could see his reflection in her deep brown eyes. Lucas inched closer, reached up and undid her hair clip. Her hair fell in luscious waves down her back. He inhaled the lavender scent, pulled her head toward him. Lucas kissed her long and passionately. To his relief she kissed him back.

They sat in Mary's small house on torn, thread-bare chairs. Light poured through the window, showing up the dusty wooden floor. Anthony threw another log in the fireplace. "Where did he go, Mary?" Gert asked her sister.

"I don't know, I told you." A tear trickled down her face. "I think he left me."

"Why do you say that?" Anthony sat down beside his wife.

"He took all his clothes. Not that he had that many, but he took all his guns and his watch that I gave him a few years ago that he never wore. All gone." She turned to face her brother-in-law and dabbed her eyes with a handkerchief. "He had money, too. I don't know how he got it but he hid it from me. I found five-hundred dollars once. He doesn't know. And shortly afterward it was gone."

Anthony leaned forward and patted Mary's leg. "I know I'm not supposed to discus my customer's affairs. But he has been moving large sums of money in and out of the bank for the last eight months now. He certainly doesn't earn it at his job, when he does work." He looked at his wife who nodded encouragement. "Are you sure you don't know anything about it?"

Mary shook her head. "Dusty had been around a few times. They always talked in secret. Ivan never brought him into the house, nor did Dusty ever bring Carrie with him. They were always sneaky. That man gives me the creeps." She blew her nose in a handkerchief. "When I asked Ivan about it he just told me to mind my own business. Can you imagine? Mind my own business about my own daughter?"

"Mary," Gert put in, "I know we haven't been close, you being five years younger than me. I regret not keeping in touch with you, more often, all those years."

"You moved away just before Father lost the farm, unable to pay the bills because of years of drought," Mary said. "It was a few years before we were settled again. No wonder you lost touch."

"Anthony and I moved here right after our wedding. You knew where we were."

"I know, but Mother became very ill. I looked after her for a year before she died." She shrugged. "Father wasn't the same afterward."

"Well," Gert sat forward in her seat. "I think Ivan has changed you. You used to be more confident in yourself, more outgoing. Sometimes I think you don't want to acknowledge that you are my sister." Gert had finally got that out. After all the slights she'd received from her sister, it felt good.

"I know." Mary looked at her hands on her lap. "I wanted to go to the parties and have afternoon tea with you, but Ivan kept telling me that I didn't belong to your social group. He said I wouldn't know how to act and that your friends would only laugh at me, and the way I dress." She studied her stained dress. "I would just be an outcast, Gert. Look at me compared to you." She looked up at both of them. "I know," she put her hand up before either one could speak. "I did this to myself. I married Ivan. I'm not blaming you two because I slipped down the social ladder."

"Can I ask you something, Mary?" Gert had waited for a long time to get up the nerve. "Is Ivan Carrie's father? She certainly doesn't look like him. And he's never paid much attention to her."

Mary looked as if she'd slapped her across the face. Finally, she answered. "No, no he isn't."

Gert watched Mary and wondered if her sister waited to be ridiculed because she wasn't married to the child's father. "Thank goodness," Gert laughed. "I'm so glad he isn't." She squeezed Mary's arm. "As you know, I've never really liked him to begin with."

A weak chuckle escaped Mary's lips. "I was in love with her father. We were young," she told them dreamily. "We planned on running away together, but he was killed. Father sent me to Kingston to have the baby. I was supposed to give her up for adoption. That's where I met Ivan." She sighed. "He was so full of adventure. It didn't matter to him that I was pregnant. He kept promising me things, like a big house, nice furniture. He wanted to travel to Europe someday.

"So we got married. But he kept losing money. Once, he lent a friend of his a lot of money, but I don't think Ivan saw that again. Then we just kept getting further in debt. At first he was very good to us, but as the years passed I think he started to resent us. We were in his way and took up whatever money he did make." She looked nervously at Gert. "Every time I suggested we visit you he'd make up some excuse; so we never did."

"Well, all I can say," Anthony told her, "is that it looks like Ivan and Dusty are up to no good. Whatever it is, they're both in it together. I just can't figure out all this money, though." He stroked his chin then took off his glasses to wipe the lenses clean.

"I just remembered something." Mary tapped the arm of her chair. "I overheard them talking one time. Before Ivan shoved me back inside the house. They said something about guns, and a shipment."

Gert and Anthony exchanged looks. "What do you mean?" Gert said.

Mary stared into space. "I don't know. It doesn't sound too good, does it?"

Anthony started to sweat as he pulled his chair closer and took Mary's hands in his. "That means they could be buying guns and re-selling them to the highest bidder. Either that, or they're getting ready for a war."

"Oh, no," Mary said. Gert squeezed her arm and gave her a compassionate look.

Anthony brought Mary a glass of water and handed it to her. "Another thing. We still can't find out whom that other reverend was who married Carrie. Or even where he's from."

Mary took a sip of water then set the glass on the table. "I've been asking around too. It seems he's just vanished. Reverend Bates had never heard of him either."

5

Major Grant Sievers sat in General Brook's office in Greenstown with a glass of whiskey in hand. It had been cold and rainy all day. The general was in his chair leaning against the wall with his feet on the desk. He swirled the golden liquid in his glass. "We have to find out who's behind this, Major, and where the guns are coming from." He uncrossed his ankles and lowered his feet. The front chair legs landed on the floor with a thump. "I want to know why they are helping the Americans. Isn't a man supposed to be loyal to his country?"

"Maybe they are Americans who happen to live in Upper Canada?"

The general emptied his glass and poured another from the bottle on his desk. "You have new orders, Grant." He searched through a pile of papers and pulled out a crisp white sheet. "Yep, here it is." He shoved his glasses onto his face. "I want you to investigate and stop these people before they get to the lake and ship more guns over." He glanced at the paper before he gave it to his major.

Grant leaned over, took the paper and read it. "Says here to bring them in dead or alive."

"We've estimated that they've smuggled at least three-hundred guns to the south already. We need to stop this, and now." General Brooks took off his glasses and leaned forward. "We need those guns, desperately."

Grant nodded. "Any leads?"

"All we have are a couple of names. Your job is to find these men and bring them in. I have others tracking down the guns and finding out how they're getting here in the first place."

Grant finished his glass. The general re-filled it.

"The names are on the bottom of the paper," the general continued.

Grant looked at the paper in his hand. "I have heard about one of these men. He's a mean son of a bitch."

"Well, you can leave in the morning. And Major, lose the uniform."

General Brooks got up and produced another bottle from a cabinet and re-topped their glasses. He sat back down. "So you were attacked by Indians on your way back?"

"Yep, up by the Big Forks."

"We haven't had any significant problems with the Indians for quite awhile now. I wonder what happened."

"I don't know, but I hear some of them were caught in that storm we had last March and were misplaced. Total villages were wiped out. I think they were after food and horses. I don't think they had anything to do with the guns, though."

"I hope not."

Grant glanced at the piece of paper in his hand. "If the Indians are involved with this..." He shuddered, unable to go on.

Lucas was the only person who had treated Winda kindly in a long time. He spoke softly and helped her as much as he could. He never hit her or spoke angrily to her. Nor did he call her names or degrade her in any way. His voice never raised in anger, except once, when he burned his hand on the hot pot of stew. He swore, at least that's what it looked like. He waved his hand in the air and then held it tight against his body, she guessed, until the sting went away.

Winda laughed at the funny sight. She watched him dance around on tip-toes. "You know pot is hot. You touch anyway."

At first, he glared at her, and then laughed with her. She watched him now as he carved up a rabbit for their evening meal. She knew he made a big sacrifice because he stayed with her all the time. He didn't do much trapping. Instead, he spent hours with her teaching her more of his language and helping her walk around the cave to strengthen her leg.

Her leg did get better, to their relief. Yesterday, he had taken her around and showed her where the closest traps were set. At least she'd have fresh meat while he was gone. Then he led her down to the river where she sat in the sun and enjoyed the warmth on her face. It had been a surprisingly warm day for late fall. Most of the trees were bare of leaves now. Lucas cut up a handful of herbs and threw them into the pot. He dropped in a handful of wild rice and stirred it. She watched his hands work. Long, thin fingers held the knife with ease as they chopped up more of the rabbit. Rough, trapper's hands that were gentle when they touched her. He had trimmed his hair and shaved his beard. She wondered if he did that for her. Alone in the woods, no one cared what you looked like. His green eyes shone when he looked up at her. She smiled back at him and shifted on the log she sat on.

"The meat looks good, Lookas."

"Thanks."

They sat side by side after the meal and faced the warm fire. Lucas bent down and threw more wood on the flames. He put his arm around her after she shivered in the cold evening.

"I think I should leave for a while, Winda," he said. "Only for a short time." He reached up and brushed the hair from her face. She looked at him, confused. "We need supplies to get us through the winter. We need more than just meat and berries. I need ammunition for my rifle so I can hunt. I need new boots and we need more blankets."

Winda looked around. They only had two blankets. One was made from different furs of small animals, sewn together to make it big enough to cover them. The other one, she knew, was from the bear that attacked her. Lucas hadn't told her this; she recognized the markings on it. "I make boots."

"Yes. I know you can. But we need to trade what furs I have for other supplies we need." He hugged her closer, worry etched on his face. "I think I'll leave in the morning."

Reluctantly, she agreed.

"I won't be gone long, maybe nine or ten days. It'll be faster if I go alone. And then I can take everything too." He gestured to the pile of furs. Winda saw that there would be no room for her in the canoe. "I hope to be back before we get snowed in here." Lucas lifted her chin and kissed her. A deep sigh escaped her mouth when they parted. Strange feelings ran through her body. Did she dare express her true feelings for this man?

Winda undid his shirt, slipped it off him and kissed his hairy chest. Lucas groaned, undid the ties on her dress, and watched her as if waiting for rejection. She smiled as she undid the buttons on his pants. He stood and pulled her onto her feet, breathing faster. She finished undressing in front of him, neither shy nor ashamed. Lucas was the first man she wanted to give everything to.

"So beautiful," he said, as he reached out and touched her arm. "Do I even have the right?"

"Lookas," she whispered as she stepped closer. She put her arms around his neck. He kissed her then lifted her up and carried her to his bed.

Lucas left the following morning, his canoe loaded high with furs. Winda told herself over and over that he would be back. He left his traps and other gear there. She watched him disappear around the bend. A blue heron flew down and followed Lucas. Its wing span stretched almost across the whole water as it passed under the trees. At the bend in the river, it swooped up and over the willow trees and was gone. She sat on the same log she did the previous day, her heart began to sink. Loneliness and apprehension swept over her. "I love you, Lookas," she said in Ojibwa.

She stayed there all morning enjoying the scenery and thinking about their love-making last night. Lucas had been gentle, not like Pakwis at all. Pakwis took but didn't give back. A smile played on her lips when she thought about Lucas. If only he didn't go away. She would love him again, soon, she hoped. How she ached for him already. She looked up at the sky and noticed dark clouds through the bare tree branches. Forcing her mind off Lucas she stood and looked down the river one last time.

Fish jumped, one was caught by a kingfisher and was carried away into the trees. A woodpecker tapped its rhythm on a nearby tree. Winda picked up a stone and studied it. It would make a good arrow head so she put it in her jacket pocket. She found a stick to lean on and headed back up the trail. Suddenly, she heard a different kind of noise and stopped to listen. Faint voices came from the river. She limped back down and hid behind some bushes. Two white men and one woman paddled up from the opposite way Lucas had gone.

A lone man in the first canoe yelled back at the other two. "This is the way Dusty. I know it."

"No it's not, Jack. We should have turned right back there. This one is getting too narrow. Damn it."

Winda watched them pull ashore. Luckily, they were far enough away that they might miss the trail to the cave. She picked her way through the bushes, watching them unload their gear from the canoes. The woman made a fire and put water on to boil. The men still argued.

"This way is shorter," the smaller of the two yelled, the one called Jack. He stood upright after he set a crate down on the ground by a pile of goods, his face had turned red.

" It's too shallow to carry our gu...heavy load."

"This is the way Iva...I was told to go, I told you. We won't make it on time going the other way."

"I'm going back." The big man called Dusty started to walk away after he threw a sack back into the canoe.

"No you can't. We can't split up." Jack looked around in a panic. He had some kind of accent. The words he spoke came out with extra guttural sounds, made them hard for her to follow. Jack had short brown hair, no whiskers, and wore a brown jacket with darker brown pants. His knife threatened the bigger man. He ran and jumped on Dusty's back, punching him. The big man threw him off, pulled out his own knife, and held it in front of him.

Dusty had lost most of his hair. His grey shirt was sweat-stained. He wore black pants and no jacket. He wiped the beads of sweat from his forehead and crouched, waiting for an attack. Jack lunged forward; the big, ugly man easily overtook him. Dusty let him go but still held his knife out. Dusty jabbed at him and cut Jack's arm.

Jack dropped his knife and grabbed at the cut. "Okay, okay. Tomorrow we'll head back the other way." He stomped over to his gear and wrapped the arm up in a rag. Then Winda watched him go into the woods, probably to sulk. Dusty went over to the fire and poured himself a cup of coffee. The woman cringed at his approach but said nothing. It looked like she was afraid of this man.

Winda backed away from behind the tree, turned, and limped back toward the trail, her leg aching. All she wanted to do was lie down and rest. Several times, she stopped and listened for the man called Jack, but heard nothing. She squinted through the trees, searching all around, but he seemed to have disappeared. She jumped when a deer ran by her then forced herself to keep walking. The trail was just behind that big rock, then up the hill and home. A dark shape flew between the trees. Sunlight filtered through the branches, blinding her. She shifted to see better, nothing, maybe her mind playing tricks on her. For a few minutes, she watched the spot where the dark shape disappeared. All was quiet. She stood and limped toward the trail.

A hard hand slammed over her mouth. Another one caught her around the waist and pulled her back into him. He pressed his mouth to her ear. "Shh. Come this way," Jack ordered. He dragged her backward and into a small clearing. She lost her walking stick and tried to pull his hands away. Her foot hit his shin which made him angrier; he only gripped harder. Tears ran down her face from the pain in her leg. She bit his hand. He gritted his teeth and let go of her mouth. She tried to scream. He hit her with something hard. Winda fell on the ground and fought to stay conscious. Her attacker was but a blur hovering over her.

Jack fell on top of her. His hand reached inside her dress and fondled her breasts while he shoved a cloth into her mouth with his other one. Winda's fists swung at him with little effect. He undid his pants, pulled them down to his knees, and then pulled her skirt up to her waist. She tried to buck him off but he just leered at her. She twisted wildly. He panted and rammed into her hard. The fight was out of Winda. She willed her mind to focus on the swaying trees above her until he shuddered and collapsed on top of her. His breath was erratic as he whispered, "That was good, eh?"

Jack pulled himself up and did up his pants. He stood over her grinning wolfishly then gave her a good kick in her side. She rolled over in pain and sobbed. He walked away.

Winda lay in the dirt cold, lonely, and in pain. She cried for all the bad times in her life. She cried from the betrayal of the man who raised her as a daughter who then took her to bed with him. She cried for lost love. Mostly, she cried for the new love she found, only to lose him because of this one act of violence. Lucas would not want her now. She felt as if she'd cheated on him and that he'd look upon her with scorn.

It was late when she pulled herself up and limped into the cave. She took a cloth and washed herself, scrubbing hard to get rid of any signs of the rape. Her hands shook as she dipped the cloth into the water, over and over. She didn't eat her evening meal but sat all night in the dark against the wall, hugging her legs, and rocking. Her eyes remained glued to the cave entrance.

"Don't let anyone take advantage of you, Winda. For once they do, they always will." Lucas had told her that one time. She hung her head in shame.

Early next morning she limped back down toward the camp and waited for Jack to wake up. When he strolled into the woods, she followed him. She watched him lean against a tree to relieve himself. He turned to find her about twenty feet away. He squinted at her, a slow grin spread across his face as if he didn't believe his luck.

"Well, you dumb squaw. Want some more, do ya?" he snickered at her. "Didn't get enough of me, eh?"

Winda ran as fast as she could. Jack followed, gaining on her. She stopped, out of breath and backed up against a large maple. Jack stopped a few feet away then slowly walked toward her.

"You are ready for some more, aren't you?" he asked, satisfaction written on his face.

Her heart pounded in her chest like mad drums as his hand reached up to touch her. He took one more step. The snap of a steel trap made her jump. It wrapped around Jack's leg, cutting into the bone. He screamed. Blood gushed all over the ground. He glared at Winda as he pulled on the trap. She ran through the woods, his screams chasing her. She kept on until her bad leg gave out on her. Winda squatted and covered her ears with her hands and cried.

The screams stopped suddenly. It was too quiet. No birds sang. No animals called. She had to know what happened. That was too quick. She went back to where she left Jack only to find him gone. Pools of blood covered the ground, too much from just the trap. Something else happened here.

She crept up to the camp. The woman sat huddled by the fire, a blanket clutched at her throat. Neither of the men were there. Winda went to look for them. After an eternity, she heard soft scraping in the dirt and peered over a bush. Dusty was filling in a hole. She saw part of Jack's shirt before it was covered up. Winda smiled, he couldn't hurt anyone ever again.

The hole was shallow with many roots in the way. Winda wanted to go up to the body and kick it to make sure Jack was dead. She rubbed her sore side and wanted to pay him back for that, too. Winda leaned against a tree and lifted her sore leg to take the weight off, ease the pain. She looked up. Dusty was watching her. Winda froze. Her brain yelled for her to run, but her legs wouldn't move. Her left one was so painful, she just couldn't run anymore.

He came closer, waving the shovel like a club. His eyes darting around, searching through the trees. "Are you alone? Where are the others?" When she didn't answer, he pointed toward the river.

She turned and limped down toward the camp. Dusty stayed close behind holding the shovel ready. When they walked into the clearing, the woman jumped up. "Who's that?"

"Don't know. But I bet it was her trap that Jack got caught in." Dusty set the shovel down and picked up his rifle. "I'm hungry. Get us some food."

The woman filled a plate of stew for him. He ate but watched both women closely, his rifle at his side. She handed Winda a plate and spoon. Winda noticed that the other woman had a black eye. The pretty, little redhead looked at her with sad, green eyes that seemed to plea for her help. The young woman had hair the colour of a red sunset, her long blue dress had dirty sleeves and was torn in several places.

Winda watched the man as she ate. Neither he nor Carrie, the woman's name, she was told, seemed upset about Jack's death. Dusty rose when she set her empty plate on the ground and tied her hands behind her back. He covered her with a blanket, scowled at her, and said nothing. She leaned back against the tree behind her and watched him through slitted eyes. Dusty pushed Carrie to where a bedroll was laid out, crawled in after her, and started to snore shortly afterward. His arm was draped over Carrie as if he held her in place. All night questions plagued Winda, keeping her awake. She jumped at every noise she heard. She thought she saw Jack in the trees and knew he'd come for her. Near dawn, she slept.

6

Dusty pushed the women hard on the long trip upriver and was seldom out of sight. His rifle never left his side. Every muscle in their bodies ached from paddling all day, every day for two weeks. At night, they were usually asleep as soon as they crawled into their bedrolls. Carrie and Winda were able to communicate with subtle sign language and eye contact. "I know some of your words," Winda had told Carrie. Carrie kept it a secret, somehow knowing it could help them in the future.

One morning Dusty took his rifle and set out hunting. They had eaten the last of their food the night before. A cold, icy rain pelted the canvas tarp that stretched overhead between the trees. Carrie watched it sag in the centre as it filled with water. Winda pushed it up with a stick and let the water cascade over the sides. Mud splashed over the crates beside them.

"What do you think is in them?" Carrie asked her new friend.

Winda turned and scanned their surroundings. "I do not know."

They both checked the woods but couldn't see too far. Evergreens grew thick on both sides of the river for miles. Their little camp was set in a clearing just above a small rapid. A fat log burned under the tarp, sizzling and hissing. Water dripped on it threatening to put it out. "Why you not run?" she whispered.

"I don't have anywhere to go." Carrie held out her hands to the fire. "I'm not smart like you, Winda. I don't know how to live out here by myself. I don't even know where we are, or which way to go. You know what plants are edible and how to set snares for meat. I don't even know how to make a shelter."

"I teach you. You can go back home."

"No," Carrie shook her head. "My father gave me to Dusty. I'm afraid of what he will do to me if I go back." A tear escaped and rolled down her cheek. Carrie wiped it away and checked up the river in the direction Dusty had gone. "Dusty will hunt me down. I know he'll find me. Then..." she shivered. "He's capable of anything."

Winda sat down against the crates. "Someday you will be rid of him, I will help you."

"Someday," Carrie repeated. "I'll find a way." She had to, before he killed her in one of his rages. She squared her shoulders. "Why don't you leave, Winda? You will be all right by yourself. You could escape during the day while you pretend to be getting water."

"I cannot run far. It is hard for me to hunt." Winda tapped her bad leg. She still limped badly and tired easy when walking. "Then Dusty hurt you more. I stop him."

It was true, Carrie realized. Dusty only hit her when no one was around to witness it. He didn't seem to mind though, that her bruises testified to that fact on their own. He hadn't been as rough when he took her to bed either, for some reason. Maybe Dusty wouldn't come back. She knew better. He always came back. He was determined to make her life miserable. She looked at the crates.

There was not a mark on either crate, no labels to tell where they came from. The size and shape of them, and the way Dusty guarded them could only mean one thing.

"Winda, I think I know what is in those crates."

Winda threw another log on the fire. "You want to open?"

They looked at each other as if to dare the other one to do just that. "If we can get one out, maybe we can defend ourselves against Dusty." Nervously, Carrie looked around for something to break open the lock. She found a large rock and walked up to the crate with a look of determination on her face. "Ready?"

Winda nodded and scanned around. Carrie raised the rock up, ready to strike. A twig snapped to her right. Carrie dropped the rock and sighed.

Dusty crashed through the trees, carrying a large deer.

Several days later Dusty pulled the canoe up to the shore and got out. Heavy snow fell as he helped the women unload the crates and drag them through the underbrush beside the river. Then they pulled branches over the trail to hide the drag marks. After they canoed another mile Carrie heard the loud roar of a waterfall. The trees thinned out on both sides of the river bank as they neared it. A saw mill stood at the bottom of a hill. The river current pushing the big wheel around slowly. It made a cling, clang noise in a steady rhythm.

They left the canoes on the bank of Black Creek, which meandered southward, hooking onto the Sydenham River, then emptying out in Lake St. Clair. The small village Dusty led them into was Blackman Falls, named after its founder, Dusty's father. Several people watched the three of them walk toward the tavern. A man stopped him and, judging by the way Dusty glowered, he wasn't too pleased about it. The stranger was tall and scruffy with a black cowboy hat perched on sandy coloured hair. His red and black plaid shirt showed under a black, unbuttoned coat. To Carrie, he looked to be as mean and rugged as her husband. She watched him warily.

The man whispered something to Dusty which made him smile. "Okay, let's go get a drink." He nodded toward the tavern.

The man followed them up the steps. Dusty pushed open the door and waved Carrie inside. As she walked through the door she saw the new man push Winda. She didn't have time to react; Dusty grabbed her arm and glared at the man. and gave the man a dark look. Suddenly, he turned to go back out.

"Wait a minute." The man took hold of Dusty's arm and held on tight. "Forget about her," he said. "She's nothing but a squaw."

Dusty gave the man threatening look. "But she's my—"

"What?" the man challenged as he stood in front of Dusty with an unwavering gaze. He let Dusty's arm go. "Indians aren't allowed in taverns."

Dusty's hand clenched tighter on Carrie's arm. She tried pulling away. He looked at her then loosened his grip. After several tense moments Dusty nodded then led them inside. Spotting a young man at the bar, Dusty whispered something in his ear. The young man downed his drink then left. Dusty took a bottle of whiskey and three glasses to a corner table and poured the first round. The new man introduced himself as Grant. The men downed their first glasses and re-filled them. Dusty gulped down another one and turned to Carrie. "Drink up," he ordered her, in a gruff voice.

"What about Winda?" she asked.

Dusty glanced at Grant then leaned toward Carrie. "I'll see to her later. She won't get far. I have someone watching her."

Dusty downed another glass and turned to Carrie. "Drink up," he ordered, in a gruff voice.

Dusty nudged her. Carrie didn't like the smell of whiskey and had never tasted it. It went down smooth enough. He egged her on. She took a few more sips and decided she didn't like it. After her glass was empty, she set it on the table, relieved that she was done. Dusty filled it up again. Carrie looked at it in horror.

She remembered her father, Ivan, drunk. His clothes reeked as he stumbled up the steps. Her mother always let him in. He would stagger around the house and break things and blame Mary when he sobered up. He'd get sick and pass out. Mary would clean up after him. Carrie didn't want to live like that. She watched her own husband and cringed. Dusty and Grant laughed about everyday things as they drank the first bottle. The bartender set another one on the table. Grant tried to hold Dusty's attention. Every time her husband turned her way, Grant told a joke or asked a question. Carrie wondered if he was trying to save her from more embarrassment.

"Drink up, Carrie," Dusty ordered again, in a low, angry voice.

"I'm hungry, she said. "I need something to eat. Not whiskey."

"I said drink up. We can eat later." He glared at her then looked at Grant. "Maybe it'll loosen her up for tonight, eh?" They both laughed. Carrie studied the floor.

She looked up to see an expression of concern in Grant's eyes. Dusty saw them exchange glances and lifted her glass to her lips. She took it from him and drank. Her throat tightened, made her choke. Her head started to spin. Her own husband picked up the bottle grabbed her by the hair in one hand and pulled her head back. Carrie batted his arm as he poured it into her mouth. Half of the whiskey ran down the front of her dress. Her head spun while she spit and gagged on it.

Grant jumped up and knocked the bottle to the floor, making Dusty lose his grip on Carrie's hair. "What's the matter with you?" Grant gave Dusty a contemptuous look. "What are you trying to do to her?" Carrie cowered in her chair to stay out of their way.

Dusty's big hand grabbed Grant's shirtfront before he could sit back down. "She's my wife," he yelled. "I'll treat her any way I want."

Grant's eyes bugged out as he gasped for air. His face turned red while he tried to push the big man away. Dusty shoved him back, hard. Grant's head hit the wall with a loud thwack. Carrie watched the man's eyes roll back inside his head as he slid to the floor.

Winda stood outside looking at the tavern door, realizing it was time to escape. Wondering if Dusty was intentionally letting her go, now that he had no use for her anymore. She had pulled herself up and brushed the dirt off her dress. That new man had pushed her down before he followed Dusty into the tavern. She rubbed her sore leg and wondered how her friend was inside. A couple of children ran up to her, pointing at her, laughing. One of them threw a stone at her, hitting her on the arm. She was surprised to see a teenage black boy chase the children away.

"I'm Sam," he told her after he stopped beside her. "My grandpa says you come with me to our house." He pointed down the street at a man standing by a tree.

Winda turned back to watch the tavern. "I need to help Carrie."

Sam shook his head. "There ain't nothin' you and me can do now. Not if she's with Dusty."

"You know Dusty?" She studied the handsome boy beside her. She had met black men before. Pakwis had traded with some.

Sam screwed up his face and let out a snort. "I know him."

He disliked Dusty. Therefore, Winda counted Sam as a friend.

Sam looked back toward his house. The old man wasn't by the tree anymore. "My grandpa would like to meet you."

"Thank you, Sam." Winda gratefully accepted the invitation, mainly because she had nowhere else to go. She followed him down the street, checking back at the tavern one last time. When they reached a small cabin and stepped onto the porch, a big black animal sat up. *Bear!* Winda pulled back.

"Don't be afraid. It's only Squirrel, my dog. He won't hurt ya." Sam patted the dog's huge head. Squirrel licked his face in turn. "You're a friend," he looked back up at her expectantly.

Winda leaned down and stuck out a tentative hand to let the dog sniff at it, his tail wagging excitedly. She patted the long-haired dog. Squirrel licked her face. She laughed and relaxed. "Hello, Squirrel."

They entered a one room cabin with a small kitchen to the left of the door. Four wooden, straight-back chairs surrounded the table in the middle of the room and a big pot of hot stew sat on top of it. To the right were an old rocking chair and three brown chairs. Two small tables sat between them with lanterns on them. Two single beds hugged the side wall with a dresser in between them. A fire blazed in the fireplace along the back.

"C'mon in," invited an old black man as he hobbled toward her, leaning on a cane. "Sit right down here. Did you eat?" Winda shook her head.

"My name is Winda," she said as she pulled out a chair. Sam handed her a bowl and spoon.

"Dig in before it's all gone." The old man laughed.

Winda enjoyed the stew and filled her bowl again after the old man prodded her. Sam cleaned up the dishes when they had finished and handed her a cup of coffee. She remembered having it with Lucas in the cave. She missed him terribly and wondered where he was.

The old man introduced himself as Jeb, "Short for Jebadiah." He was tall and lanky with wispy white hair and stubby whiskers. His brown eyes dancing with mischief. He wore a long-sleeved, tan shirt with black pants and suspenders.

Jeb chuckled and patted his right knee, "Art-right-us, gets worse in cold weather."

While Jeb drank his coffee, Winda turned her attention to Sam. He was quite a bit lighter in colour than his grandfather. Must be some white in there somewhere. Sam was fifteen. His hair was wavy and not tightly curled like most black people had. The prettiest blue eyes she had ever seen mesmerized her. And on a black man. He had beautiful, white, crooked teeth that didn't take away from his good looks. Like his grandfather, Sam wore a tan shirt but with blue pants and with dirty knees.

Winda looked back at Jeb and smiled, noticing how comfortable she felt. "Thank you," she said.

Grant came to a few minutes later and found Dusty and Carrie gone. He rubbed his sore throat until he could swallow without choking, and wondered why no one had helped him. Everyone turned away when he looked at them, even the bartender. Grant leaned against the wall and tried to piece things together. Dusty Blackman was the man he had heard of before. Grant was right; the man was as unpredictable as they came. He had walked up to the ugly bald man and whispered to him that General Walton had sent him. Dusty wasn't pleased to meet a new recruit for their operation.

Dusty had studied him with suspicion. Grant talked to calm him down and ease his mind. After he offered to buy Dusty a drink, the man's whole attitude changed. When Grant pushed the Indian lady down, he'd felt bad. He did it to impress Dusty. But he didn't intend to push her that hard.

Inside the tavern, Dusty had acted like the worse specimen of a human being he had ever met. He gulped down the whiskey; let it drip down the front of him. And the way he treated his wife was appalling, making her drink liquor when it was apparent that she didn't want any. Dusty also talked too much, bragging about exploits that Grant was sure weren't true. Grant was soon tired of him as he rambled on.

Grant felt sorry for Dusty's wife, Carrie, and wanted to know how she ended up with the likes of Dusty Blackman. Grant saw a beautiful, freckle-faced redhead under the dirt and bruises, much younger than her husband. He had watched her frightened green eyes dart around the room as if she was looking for a saviour. When Dusty poured the whiskey down her throat, Grant lost control. Dusty's knuckles had dug into his throat and cut off his air. Grant knew he'd have a bruise there. The last thing he saw was

Carrie's frightened eyes when he collapsed. He rubbed his throat now until he was able to swallow without the scratchiness.

A glass fell and shattered on the floor when Grant pulled himself up. He leaned on the table to get his bearings. The other patrons ignored him. The barkeeper watched him stumble to the door and smiled at him like an old friend. Grant wondered why nobody had helped him, coming to the conclusion that Dusty told them not to.

A light snow dusted the street as he staggered toward the boarding house in the dark. The Indian lady was gone. He wanted to apologize to her. A man and lady walked by and looked at him in disgust. He wanted to yell at them, tell them that he wasn't drunk. But he couldn't, his throat was just too raw.

It irked Grant, to think that he had to be nice to Dusty until he'd accomplished his mission. He made his way around the corner to the boarding house and his rented room, and climbed the stairs, banging the door angrily behind him.

Grant paced back and forth in the dark. Carrie's sad, green eyes haunted him. Minutes later he punched his pillow. Feathers flew everywhere.

Sam jumped up after the meal and fed his dog. Winda watched him put fresh water into his bowl and set it near the door. Squirrel lapped it up noisily, wagging his tail all the while, his long ears wiping the floor.

"You know Dusty long?" Jeb asked her.

"No, only..." She tried to think of the number but didn't know it. She held up the appropriate number of fingers to show him.

"Eighteen days?" Jeb asked. Winda nodded. He sat across the table from her while Sam played with his dog. "You a friend of his?"

"No," she told him a little too forcefully. "I had no choice, to come here with him." She rubbed her leg to steady her nerves. Sam saw her, lifted it up and rested it gently on another chair. "Thank you, Sam." He beamed at the praise and sat across from her.

"Don't trust him," Jeb warned her vehemently. "He isn't what he pretends to be. He's dangerous." A long, thin finger shook at her. "He's a killer! Don't trust him."

"I do not," Winda told him. "I do not like him."

Jeb forced himself to settle down. He apologized for his outburst. "Who was that other woman with him?"

"That's Carrie, his wife."

"What?" He bolted out of his chair and slammed the table with his fist. Both Winda and Sam jumped. Sam's mouth popped open. Winda looked from one to the other. Sam shrugged. Jeb's leg gave out. He fell back down and yelped. "His wife?"

Winda nodded. "What's wrong?"

Jeb sat back into his chair and rubbed his scruffy chin. "She can't be. He has a wife."

Winda looked at him in astonishment. "What do you mean?"

"Well, as good as anyway. He's been living with Kate for about eight or nine years now."

"The truth, Jeb?"

"Yep, and that ain't all." He leaned in closer. "They have two little boys too." A slow menacing smile spread across his face. "That won't go over good. No, that won't go over good at all." He chuckled. "There's going to be war over this one." Jeb rubbed at his sore knee. "Kate considers herself his wife. And rightly so, I guess." Then, he laughed so hard, tears blinded him. Sam laughed with him.

Winda didn't find it funny at all. "What will happen to Carrie?"

Jeb wiped his face with the back of his hand and shrugged. He reached across the table and took her hands in his. "You got a place to stay tonight?" She shook her head. "You can stay here, Winda. We will be glad to have ya." He pulled himself up on his feet. "This old man needs his rest. I'm going to turn in. Sam and me will share my bed. You can have his, okay?"

Sam followed his grandfather into the corner. Winda looked the other way and waited until they were settled. She quickly pulled on an old nightshirt that Jeb lent her and crawled under the covers, tossing and turning most of the night. Sometime in the early dawn, she slipped down to the floor and slept.

"I still haven't been able to find out who that reverend was," Anthony said as he stabbed his fork into a pork chop and lifted it off the platter. "No one has seen him since." Mary's face paled. "I'm sorry, but I checked all the towns nearby." His pork chop slid off his fork and landed with a plop onto his mashed potatoes. He wrinkled up his nose as he looked down at his splattered chest. "Oh, no. I just bought this shirt."

Gert set her napkin on the table and stood up. "Go and change it. I'll set it to soak so it won't stain." She shook her head at her sister as she followed her husband. "Men can't seem to keep clean, even at the supper table." Mary let out a little snicker and then went back to her meal. Gert glanced her way as she rounded the corner to go up the stairs. Once in their room she waited for Anthony to slip out of his shirt. "I don't think Mary eats very much at home. She's stuffing herself down there now."

"She probably can't afford to." Anthony handed her his shirt and slipped into another one. "Maybe we should have her here more often."

"As long as Ivan doesn't come with her." Gert took the shirt and headed back downstairs. She went into the back room and filled a bucket with water and dunked the shirt into it. Then she joined the other two in the dining room. "Sorry," she said to Mary. "Anthony's clothes have to be clean. It won't do for him to have a stain on his shirt while he's meeting clients, now would it?"

Once again, they settled into the meal. After they'd finished Gert served them tea and little vanilla cakes. "Have you heard from Carrie?" she asked as she cut a piece of her cake with her fork.

Mary swallowed the cake in her mouth. "No, and it worries me. I haven't heard from Ivan, either."

"It must be hard." Gert patted Mary's hand as she gave her husband an uneasy look. "I'm sure Carrie's settling in someplace and she will contact you when she is."

Mary shook her head. "I would have thought she'd be settled in by now." She let out a long sigh. "Maybe she just doesn't want anything to do with me anymore."

"Now why would you say a thing like that?" Anthony asked as he tucked a napkin under his chin before he lifted his cup of tea.

Mary shrugged. "I don't know. It's just a feeling I have."

Carrie woke up the next morning with a headache, her stomach churning. She rolled over and buried her head into the pillow. She peeked out over the covers and realized she was in a small room. Grayish wallpaper covered all four walls that had stained yellow. A night stand with a pitcher and bowl stood beside the window along with a wooden rocking chair. Another straight-back chair stood by a desk with a bible on it. Small logs burned brightly in the fireplace. She figured she was upstairs in the tavern.

The door banged against the wall when Dusty entered with a tray. She jumped and grabbed her head.

"Here's your breakfast," he called to her cheerfully. He set it down on the table beside the bed, pushing the lantern to one side. He threw open the curtains, letting the bright sunlight blind her. She lifted the blanket over her head. Dusty pulled the blanket back, grabbed her arm, and pulled her up. Her head started to thump as she pushed her legs over the side of the bed. She tried to lie back down. He held her up.

"C'mon, Carrie, now eat something." He sat next to her, reached over and picked up the tray, eased it over, and set it on her lap. He lifted the lid off her plate and set it aside. Carrie smelled the greasy bacon and watched the slimy eggs float around, and vomited all over her husband.

"Why you little…" He didn't finish but jumped up and stormed out of the room.

Carrie set the tray aside. After she cleaned herself up, she lay back down and prayed that she would just die.

She slept all that day and throughout the night. Dusty didn't return. The second morning she felt much better. The slight headache she had now was easily dismissive. Carrie crawled out of bed slow and easy. Someone had brought up her sack and left it inside her door. She reached in and pulled out her worn, green coat. Carrie picked up the tray and took it downstairs.

The tavern was empty, except for the barkeeper who took the tray from her and disappeared into the kitchen. Carrie sat at a table and laid her coat on the chair beside her. She planned to get some fresh air later. When the barkeeper returned she ordered ham, potatoes, and bread; nothing greasy. She hadn't eaten in two days and gulped down her breakfast. When her plate was empty she sat back to enjoy her second cup of coffee. Her headache was gone and she felt much better. She took a sip of coffee and savoured the warm liquid as it slid down the back of her throat.

Winda's disappearance didn't disturb her. Carrie knew that Indians weren't allowed in places like the tavern. Her mind wandered as she sat there from how Dusty treated her to that good looking guy named Grant. She straightened herself up and wondered where that came from all of a sudden. And just as bad as her husband, she chided herself. She was a married woman and shouldn't have these thoughts about another man, but just the same.

Someone tapped on the window next to her and woke Carrie from her fantasy. Winda motioned to her. Carrie threw on her coat and headed for the door. The barkeeper looked up from wiping the bar and said, "Don't try to leave town, missus."

Carrie glanced at him and tried to ignore the stab in her chest. She knew then, that Dusty was having her watched. She stepped out, squinting into the bright sunlight. Winda took Carrie's hand and led her down the snow covered street to a small cabin. A huge black dog sat up when they walked up the porch steps.

"This is Squirrel," Winda introduced them. "He's big, but very gentle."

Carrie patted the dog's head. "I like dogs."

Winda led Carrie inside and introduced everyone. "Sam saved me the other night. I've been sleeping here."

"I'm glad you found a place, Winda. I didn't know where you went. I looked for you, but you disappeared."

"That man Dusty met pushed me out of the tavern."

Jeb motioned for the ladies to sit at the table. Sam shook Carrie's hand then ran outside to hang out with his friends. Winda made a pot of tea and poured them each a cup. She looked relieved that her friend was safe.

Jeb told Carrie about Kate and the boys. "Dusty is their father, unfortunately. He's always had a mean streak in him." Jeb shook his head. "He brought her here about nine years ago. I thought he would settle down. Boy, was I wrong." He looked at Carrie. "They are good kids. Kate sees to that. She's a good woman. I just don't know what she sees in him, is all."

Carrie sat there stunned. Winda poked her. "Breathe, Carrie. You turn white."

She let out a long sigh. "You mean Dusty is already married, to a girl?"

"Yep," Jeb acknowledged. "But not legal though. They just live together."

"But we are legal. My father made sure of that." Carrie told them about her wedding. "What I don't understand is why my father would do this to me." Tears threatened. Winda hugged her.

Jeb studied Carrie. "Dusty's father owned the tavern and the saw mill at the other end of town. He gets inheritance from both of them."

"So that's how he can afford to keep me there." Carrie shook with rage. "Where is Kate? I bet she's not too far away is she?"

"No, she ain't," Jeb told her compassionately. "They have a farm about ten miles north of here."

"What do I do?"

Winda shook her head. "I don't know, Carrie. We need a plan."

Carrie watched Winda get up and make more tea. "This is a very unusual situation."

They sat in contemplation until the tea had steeped enough. Winda poured another round.

"You can look after this old man anytime, Winda,"Jeb laughed, his eyes sparkling as he watched her.

She smiled at him. "I am just happy for someplace to stay, Jeb."

Carrie looked at her friend. "I thought you were going to find your people, Winda?"

Winda took a sip of tea then set her cup down on the table. "You need help here, I can wait."

Carrie's eyes filled with tears. "Thank you, both of you."

7

Lucas steered his canoe toward shore and jumped out onto the slippery bank, a week late. He tied it up and grabbed his gear. The sun hovered above the trees. A light dusting of snow covered the ground. *Winda's probably started her evening meal about now.* He smiled in anticipation as he trudged up the hill toward the cave. He wanted to get there before it got too dark to see his way through the trees. The path had overgrown and was hard to follow. He didn't notice; his thoughts were on Winda.

Wearily, he staggered up the slope and into the clearing at the mouth of the cave. He stopped on the top of the hill and set the sacks down. There was no light from a fire. Inside the cave was dark and quiet. His feet carried him inside but he didn't remember the walk. Everything was the same as when he'd left her. He felt the coals; cold. He noticed that all of her things were still there. She left in quite a hurry. Her blue hair clip lay on the bed. Her bone comb he had used on her long, silky hair lay beside it. He picked it up and studied it. A tooth had broken off, left a gap in the middle of the evenly spaced tines.

Lucas sighed and sat on the bed. He could see her smile up at him as she combed her beautiful, long hair. He could smell the lavender scent of it, could see her flip it this way and that to comb every knot from it. He saw her laughing, together with him. He could almost feel her warm lips on his. His arms felt empty. He wanted to feel her arms around his neck. But he sat there, empty and confused.

He stared angrily down at the comb in his hand. He shouldn't have left her. Angry with himself, he whipped it across the cave. It bounced and landed near the fire pit. Wearily, he sunk down on the bed and buried his face in his hands.

Lucas stayed in the cave for several days hoping that Winda would return. One morning he set out to hunt. Lost in thought, he tripped and nearly fell. He cursed the tree root hidden under the dead-fall. But when he looked down, he saw something buried under the leaves. Lucas pushed off the debris, uncovered a human arm and jumped back. He stood there and blinked at it while his heart hammered in his chest. A silent prayer went up to his maker. *Please, don't let this be Winda.*

With a shaky hand, he brushed off more leaves and dirt. A man lay there. He looked around and wondered if he should dig it up. Suddenly, he came to a realization that they'll think he did it. That was his trap around the man's leg. He was a killer of animals, not of men.

Hastily, he covered it back up and ran up to the cave. Everything went into the canoe in hurriedly packed sacks. Several trips later, he stood in the middle of the empty cave. Leave no evidence behind. Lucas checked the trail one last time to make sure he didn't drop anything. He made sure he had all of Winda's belongings too. Nobody could tie her to a murder, even if she did this. He knew her, or at least he thought he did. She would never do something like this, unless she had no choice.

After another quick glance around, Lucas jumped into the canoe and paddled as hard and as fast as he could. It was best to leave now, before the river froze over.

Winda needed some fresh air and borrowed a heavy coat from Jeb after Carrie left. She stepped outside into the cool evening. Her own coat was still in the cave. She wished she had that one, it was warmer. Squirrel bounded up the steps to greet her. She bent down and petted him and ordered him to stay. When she looked up she saw Dusty walking by on the other side of the street. He didn't see her so she followed him. He turned down between two buildings and knocked on a door at the back of the general store. Someone let him in. Winda crept closer.

She heard voices. A small window was slightly ajar so she crouched down under it and listened. A woman's voice yelled at Dusty in anger. Winda peered through the dirty glass. He stood in what looked like the storage room for the store. It was full of crates and boxes. Shelves around the room held blankets, cans of food, utensils, pots, seeds for panting and various other items for sale. Shovels leaned against the wall to her right, barrels and crates stood along the wall to her left.

Dusty had his arms up and talked softly as if trying to calm the woman down. She picked up a small object and threw it at him. He ducked, it crashed against the wall. Winda watched them argue, unable to tear herself away. Dusty pleaded some more and took a step toward the woman. She glared at him and he stopped.

The woman was almost as tall as he was with long, dark hair that flowed down to the middle of her back. She seemed muscular for a female, her arms bulged out against the sleeves of her green dress. Winda couldn't make out her fine features from where she was.

"Please. Listen to me, Kate," Dusty pleaded. "It's not what it seems. She won't be here long, I swear."

"How dare you, Dusty. How dare you bring another woman home with you."

He tried to put his arm around her. She pushed him away and backed up. "I'm just watching her until Ivan pays me. That's all, Kate."

"I'm sure," she spat at him. "I'm tired of this, Dusty. If you don't get rid of her soon, you will never see your boys again."

He shook his head, "Please, Kate. She won't be here long. Just until our last deal goes through. I promise." Kate let him hug her. "Let me tell you about the deal I made this time." He kissed her tenderly, stroking her back. She buried her head into his shoulder. He looked behind her and smiled.

Winda backed away shaking her head. "That man tell lies," she said as she headed back to Jeb's.

Sam opened the door the next morning and let Carrie inside. She shivered as he pushed the door shut against the snow that blew in sideways. He took her coat and hung it on a peg while she blew on her hands to warm them up. "Smells good in here," she commented after she tousled his hair.

"Winda made it," Sam told her proudly. "I'm teaching her."

"Good for you."

He led her to the table with plates full of bread, bacon and eggs.

"Breakfast is ready, Jeb," Winda called him to the table.

He threw more wood on the fire, limped over, and nodded at Carrie. "Morn'in Carrie. Not a very nice day out there, is it?"

"No. The wind almost blew me across the street on my way over here." She looked out the window. "I hope it dies down before I go back."

Winda motioned for everyone to dig in. Carrie filled her plate. She lifted a hesitant fork full of egg to her mouth and swallowed. Her stomach didn't protest this time so she dug in. Jeb smiled at Winda when she got up and poured everyone, even Sam, a cup of tea.

"You know where Dusty is now?" Winda asked Carrie as she set the teapot down.

Carrie shook her head.

Winda looked from Carrie to Jeb then back again. "I saw him last night arguing with Kate. This morning, they left in a wagon full of things. I don't know where they went though."

"Did they head north?" asked Jeb.

"Yes."

"Kate was here?" Carrie asked. "Does she know about me? Does she know who I am?"

"Yes," Winda told her sympathetically. She cleared her throat. "I heard them talk. Dusty told her."

"I bet that didn't go over so well," laughed Jeb.

"No. It did not. She said she would take the boys away from him." Winda took a sip and set her cup down slowly.

"Something has to be done about this situation," Jeb surmised. "But just remember, this is Dusty's town. He has a lot of friends here as well as enemies. I don't know who we can trust."

Carrie turned toward Jeb. "Why are you helping me?"

"Because." He sniffed. "I'm too old to put up with his antics anymore. And because he killed Sam's parents, my daughter and her husband."

"What happened?" Winda saw a tear in Jeb's eye.

"He blamed my son-in-law for stealing. Dusty and some of his friends set fire to their home. Both of them died, burned to death." Tears ran down the old man's face. "Sam just happened to be with me at the time, or else I would have lost him too." He squeezed Sam's arm. "I know he didn't steal anything." He looked pleadingly at the women. "He just wasn't that type. I know he didn't steal anything."

Carrie and Winda exchanged glances. Winda asked. "Why you stay here?"

"I was Dusty's father's slave. I was freed after he died." Jeb looked around the cabin. "I get enough money to live on. Me and Sam live here free. I can't afford to live no where else. It was in his father's will." Jeb watched Sam drink his tea. "I don't know what will happen to Sam when I'm gone."

Sam patted Jeb's arm. "I can look after myself, Grandpa," he said bravely. "I'll be all right."

Winda figured his insides rolled like a mad river, though.

Jeb turned back to the women. "I hope that some day I can get Dusty back for what he done."

Carrie entered her room two weeks later to find Dusty in there. He was sitting on the edge of the bed, gulping down whiskey from a brown bottle. He glowered at her for a few minutes then tipped the bottle up and finished it, but kept it clutched in his big hand.

"Where have you been, you little harlot? I've been waiting here all day for you." He weaved around and hiccoughed.

"I've only been gone a couple of hours, Dusty." Gently, Carrie set her packages down on the desk and faced him.

"You're supposed to wait here for me. Not out traipsing all around town." He staggered toward her, backed her into a corner. She stared to shake. "What have you been up to? Seeing someone behind by back?"

The slap across her face shocked her. She rubbed it tenderly, fighting back tears. She should be used to this by now. "No, Dusty, I just needed some fresh air. That's all."

He glared at her for a long time. She watched him strain to keep his temper in control. "Well, it better be," he threatened. Dusty backed off and stood in front of the window. He parted the curtain and stared out into the darkness. He dare accuse her of what he was guilty of? But she dare not confront him about it. She watched her husband tip the bottle back to suck up the very last drop. He dropped it to the floor; it rolled into the far corner.

He turned, still glaring at her, then walked toward the bed and undressed himself. "Come on, now."

Wide-eyed and frightened beyond measure, she joined him. She could smell the stale whiskey on his breath and held back the vomit that rose to her throat. His brutal strength was the only thing that kept her in bed beside him. He was foul and slobbered all over her. She cringed when he put his grubby hands on her.

As soon as he was done, he passed out. Carrie got up, careful not to disturb him, and undid one of her packages. She pulled out and loaded a small pistol, pointed it at him. Her hand shook. She wrapped her other hand around it to help steady the strange object in her hands. Sweat poured down into her eyes. Her heart raced. For a few seconds, she actually thought she could do this.

She lowered the pistol and stuffed it back inside her package, under the rest of her belongings. With shaky fingers, she undid the other package and took out a pair of pants and a blouse and set them aside. She slid back into bed and cried herself to sleep.

Dusty rose the next morning and cradled his head in his hands. Carrie was in a chair by the window with a new book in front of her. He groaned when he sat up and leaned against the wall. She didn't move.

"Read to me, Carrie. Please? You know I like it when you read me a good story." She flipped back to the start of the book and read aloud in a shaky voice. Several chapters later, Dusty pulled himself up and got dressed. "Let's go down and get breakfast."

Carrie banged the book shut. Dusty grabbed his head. "You go, I'm staying right here," she told him and didn't look up, but watched him from the corner of her eyes.

He stepped back, eyes darting around the room. She waited for the next blow. When it didn't come, she dared to face him.

"What's that?" he asked and pointed to her new clothes.

"Clothes. I bought them for travelling. Don't you think I need decent clothing to wear, Dusty? Have you seen the shape my dress is in? Do you want your wife going around looking like a beggar?"

"Ah, yeah, ah no, well, we aren't going anyplace." Sunlight filtered into the room and made Dusty squint.

"Oh, okay then." Carrie opened the book stared at it. She jumped when he made a sudden movement.

"How are you paying for all these things."

"Charging it. It's a wonderful thing." She might not be able to leave town, but she'd make him pay for keeping her there.

"Charging it, to who?" He squinted at her as if he knew the answer.

"To you, Dusty. As my husband, you can support me, can't you? How else do you expect me to live?" She faced him then and watched his neck turn red.

His eyes glazed over. Then he blew out a loud whistle. "Ya, well, I guess. You're right. You do need some things, don't you?"

She watched him fight his emotions. Normal colour slowly returned to his face. His laboured breathing calmed. He gave her a sly grin. "Okay. But, don't you dare spend too much. I ain't a rich man, Carrie." He reached for his hat and headed toward the door. In a carefully controlled, calm voice he addressed her. "I'm going down for breakfast, you coming?"

Carrie gently closed her book, set it on the middle of the table and followed her husband out of the room.

Icy wind blew across a small lake at six wigwams crowded along the northern butte. People huddled around small fires and tried to keep warm. An early winter snow had piled up outside the stick and fur dwellings up to three feet high. A child cried of hunger.

Little Blossom put another log on the fire, her eyes never leaving the hide cloth over the doorway. It flapped and twisted on its ties and threatened to blow off. She had prayed to her spirits several times in the last four days to bring her new husband home safe. To lose another one so soon would be unbearable. The last big storm had claimed the lives of her husband and two small sons. Her new husband had been out hunting for three days.

The storm had started late last night when Pakwis was supposed to return.

The weather had turned quickly. Just yesterday, she watched the children play on the ice. They used an old hide where one would sit on it while others pulled them across the small lake and back. Sometimes they would run around in circles, spinning the fur around. Their laughter was contagious. Some of the children looked a little dizzy afterward.

Little Blossom sat up straight when she heard snow crunching outside under footfalls. Pakwis opened the flap and carried in a deer. He smiled through a frozen, white face, then dropped his mitts and blew on his hands. Little Blossom secured the door.

Pakwis gave her a kiss. "Night Wind got another one. We will both share. Everyone will eat plenty tonight."

Little Blossom undid his snowshoes and waited for him to step out of them. She leaned them against the wall while he took off his wet coat and leggings and hooked them on pegs to dry out. He pulled a buffalo-hide blanket around his shoulders and stood by the fire.

"Welcome home, my husband." Little Blossom handed him a cup of tea which he took in both hands.

"Happy to be home. The wind spirits are angry this day. We did not know if we would make it back." He sat down and stretched out his feet to the fire. His face was raw from the icy wind. His teeth chattered. The tea would sooth his throat as the warm liquid slid down. "Thank you, Little Blossom."

"You are welcome." She patted his arm. "I will cut up the deer now." She dug into her basket by the door for her knife. She didn't want to butcher the animal inside her home, but the weather outside was too bad. She pulled it over to one side and cut it up.

By the time she was done Pakwis had warmed up. Little Blossom handed him several baskets of meat, which he took over to their neighbours. She put some in a pot for their evening meal. The rest of the meat she'd cook for later.

While the stew cooked, Little Blossom wiped up the blood with a cloth, and then rinsed it out in melted snow. She took a flat piece of wood and scraped the hard-packed dirt floor and threw the remains outside. When she was satisfied that her house was as clean as she could get it, she threw the piece of wood into the fire.

Pakwis returned with a small bowl of wild blueberries. "Sleeping Rabbit sent these as a thank you gift." He beamed at his new wife. "I am glad to have this tasty treat to go with our meal."

She dropped a handful into the pot. "I will thank her the next time I see her."

Pakwis sat on the hard ground and waited while his meal cooked. He watched his wife as she stirred the stew and flipped over the lines of venison strips that would sustain them for a few more days. He felt lucky to have Little Blossom as his wife. His love for her had grown with each new day. She too, seemed to be very happy in their new relationship and told him that she loved him. The age difference didn't even bother her as he once thought.

He had married Lanick more out of duty to help keep peace between two of the clans and soon regretted it. He tried to love her, but she made it so difficult for him. She would lay stiff in his bed when he tried to make love to her. She always complained and ridiculed him.

Pakwis smiled slightly. His slave girl, Winda, responded better, even though she tried hard not to. He felt her hold back. In the end, though, she actually started to respond to his touch. Of the two women, he missed her the most.

Little Blossom set the stirring stick on a rock and sat back, smiling at her husband. Pakwis leaned over and pulled the tie on her dress. "I love you, Little Blossom, always."

"I love you too, my husband." She bent over and pulled him toward her. Winda faded from his mind.

8

1801. Lucas had pulled his canoe down the frozen river as far as he could. He had taken the right fork, only because it was wider. Not knowing that the left one would have led him to Winda. A late spring snow storm that hit four days ago, froze everything, again. His shoulders and back ached because he'd hauled his heavy gear all over the damn place. He found a good spot to camp and set up his tent. He had enough and didn't want his feet to slip and slide all over the ice anymore. Now, he told himself, he wouldn't go anywhere until the river thawed.

His canvas tent stood behind him on a rise above the water so it wouldn't flood. Lucas sat on a stump, poured himself a cup of coffee and scanned the river, both upstream and down. He felt like he was the only person in the world and desperately needed someone to talk to. Then he chuckled to himself. He was getting tired of his own company. He felt so lonely after months by himself in the wilderness.

He looked out across the half frozen river three days later to the eastern hills past the meadow before him. Snow started to melt where the sun's warm rays shone along the bottom of the hill. Sprigs of grass shot up here and there in the meadow. Water dripped off the trees behind his tent. Every day he walked up and down the river and poked the ice flows with a stick. He hoped that in four or five days he could canoe it. Lucas itched to get out of there.

Songbirds had arrived a week later when most of the snow and ice had melted, calling for their mates. He had seen his first robin, the sign that spring was officially here. A bear meandered along the bottom of the hill. It reminded him of Winda. He missed her so much, his heart ached. The memory of the bear that attacked her flashed before his eyes. Where are you, my love? Did she miss him as much as he did her? He hoped to leave there in two days to look for her.

The bear disappeared through the trees on the far side of the meadow. For some reason he was sad to see it go. A black spot moving down the hill caught his attention. From where he sat, he couldn't make out what it was. It grew as it got closer. Then it split into two, then five, then more. Lucas braced himself, ready to run and hide. Then he thought, what for? If they want to, they'd hunt him down anyway.

When the group got closer, he saw that they were a band of Ojibwa. He sipped his coffee and waited. They crossed the river, jumping onto the last of the ice, then off on his side. Men helped the women and children with their packs. It seemed to take them forever before they trudged up the rise and into his camp. One man stepped forward and gave the universal sign of hello, he was a friend. He stood tall and straight and looked him right in the eyes. This was the man of power, Lucas thought.

In crude English, he introduced himself as Pakwis. Lucas looked up at him in surprise. Was this the one Winda had told him about? He looked to be about fifty. Lucas expected a much younger man. He could tell that he was taller than the Indian and thinner. Pakwis watched him through dark eyes that pierced right through him. His chiselled face remained unreadable. Pakwis wore his grey-black hair in a bun to one side with two feathers stuck in it. A red bandanna was wrapped around his head. He was the only one who wore a cloth shirt under a fur coat and had tucked his leather pants into high rabbit fur boots. Lucas also noticed that the man carried his rifle, pointed down in a non-threatening way.

Lucas watched as the crowd formed around his camp. Hungry eyes stared at him. The sight of the ragged children that looked half starved tore at his heart. He set down his cup and pointed to the moose he had hung in the trees to keep predators at bay. He smiled as the women rushed to it and cut it down. They need it more than he did.

A brave, about Lucas's age sat down beside the one he believed to be the chief. Hard stern eyes watched him. Lucas felt that this man would just as soon shoot him. It didn't frighten him though. He didn't really care what happened to him at this point.

Pakwis similarly studied the white man as he walked into the camp. His hair was the colour of dried wheat, his face shaggy. The bright green eyes fascinated him, the colour of grass in the sunlight. Buckskin covered the man from head to toe. The white man showed no sign of fear, which impressed him. The man's rifle leaned against his lodge ten steps away. Pakwis relaxed and faced the white man after the offer of the moose was given. "It is a good day. Thank you, my friend."

The two upside down canoes lay on the riverbank at the edge of town. Dusty hadn't used them since last fall. The river ran free of ice but a heavy frost covered the ground. The sun had just peeked through the trees when Winda pushed one into the water.

After she threw in her sack, she jumped in and guided the canoe downstream. The current carried her along silently. All she had to do was steer. She kept the craft in the centre to avoid rocks and tree roots. Winda managed this with expert ease. Even though she was anxious to get to her destination, she enjoyed it out on her own. It was a time for reflection and hard exercise after the long winter.

At night she would tie up and make a small fire to cook her evening meals. Then she would relax and enjoy a drink of mint tea. Winda threw another log on the fire and watched the sparks disappear into the blackness. She had inquired about her parents when she met other Cree. No one seemed to remember them. Only one person told her that they had died years ago of the smallpox. She took a sip of tea in deep thought. She didn't remember any Cree legends or stories anymore. All she knew were Ojibwa ones. Even if her parents had been alive, they would be as strangers to her now. She came to the conclusion that her parents must be dead. If they could have rescued her, she's sure they would have at least tried. Winda resigned to give up her search for them.

She thought about Jeb and Sam, and had come to love her new family. Then the thought of Carrie made her shiver. She had looked so young and vulnerable when they met. Winda's stomach knotted when she thought of Dusty. His hard grey eyes wore through her soul when he glared at her. She still didn't know why he just let her go when they reached Blackman Falls. He just ignored her after she helped deliver those crates. He cast her aside like she was an old tool that was no longer of use. Now she retraced the route they'd taken in one of his stolen canoes.

Trillium and May apples overgrew the path to the cave several days later. Winda picked her way up the hill under a green canopy of maple, birch, elm and oak. She loved this time of year. Everything was new, fresh and alive.

Bushes blocked the entrance to the cave. Winda pulled some out to gain entry. She went straight to the pit and lit a fire. It was empty. Lucas's image floated on the rock wall before her as if he were there to comfort her. *"I'll be back as soon as I can,*

Winda. I promise," he had told her before he left. Tears rushed down her face as she sat cross-legged by the fire. She hoped that it was Lucas who had all their belongings and that they hadn't been robbed.

She stayed there for several days just to be alone with her thoughts.

The next morning, Winda picked up her sack and walked to where Jack's body lay. She was glad to see that the animals had chewed at it. His spirit would forever roam with no proper burial. She didn't fear him anymore, or his spirit. She just stared at the decomposing body, satisfied that he could hurt no one else.

She went down to the river, threw her sack into the canoe. She got in and pushed the craft away from the shore. This time she had to fight the current as she paddled upstream. On the second night, she pulled the canoe up onto a small sandy beach and made camp. After eating the rabbit she'd shot with her bow and arrow Winda sat by her fire and thought about her new friends again.

Jeb and Sam treated her like one of their own. Sam was like a little brother to her. She was teaching him to hunt and fish; at least the skills he didn't know, and enjoyed it. He was so eager to learn. She had seen him look up at her with such adoration in his eyes.

Jeb seemed to have adopted her, treating her like a daughter. She looked down at the hands on her lap. He'd aged so much since she first met him. His knee was a constant concern now; he bent lower on his cane and hardly left the house anymore.

Winda supplied them with meat and whatever she could trade for. The man at the general store seemed to enjoy bartering with her. They had become friends. Even other people in town had started to recognize her. Some still treated her with indifference or even disdain. But overall, life was good.

For three days it had rained and snowed. Carrie needed the fresh air of early spring after she had been cooped up in the tavern all winter, most of the time without Dusty. On the fourth day, the sun had set behind the livery stable when she finished her new book. She went out for a short walk. Her new clothes she bought fit her perfectly. She liked the freedom of movement that the pants gave her. A satisfied grin spread across her face because she bested one over on Dusty. Carrie planned to charge more items to him just to make him pay. She chuckled to herself at the barkeeper's look of shock when she threw her old tattered dress into the fireplace in the tavern.

Carrie fingered the envelope, making sure it stayed hidden in her pocket. Sam had gotten a piece of paper, ink well and a pen. She'd written the letter in the cabin. The time had come to find the man that Jeb told her she could trust. "*The man who runs the general store hates Dusty. And he travels east once a year for new supplies for his store. His wife runs it while he's gone.*" He'd be leaving shortly, as far as Jeb knew.

Carrie glanced around, making sure the man she'd seen follow her on occasion wasn't around, then she slipped into the store just before it closed that evening. She was glad she was the only customer. The owner set a heavy sack on the floor by the corner then stood up straight. He smiled at her. "What can I get you, Ma am?"

Suddenly Carrie wasn't so sure she could do this. She fingered the envelope again inside her pocket. But the man in front of her was looking kindly at her. "I need to send a letter," she spurted before she lost her nerve.

The man narrowed his eyes as if he finally recognized her. "Ain't you Dusty's woman?" There was a threat to his tone.

"I am. But against my will. Jeb said you'd help me." She took the envelope out of her pocket and held it up. "I need to let my aunt and uncle know where I am." She started to shake. "Maybe they can come and get me."

"And get you away from Dusty?" He said softly.

"Yes."

The man stepped forward and took her letter. She almost grabbed it back. "I leave in a couple of days. I'll make sure it gets posted in the nearest city that has a post office."

"Thank you," she muttered before she left the store.

The crisp, clean air slowly rejuvenated her as she wandered around aimlessly; until she stopped in front of the livery stable. The barkeeper had told her that if she tried to rent a horse or buy a ticket on the stagecoach, Dusty's men would detain her until he got back. She felt her cheek in the spot where he'd hit her last.

She sighed then went down a side street, past a few houses and a church; she rounded another corner, her boots splashing in the mud. A cat jumped out and startled her. She laughed at herself and bent down to pet it, talking to it while it purred and rubbed against her leg. When she stood up, something caught her eye. At the other end of the street, Dusty was talking to another man.

Carrie hugged the building and crept closer. She knelt down against a barrel behind a warehouse. The two men went inside a small door at the other end of the building. They emerged a few minutes later with a crate. It looked like one of the ones that they had hauled all the way from York.

She watched them lift it onto the back of the wagon with another long crate and throw a tarp over the cargo. It was too short and didn't cover the end, but it would keep the rain off. The man Dusty helped walked back into view. He was shorter than her husband. His long brown hair lay over his collar. The way he walked seemed familiar.

"That's the last one for awhile, Dusty. See ya next month." He handed Dusty an envelope. "I gotta get moving. General Walton is waiting for these guns."

They shook hands and the man jumped up onto the driver's seat. Moonlight illuminated the man's face. Carrie crouched lower. Ivan clicked his tongue and the horses pulled the wagon toward her. Ivan? What was he doing here? The shock of seeing her father almost made her cry out. Then, as her heart settled from tapping against her chest, she realize she needed to get out of there before Ivan saw her. Something was not right. She glanced around and saw that she had nowhere to go. She could not squeeze between the barrel and the wall. If he looked back he would see her.

Dusty shoved the envelope into his coat and jumped up on his horse. The gelding neighed and stepped sideways. Ivan looked back. "Hey," he yelled and pulled hard on the reins. The horses stopped. Ivan jumped down and ran toward Carrie. Dusty galloped to where Ivan pointed.

Carrie tried to run. Ivan caught her and held her tight, his fingers digging into her arm. "What are you doing here?" He shook her. Her head bounced around on her neck.

Dusty's horse skidded to a stop, splashing dirty water all over them. Ivan hit her repeatedly. She screamed. He raised his hand again. "You're going to ruin everything."

Dusty grabbed his arm in mid air and held on. "Think." He stared angrily down at his partner. Ivan blinked up at him and slowly relaxed. Dusty let go. Both men looked around nervously. "We're making too much noise, Ivan."

Carrie's father pushed her toward her husband. "She's your responsibility. You deal with it." Carrie started to snivel. Ivan pushed her up on the horse in front of Dusty.

Dusty grabbed her by the hair. "Shut up." She stopped. Ivan walked back toward the wagon.

"Why are you doing this to me?" He didn't stop. "Father?"

"Because I can." Ivan turned back to face her. "I'm not your father, Carrie." Ivan stood stone still and watched her stricken face. "You were only a baby when I married your mother. But no, I'm not your father." He turned and jumped up on the wagon and raced away.

"Well," Dusty hissed through clenched teeth. "There's only one place I can take you now to keep you out of trouble." He kicked the horse hard and raced out of town.

The horse skidded and slipped through the slush at breakneck speed. Dusty's strong arm held Carrie so she wouldn't slide off. They rode up a steep hill and down again. They didn't even slow down for the bend in the road. A wooden bridge shook and bounced when they flew over it.

They barrelled up a long lane and didn't slow down to turn the tight corner. They passed a small stand of pine trees and stopped in front of a two-story, frame house. Dusty jumped down and pulled Carrie off. She staggered. He steadied her then dragged her inside. Carrie heard the horse snort and looked back. It stood there with its head down. Its side heaving in and out. It teetered sideways, but held its ground. Its lower legs bled from cuts from the thorny bushes they'd passed.

Dusty banged the door open and pushed her onto a kitchen chair. A woman standing by the stove turned with her spoon in hand. A sweet smell hung in the air. Carrie's stomach rumbled.

Two little boys bounded in from the other room, "Daddy, Daddy." They ran up to hug Dusty. He bent down, smiled, and picked them up one at a time and hugged them.

"You men looking after your ma?"

"Yep, we're big boys now, Daddy. We can look after her." The biggest one eyed Carrie curiously.

The smallest one showed Dusty his finger. "I hurt my finger. Mommy made it better. She put stuff on it." Dusty inspected the scar and told the boy, "Well I guess you'll live then, eh?" The boy nodded and looked back at his finger.

Carrie watched the woman by the stove through the corner of her eyes. She wore her long, black hair in a bun at the back of the neck. Her green dress showed a purplish stain in the front. She had a long, thin nose and thin, straight lips that scowled at them. Her blue eyes bore right through Dusty.

"Kate, I ah, this here is Carrie," he told her in a raspy voice. He turned to Carrie. "This is Kate. And these are my boys, Adam and Johnny."

Carrie nodded to the boys who smiled at her. They looked to be about eight and five years old. She didn't want to look at the woman's hate-filled eyes. Instead, she flipped her hair over her face to hide from the scornful looks Kate gave her.

Kate set the spoon on the stove, pulled out a chair, and slid into it. "Boys, go play in the other room. I'll come tuck you in, in a few minutes." They ran off, sensing the hostility in the room.

Carrie sat in Kate's kitchen afraid to look up. Dusty cleared his throat and faced Kate. "I had no choice. She saw us, me and Ivan, ah, working. I couldn't leave her in town." He leaned on the table as if to steady himself.

Kate spat at him. "But to bring her here, of all people? Here, Dusty?" Her face reddened. "How dare you!" The chair toppled over when she sprang up and stomped into the other room.

Seconds later they heard a loud thud from outside. Carrie followed her husband out. The horse they had ridden had fallen over. It lay in the wet snow and mud, its eye bulging out, its stiff tongue stuck to an icy patch of ground.

"Just great," Dusty huffed and pushed Carrie back inside the house. Kate returned a few minutes later.

He asked her if the boys were in bed. She nodded, her face puffy and red. "I don't want that, that woman in my house, Dusty. It's either her or me. You choose, now."

Dusty held up his hands. "You know the answer to that, Kate. I've told you."

"But to bring her here, how could you?"

He shrugged. "I'm going to put her in the back room." He walked over and removed a key from its hook and pulled Carrie by the arm. He led her up the stairs and down a short hall and opened the door at the far end. He gave her a sorrowful look before he pushed her inside the room. Carrie heard the key grate in the lock.

Grant had put down his fork and listened. Yes, he did hear something, a horse's neigh and someone yelling. Which alerted him to trouble. He threw on his coat and boots, grabbed his pistol, and ran down the stairs of the rooming house. He could have stayed at the tavern, but Dusty owned it. Grant also wanted peace and quiet. He figured it was the reason no one had helped him that day when Dusty cut his air off. Dusty probably threatened them if they did. Dusty could keep Carrie there for as long as he wanted. And Grant would know where she was. He also didn't want to blow his cover. Carrie would be too much of a distraction.

He had crept to the back of a building and peeked around the corner. At the back of the old warehouse, three people were arguing. One man hit a smaller one. Then the two rode off in the other direction in a hurry. One of them was Dusty.

He recognized Ivan Tanner who raced toward him in a wagon. When it slowed down Grant jumped into the back and slid under the tarp. It nearly tipped over because they took the corner so fast. Ivan glanced back when he felt the wagon jar but kept on. Grant had rolled up against a crate, out of the driver's sight. A small hole in the tarp allowed him to keep an eye on the driver.

Ivan whipped the horses as they sped through town. They flew past the tavern, the saw mill, and over a bridge. The wagon bounced and jostled down the road bruising Grant's arms and legs. After a few miles Ivan slowed the horses to a comfortable walk. He looked back over his shoulder several times, nervously. Grant peered out between the slats on the side of the wagon and watched the scenery go by. They turned off the main road and onto a hidden trail. Tree branches scratched the side of the wagon as they travelled down a steep hill and twisted and turned through the woods.

Grant couldn't sit up so he lay on his side and bounced around. When it got too dark for the driver to see the wagon stopped. Grant rolled out of the back and hid in the underbrush. Ivan jumped down with his rifle and checked the back of the wagon. Grant watched as Ivan took out his bedroll and settled down for the night. Grant settled for a night on wet leaves.

Dawn slowly crept in after a long night. Bullfrogs serenaded them after they had hibernated all winter. Grant hopped onto the back of the wagon as it pulled out, watching through the hole in the tarp. Again, Ivan feeling the thump, looked back, saw nothing, and kept on. Grant chuckled to himself at the man's bewildered look.

They passed the swamp and drove up a muddy slope through some low growth. Ivan stopped in the late afternoon and set out with his rifle to find his supper. Grant took the opportunity to pry open a crate with a bar he found for just that purpose. He lifted out a long sleek rifle and shouldered it. A smile crossed his face as he aimed it, pulled the trigger and heard the soft click. Grant turned it this way and that, admiring the sleek new look. It was lighter than the Brown Bess and was easier to handle. He replaced it and put the lid back on tight.

A twig snapped behind him. Grant dove for cover just as Ivan stepped into the open with two wild turkeys. While the driver prepared his meal, Grant sneaked out to find his own. After an hour, he had only one tiny ptarmigan. He chanced a small fire behind a grove of cedars to cook it, and kicked the fire out as soon as his meal was done, which wasn't long. He ate it in about ten bites. His stomach growled for more.

The sun had set behind a group of poplars when Grant returned to the wagon. Ivan had just settled in for the night. He waited until he heard Ivan snore before he allowed himself a few winks.

Grant lay on his back, looking up through the branches at the stars. He had seen Dusty with this man earlier and knew that he was the other man named on the list General Brooks had given him. He had hidden behind a buggy two weeks ago when he heard them talking about General Walton and the guns. The description fit too. Grant had gone back to his room before Dusty discovered him. He wasn't surprised to see them together behind the warehouse again. Now he had to find out who that other man with Dusty was; it was just too dark to see clearly. And of Dusty, what about that pretty, little wife of his?

The room was dark, illuminated only by the full moon. It gave Carrie enough light to make out where the furniture was. Fully clothed, she curled up on the bed and wept until she fell into a fitful sleep. She woke the next morning to the sound of a rooster's crow and wiped the sleep from her eyes. The room she was in was small with bright yellow wallpaper that looked fairly new. A wooden rocking chair hugged the far corner beside the door. A small dresser with a lace doily stood beside the bed. Long lace curtains hung to the floor over a tall window. On the other side of that was a small wooden straight-backed chair. Pictures hung on two of the walls, one above the bed. Both were of simple scenery which appealed to her.

This was the nicest room Carrie had ever stayed in. Dusty must have money to be able to decorate a room like this. The whole house was done up nice. Then she wondered why he kept her in a run-down tavern when he could afford a better place. The answer hit her like a tree branch on the head, because to him, she was not worth it.

The key grated in the lock. Dusty pushed it open and set her breakfast tray on the dresser. He left without a word, locking the door behind him. His footsteps fading. Then silence.

Carrie lifted the lid off the tray. A big helping of sausages, eggs, and potatoes filled her plate. Two pieces of bread and a small dish of jam sat to one side. That must have been what Kate was making last night, it sure smelled like it. She surprised herself and ate every bite, then took her steaming cup of coffee and sat in the rocker. She liked the room she was in. If things had been different she wouldn't mind it here. But it wasn't. She was a prisoner. She had always been Dusty's prisoner.

Squeals of laughter floated up from downstairs. She wondered if Dusty was playing with his boys. Then she heard the door slam. Minutes later she heard the boys outside. Both Adam and Johnny were out back wearing heavy jackets. The grass looked wet as if it had rained during the night. The sunshine that came into the window now made Carrie shade her eyes. She sat in the chair and watched the boys run around chasing each other.

Dusty's loud voice carried up the stairs. "It won't be long. I told you. Only a couple of weeks, till we get this shipment done." Carrie smirked to herself, Ivan had said that there wouldn't be another one for a month. "I'll take her…" his voice faded. Carrie walked over and put her ear to the door.

"She's supposed to be gone already, Dusty," Kate yelled back at him. "Don't you dare leave her here for me to look after."

A slap, Carrie smiled. So, all was not well with them either. She couldn't hear anymore so she sat back in the rocker. Some men had two wives, she knew. There would be one in the city and one, usually an Indian, out in the wilderness. A trapper or voyager could be gone from home for years at a time. Carrie couldn't think of how Dusty thought he would get away with this. She certainly didn't want to be Kate right now either. It was as if Dusty were flaunting his mistress at her. She took several shallow breaths and thought about her wedding day. Then she wondered why no one had told her about Ivan.

Jeb enjoyed Winda in his house. They both limped around and joked about it. Jeb's arthritic knee ached constantly. Winda's left leg was slowly healing from the bear attack. Her limp was less noticeable. Two long scars stretched pink and white down from her inner thigh then wrapped around the leg to the outer ankle. Sometimes they got itchy so she had to keep a soothing salve on them.

He had offered her a place to stay for the winter, hoped she would stay for good. "Stay until the weather improves. *You don't want to get stuck in the middle of a storm,*" he had told her. Winda thought about it and had accepted his kind offer. Now that spring was there, he hoped she'd forget to leave. He worried about his health and what would happen to Sam if something happened to him, and hoped that she would take him in when it was time. Jeb knew she was happy there.

He looked around the room. It was cleaner than he and Sam kept it. They didn't worry about the little things like Winda did. She chastised Sam just that morning because he didn't wipe his boots off when he came inside. She left after that to go hunting, as she often did, and took her bow and arrows she made. She'd be gone for most of the day. Jeb felt empty then, the cabin colder until her return. He relied on her too much already. He noticed that Sam followed her around like a lost soul. He would surely miss her if she left.

Winda told him about her capture and life as a slave. He in turn told her of his life as a slave to Dusty's father. He knew that she wanted to find her parents. Yet part of her realized that they were dead. She told him that she didn't know if she believed that or not. And that they wouldn't have anything in common anymore. Her parents were Cree, Winda was raised Ojibwa. Jeb would watch her contemplate her future. A sad expression would wash over her face. He knew she felt hopeless and he ached for her.

Jeb looked over at Winda's corner. He and Sam had hung a sheet across it to give her privacy. She had made a bed on the floor by the wall. A pile of furs hugged the other wall, some sewn together as part of a new winter coat. Winda still wore the one he gave her last fall.

Sam ran in, slamming the door behind him. Squirrel at his heals. He leaned on the table out of breath and squinted over at Jeb who sat in his chair spit-polishing his boots.

"Carrie's gone."

"What do you mean, gone?" Jeb dropped his boot and rag. His knee crunched when he pulled himself up.

"Last night. She didn't go back to the tavern after a walk. The cleaning lady says she wasn't there all night." Sam puffed to get his breath back. "Her bed hasn't been slept in. Her things are still there."

Jeb grabbed his cane and shuffled closer to his grandson. Squirrel nosed him for a pat on the head. Jeb complied automatically. His knee jabbed in pain, seemed worse today for some reason. Probably from the cold.

Sam straightened. "What should we do, Grandpa? Maybe Dusty took her someplace?"

"If he did," Jeb said, "wouldn't he let her take her belongings? He has so far." Suddenly his knee gave out. Sam helped him to his chair. After the pain subsided he shook his head. "I don't know, Sam. I just don't know."

9

Ivan drove the wagon across the swollen creek. The horses jumped and pulled at the reins. The current threatened to drag them downstream and over the falls. He whipped the horses and steered them toward the only clearing where the wagon would fit. At last, they dug in and flew out onto shore, splashing icy water all over him. He stopped the wagon on a high bank so the horses could rest. Grant rolled out of the back and ditched under some bushes, grateful that he'd remained dry under the tarp. Ivan was soaked and built a fire, stripped, and stretched out his clothing on the ground to dry. He reached into the back of the wagon and pulled out a blanket and sat in front of the fire to warm up. Grant stifled a sneeze. Ivan looked around, saw nothing move from where he sat, and then dozed in the afternoon sun. A few hours later Ivan re-dressed and continued on his journey. Two days later he drove the wagon along the top of a small hill. Grant saw a small shed at the bottom of the hill to his right. When the wagon headed toward it he rolled out of the back. He hit his head on a rock and almost cried out.

When the wagon got close to the building three men emerged from it and greeted Ivan enthusiastically. Two of them unloaded the crates and took them inside. Ivan and the older man followed them. Grant took out his pistol and crawled up to the door and put his ear against it to listen.

"Nice to see you made it, Ivan." Sounded like the older man, a man of authority.

"Ya, it was easy this time, General; except crossing the river. The guns never got wet though."

"Are you sure you weren't followed?"

"No. I was extra careful."

Grant heard them open the crates. One of the men whooped. "Look at these beauties, General Walton."

"Yes, they are. Put them away, we can't dawdle." General Walton asked Ivan if he was hungry. It sounded like they all sat down to eat. Grant's stomach growled from hunger, but he stayed and listened until he heard someone approach the door. He ran around the building and hid behind the horses in the corral. He knew immediately that he would be out in the open too much. There was nowhere else to hide.

Ivan strolled out and headed right toward him. Grant slid back and dropped to his stomach. Ivan got within a few feet from him and stopped. He pulled out his pistol and aimed it at Grant. At the same time the other three walked out and around the corner of the building. The general called to him. Ivan turned with his gun drawn and pointed it at them, confused. All three pulled their weapons out and fired. Ivan fired back twice before he fell backward against the corral. The horses sidestepped around nervously, one nearly stomped on Grant.

Ivan and one of the other men lay dead. The general clutched at his chest while his last man helped him back inside. "I didn't think he'd turn on us." He looked back at the bodies with a bewildered expression. "What got into him?"

Grant waited until the skittish horses settled down before he stood upright. He searched Ivan's pockets and found a brown envelope full of cash. He looked after the men. It must have been payment for more rifles. He pocketed it, lifted a saddle off the rail and threw it on a horse. Grant led it away quietly. No one followed so he jumped up and galloped over the hill.

Dusty had stayed at Kate's for three days. Then Carrie didn't hear his voice anymore. On the fourth day, Kate unlocked her door, leaving it wide open then went back downstairs. Carrie lifted the tray with her dirty dishes from the night before and followed her. She set the tray on the counter and turned to face Kate. Kate was leaning against the table, arms folded across her chest. She threw daggers at Carrie. "Dusty wants me to keep you locked up till he gets back," she said. "But I ain't no jailer. So, this is how it's going to be. You will help me with the chores. And if he doesn't show up within the two weeks, when he said he'd be back, then you walk back into town."

Carrie glanced at the door hoping that Dusty wouldn't come back for her. Fearing that he would.

"You can have him." Kate let her arms drop. "I don't care what he does anymore. He's gone more than he is here anyway." Her demeanour softened slightly. "He won't stay away from his boys forever, though."

Carrie didn't miss the innuendo behind that. While Dusty visited his boys he'd be with Kate. It didn't matter to him that he was married. Carrie leaned back against the counter, fighting back tears. "It doesn't matter what we want, does it? He'll just do what he wants anyway."

"You ain't the first woman I've caught him with, you know." Kate pulled out a chair and sank into it.

"Then why do you sit here waiting for him?" Carrie joined Kate at the table.

"I'm not waiting for him," Kate said, almost defensively. "This is our home. It's where the boys were born."

"Then I'll get a divorce."

Kate laughed. "Not in Blackman Falls, you won't. Most of the people there are afraid of Dusty."

The boys ran down the stairs and stopped beside their mother, eyeing Carrie. Kate put her arm around the youngest one and said, "Carrie is going to make breakfast this morning."

They came in the early dawn of a new summer, yelling and screaming. Pakwis, Night Wind, and Lucas grabbed the only three guns they had and fired into the morning fog. Ghostly figures ran from tree to tree throwing spears and shooting arrows at them. Pakwis aimed his rifle at a youth who brandished a tomahawk. His shaved head had a fuzzy strip down the centre and a long tail down his back. He wore only a breech-cloth as so many did this time of year. Pakwis pulled the trigger. The boy flew backward.

Lucas ducked down behind a tree and shot at anything that moved in front of him. Sometimes he just fired, hoping to hit something. He sensed someone sneaking up toward him. A man came at him from behind. Lucas grabbed at the spear before it skewered him in the gut. The warrior yelled and twisted it out of his hand. Lucas fell backwards, landing hard on the ground. He picked up a rock and threw it, hitting the warrior in the temple. The man fell back, onto the rocks. A pool of blood seeped from under him. Lucas picked up his rifle and fired at another one. The man stumbled and fell forward in the mud.

Lost Boy, a teenager, aimed his bow and arrow at his second target and fired. The arrow hit the intruder in the throat. Blood pulsed out at every heartbeat. The man fell and jerked for several seconds on the ground. Lost Boy shuddered as he watched the man's eyes bulge out and stare up at him. Lucas smiled encouragement at the youth.

The fog slowly lifted. Gunshots ceased. All was quiet once more. Lucas stood and watched through the woods for stragglers. Pakwis walked over to him. One by one the women and children returned to camp. No one seemed to be seriously injured. Night Wind had vanished.

Gunfire in the distance made everyone brace for another attack. It didn't come. Then all was silent once more. The sun poked out. A wolf howled from across the lake. Lucas lowered his rife and thought that they only howled at dawn. Little Blossom bandaged a scratch on Pakwis's arm and helped Sleeping Rabbit with the injured. They all waited nervously for Night Wind.

Lucas and Pakwis exchanged looks. They knew that the Mohawk attacked them to gain more of their land. The fur trade was big business for both tribes. The one with the most land could harvest more furs and become richer. "This small village cannot keep them away forever," Pakwis told Lucas before he walked off.

A lone rider crested the hill and raced down toward the small band of Indians as they travelled north. He let out a war whoop and raised his rifle. Night Wind laughed when he rode up to Pakwis and Lucas. "They will not be attacking us anymore." Lucas grimaced when the warrior showed him a string of scalps.

Winda leaned against the wall of the blacksmith shop. The rhythmic hammering from inside soothed her frayed nerves. All day she had watched the tavern across the street. She had just found out that Carrie had been gone for several days. She shouldn't have gone to the cave. Now Carrie was missing. She stepped out from the shadows into the late afternoon sun, thinking her vigil was done for the day. Then she jumped back as Dusty rode up pulling another horse. Winda watched him enter the tavern. Fifteen minuets later he came out with Carrie's bags and loaded them on the pack horse. Winda waited until Dusty rode out of sight before she stepped out into the sun. Strong arms pulled her back. A hand clamped over her mouth before she could scream.

"Shh. Winda. I won't hurt you. Promise me you won't scream. I just want to talk to you, okay?" the man whispered into her ear. She nodded. The hands released her. When she made no move to run the man's shoulders relaxed. "First of all, I want to apologize to you for pushing you down when you arrived. Remember?"

"You are Dusty's friend." She stepped back away from him.

The man shook his head. "I'm Major Grant Sievers of the Twelfth Militia." He hurried to explain everything to her. "I didn't mean to push you so hard, but I had to make it look good."

Bewildered, Winda asked. "Look good, for what?"

Grant guided her around the corner behind the building. "I'm investigating Dusty Blackman. We think." He shook his head again. "We know he's smuggling guns to the Americans."

Winda's eyes lit up. "I was right then, about those crates? They have guns in them?"

He nodded. "I'm pretending to be his friend until I have enough evidence to bring him and his partners to justice." He said this in a way to make absolutely sure she understood. "Did he force you and Carrie to haul loads for him?"

"He made Carrie help him with two crates all the way from York. He kept her apart from people so she would not tell anyone." It all started to become clear to her. "He held guns on both of us until we got here. And he tied me up at night."

"I thought so. From what I've put together, neither of you were willing participants in this." He smiled, as if satisfied with himself. "Carrie is really innocent then." He shuffled his feet. "Do you know where the crates are now?"

"No. When we arrived, he had us hide them down stream. They are gone now."

"He has a farm not far from here, doesn't he?"

"Yes. But I have never been there," she told the major. "He and Kate have children, you know?"

"What is he doing with all these women? He can't be married to both of them?"

Winda watched him look off into the distance and wondered if he had feelings for Carrie. She didn't tell him that Carrie had disappeared, she couldn't trust him yet. She was on her own hunt and planned to follow Dusty out to his farm.

Both Jeb and Sam were asleep when Winda returned to gather some supplies. She was gone again when they woke up the next morning. Neither of them had been able to tell her of Carrie's disappearance. They weren't worried about Winda yet. She was often gone for days at a time and Jeb knew she went back to the cave to look for her friend, Lucas.

She could be out hunting. Jeb was grateful for the meat and trade goods she supplied them with. He also liked her generous ways with him and Sam. She was a wild creature and needed to be out in the wilderness by herself. He respected that. She had the right to her new-found freedom.

Sam went outside to practise with his new bow and arrows that Winda had made for him. Jeb watched and listened from the open window at the back of the house, just above Winda's bed. "You have to hold this just right," Sam told his dog. He positioned himself, took careful aim and shot. "I hit it. Squirrel, I hit the bull's eye."They had painted a big red circle in the centre of a scrap piece of wood and leaned it against a tree in the back yard.

Squirrel tried to catch the arrows in mid-air. Sam yelled at him to get out of the way. Jeb laughed at the dog's antics. Sometimes Squirrel ran away with an arrow. Sam would chase him. Squirrel eventually gave it up and waited for the next one.

"I'm getting hungry now, Squirrel. Let's go get something to eat." Sam picked up all the arrows and headed inside.

Jeb had been frying up chicken and had the meal ready when Sam walked in. A big bowl of biscuits sat in the middle of the table. Sam licked his lips. "Smells good in here."

"Wash up. It's almost ready." Jeb wiped the sweat from his forehead. "It's just too hot today."

Sam poured water into Squirrel's dish before he washed his hands and sat at the table. Jeb spooned them out some beans and plopped a chicken leg on each plate. "You say grace tonight, Sam." They bowed their heads in prayer. Sam blessed everyone he knew. Jeb got restless and cleared his throat for him to stop.

He watched his grandson eat. Sam looked up at him. Jeb raised his right eyebrow, which, he did when he was pondering something. He cleared his throat again. "I'm going to ask you to do something tonight. You don't have to if you don't want to, okay? It might help us find Carrie."

Sam set down his fork and gave Jeb his full attention. "What do you want me to do?"

"I saw one of Dusty's friends ride into town earlier today, when you were out back. Usually that means he's meeting Dusty in the tavern. Dusty hasn't showed up yet, so I'm betting the meeting is tonight." Jeb hesitated. "If you could sneak around there after it gets dark, maybe you could find out something."

Sam gulped. "If we find Carrie, then we will be helping Winda, won't we?"

"Yes we will, Sam. I still don't know if she realizes Carrie is missing. Or, it could be why we haven't seen her lately. I don't know, but we can try."

Jeb got up and leaned on the table until the pain in his knee subsided. He hobbled over to his chair and sighed. Sam cleaned up the kitchen and threw Squirrel some bones. He made some tea and handed his grandfather a cup, careful not to spill it.

"Wait until dark," Jeb told him. "Change into dark clothes. And leave Squirrel here."

"I will, Grandpa." Sam gave Jeb a bright smile. "I can do it. I know I can."

Jeb gave Sam hug. "I know you can, Sam."

Hot, humid air made it hard for Jeb to breathe later that evening. He sat in his chair and fanned himself with a piece of wood. "I think we're in for a storm, Sam. My knee is paining me something fierce." His voice came out wheezy.

Sam bent down and hugged him. Jeb complained about his health all the time now. Sam worried about him. He prayed that God let Jeb live for a long time yet. "I'm ready, Grandpa."

Jeb pulled him around in front of him. Sam was all dressed in black. With his dark hair and skin, he should do fine. "Just remember one thing. It's important."

"What's that?"

"Remember, don't smile. Your big, white teeth will light up like a beacon."

Sam looked at him surprised. "Funny, Grandpa."

Jeb laughed.

Sam left, kept to the shadows, and eventually stood next to the tavern. He crouched down between an open window and a small bush and lifted his head up to peer inside. Like a shot, he ducked back down. Dusty was sitting next to the window. He could reach out and touch him. Very slowly, Sam lifted his head up. Dusty had put his hat on the table near the window which gave Sam something to hide behind. He heard Dusty call out. "Over here, Grant."

Footsteps approached. A bottle landed on the table then two glasses. Dusty uncorked the bottle and poured the gurgling liquid. He lifted his glass and tossed the whiskey into his mouth. "He sure enough likes his whiskey," Sam mumbled to himself as he wiped the beads of sweat from his forehead with the back of his hand. Grant settled himself across from Dusty.

"You look a little nervous," Grant said.

Dusty studied him through glassy eyes. "So, General Walton wants you to go on the next shipment, does he?"

"Yep. There's been trouble. We lost a couple of men. It's just for extra insurance. The general doesn't want to lose anymore guns."

Dusty gulped down another glass. His grey shirt was soaked in sweat, his bald head glistening. The red scar over his right eye seemed to have popped out. Sam watched Dusty take out a rag and wiped his whole head with it.

"I haven't heard from Ivan. He's four days late," Dusty said.

Grant seemed surprised by the news. "Maybe he just got held up."

"I don't know." Dusty sounded doubtful. "It's not like him."

"Maybe we'll find out when we see General Walton."

Dusty sat back in the chair and studied Grant closely. "We leave tomorrow at dawn. Meet me by the saw mill. Don't be late, or I'll leave without you."

Dusty grabbed his hat and staggered out the door. Grant poured another glass of whiskey and sipped on it. Sam memorized the man's features so he could report them to his grandfather, and then ran for home.

The next morning Grant jumped into the wagon next to Dusty. He had waited over an hour for the big man to show up. Without a word, Dusty flicked the reins and headed south-east toward their rendezvous with General Walton.

Wind and rain came down in a flash, making them scramble to put on their rain gear. The tarp across the back of the wagon whipped up and down wildly. Grant remembered when he hid under one just like it when Ivan delivered his last load of guns to the general. He smiled to himself. The envelope was still in his room at the boarding house. Two thousand dollars. He had pondered what to do about it. He knew he should turn it in, but also knew that it would be very unlikely that anyone would come looking for it. No one knew he had it.

They rode through most of the night, and then slept under the wagon out of the rain. All too soon, Dusty jabbed him and rolled out. Grant jumped up beside the big man, Dusty handed him a piece of jerky. They ate in silence, bouncing and jostling down the trail. The sun beat down on their heads as Grant tried to engage conversation, but Dusty either ignored him or answered in short non-committal sentences. Grant couldn't get any details from him.

Another thing Grant had to consider was General Walton. He knew who the general was but the general didn't know him. He hadn't told Dusty that Ivan was dead either. He'd leave that up to someone else.

It rained the third night and all the next day. The wagon rolled along through the mud. Grant sat in his seat enjoying the ride. Suddenly, the wagon tipped sideways, pulling the horses back. Grant slid into Dusty, who swore at him. Both men jumped down and found that the front wheel had worked its way off the axle. They unloaded the cargo in order to lift the wagon high enough to slip it back on. Once secured, they rested.

A bottle of whiskey appeared out of nowhere. Dusty offered Grant a drink; he took a swig and handed it back. Dusty drank half the bottle before he offered it again. Grant took a couple of swigs. Dusty drank the rest and then started to weave around. Grant decided they couldn't go anywhere for the rest of the day so he started a fire and asked Dusty if he was ready for supper.

"You bet," he slurred and drained the bottle.

Grant sat on the crates and watched his partner get drunk. Usually that would loosen up the big man's tongue. He made a quick meal for himself while Dusty danced around hollering and laughing. He pointed at Grant and sang a made-up song.

"You got no wife, I got two.
You got no kids, I got two.
When this is all over, I'll get you."

Grant couldn't tell if there was a threat there or if Dusty was just trying to rhyme his words. With an exaggerated bow, Dusty swept off his hat and waved it, stumbled forward, hit the ground face down and passed out.

10

"Mrs. Paterson. Mrs. Paterson." A young clerk rushed out of the postal office as Gert strode by. She stopped at the sound of her name. He ran up and handed her an envelope. Who would send her a letter? She tipped the clerk and looked at it. There was no return address, no tell-tale sign of where it came from. She shoved it into her pocketbook. She'd just have to read this later tonight when she got home, she told herself as she continued down the street.

The little white house showed signs of neglect. Tall weeds filled the front lawn. Dead flowers lined the front garden. "Why doesn't Mary pull those out?" Gert walked up the steps and knocked on the door.

Mary opened it, her face swollen, her eyes red. She dabbed at them with a handkerchief. Gert knew that something was terribly wrong. Mary plopped down on a chair. She seemed almost comatose.

"What happened, Mary?" Gert knelt beside her.

She blew her nose first. "Ivan is dead!" Mary looked at her sister. "I know I should hate him for what he put me and Carrie through." She hiccoughed. "But in some ways he was good to us."

Gert hugged her. "I'm sorry, Mary." Inside she was glad that Ivan was dead.

"I know you didn't like him, Gert. I was starting to wonder why I married him in the first place."

The older sister stood. "Let me make some tea. Everything seems better with a cup of tea. I'll be right back." Mary reached for another handkerchief.

Gert leaned against the wall in the kitchen and hugged herself. She had wished for this for years. So why then, did she feel bad? She used the same tea set that Carrie had used, the day that she brought her wedding gift over. Gert wondered where her niece was and how she would feel when she found out about Ivan's death. The cups rattled as she set the tray down on a small table and poured the cups full. She noticed that her sister had aged a great deal in a short time. The creases under her sad, brown eyes were deeper. More spread around her mouth. Her dress hung on her like a rag, she had lost so much weight.

Gert, on the other hand, had gained. She had to let out her dresses again, and hoped that Anthony wouldn't notice. She had tried to keep slim, like she was all those years ago when they first married. But through the years, her waistline expanded slowly. For her it was a battle she couldn't win. She enjoyed a good meal. Anthony did too. He, however, stayed the same weight. She wondered where all those years went. Anthony's hair had receded too, and was grey now. Her own hair had stayed a dull brown with only wisps of silver at her temples.

The rattle of the tea cup that hit the saucer startled Gert. She took a sip from her own cup and sat down next to Mary. Mary picked up a pocket watch off the table. Her fingers caressing the glass face of it.

"A man came by earlier and gave this to me. It was Ivan's. I gave it to him for Christmas one year when things were going good. We had a little extra money then." She looked over at Gert. "They buried him, you know? Somewhere down near a place called Cobble Hills. He told me that Ivan was killed in a gun fight. That was last spring. He's already been dead almost five months."

Later that day, Kate and Carrie were gathering water from Black Creek, beside the house, to pour over the vegetables in the garden. The boys helped to pull out weeds. Weeds grew no matter what. Kate looked up and pointed. "Look!"

A huge black cloud swirled down over the trees toward them. Carrie yelled, "Tornado!"

The closest building was the barn. Carrie and Kate pushed the boys inside and huddled in the farthest corner. The temperature dropped significantly in just a few minutes. Carrie started to shake. Torrents of hail bounced off the corn. Wind whipped through the area so strong that the windows in the house smashed. Part of its roof flew off.

Kate used her body to shield Adam while Carrie hid behind the plough. Johnny crouched down beside her, his eyes full of terror. Carrie covered her ears with her hands against the noise that deafened her. They watched in horror as the barn blew apart around them. Debris flew everywhere. A goat missed Carrie by mere inches. Dirt and hay scratched at her eyes. Johnny screamed in silence. Carrie inched her way over to him and took him into her arms. He clung to her with all his might.

It seemed like hours but it was only a few minutes. All that crashed, banged, and cracked had suddenly come to a stop. An eerie silence filled the air after all the dust slowly settled.

Carrie pushed debris off her and stood up, Johnny crawled out with her. They couldn't find Adam but could hear him whimpering. Carrie called to him until she found him as he squirmed under a wagon. One wheel still spun around in mid-air, squeaking at each turn. Most of the wagon was in shatters and lay on top of the little boy. Frantically, Carrie threw off pieces of wood, metal, leather strapping and a dead pig before Adam appeared.

He screamed when she tried to pull him out. "My arm, my arm."

Johnny found a rope. Carrie tied it around the beam that had Adam pinned and then Johnny helped her pull it off. Adam screamed again and grabbed his broken arm. Carrie lifted Adam up and carried him out into the yard to check him over. He writhed in pain and cried for his mother. Tears ran down Carrie's face at the sight of the little boy in so much agony. Johnny stood beside her, his whole body shaking.

On shaky legs, Carrie stumbled back to the corner of the barn, climbed over beams and broken pieces of machinery to get to Kate. She almost fainted when she saw the iron rod that stuck out of Kate's chest. She retched and coughed up dried phlegm, and then told herself that she had to be strong. After several deep breaths she reached down and tore off a piece of Kate's dress and went back outside. Johnny was kneeling beside his little brother, stroking his hair. Silent tears soaked the front of his shirt and smeared his blackened face. Adam had passed out.

Carrie ripped the cloth into strips and wrapped Adam's arm in it. She found leather strapping which she used as a sling. She brushed back Johnny's hair and gave him a kiss on the cheek.

"He's dead, isn't he?" he asked her, eyes glued to his brother.

"No, Johnny. He's just unconscious. That's all."

"What's un-con-sos?"

"It's like a deep sleep so he won't feel the pain. Sometimes it's a good thing."

"Oh." he turned toward the barn. "What about my mom?"

Carrie looked at the barn. "I'm sorry, Johnny. She didn't make it."

The boy started to convulse, violently. Carrie hugged him tight, rocked him, and cried with him. When he slowed to a whimper she stood him at arm's length. Carrie noticed then that he was full of cuts and bruises but none seem too severe.

"I'm going to need your help, Johnny. Do you think you can help me? We need to get Adam help for his arm." He stood there in shock. Carrie lifted Adam up and started toward the road. Johnny followed in a daze.

Very little was left of the barn. Only part of the wall stood jagged against the clear blue sky. The whole roof was gone. Carrie and Johnny climbed over and walked around lumber, trees, clothing, glass and furniture.

The tornado had demolished the corn, squash, wheat and even the fences. The house was in shambles. The roof had blown off. Part of the porch had collapsed into itself. All the windows were broken. A huge tree protruded from the kitchen. Its leaves silent and still where only minutes ago they whipped around madly.

Carrie looked down at Johnny's stupefied look. His eyes were huge as the made their way past his home. He grabbed her shirt and walked as if in a trance. It had only taken a few minutes but destroyed a home and a family.

Blackman Falls had been on the edge of the storm and had received only minor damage. The day after, Jeb hobbled down to the new postal office and had the clerk write a letter for him. It had taken him forty minutes when it should have only been fifteen. But he had been determined, and he didn't want anyone to know he did this. Sam had gone off somewhere with Squirrel, it was the right time. He addressed it to General Brooks in Greenstown, put his mark on it, and watched the young man stuff it into an envelope. He made sure the letter went into a mailbag to go out that very day. The clerk smiled at him and said, "I don't like Dusty either, Mr. Horne. I hope they get him."

They were near the road when Carrie recognized something in the middle of the pine trees. One of her canvas bags had blown way out there. It was on its side against an old stump. She asked Johnny to fetch it for her. He picked his way carefully through the debris to bring it to her. "Can you carry it for me? Please, Johnny?"

"I can do that. I'm the man now, ain't I, Carrie?"

"Yes," she agreed, "you are quite the man."

He smiled sadly up at her. They continued their walk down the dusty road. Adam's weight grew heavier with each step. Her shoulders and back ached. Her feet were sore. She needed a bath and wanted to wash her hair. Carrie was exhausted and just wanted to lie down and sleep. But she couldn't. She had to get help for the little boy she carried.

The bridge hung precariously twisted over the creek that flowed twice as fast now. She watched a goat float down it as the waters churned and splashed. They could cross over on the right side where she could get enough footing. "We can make it," she told Johnny, and tried to sound confident.

Carrie laid Adam down on dead grass and helped Johnny across. She held his hand and guided his every step. Inch by agonizing inch they skirted the slippery edge. Once on the other side Johnny collapsed on the bank. Carrie set her bag down beside him. "I'll be right back." She hugged him then made the treacherous journey back across the bridge.

Adam's breath was shallow and slow when she reached him. He was still unconscious which she figured would make this easier for her. She undid the sling and tied his wrists together then slung him over her shoulder. This way, she would be able to use both hands. They were almost across when her foot slipped. Her knee scraped on the wood, making her cry out in pain. Her hand flew out to steady the little boy on her back. She choked as Adam's hands dug into her throat. Her foot found something solid to rest on. Carrie froze.

Johnny appeared above her and grabbed at her arm. "I'll help you, Carrie. Don't let go."

His little hands pulled at her while he leaned over the top of the bridge. "It's just a little further, Carrie. You can do it. I know you can." He begged her as tears ran down his stricken face. She could feel Adam slip and adjusted him again.

She lifted her arm from Adam and with Johnny's help, pulled herself along. Adam swung precariously on her back. She steadied him again and took a deep breath then crawled along to safety. Johnny helped her lower Adam onto the ground. Carrie collapsed down beside him. Her body shook while she cried from exhaustion and despair. Johnny sat beside her in silence and stared at the bridge. Tears ran down his smudged face. He was no doubt thinking of his mother.

Lucas stood on top of a high waterfall looking down at solid rock. Night Wind stood beside him in prayer and offered the spirits a pinch of tobacco. Both men watched it disappear in the wind. In the distance, a line of wagons headed south. Night Wind scowled. "More and more white men coming to take our lands." He fixed his gaze on Lucas as if to say, "You included."

Lucas started back down the hill. Leaves had started to turn colour. Plants died off for the winter season. Sleeping Rabbit was picking mushrooms. She smiled at him when he walked by. Out of the corner of his eyes he saw that Night Wind had followed him and gave Lucas a dirty look.

Pakwis found a place where he wanted to camp. Lucas and Night Wind lifted the canoe over their heads and followed. They crossed the flat ledge then headed down a gentle slope. Night Wind pushed Lucas faster than he should have. Lucas almost lost his balance and nearly ran over a couple of the children. Pakwis turned and glared at them. Their mothers looked back and scowled.

Heads hidden under the white man's canoe neither one saw the cloud of dust in the distance. Pakwis ordered everyone back into the trees until they knew what it was. The upside-down canoe followed them. Lucas and Night Wind flipped the canoe upright and set it down gently. Lucas flexed his shoulder muscles. A young man threw the paddles down into the canoe. "Thanks, Lost Boy."

Lost Boy was an orphan; his parents and sisters had been killed in the big storm. His father had been out hunting with Pakwis and Night Wind. Lucas learned that his mother and two sisters were inside their lodge when a huge pine crashed through the roof. Lost Boy had been closer to the door. Big branches of the tree landed on both sides of the terrified boy. His cuts and scratches had healed long ago.

Lost Boy lived with Sleeping Rabbit now and considered her his new mother. She was kind to him and treated him like an adult, which Lucas was sure Lost Boy was grateful for. After all, he'd killed his first big game. He also had killed his first enemy in battle and had his initiation ceremony into manhood. Now he was tall and lanky and started to fill out. His voice had begun to change, becoming deeper. The young girls smiled at him and vied for his attention. At fourteen summers, Lost Boy followed Night Wind everywhere and Lucas knew he hoped to use the rifle again. It was a long shot though; lead balls and powder for it were scarce.

Lucas smiled at him "You have been a big help, Lost Boy. It makes our load lighter when you help us like that."

The boy beamed at the praise. "I am going to be the best hunter of all when I get my own gun," he promised while pointing at Night Wind's rifle.

"I bet you will."

Pakwis strode up to them then pointed to the dust cloud. "We better see what that is over there. Night Wind, I want you to stay with the women and children. Lucas, come with me."

"No," Night Wind balked.

Pakwis took him aside and whispered, but Lucas overheard them. "You are the only other one with a gun. I need you here just in case of trouble." He glanced over at Lucas who looked off in the distance. "Besides, I have to keep an eye on him yet, just in case he deceives us."

Night Wind stood up to his Chief. "I do not trust this white man, Pakwis. I will watch your back. But I will not hide in the woods like a coward." He walked away in anger.

Anthony watched his wife as they stood at the grave. She had her eyes open and watched her sister when they were supposed to be praying. He knew that Gert wouldn't pray for Ivan. Neither would he. But they pretended, for Mary's sake.

Why she insisted on having this ceremony was beyond him. Ivan had been dead and was buried some five-and-a-half months ago now. It was long over with. So he shuffled his feet when the prayer was over with and gave Mary a hug. Reverend Bates read one last passage from the Bible and then that was it.

They went back to their place where some of the church ladies had the dining table full of food. Anthony was starved, but ate sparingly so he wouldn't embarrass his wife. Later he'd get his fill. He hoped that there would be some of that great looking apple pie left. He set his plate aside and waited until everyone went into the other room. Then he plopped a tart into his mouth and chewed it with a smile on his face.

"Mr. Patterson?"

He turned to see Reverend Bates walk up to him. Anthony wanted to savour the cherry and the pastry, but instead he swallowed the tart whole and shook the reverend's hand. "That was a nice service today."

"Thank you." Reverend Bates snickered and reached for a tart. "These are good, aren't they?"

Anthony almost licked his lips as he watched the reverend eat his tart. He wanted another one; he wanted to taste it and not swallow it whole. Except that good decorum forbid him to eat gluttonously.

Reverend Bates wiped his hand over his mouth and swallowed the last of his tart. Then he turned to Anthony. "As you are well aware, the donations from the spring bazaar weren't what we expected. The church is low in cash."

Anthony nodded. "Times are tough, aren't they?" He leaned against a chair in an effort to hide the lie he just told. Last week he had persuaded old man Zuker into donating three-thousand dollars just before he passed away of pneumonia. Anthony's bogus charity had been doing quite well lately.

"Well, I was wondering if your bank could make a sizable donation this year."

Anthony glanced at the doorway and then pulled Reverend Bates closer. "I'll see what I can do. But as you know, Gert and I are helping Mary out." He could afford to donate a few hundred dollars to the church. Reverend Bates would be grateful to him. Anthony needed to keep up appearances after all.

"Yes, yes." Reverend Bates put his hand on Anthony's arm. "I'm well aware of her circumstances. And am glad that you can help her, it takes a burden off the church." He let out a big sigh. "Anything you can do will be greatly appreciated, Anthony."

"Like I said, I'll see what I can do."

Reverend Bates nodded. "That's all I ask." He headed toward the parlour. "Enjoy the tarts."

Lucas and Pakwis lay side by side with their rifles pointed down the grassy knoll in front of them. The land dipped down and disappeared into a small lake which glistened in the morning sun. To the east, a marshy area stretched over a mile. Tall cattails waved in the light breeze. Fluffy white clouds drifted overhead. A small heard of cattle roamed the bottom lands. They counted four men on horseback that drove the cattle southward along a ridge that turned westward. The cattlemen would pose no problem. They could just let them pass on by.

Pakwis shifted his rifle. "I think we will eat big tonight. We can kill these men and take the cows for us."

Lucas gave his friend a bewildered look. "They're no threat to us. Why not let them be?"

"We need the meat." Pakwis gave him a stern look. "We need the hides for clothing and shelter. Winter will be here soon enough. We will not go hungry this time."

Lucas remembered when he first saw these Indians walking into his camp. They had been dirty and half starved. He gave them food and had helped them ever since last spring. His extra rifle had made a big difference to their survival.

At first he didn't really care what happened to him. He was lost and felt empty. Now he had found purpose again. These people had accepted him, for the most part. They let him stay with them on their journey to find a new home. He had even fought in battle alongside them. They celebrated his bravery. But he knew he was still an outsider, especially to Night Wind. Sleeping Rabbit had sought him out on a few occasions; let him know that she was available. He liked her but she didn't interest him in a romantic way. He was grateful for her friendship, though.

A loud explosion erupted in his ear. Pakwis jumped up hollering after firing his rifle. Lucas followed on instinct and ran toward the herd. He shot one man and watched him fall from his horse. Pakwis jumped on it, turned it around, and charged at the others. The cattle scattered in all directions. Lucas ran in, dodging the cattle as they all turned at once and stampeded toward the band. He shot another man whose horse reared and vanished into the marsh after throwing the cowboy off its back. Several warriors were chasing after the cattle.

The last man galloped toward Lucas, his rifle aimed at him. Lucas squatted and fired a shot, missing the man. The cowboy let out a frustrated yell as he barrelled down on Lucas. Hurriedly Lucas tried to reload. The horse was almost on top of him when the cowboy fired. Lucas saw the smoke from the rifle then felt his side explode. He flew backward landing on a thistle. The cowboy turned his horse and charged his next enemy with an empty rifle. He flipped it around and held it like a club.

Night Wind pulled the cowboy off his horse and punched his face. The cowboy dropped his rifle and took a swing at the warrior. Night Wind ducked then pulled out his knife. The cowboy charged at him only to get his throat slit. Blood squirted out all over. Night Wind's triumphant yell echoed throughout. He jumped on the cowboy's horse and galloped up to Pakwis.

Lucas lay on the ground in extreme pain. It took all his effort just to breathe and stay conscious. "Where's Lucas, have you seen him?" he heard Pakwis but couldn't see him. "Did he desert us?"

"No. I saw him awhile ago," it was Night Wind's voice. "He was helping you."

Lucas's eyes flicked open when Night Wind knelt down beside him. Pakwis dismounted and walked up to them and said, "We better not move him." Pakwis leaned down to examine the wound. " He has been shot."

11

Night Wind leaned against a tall ash tree and watched Sleeping Rabbit tend to Lucas in the firelight. Gently, her long fingers applied a poultice to the white man's wound. A bullet had passed through his flesh between his ribs and out the back. Night Wind stepped forward to help her roll the lifeless body onto its side. Lucas had passed out. She smiled up at him, thankful for the help. He saw sorrow in her eyes.

Sleeping Rabbit dipped her finger into a bowl of black mush and smeared more poultices on the exit wound. Together, they rolled the body back and forth, wrapping it in a clean cloth. She felt Lucas's forehead. "Fever is down. He will live, thank the spirits."

Night Wind smiled at her uncertainly. Lucas had helped them in their troubled time. Yet he felt threatened by him. He didn't like the way these two spent hours together, alone. So far though, he was certain they hadn't shared robes. It was only a matter of time, he was sure. She enjoyed the white man's company a little too much. If it weren't for Pakwis, he would have challenged Lucas a long time ago.

Pakwis had ordered Night Wind not to harm Lucas. "He is too much of an asset to us right now. We are not going hungry. And a white man in our favour could be useful in the future for better things."

Night Wind looked over at Lucas's canoe. It was made entirely of wood but was a lot heavier than their birch bark ones. Through the months he had noticed that it stood up better than his and it didn't need to be repaired after every time it was used. The sturdy craft bounced off rocks that would tear holes in theirs. He had hoped that Lucas would teach him how to make one like that some day.

He looked down at the unconscious man. Lucas had only wanted to be his friend. But he discredited Lucas every time he could. It was Lucas who got the ugly looks when he pushed them down the hill that day, under the canoe. That morning, Night Wind had seen those two together again as they sat side-by-side, laughing at their private jokes. His chest had tightened. He wanted to kill Lucas then. But instead, he walked away and returned to camp after his temper had cooled down.

Sleeping Rabbit sat back on her heals and watched the white man's chest rise and fall in shallow breaths. Night Wind reached down to her. "Come, Sleeping Rabbit. I wish to talk with you," he said in a soft, low voice. For awhile, she didn't respond. He thought she didn't hear so he asked her again. She reached up so he could pull her to her feet. Her eyes remained on Lucas.

Night Wind's heart broke at the dedication this woman had on another. He hoped to fix that. He led her through camp and down a slight incline and over to a patch of wild blueberries. A half moon hung high in the starry sky, lighting their way. A light, warm breeze drifted over the cattle that lulled nearby.

Out of earshot from the others Night Wind stopped and faced Sleeping Rabbit. "I know you care for this white man, Sleeping Rabbit. I do not think it wise to get too close to him."

Big, doe-like eyes looked back at him. "Why not? We are both old enough to make up our own minds."

He stroked her long, black, silky hair. "Because, one day he will leave you alone with a child to raise by yourself," he stammered and then wondered where that came from.

"You know this for sure, Night Wind?"

He took her into his arms. "I just do not want to see you getting hurt."

"And you can prevent this?" She pulled back and narrowed her eyes.

"Yes, I can." He waited for her to say more but she didn't. "Marry me, Sleeping Rabbit." His arms tightened around her. He bent down and kissed her soft lips. "Become my woman," he said afterward.

She looked as if she didn't know how to respond to this. "Did you order me to marry you?"

"No, I am asking."

Little Rabbit regarded him. "I need time to think about it. This is too sudden." She pushed away from him and ran.

Night Wind chastised himself. He hadn't intended to push her so. He only wanted to court her, and turn her away from the white man's attention. He kicked at a rock. The moccasin didn't shield his toe from the pain. Night Wind hopped around on one foot and swore, a cow bellowed and side-stepped. He didn't want to start a stampede so he stomped off into the darkness. "I didn't even tell her I am in love with her."

Johnny pointed down the road ahead of them. "Look."

Carrie lifted her head and peered through heavy eyelids. A human form stood at the side of the road. She shifted Adam's weight and willed one foot in front of the other. Johnny had stayed by her side all night. Dawn slowly made things visible again. The sun peeked over the horizon in front of them, shining directly into Carrie's eyes, making her squint. It put the human figure in dark shadow. Johnny grabbed her sleeve and ducked behind her. "It's an Indian," he whispered fearfully. "She might scalp us." He tried to pull her back. "My dad says Indians kill little boys and eat them. Carrie, don't go."

She reached down with a cramped arm and gave him a light hug. "I won't let anyone eat you, okay?" He looked up at her uncertainly. She took his hand and trudged along. Carrie stumbled and nearly dropped Adam; she took a few seconds to collect herself. Johnny kept his eyes on the stranger ahead of them. Adam groaned, his weight almost unbearable.

"Carrie?"

"Yes, Johnny?"

"Are you my new mom?"

Surprised, Carrie held her breath for a few seconds, didn't know how to answer him. She wondered if her marriage to Dusty made it so, and what he would think about it. She knew these kids had nowhere else to go. Was she ready to be a mom? "Did you say that's an Indian woman up there?"

"Yep, it's a squaw all right, she's just standing there."

Carrie cringed at his choice of words but said nothing to him. Obviously, Dusty had taught him those things. She would have to correct them. As they got closer the form came into focus. Johnny started to shake. Carrie looked down at him and smiled. "That's my friend, Winda."

"You have an Indian friend?"

"Yes, I do," she answered seriously. "It shouldn't matter who they are. Anyone can be your friend."

"Oh."

Winda smiled and hugged Carrie when they approached. She reached up and took Adam's lifeless body then laid him on the ground under a tree. He was still unconscious. "I was worried about you." She watched the young boy beside Carrie.

Winda held a hand out to him. "My name is Winda."

"Johnny." He put a stiff hand into hers and looked over at Carrie who nodded encouragement. Johnny sighed loudly. "And that's Adam. He broke his arm." They pumped their hands in unison.

"Glad to meet you, Johnny. Do you think we can be friends? I could use another friend."

Again, he looked at Carrie for guidance. She smiled tiredly at him. "You can never have too many friends."

That evening, Squirrel stood at the door whimpering. His head turned one way then the other as he listened with pricked ears. "Quiet, Squirrel." Sam grabbed him on the back of the neck and pulled him away form the door. He looked nervously at his grandfather. It was too late for company to come visiting.

Jeb stood behind the kitchen table with Winda's spear in his hand, ready to defend them from whatever lurked around outside. Sweat poured down into his eyes. His hand shook. Squirrel broke loose from Sam and scratched the door. Another thump from outside and Squirrel's tail wound up faster as he danced around excitedly. Jeb watched him closely. Must be someone they knew or else he'd be growling. He lifted the spear higher. Just in case. Sam tried to pull his dog back again. Squirrel refused to budge. He barked and whimpered louder. The door flew open and banged against the wall. Winda and Carrie rushed in, each carrying a small boy. Carrie ran straight to the back and laid Johnny on Sam's bed. The boy's eyes fluttered before he rolled over and slept. She dropped her canvas bag and turned down the covers on Jeb's bed. Winda lay Adam down then covered him up, his arm bandaged. A thin piece of material was wrapped around him, holding the arm to his body.

"What happened to his arm?" Sam asked.

"Broke it," Carrie answered.

Jeb realized he still held the spear and set it down against the wall behind him. He hobbled over to Carrie and led her to his chair. "You need rest, Carrie. Me and Winda will look after the boys. You just rest." She looked so exhausted. Jeb limped back to the table and joined Winda there.

"Carrie said that Dusty's farm was hit with the tornado," Winda told them. "Kate is dead."

Sam looked back at the boys with a sad expression. "Kate was a nice lady."

Squirrel had settled down as soon as the women entered the cabin. He seemed to sense that no one was going to pet him tonight. He let out a loud sigh then curled up on the floor in front of Carrie.

"I made Carrie take Johnny for a walk," Winda said, "while I set Adam's arm."

Jeb just nodded.

Carrie started to snore. Her head tilted to one side, an arm dangled over the side of the chair. Sam rose, found a blanket and laid it over her, tucked it in so it wouldn't fall off. He turned to the adults at the table. "What are we going to do, Grandpa? Dusty ain't going to like this." He shook his head from side to side. "No, he ain't going to like this one bit."

Grant knew that Dusty didn't like him by the way the big man watched him. They had kept to an indistinguishable trail and avoided towns and settlements. Talk was at a minimum and only at the task at hand. The man could be smart when he wanted to be. As he rolled up his bedroll, Grant watched Dusty. He hadn't given anything away about the guns or how they got them.

Dusty hitched the horses to the wagon and seemed eager to go. He then threw his bedroll into the back of the wagon after Grant's. Together, they covered up the load with the tarp and fastened it down. Today was Grant's turn to drive. Both men hopped up. Grant took up the reins and steered them up and over a grassy knoll and across open flat land.

As each day passed, Grant became increasingly nervous. He didn't know what would happen when they met up with General Walton. He tried to figure a way to fake it as being one of his men. Maybe he'd just have to play it out as things went along? Mile after mile the wagon bounced and jostled, Dusty pointing the way. In the cool afternoon he pulled out a pipe and smoked it with his feet up and hat shoved low over his eyes. He leaned back in his seat and puffed leisurely as they went.

Grant could feel those mean grey eyes on him and tried not to squirm. Dusty remained silent. It must be how he tortured people, by glaring at them all day. Maybe he wished Ivan was here instead. The horses turned left between a hill on one side and a downward grade on the other. They rode in between on a flat plateau. Dusty pointed to the left. Grant turned the wagon and they followed along the base of the hill and through some trees. The leaves had turned again; some of them fell on them as they drove through. The fall colours didn't seem to be as bright this year for some reason. They crossed over a small stream and through a patch of goldenrod. Grant drove through a harvested field of hay. The farmer had it stacked in large piles all over the fields. A house and barn stood in front of them. No one seemed to be about. Grant stopped the wagon in front and both men jumped down. They walked toward the house, rifles in hand.

At Dusty's nod, they sneaked inside, pointing their weapons. It was quiet. They checked every room down stairs then headed up. A step creaked under Dusty's weight. They stopped and held their breaths. Grant noticed the sweat on the big man's forehead. Nothing stirred so they continued cautiously. They checked all the bedrooms upstairs until only one remained. Grant used his rifle to push open the door. The bed creaked when someone shifted their weight on it. They charged in. Dusty let out a big sigh of relief and set his rifle down against the wall. Grant lowered his but hung onto it.

Dusty smiled and stepped up to the bed. "Hello, General."

"Oh Dusty, How are you boy? Come here. Let me get a good look at you."

Everyone in the cabin slept in late the next morning. Sam had crawled in beside Johnny. Jeb dozed in another chair near Carrie. Winda slept on her mat in the corner. No one disturbed Adam when he moaned and whimpered in his sleep.

In the morning, Winda watched as Carrie stretched and looked over at her, and then rolled her head around and around then from side to side to loosen a kink in her neck. Winda and Jeb sat quietly at the table drinking coffee. Carrie pushed off the blanket and joined them.

"Morn'in,"Jeb greeted her with a big smile. "How did ya sleep?"

"All right, I guess, just a little stiff." She stifled a yawn.

"Well, I think you had a great sleep," he teased.

"What do you mean? I didn't sleep all that well."

"You snored so loud that Squirrel couldn't hear the mice underneath the floor."

Winda spewed out a mouthful of coffee. Some ran up her nose, she choked and coughed. She wiped her mouth with the back of her hand and then laughed.

None of the boys stirred so Jeb bent in to whisper. "Dusty and his friend left two nights ago. Just before the storm. I think they're meeting a General Walton at some place called Cobble Hills."

"I didn't realize Dusty was still here. He hadn't been home in weeks," Carrie said angrily. "Me and Kate were doing all the work. That's how he does it. He starts something and sits back while others do all the work for him."

"That friend," Winda conspired, "isn't what you think." She wanted to tell her friends the truth about Major Grant but kept her promise to him instead. "He's on our side."

"Then why is he helping Dusty?" Jeb wanted to know.

"He asked me not to tell anyone who he really is. All I will say is that he wants to catch Dusty."

Jeb looked at Winda. "Then he must be some kind of agent or something."

"That means," Carrie gulped, "that I can get arrested too, for helping him."

Winda held Carrie's arm. "No, Carrie. He knows that both you and me had no choice. He does not want us." She leaned back. "Maybe we can help him, though."

Carrie took a drink. It seemed to settle her nerves. "I know that Ivan is involved. I saw him take a load of guns and he gave Dusty an envelope. I bet there was money in it." She looked at Jeb. "Where would he get that kind of money?"

Winda poured another round of coffee. She set the pot back on the stove and glanced out the window into the late cloudy morning. "The tornado didn't hit here very hard, did it?"

"No. We were lucky, just minor damage around town. I think we were just on the edge of it." Jeb stretched and yawned. "Some roofs need repairing. Some things blew away, but that's all."

Both Jeb and Winda looked sympathetically at Carrie who studied the cup in her hands.

The tiny cabin was crowded. They pushed Sam and Jeb's beds into the corner. Adam and Johnny used a pallet to sleep on which they leaned up against the wall during the day. The two women shared the small space behind the curtain. Carrie had gotten so she could sleep anywhere.

She sat cross-legged on her bed and opened her canvas bag that she'd saved after the tornado. Carrie pulled out her coat and boots in preparation for the upcoming winter. Next, she lifted out the small pistol she hid from Dusty. Carrie stared at it. All those long lonely days and nights she'd spent since they'd been married came back to her. Worse were the days he did show up. She turned the pistol over in her hand and wondered if he knew about Kate. Carrie looked up at the wall beside her and realized that here in this tiny cabin was the happiest she had ever been. Somehow she knew that Dusty would be the one to destroy that happiness. She buried the pistol under her bedding and hoped that she would never have to use it.

Three books came out next. Carrie set them aside. Dusty couldn't read. He often prodded her to read to him. She told herself that she would teach the boys and give them this advantage in life.

The last thing in her bag was the quilt that Aunt Gert had made for her. Tears slid down her face as she held it to her chest. Carrie unfolded the quilt, admired the grey, blue and burgundy patchwork. Aunt Gert put this together just for her, every stitch done by her arthritic hands was fine and even. Great care made this quilt. Carrie's fingers gently slid over her only possession of value. She didn't even know she had an aunt and uncle until they moved to York. She wanted to ask her mother about that, and about Ivan. She wanted to know about her real father.

Her aunt Gert came into her mind. She missed her and Uncle Anthony. They had let her stay with them when Ivan drank too much and fought with Mary. She'd run across town, even in the rain, and knock on their door. Her mother would come and get her the next day after things cooled down again.

The curtain opened letting in the light from the fireplace. Winda sat down next to her. "What a beautiful blanket. Your mother make it?"

"No," Carrie shook her head, "my Aunt Gert made it for me as a wedding gift. My mother never gave me a wedding gift."

Winda gave her a quick squeeze. "Your aunt is a special person to you?"

"Yes. I miss her more than my own mother."

12

Even though it was mid-day, Grant tried to stay in the shadows of the small room. General Walton lay before him, his chest bandaged. The older man had salt-and-pepper hair and a silvery grey moustache that needed a trim. His big hands were folded together on his bare chest. A light sheet covered him from the waist down. A cool breeze folded and unfolded the curtains on the opposite wall. Despite it though, the man looked feverish. His skin glistened with sweat and his yellowish face looked drawn into itself.

The bed squeaked when Dusty sat on the edge. He shook hands with the sick man. "Good to see you, General."

General Walton coughed, his whole body jerking.

"What happened?" Dusty poured him a glass of water from the nightstand and tipped it into the man's mouth.

The man sipped and then coughed. He wiped his mouth before he spoke. "Got shot, Dusty; a nasty one." He closed his eyes and waited a minute before he opened them again. "Then fever set in, haven't been able to shake it.

"When was that?"

"Last spring."

Dusty stood and paced the room. "Last spring. That's at least four months ago? You've been like this for four months?"

"Yep, actually closer to five." He started coughing again. When he settled down Walton turned his attention to the other man in the room. "And who are you, sir? Come closer so I can see you."

Grant forced himself out of the corner and walked toward the bed. Dusty watched him closely, his big hand slipped down to the pistol at his side. Grant knew that he could be shot at any second.

As Dusty did, Grant sat on the edge of the bed. Walton studied him and seemed confused. "How do I know you, son?"

"Don't you remember, General? Down by Sandy Creek?"

The old man studied Grant but still seemed unsure.

Dusty jumped and checked out the window. Horses galloped up to the front of the house. Someone yelled. The big man ran down the stairs. Grant followed at his heels, glad to be out of the bedroom. He didn't know if his cover had been blown. Now another threat faced him.

Three cowboys pulled up by the wagon. One of them checked under the tarp. "Yep, he's here all right." The men jumped down off the horses and strode into the house. Dusty and Grant set down their rifles as the men entered one at a time.

Dusty shook hands with all three, calling the first two by name. His mood lightened considerably as the men joked and made fun of each other. He introduced Grant to them, except the third man, who he didn't know.

Grant shook their hands. The last one however, hung on just a little too tight. He was about to say something but studied the scruffy young man a little closer.

The other three headed into the kitchen. The young man grinned at Grant. "It's me, Major Sievers," he whispered, "Lieutenant Egelton."

Relieved, Grant smiled. "Lieutenant? Well, congrats." Grant led his friend into the kitchen after the others.

Night Wind watched Sleeping Rabbit care for Lucas while he healed from his wound. The bullet had entered under his right arm, between his rib-cage and straight out his back. Lucas sat upright against a tree and ate his meal that she had made for him.

Night Wind frowned at them from across his own fire. Lucas said something that made Lost Boy laugh. If only Sleeping Rabbit looked upon him like she did that white man. He had kept his distance from her since that day he humiliated himself because he ordered her to marry him. Now he had to start all over with her. Night Wind watched her clean up after their evening meal and then head out of the camp for a walk. He followed from a distance. A bright, full moon hung low over the autumn sky. No clouds hid it tonight. Thousands of stars twinkled above them. The air was crisp and still. His moccasins crunched on dead leaves as he climbed to the top of a small hill and stood behind her. Sleeping Rabbit heard him and turned to face him.

"Sleeping Rabbit, I want to apologize to you for the way I have been treating you." He looked so sincere that she smiled at him. *Spirits above, she's beautiful.* He took in her round face, her full lips that invited him to kiss them. He loved her huge, expressive eyes. She had braided her black hair into one thick strand that hung down the middle of her back. She held the cow-hide blanket tight around her shoulder.

"I accept your apology, Night Wind." She shivered slightly.

He held back and didn't take her into his arms; he didn't want to scare her away again.

"Will you consider me as one of your suitors, Sleeping Rabbit? I would be most honoured if you would." He held his breath while she studied him closely. She took too long to answer!

"How many suitors do you think I have?"

"Well, what about Lucas? Isn't he trying for your hand too?"

She creased her forehead. "Is that really what you want to know, if I am interested in Lucas?"

"No. Well yes." He threw up his arms. "All I want to know is if I have a chance with you, Sleeping Rabbit."

She backed away from him.

"Lucas makes no advances toward me. We are only good friends, Night Wind." She looked at the ground and added. "I think his heart yearns for someone else."

He watched her emotions flit across her face. "You are in love with him though, aren't you?"

She cringed as if he'd slapped her. "I have feelings for him, I cannot deny that." She looked back up at him. "I also have deep feelings for you, Night Wind."

Night Wind gave her his best smile. "All I am asking is that you give me a chance." He held out a hand to her. She put hers into his. His heart swelled.

"Lucas is only trying to be friends. Do not act so mean to him."

He tried to joke. "I am jealous of any man who looks at you."

She pulled her hand back. "I do not want a man who is so jealous that I cannot breathe." She turned and walked purposely back toward camp.

"Why are you so touchy when it comes to me?" he yelled at her back.

She didn't stop. He ran up to her, caught her arm and turned her to face him. "Sleeping Rabbit, my heart yearns for you." He could see the tears that threatened. "I love you. I hope that someday, you will return that love to me." He gave her a soft kiss on her cheek, looked deep into her eyes. Night Wind didn't want to push things too far or too fast, he let her go. She walked back to camp, slowly, as if in thought. He watched her and felt a little more hopeful than before.

Dusty, as usual, found a bottle of whiskey. He and his two friends had settled in the kitchen and filled their glasses. When Grant and Bill entered he ordered them to unload the crates from the wagon.

"Let them party," Bill said. "That's all Dusty wants to do. All he's interested in is guns and whiskey."

"Yeah, and a few other unscrupulous things."

They worked together, undid the tarp and folded it up to set in behind the crates. Each man lifted his end of the first crate and carried it into the parlour. Laughter floated out of the kitchen as they set the crate along the wall. When they were back outside, Bill glanced toward the house. "They're getting the guns from Montreal. They're being shipped up the St. Lawrence, and then somebody buys them and ships them to General Walton. He sends them down to be shipped across Lake Erie."

They lifted the second crate. Grant was sure he saw the curtains move from the upstairs bedroom. General Walton lay in the back room. That one was empty.

"Is there a ship docked down there waiting?"

"No. They anchor out in the lake and use a couple of canoes to row the crates out to it. They have a set date to meet each shipment." Bill's hand slipped off the crate. Both men scrambled not to drop it. He caught his end. They looked at each other in relief. "I've seen three loads go out so far."

"Then this one should be the last one until spring?"

"Hurry up, ladies! We don't have all day," Dusty yelled from the doorway. He frowned at them, sipping his drink as they climbed the stairs. He took a step back to let the men pass.

Grant and Bill exchanged nervous glances. They set the crate on top of the first one. The other men came into the parlour with a new bottle. Bill smiled. "Hey Dusty. How many wives you got now?" Everyone snickered.

Grant did too, but his stomach knotted when they made fun of Carrie.

Dusty grabbed the bottle from his friend and drank. Then he wiped his mouth on his sleeve. "Still just two, kid. Why? Can't you get one for yourself?" Everyone roared.

Bill drank from the bottle Dusty offered him. He handed it over to Grant.

"Drink up, cowboy," Dusty ordered. "Drink like a real man."

Grant took a long drink and handed Dusty back the bottle, who grabbed it forcefully and led the others back into the kitchen.

"Bill," he yelled back. "Think you can cook us up something?"

"Yes Dusty, I'm coming." Bill shrugged and disappeared through the door.

Grant went back outside and unhitched the horses, led them to the corral and fed them. A light snow started to fall in the grey evening. The days were warm yet but the nights were cold. He knew that Bill had more to tell him. He hoped that he got that chance.

Gert chastised herself. "How can I be so stupid?" The rocking-chair on the front porch creaked as she pushed it back and forth. Anthony sat in his, watching the leaves fall from the big maple in front of their house on a cool autumn day. He didn't want to answer that one.

The letter she received a month ago lay on her lap unopened. She picked it up and waved it in front of her. "With Mary insisting on giving Ivan a funeral and looking after her, I completely forgot about it."

"Well, open it, Gert," Anthony implored. "I'm just as curious as you are."

A finger slipped under the flap and tore the envelope along the top fold. Gert pulled out a single stained sheet of paper and unfolded it. "Why, It's from Carrie." Her other hand went up to her chest. The chair stopped and stood still. "Oh, Anthony. Why didn't I open this long ago?" Red faced and furious with herself she read it aloud.

Tears ran down Gert's face, dripped on the paper as she read and barely got out the last few lines. She took out a handkerchief from her pocket and wiped her eyes. "That poor girl doesn't sound happy at all."

"No, she doesn't. And she doesn't know that Ivan's not her father, or that he's dead."

Gert blew her nose in a handkerchief. "What about the guns? This must have something to do with all that money he was moving in and out of the bank."

Anthony sat back into his chair and shivered against the evening breeze.

"Yes, I know," he said mostly to himself. "And there is still some in there too." He rubbed his chin in thought. "Nobody has come to collect it either."

"If we cross the river we will be in Mohawk territory," Pakwis said as he scanned the horizon. "I for one do not want any trouble right now." He remembered that not too long ago all of this land belonged to the Ojibwa. He himself had fought their enemy to keep it from them. The Mohawk grew stronger. His band got weaker. He feared that soon there would be no Ojibwa left. The fur trade made the Mohawk richer and bolder. "I think we should head back up to Twin Hills for the winter." Night Wind nodded. Pakwis knew he didn't want to fight. He wanted to spend his time with Sleeping Rabbit.

"I think it is a good place to live," Night Wind agreed. " I for one would like to live there for good."

Twin Hills were two high bluffs that ran alongside each other. One sloped down more easterly while the other one dipped toward the north. Along the base and up the slope, a variety of bushes and trees grew which would provide them with food and shelter. Pine, spruce, maple, birch and others grew along the southern slope. A nearby creek that flowed along the base of the western hill would provide water. Guards that watched from the hilltop could see for miles because the vegetation thinned out toward the east where long grasses, herbs and wild flowers grew. Southeast of the hills was a marsh. Anyone who approached had to go around it. There was only one way into the valley.

"We better go then, Chief," Night Wind said. "If we are going to make it before the bad weather comes."

"Yes, right after the morning meal."

Pakwis pulled his buffalo hide blanket tighter. His small band had survived and prospered since the big storm two winters ago. Three babies had been born, two still lived. He watched his wife, Little Blossom as she prepared their first meal of the day. Her thick waist pulled tight at the dress she wore. Her cowhide blanket had fallen to the ground when she bent down for more firewood. She threw the sticks into the flames and picked up her blanket. She noticed Pakwis's smile as he watched her.

He walked up to her, they embraced. "You look more beautiful every day, Little Blossom."

"And you more handsome, my husband." She patted her swollen belly. "And our son will be just as handsome as his father."

"Or, our daughter just as beautiful as her mother." He kissed her passionately then said, "We will leave after our morning meal." He gestured toward the cooking pot. "I think we will make our new home at Twin Hills."

Little Blossom agreed. "It is a good place to raise our children."

He held her at arms length. "I will tell the others"

She grabbed his arm. "Eat first. It is ready."

Lucas was packing his gear when Pakwis walked up to him. "You look like the fox that stole the duck's eggs," he said as he stood up.

"I guess becoming a father does that to a man," Pakwis laughed. He saw the pile of sacks in the white man's canoe. It bobbed in the nearby river half full. More gear sat ready to be loaded.

"I'm going to be leaving, Pakwis. I've made up my mind. There is someone I need to find."

The chief nodded. He half expected this would come some day. "You will be welcome here Lucas, if you want to come back."

"Thank you, Chief. This is something I have to do." With a shrug he picked up another sack. A small object dropped out. Pakwis picked it up and studied it, his face whitened as he twisted the delicate object between his thumb and forefinger. It was made from two tiny deer bones wrapped together with a thin string at one end so that it could be pushed into the hair. The blue bones had colourful beads inserted into it to make it a striking piece of jewelry.

"Where did you get this?" Pakwis eyed Lucas suspiciously.

"Oh," Lucas stammered, "I didn't steal it if that's what you mean. It belongs to a friend of mine."

"The one you look for now?"

"Yes," Lucas paused. "I need to find her."

Pakwis raised his eyebrows. "How did you get this?" He waved the hair clip at Lucas.

Lucas looked at him as if unsure what the accusation was. "I found a woman who had been attacked by a bear and nursed her back to health." He hung his head. "I left her alone to trade my furs and replenish our supplies. When I got back to our cave she was gone. I don't know what happened to her." He looked imploringly at the chief. "That's who I want to find."

"Why?" Pakwis shot daggers at Lucas. The white man looked out in the distance and didn't notice.

"I want to see if she will become my wife." Lucas said softly.

Pakwis took a step back. "And who is this woman you speak of?"

"Her name is Winda."

Pakwis' stomach did a flip. He had recognized the hair clip as Winda's the moment he picked it up. He had thought of her as dead. He tried to put her out of his mind. Then this. There had been no sign of her after the storm. He couldn't look for her; he was chief and had to stay with his people. She had escaped. He didn't know what to do now. Winda had been his since he captured her in her youth. He captured her. He raised her. Then he took her as a wife.

He studied the ground at his feet. But she was still a slave. Lanick saw to that. Winda's big, sad eyes came into view, her long shining hair, her beautiful face, and her long, slender legs. He envisioned her full, soft breasts and smooth skin.

"Pakwis." Night Wind shook his arm.

He jarred awake. "What?"

"We are ready to leave." Night Wind watched Pakwis with a sympathetic look, as if he knew how it felt to be love-sick for someone. "Are you all right, Chief?" Pakwis watched his people trudge by him. Slowly their shapes emerged as he began to focus. His new wife watched him, unsure of her place now. Everyone had heard that Winda was still alive. Pakwis was glad for the blanket he held over him. His sudden yearnings made it hard to concentrate. He nodded to Night Wind and jumped up onto his horse.

Lucas had become very comfortable with these people and swore at himself because he lost the hair clip. By the look on Pakwis' face, he hadn't gotten over Winda. Lucas didn't want to think of her in his friend's arms. The image of the two of them together haunted him all day. He was sure Pakwis didn't want to let his slave go. Maybe he would have to kill his friend for her. He mulled this over in his mind and didn't pay attention to where he went. Automatically, the paddle pushed the water back in long deep strokes. Lucas didn't want to think that something bad had happened to her. The corpse at the cave told him that something terrible had occurred. He had to find out where she was.

Lucas had decided to head back up to the cave. This time he would search harder for clues as to what did happen up there. Then he'd decide what course of action to take from there. The band travelled in roughly the same direction as he was. Lucas wanted to be alone to think things over, especially now that Pakwis found out about Winda. He was jealous. Lucas saw it in his eyes.

He canoed up the same river that the starving band found him on. He still felt a sense of melancholy as he did the first time. Lucas was so deep in though that he took a wrong turn and didn't realize it until two days later when he stood on top of a small waterfall. The way to the cave didn't have one. He didn't care where he went and decided to test out this new route. Hell, he had to get lucky sometime.

13

They partied well into the night. Dusty was the last one to pass out at the kitchen table. One of his friends snored as he lay on the floor. The other leaned against the wall still in his chair, with his tongue out. Dusty's eyelids closed before he slumped forward and landed face down on the wooden table.

Both Grant and Bill had limited their intake of whiskey, played along with the rest, laughed and joked with them. Only once did someone check on the general upstairs. They sneaked outside. Rain fell heavily so they stayed on the small porch. Often, they checked through the front window for any movement.

Bill told Grant, "I think this is the last shipment this year. The lake will soon freeze over. They can't wait any longer; they have to do it soon."

"How long will it take them to get these crates to the ship?"

"About a week, maybe more. The ship will have to be right there to meet them. Any delays could hold them up till next spring."

"How much does General Brooks know?"

"All of it. He's the one who instructed me to fill you in with the details if I saw you. He wants you kept up to date."

Grant checked inside the window.

Bill continued. "We hope that by next spring we can put an end to all of this. General Brooks sent a dispatch to the authorities in Montreal to stop any more shipments entering the country. I think we may need to wait until spring for the next one to reach port. According to Brooks, they have narrowed it down to just a few ships. They'll keep an eye out for it."

"Good. When can I arrest these men?" Grant checked the window again.

"General Brooks wants us to wait till spring so we can get as many of these men as possible. We're compiling a list of names." Bill shuddered and shifted closer to the wall. "We want to make sure we get all the organizers of this mess."

"Well, we know one thing, Dusty is one of them. I think Ivan was too."

"Yeah, he sure moved a lot of money around, didn't he?"

"Yes, it's rumoured that he hid some of it someplace," Grant said, just in case they start to look for the two thousand dollars hidden in his room.

"Now that we know where General Walton's hideout is, I'll send some men to keep an eye on it."

"And I will keep a very close eye on Dusty." And that will keep him close to Dusty's wife.

"I think we better get back inside. Besides, I'm freezing."

Grant followed Bill back into the kitchen. They had just sat back down in their chairs when Dusty lifted his head and looked at them through blurry eyes.

Lucas pulled his canoe up on shore at the edge of a small town three days later. His canoe lay beside three others in a row above the flood line with all his gear in it. He blew on his hands as he walked up a small hill toward the main street to find accommodations. His right side ached. Sleeping Rabbit had done a good job stitching him up, though. Every once in awhile, like today, he would overdo it and pain would shoot through his side. Lucas looked back down at the river. It had started to freeze over. It was a good time to get off the water for awhile.

He walked down the street and took stock of the shops and services that he might need someday. The biggest structure and the first one he saw was the saw mill. It was a three story wooden building with a huge wheel that turned slowly with a *thump, thump, thump*. Down the road from it was a two-story tavern with a long front porch. Across the road from it that was a blacksmith shop. Its huge doors stood open even in this cold. The *clang, clang* of a hammer over the anvil echoed throughout. Next to it was the livery stables, then a restaurant, a seamstress shop, and then several houses.

People greeted him as he strolled through the streets. He smiled and nodded back. He passed the tavern then an empty lot. There was a butcher shop and a hardware store. Next were the bank and several other shops and businesses. Near the far end was the general store, and the silversmiths stood across the street from a livery stable. Several houses lined both sides of the street. One stood out, which he thought was charming. A lone, log cabin nestled in between two large framed houses on a deep lot. It seemed out of place, yet it seemed to be the only thing that belonged.

Lucas turned right at the corner and passed a bakery and a church. Houses filled in the rest of the street to a dead end. Huge trees lined both sides of the street, most of them bare of leaves. People filed out of the church as he passed by it. He watched as they huddled against the cold. Lucas nodded to them and turned down an alley.

He walked by a huge warehouse behind the church which took up most of that side of the block. A woodworking and furniture shop stood at the far end and backed up to the blacksmith shop he saw earlier. Across from it stood a boarding house and more houses. Farmers' fields stretched out on the same side of the street he stood on.

The boarding house invited him, so Lucas went inside and secured a room. The lady looked up at him and smiled warmly. She didn't even check his signature when he registered. Lucas returned to his canoe and made several trips to bring all the gear inside. He didn't want to stay in the tavern, it did not appeal to him. He wanted peace and quiet.

He had just settled in when the woman brought up hot coffee and some baked goods to his room. She introduced herself as Hazel. She took her time to light the fireplace for him and smiled sweetly at him.

"You need anything, just let me know." Hazel sidled up to him and rubbed her hand on his arm. "Anything at all." She stood close to him, a little too close. He could smell her cheap perfume. He could see down the front of her dress. But his side ached. He was tired and hungry. She didn't do anything for him at all.

"Maybe later," Lucas told her, trying not to hurt her feelings.

"All you have to do is knock on my door, ah...?" she ran her fingers up his chest.

"Lucas."

"Lucas." She sashayed out, and left him with a smile of amusement on his face.

He poured a cup full of coffee, took a baked good, and stood at the window watching the new snow swirl around in the field. After he finished it, he took out the little blue hair pin that Pakwis had found. Mixed emotions played on his soul. His gaze went over to the gear in the corner. He had carried Winda's things around with him for over year. Her new winter coat she had made was in there, along with her leggings. He even had the dried herbs she had collected and laid out in the sun or tied together and hung upside down. Then he looked down again at the object in his hand and wondered how long he should hang on to her things. When was it time to let go?

The aroma in the small cabin made Carrie's mouth water in anticipation. She sat at the kitchen table peeling carrots while Winda cut up potatoes for supper. A turkey slowly roasted in the iron stove. Adam asked when they could eat for the third time in an hour.

"This is a special day, isn't it, Carrie?" Johnny eyed the freshly baked bread on the counter that Winda had made that morning.

"Yes it is. It's Jeb's birthday. He turns eighty today."

Johnny looked at Jeb with an open mouth. "That's old!"

Jeb laughed. But to Carrie, he looked tired. She was sure his memory was fading; he forgot when Sam was born. It took him longer to get dressed in the morning too. His shaky hands fumbling with the buttons on his shirt.

"Don't you think you'll get that old, Johnny?" Winda asked while she put the potatoes on the stove.

"I don't know. That's a long time."

"I'm going to live to be a hundred," Adam piped up. He wore a big smile today. Earlier, Winda had removed the cast off his arm. He was so glad that he gave her his biggest hug.

"You need to be careful with that arm for awhile yet," Winda warned him.

"Or I'll break it again?" Adam looked up at her with big blue eyes.

"You might, but that would take some doing. It will hurt easier now if you bang it. Just be careful, okay?"

Both boys were used to Winda now, accepting her strange ways. They weren't afraid that she might eat them anymore. Carrie put the carrots on the stove and checked out the window. "I wonder what's taking Sam so long." He had taken Squirrel for a short walk and was to stop at the general store to pick up a side of bacon for breakfast tomorrow.

Johnny helped Winda set the table. Adam sat in his usual spot. "It's going to be awhile yet, Adam. Why don't you and Johnny go play? We will call you when it's ready," Carrie coaxed them.

Both boys left the table and ran over to pester Jeb. Sam came in and handed Carrie the bacon and her change. She smiled to herself. She was able to withdraw money from Dusty's account at the bank. He didn't even know it yet. Little by little, she was hoarding some of his money. Someday she'd be rid of him. A serious look came over Sam as he walked over to Winda. "There is a man outside. He wants to talk to you."

She stirred the potatoes then turned to face him. "For me?" She gave Carrie a nervous look. "What does he want?"

"I don't know." He reached in his pocket and handed Winda a strange object.

"Oh!" She grabbed the back of a chair and started to weave.

"What is it, Winda?" Carrie set the bacon down. "What's wrong?"

"It's my hair pin. The one I left at the cave."

"What did the man say?" Carrie turned to Sam. "Did he give you his name?"

Sam shook his head. "Just that she would know where it came from." He shifted from one foot to the other and glanced back and forth. "Did I do something wrong? Maybe I shouldn't have brought that man here."

Tears welled up in Winda's eyes. "Lookas."

"Well, don't just stand there, girl. Go let him in." Carrie pushed her friend toward the door. They all had heard the story of Winda's hero and she suspected that Winda was in love with this man. Jeb pushed out of his chair, stood beside Sam and leaned on his cane. They all waited for Winda to open the door.

Lucas caught his breath when Winda opened the door. She was even more beautiful than he remembered. Her long black hair still hung to her waist, he detected a hint of lavender. He searched her eyes for what she might feel for him. "Hello Winda," he said at last.

He caught her when she jumped into his arms. "Lookas!" She plastered kisses all over him. "I missed you."

Lucas laughed. "I can't believe my luck. I found you. Oh, Winda, I searched for you all over the place." She hung on to him so tight that he started to choke. He let her down and grinned at her.

"I have prayed every day that we would be together again," she told him.

"I have too." He glanced into the open doorway. "I hope that this time we can stay together."

Lucas saw the shape of a man standing in the shadows and frowned. He couldn't make out who it was. His heart sank. Winda grabbed his hand and led him inside. He quickly realized that the man was too old to be Winda's lover. He relaxed after she introduced him to her new-found family. Lucas shook hands with everyone and patted Squirrel's head, who licked his face when he bent over.

Sam laughed. "He likes you."

Carrie sprang back to the stove to rescue the carrots that were over-boiling. Winda hung on to Lucas as if afraid to let go in case he vanished again.

"It's Jeb's birthday today," Johnny informed him. "He's old."

They all laughed, including Jeb who started to cough. Sam helped him back to his chair. Carrie put another plate on the table. "Now you have to stay and celebrate with us."

After the big meal, the boys cleared away the dishes. Jeb praised the women. "Supper was perfect. I won't be able to eat for at least another hour or so."

Carrie got up and pulled out a chocolate cake and lit one big candle on it. "Make a wish, Jeb."

Jeb's tearful eyes scanned around the room. "I can't remember the last time I had a birthday cake." He thought for a few minutes before he leaned over and blew the candle out.

"What did you wish for?" Adam wanted to know.

"I can't tell you," Jeb said. Adam's face dropped.

"Is that right?" Johnny asked as if he tried to rescue his brother.

"Yep, that's the way it goes. I can't tell you or else it will break the wish and it won't come true."

Adam's face lit up again as he watched Carrie skillfully cut the cake up into sections. "Can I have a big piece?"

Grant and Dusty were on their way back home after they delivered the crates. Bill Egelton and his companions were on the way to Lake Erie to load the crates onto the ship. (Actually, he'd confiscate them before that.) The wagon became stuck in a winter storm. The horses were knee deep in hard, wet snow. They had lost the trail in the blinding wind.

"We've got to get out of here," yelled Grant, "or we will freeze to death."

"Can't see anything," Dusty shouted back.

"The horses are freezing to death." Grant tried again in order to get his highness off his fat ass. "Look!"

"Over by that ridge." Dusty squinted in the direction where Grant pointed.

"Okay," Dusty finally agreed. "You grab the gear. I'll get the horses."

Both of them jumped off the wagon. Grant reached into the back and lifted out a sack. Dusty felt his way to the front of the wagon to unhook the horses. He stepped into a hole and couldn't move. Grant barely saw him through the snow and didn't help his partner when he got himself into trouble. He pretended he didn't see him. Dusty yelled for Grant but he acted as if the big man's voice didn't carry in the wind. Slowly, inch by inch, Dusty pulled himself up onto the wagon and freed himself.

Grant watched Dusty crawl over and jump off the other side and try again. With frostbitten fingers, Dusty unhooked the horses and led them out of the wind. Grant threw Dusty a blanket he had dug out of the sack and pulled one out for himself. They huddled against the ridge to wait out the storm.

Grant stewed as he sat against the dirt wall. He had wanted to stop a long time ago, before the full fury of the storm hit. They watched the sky turn dark, felt the wind pick up and blind them. They could have driven off a cliff.

Dusty had been in a foul mood ever since he found out that Ivan was dead. He pushed them in spite. Grant glared at the big man. If they got out of here alive, he'd kill the son of a bitch. Grant shivered. His teeth rattled and his feet were numb. The leather gloves he wore had stiffened over the edge of the blanket. He couldn't move. Dusty's head dropped onto his chest, he started to snore. Minutes later, so did Grant.

Grant woke up to a grey depressing day. A chickadee flitted from branch to branch in a nearby bush, serenading him. He ordered his fingers to move in his mind. He was able to lift one, then another one. Eventually, everything moved. He tested his legs one at a time and stood up. He still couldn't feel his toes. It saddened him when the bird flew away.

Dusty was up and was checking the horses; he rubbed his hands down each leg. "They're fine," he announced when he saw Grant approach him.

"Can't say that about the wagon."

Dusty turned to look. The wagon had blown over onto its side, half buried in the snow. The contents had blown all over the place. The men tied the horses to it with a couple of long ropes and pulled it back up onto its wheels. Grant gathered all the gear while Dusty hitched up the team. They jumped up. Dusty pulled out a piece of jerky and handed one to Grant. Grant took up the reins.

"Let's get out of here," ordered Dusty

Grant still couldn't feel his toes.

Night Wind beamed as Lost Boy put the final touches to his outfit. The young boy stuck three eagle feathers into the warrior's hair and arranged them just so.

"Like a man to the slaughter," Lost Boy snickered.

Playfully, Night Wind backhanded him. "I am ready."

Dressed in his finest, Night Wind listened to the drums beat his wedding march. His stomach knotted, the palms of his hands were sweating. Lost Boy opened the door-flap and checked outside. "They are ready."

Night Wind nodded and gulped before he followed Lost Boy outside into the snow. The whole village waited excitedly as he passed by them to stand in front of Pakwis. He smiled as he went, noticing that everyone had worn their best for this day.

Pakwis said a short prayer over Night Wind then nodded to Little Blossom who opened the flap to another wigwam. Sleeping Rabbit ducked out into the sunshine. She wore a pure white deerskin coat over a beautifully beaded dress of that same material. The intricate patterns on her coat sparkled as she walked. Her long hair hung loose down her back like a dark veil. High rabbit-skin boots covered her tiny feet. The snow glittered around her as she walked up to Night Wind. He had never seen such a beautiful sight.

Pakwis nudged him. People giggled. "I will repeat. Take her hands into yours and face each other."

They said the words that would make her his. Pakwis blessed the newly married couple. Night Wind picked up his bride and carried her into his wigwam, set her down gently. Night Wind kissed her before he walked back to the door and secured the flap shut. The crowd danced around the wigwam singing and laughing until they tired out.

Night Wind led his wife to his bed.

The rest of that winter was mild. No more big storms blew over the hills. Pakwis sat on his horse on top of the north ridge that overlooked the village. He rode up there that morning to watch the sun creep across the snow and illuminate the lodges below him. He tried to tell himself that he was guarding his people from enemies. He couldn't deny the real reason he was up there. The horse stayed still as he opened his arms to the heavens.

"I have prayed to you, Great Spirit to give me a sign. Please show me what to do. Do I challenge Lucas for Winda or do I let her go?"

Pakwis brought his arms down, watched the women light the cooking fires below him and begin their morning chores. Little Blossom stood outside, big with child. His emotions fluttered between lust for Winda and love for Little Blossom.

He knew his wife worried about him. His obsession with his former slave seemed unnatural to her. He could hardly think of anything else. He missed Winda's shapely body. Then he'd feel guilty and act foolish with Little Blossom. He had spent most the winter in a haze. The way his wife watched him made his skin itch. He couldn't help himself.

He closed his eyes. Pakwis took a deep breath, let in the clean crisp air. When he opened them again, he noticed that something was wrong. Sleeping Rabbit was bent over Little Blossom. Night Wind raced toward him on a horse. Pakwis hung his head in shame and wondered what he'd missed. Was he so engrossed with thoughts of another woman that he put his wife in danger?

He raced his horse along the ridge top and down the trail and met Night Wind. "Little Blossom is having the baby," the warrior told him.

It felt like a punch in the stomach. Pakwis couldn't breathe. Finally he mumbled, "Baby?"

Night Wind smiled at him sympathetically. They rode down the hill to the village. Pakwis jumped off his horse just as Sleeping Rabbit led Little Blossom into the birthing hut. What a fool he'd been.

14

1802. The lady at the boarding house scowled at Winda as she led the squaw up the stairs. It wasn't proper for a lady to visit a man in his room, alone. Especially one so handsome. She never included herself, she owned the place. Hazel usually got any man she wanted. She was used to the easy pickings that her establishment afforded her. And, she wanted Lucas. But her charms hadn't worked on him. Hazel prided herself on her good looks and shapely body. She had powdered her face and coloured her lips and slipped into her low-cut dress just for him. He ignored her. She looked over at Winda and frowned. They stopped in front of room number six. Hazel rapped on the door.

"Come in," his deep, sexy voice answered.

Before Winda could reach for the knob, Hazel pushed her way inside. "There is a," she stammered, "lady here to..."

Winda had followed her inside. Lucas rose from the chair. "Thank you, Hazel." He led her out and shut the door behind her. Hazel's hand flew to her mouth.

"Well I never!" She stood there in the hall, shocked. Minutes later, Hazel turned and stomped down the stairs.

Lucas took three long strides until he stood in front of Winda. "Good to see you, Winda." He kissed her deeply, then stepped back and lifted her hair and smelled the lavender. He smiled then purposely sat on the chair at the desk. "I'd better behave myself. I think Hazel hears everything that happens in this place."

Winda sat on the edge of the bed and took off her mitts. She noticed the sacks in the corner. The coat she had made in the cave stuck out of one of them. "Why you carry my things all this time?"

Lucas glanced at the corner. "Because, like I said, I looked for you all over the place." He told her how he went back to the cave. How he wandered around and felt lost without her. Then he told her that he had met Pakwis and the rest of the village after the big storm and how desperate they were.

In turn, Winda told him of the rape and how she expected him to turn away from her in disgust.

He knew she must have felt dirty and ashamed. Lucas knelt in front of her. He saw the fear in her eyes. "Oh, Winda, my love. I'm so sorry. I shouldn't have left you there by yourself. It's my fault. Not yours."

He pulled her head down to his and kissed her tenderly. Then he looked into her eyes and asked about the dead man he found with his trap wrapped around his leg. "Is that the man who raped you?"

She told him how she set the trap and buried it under leaves and how she lured the evil man to it. Lucas held her as she cried. "I will never leave you like that again, Winda."

The following day Dusty pulled the wagon up in front of the tavern. Grant reached into the back for his gear and jumped down. He watched Dusty enter the front door. That man's biggest love was the bottle. Tired and hungry, Grant walked down the icy street to his room in the boarding house. All he wanted was hot food and a good night's sleep.

Hazel greeted him cheerfully when he entered. She was using a feather duster to clean pictures in the little hallway at the bottom of the stairs. "Good day, Mr. Sievers. Glad to see you back."

"Afternoon, Hazel. Can you send up a hot meal and coffee to my room?"

"Certainly." She sashayed down the hall toward the back of the house. "I'll bring you up a juicy steak. How about that?"

Grant watched her walk away. It seemed that she swung her hips just a bit too much. "Fine." He shook his head and climbed the stairs up to his room. After dropping his gear inside the door he sat down on the edge of the bed and pulled off his boots.

Grant jumped awake when someone knocked on his door. For a second he didn't realize where he was. He opened it to let Hazel slide by him and set a steaming tray on the table by the window. She licked her lips seductively while she lifted the lid off his plate and unrolled his utensils from the napkin. He watched her place his knife and fork by the plate, his napkin on the chair. She even poured his coffee from the pitcher on the tray. He just stood there with his arms folded across his chest and smirked at her. "There you go, Grant." She blinked at him. "All set." He didn't move.

Hazel walked up to him and ran her fingers up the front of his shirt, playing with his buttons. He swallowed hard and looked down the front of her dress. She smelled of spring flowers. Her breasts rubbed up and down his arms. "How about a little something before supper, eh cowboy?" She leaned into him.

His stomach growled. The food smelled heavenly. He looked over at the table. A large, thick, juicy steak waited for him. Potatoes dotted with butter and creamy corn called to him. His mouth watered.

Gently he pushed her aside. "I'm sorry, not now." He sat down at the table, cut a big chunk of the meat and savoured it. A bite of corn was next. His stomach thanked him. He ignored the seductress as he ate the delicious food, and felt better with each bite. Hazel huffed and stormed out of the room.

Lucas climbed the stairs two at a time. He had had his supper in the little restaurant around the corner. Hazel sped by him, nearly sending him back down the stairs and barely glanced at him. He looked down the hall. As far as he knew, there were only two boarders there at this time. Winda told him that a man named Grant had a room there. His heart raced when he heard. He didn't say anything to her; he wanted to be sure first. The floor in room number two creaked.

He knocked. The door opened slowly. Grant's eyes widened. Lucas stepped inside. "Hello, big brother."

"Lucas. Where did you come from?" Grant hugged him and patted him on the back.

"End of the hall."

"Well, look at you. You're getting fat."

"It must be love." Lucas turned a chair around and leaned on the back. "I'm thinking of getting married."

Grant's eyes narrowed. "Not to that "any man will do" from downstairs, I hope."

"No, no." Lucas laughed. "This one doesn't throw herself at every male in her vicinity."

Grant told his little brother how she delivered his supper and how he turned her down.

"So that's why she almost sent me flying down the stairs."

Grant sat back down at his table to finish his supper.

"I've turned her down too, on occasion." Lucas sighed. "Must admit though, it's pretty tempting, isn't it?"

Grant nodded and looked at his empty plate. "Yeah, but the steak won out this time." He smiled at his brother and commented on the buckskins he wore. Lucas just grinned. "So," Grant prodded, "who is this lucky lady you have your heart set on?" He sipped his coffee.

Lucas watched Grant. "She's Indian, a Cree raised as an Ojibwa." He hoped that Grant wasn't going to turn away in disgust. "Her name is Winda."

Grant let out a long whistle and smiled encouragement at him. Lucas relaxed. His brother wasn't a hypocrite. "How did you meet her?"

Lucas told him the whole story about them. He told Grant how they had been separated and of his search for her.

"I've met her, I think. At least I know a Winda."

"Yeah, she's the one who told me you were here. I wanted to check it out before I let her know that you're my brother."

Grant's face paled. "I pushed her down." Lucas balled his fist. "I didn't mean to push so hard. I did apologize to her." Grant started to trip over his tongue. "I just wanted to make my undercover look convincing."

Lucas flexed his fingers. Grant tried to explain before his brother hit him. "I did apologize to her," he repeated. "I'm investigating Dusty Blackman for gun smuggling." Lucas relaxed. "I didn't mean to hurt her. She knows who I am now, I told her."

Grant told his brother how he'd met Winda. How she had watched Dusty from across the street. He had questioned her, her big brown eyes watching his every move. She stood ready to bolt, but stayed and listened to him babble on. "And this beautiful creature had fallen for my brother," he teased and was swatted. "Well, there goes any chance I might have had."

Lucas kicked him. "Well, what do you think about it?"

Grant nodded. "Yes. I can see it. She's the right kind of woman for you Lucas, from what I've seen. Being Indian makes no never mind to me. Hell, I've thought about it a time or two myself." He smiled. "I'm glad you found someone."

Grant saddled his horse and headed out of town two days later. The snow had begun to melt. The last few days had been mild. It was a perfect day for a ride. He stopped at a hastily made ramp set across a creek. The old bridge stood twisted and half submerged in the icy water. The new one lay beside it with no rails. Grant led his horse across the slippery surface.

Dusty's farm wasn't that hard to find. It was the only one out there for miles, right past Black Creek. He rode slowly down the lane. The sight was unbelievable. He had wondered about the tornado. To see the devastation in person sent shivers up his backside. And Carrie survived it. He had seen her in town. She was living at Jeb's place with Dusty's kids. He wondered why Dusty wasn't with them.

He looked at the barn. It stood jagged against the sky. Half of the house was gone. A huge pile of lumber stood in the yard. Someone had been tearing the house apart piece by piece. He slid off his horse and walked around the corner. Dusty threw broken furniture and debris into a bonfire that smoldered with thick black smoke.

"What the hell do you want?" coughed the big man, who squinted angrily at Grant.

"Nice to see you too, Dusty," Grant didn't let Dusty rile him. "I just came to see if we have new orders yet. And to see if you need any help."

"Nope and nope. Now leave." Dusty gave him look of contempt and threw more stuff on the pile. He walked over behind Grant and picked up a tree limb. Grant assumed that it would go into the fire and didn't pay attention. The fire caught and flared up, sending Grant backwards a few feet. Dusty raised the tree limb and brought it down over Grant's head. Grant blacked out before he hit the ground.

Hours later, Grant pulled himself up from the wet ground and groaned. His head felt ready to explode. He tried to stand, but had to lean over and hold it with both hands until the pounding stopped. He opened his eyes and squinted into the dusk. Dusty was gone, stolen Grant's horse. He straightened and became dizzy, staggering sideways a few steps. The fire had died down but was still smoldering. Grant walked over to warm up. Something unusual caught his attention. He bent down closer to see better and saw a human form buried under tons of rubble.

Grant backed up, fell on his butt, and crawled backward like a crab and onto the snow. He had to wait until his head stopped pounding before he crawled on all fours to look again. The body was still there. It wasn't a dream.

With brute determination, he kicked at the fire, threw snow on it, and pulled it apart, anything to put it out. Fire crawled up his sleeve, sending excruciating pain through his skin. Grant dropped down and rolled in the wet to get it out.

But he body was still there, on fire. He forced himself up and threw more stuff off it. Grant grabbed a leg, pulled it out, and dragged it away from the red hot embers. He took shallow breaths to ease his painful chest and stood on wobbly legs. Every fibre of his being cried out, "*No,*" when he recognized the corpse.

He had met this old man. Everyone spoke highly of him and Grant couldn't figure out why Dusty would want to kill this gentle soul. He wondered what he had on Dusty to end up like this. Grant had heard stories of who really built Blackman Falls. It was on the back of this old man. In his younger years, the big, black slave had the strength of two men. He did the heavy lifting to clear this land and build the saw mill and the tavern for Dusty's father.

He also found out that Dusty's father died just after he and his son had a big fight. Maybe that was when Jeb gained his freedom.

Grant shook his head, and regretted it. He looked down at his tattered coat and blackened fingers he sustained from pulling the body out of the fire. Burned grass was what his hair smelled like and the front of his pants smoldered. His mind started to spin. Grant grabbed his head and screamed. "Dusty, I'm going to kill you."

He stumbled. The world swirled around then went black.

Lucas woke up from a deep sleep as someone pounded on his door. He dragged himself out of the warm, cozy bed and opened the door. Winda burst in and started to babble hysterically.

"What is it? What happened?" Winda wasn't the type to get all emotional on him; she was as levelheaded as you could be. Automatically, his arms encircled her.

"Jeb, he's missing," she huffed between shallow breaths.

"What? What do you mean missing? He can't walk down the street by himself."

"I don't think he went on his own." She sniffled and wiped her eyes. "He's been gone all night."

She trembled as Lucas guided her to the edge of his bed and threw on his clothes. Winda gave a short laugh at him because he tried to put his pants on backwards. If it had been any other woman, it would have embarrassed him. With Winda though, he just shrugged it off and flipped them around.

"What do you mean gone all night? How could you not know he wasn't there?"

"Carrie told me that Jeb was out on the front porch when she went to bed last night. When I left you and got home everything was in darkness. I thought he was in bed like everyone else." She lowered her head. "He wasn't even there."

Lucas held her and let her cry herself out. "I should have checked," she sniffled.

"It's not your fault. It's normal that you assumed he was there." Lucas kissed her forehead and dried her tears with his blanket. "We'll find him, I promise." He waited for her to settle down. "Come on, we'll get Grant." He led her down the hall.

"Grant? The man I told you about?"

"Yes. He's my brother." Lucas knocked on the door. No sound came from within. He banged harder. "Come on, Grant. Open up." Still no answer. He pounded with his fist. "Grant. Wake up."

"What's going on?" Hazel ran up the stairs. "You're going to wake the whole town."

Lucas watched as Winda stifled a scream. Hazel wore a long, white cotton nightgown with no makeup and hair rolled up in curlers. To him, she looked like a porcupine. He muffled a laugh. *This was the sexy made up lady who tried to seduce me?* He turned back to the door.

"He's not answering." Lucas stepped back, ploughed through the door, and landed on the bed. It was empty. There was no sign of Grant. No one had slept in the bed all night.

"Oh no." Winda threw up her hands. "Now we have two people missing."

Carrie paced back and forth tying not to panic in front of the boys. Sam lay curled up in a chair sobbing. Johnny and Adam sat together on the floor and watched her with big, sad eyes. Adam petted Squirrel unconsciously. The big black dog greeted Winda and Lucas when they entered.

"What happened?" Lucas asked Carrie.

Carrie told him the same thing Winda did. She waved her hands and spoke quickly. "I fell asleep in the chair. I thought Jeb was in bed when I woke up. So I went to bed. When we got up this morning he was gone."

Lucas shook her. "Settle down, Carrie." He led her to a chair. "I'll go have a look."

She rambled on. "He was just sitting outside in his rocker. Where could he have gone?"

"His chair was tipped over." Winda informed her friend.

Lucas watched Squirrel sidle up to Sam for attention. "Where was Squirrel? Surely he would have heard something?"

Carrie pointed to the corner. "He was sleeping with Sam." She looked at the dog. "I think his hearing is going."

Winda agreed. "I've noticed that too. You have to talk louder before he will obey orders."

Lucas went outside. The sun had just risen over the church steeple. A flock of swans flew over head. He watched a cat pounce on something invisible to him on the neighbour's yard. He waved to a man walking by. Everything seemed so normal.

A blood stain near his foot caught his attention. More blood dotted the snow. Quickly, he covered them up. He turned to go back inside when he spotted something in the slushy snow by a tree. He bent down and picked up Jeb's cane.

When Sam saw it, he ran to Lucas and hugged him. His whole body shaking violently. Lucas held him tight. "We will find him, son."

Winda had prepared a quick breakfast for the boys. Johnny and Adam sat at the table and stared at the food. Neither one had an appetite. Sam took the cane and sat down on his bed to be alone.

Lucas called the women over by the door. "There was a lot of blood out there. I covered it up." He nodded toward the boys. Carrie thanked him for his consideration. "It looks like Jeb was dragged out of here and put on a horse. Tracks lead northward."

Carrie looked at him shocked. with fear in her eyes. "Does that mean Dusty's behind this?"

"Could be," Lucas answered. "I wouldn't put it past him."

Winda looked at Sam as if her heart broke. "This is not good."

"Well, I'm going to find out for sure." Lucas opened the door.

"Wait. I am coming with you." Winda gathered a few supplies then slipped into her coat.

"I'll keep a close watch on the boys." Carrie promised. "They'll be fine," she said before she closed the door behind them.

15

Lucas led them up the north road. When they reached the bridge they dismounted and led the horses over the ramp one at a time. Winda walked across and studied the old one beside it. She tried to picture Carrie as she crossed it with the boys. How she managed to do so, Winda couldn't fathom. It stood straight up in the air. There wasn't much she could get a footing on.

Lucas took her hand and led her across. They walked down the road side by side. He told her about Grant, and that he was a major in the militia. And about their childhood and how their parents died.

"Grant's looked after me since I was thirteen. He was only fifteen, but managed. We didn't want to separate at that time. Then when he turned eighteen he joined the militia. That's when I started trapping."

"I hope," Winda said, "that Grant kills Dusty if he has Jeb."

Lucas squeezed her hand. "We'll find out soon enough."

They got back up on the horses now that they were rested and rode in silence. Neither spoke much. They didn't need to. They just wanted to be in each others' company. "You're a brave woman, Winda," Lucas finally said.

She smiled at him. He lifted her hair and smelled the lavender scent of it. They rode together stealing kisses as they went. Lucas tried hard not to show how much he was worried about his brother. With Dusty around things could turn very bad in a hurry. He looked over at Winda and decided right then that he would make sure he'd never lose her. Impulsively, he slid off his mount and asked her to do the same. He took her in his arms. They stood in the middle of the road in a deep embrace. The caw of an eagle close by startled them. Lucas shifted from one foot to the other.

"Winda, I can't tell you how much I love you." He forced himself to get up the nerve. "Will you? When this is all over, that is." He started over. "Please say you'll be my wife?" He waited, watched her face show surprise, then acceptance, then the love that he hoped she would only show to him.

"Yes, Lookas, I love you too." She jumped into his arms, laughing hysterically. He swung her around grinning from ear to ear.

Lucas set Winda down. Both of them stopped laughing as they became serious again and concentrated on finding Grant and Jeb. They hurried down the road.

Ten minutes later they held their weapons at the ready as they rode down the long lane past the house. "I smell smoke," Winda told Lucas who kept his eyes glued to the corner of the house. They left the animals and walked around to the back. "So this was Kate's house? I wondered how she could live way out here with just the two boys as company. Dusty left her alone a lot too, like he did with Carrie."

Lucas stopped. Winda looked down from staring at the house. Grant lay on the ground, still and lifeless. Small fires burned around him, scattered around the yard. Debris lay everywhere, smoldering and turning the air rancid. Winda ran up and knelt beside Lucas's brother. Grant moaned. Lucas let out a breath of air and bent down to inspect his wounds and almost cried aloud.

Grant had suffered severe burns to his hands and face. His clothes were charred. Yet, he still lived.

"He has a fever. I will give him medicine," Winda told him. "We need to get him out of here."

Lucas nodded toward a small cabin at the back of the yard by the trees. He reached out to pick Grant up. "What happened here, Grant?" Grant swung his good arm out and blocked Lucas, who stood up, confused. "Don't you want help, Grant?"

"Dusty." Grant swallowed more soot into his lungs and coughed. "Burn…man." He raised his arm, fought the pain, and pointed to a charred heap of coal a few feet away. Lucas walked over and turned it over.

Winda screamed behind him, "Jeb! Oh no, Jeb!"

Lucas turned and grabbed her tightly and led her away from the gruesome sight. "I'm so sorry, Winda. I'm so sorry." He shook and cried with her.

Lucas jabbed the shovel into the hard dirt, angrily swearing aloud. "Why did that ugly, bald man have to kill Jeb? What did that gentle, old man ever do to him?" He threw the dirt out of the grave haphazardly. "How many more times is he going to try and kill Grant?" *More importantly, would he eventually succeed?* He hit a rock, bent down, and heaved it out of his way. He didn't watch, or care, where it went; the offending object hit the cross next to him. "Kate. It had to be. Who else?" She was another one of Dusty's victims?

"What did she ever see in him? And why did she wait for him after all this time?"

Several minutes later he hit a bigger rock. He dug around it until he could pry it loose. Lucas heaved it out of the hole. Sweat poured down his bearded face. His hair hung long and damp on his shoulders. His arms ached. Lucas stopped to take a breath.

Kate's grave had no inscription on it. "I'm going to put one on there for her. She deserves that much," he told the mound of dirt.

As his laboured breath became easier, Lucas still talked to himself. "How many lonely graves has Dusty left behind him? What about the one at the cave?" He was sure that Dusty had killed that man too, even if it was just to put the man out of his misery. He's still another one of Dusty's throwaways.

"And what about Carrie?" Lucas's heart went out to the pretty redhead. "Look what that bastard put her through. I wouldn't blame her if she shot the son of a bitch." He dug until the hole was big enough then took a break. "And what about the boys, what will happen to them?" He threw the shovel. "Where would they go from here? I hope they don't end up with their father."

Winda walked up and handed him a cool drink. "Jeb's body is ready." Her voice was scratchy, her face blotchy red.

Lucas took several gulps and poured the rest of the water over his heated head. And then there was Winda, another victim. Suddenly, he couldn't get his breath. His chest thumped against his ribs. He started to get dizzy. *What if he killed Winda*? Lucas clamoured out of the hole, wrapped his arms around her waist and hung on with all his might. He couldn't let go of her.

Winda squirmed. "Lookas, I can't breathe." He loosened his grip and stepped back.

"Oh, sorry," he apologized sheepishly. "I don't know what came over me."

She waited until he pulled himself together then put her arms around him. "You had a panic attack. I get them too, sometimes."

Together they laid Jeb's burned and broken body into the grave. Winda had wrapped him up in a clean cloth. Then she put food and her own bow and one arrow on top of him. "This will help him in the afterlife," she told Lucas. She prayed as he filled in the grave.

Lucas planted a cross with Jeb's name and a small inscription, *Here lies a gentle man who was murdered.*

Lucas said his own prayer before he walked back to the leaky cabin to check on his brother.

As each hour passed Sam looked worse. Carrie had tried to keep up his spirits, and hers, but eventually gave up. She shivered and sensed evil in the air. It had been a long time since she had felt this way and it frightened her. She was usually right.

"I'm going to get some air." Sam's drawn-out face looked at her sadly. "I just need to do something besides sit here." He threw on his coat and called his dog. "I won't be gone long."

"At least he has Squirrel for protection," Carrie said after he left.

She sat in Jeb's favourite chair and sighed, too tired to think straight anymore. Carrie closed her eyes and hoped she could get some sleep. Her mind raced though. All she ever wanted was a good husband and family, to live a nice quiet, simple life with the ones she loved. *Was that too much to ask for?* She pushed the hair out of her eyes noticed that it needed to be trimmed. She just hadn't had the energy to do it.

Adam and Johnny had been especially good. They made her honey on bread and brought her a cup of tea. "Thank you, boys." She smiled at them to ease the haunted look in their eyes, then she ate and drank it but didn't taste it. She felt nauseous but didn't let on so she wouldn't disappoint the boys.

Carrie opened her eyes and yawned loudly, glad to have slept. Adam was asleep across from her in the dark room. His knees were up, his head hung over the side of the chair. She looked around the room, still feeling exhausted. Johnny slept on top of her bed, the curtain hung wide open. There was no sign of Sam or Squirrel.

She stretched, straightened Adam up then started to build a fire in the fireplace. She banked the coals and lifted a log up to lay on it. A thump outside startled her. She stood and waited for Sam to come in. Nothing happened for several minutes. She clutched the log in her hand. Carrie jumped when the door banged open. Both boys screamed. Adam flew over to Johnny and hid behind him. A dark silhouette filled the doorway, illuminated from behind by the moon.

"Drop it, Carrie," that deep menacing voice ordered her again. Dusty slithered in, gun pointed at her. The log hit the floor with a clatter.

"What do you want, Dusty?"

"My family. You're all mine." He waved the gun at the boys as he spoke. "You're all coming with me."

She looked at his wild eyes. "No Dusty, we live here now." She surprised herself at her defiance. He stomped up to her and slapped her face. She grabbed the back of the chair, her world spun. The boys cowered into the corner.

Dusty shook her. "You're coming with me. You're all mine." He pushed her toward the door.

"You've gone mad," Carrie screamed at him.

He hit her on the head with the butt of the gun. "Get moving."

Everything went hazy. She fought to stay conscious and on her feet. A loud bang exploded. Dusty stumbled but held his ground. Carrie looked back into the corner. Johnny stood on her bed with her small pistol in his little hands, pointing it at his father. Tears running down his face. "Don't hurt her. You can't hurt her anymore."

Dusty's face changed from surprise, to anger, to carefully controlled rage. The bullet had only grazed his arm. He ignored it and let it bleed down his coat sleeve. Johnny let the gun slip from his fingers.

With the stealth of a cat, Dusty picked Adam up, who kicked and screamed and then he pushed Johnny toward the door. "Get your things, we're leaving."

Carrie grabbed their coats and shoes and walked out in front of her husband while he held his gun on her back. "Get up," he told her, pointing to the buckboard outside. "Take the reins."

Dusty dumped Adam in the back and lifted Johnny in with him. Carrie sat in the front. Dusty jumped up beside her and gave her a wicked smile. Carrie took up the reins. Across the street, behind a tree, she glimpsed Sam holding Squirrel back by the neck.

"Mary, get up off the floor!" Disgusted, Anthony pulled at her arm. He had let himself in to her house when she didn't answer her door. He could see her through the window and knew she was home. "You've been hiding in here for too long. You need to get out." He grunted and struggled with her weight as he lifted her, even though she was as thin as a post. "I'm too old for this," he complained while he dumped her into a chair.

Anthony wrinkled his nose up at the stench. He swatted at a fly that buzzed around his head. An overturned chair was set up right. A lantern had rolled into the corner. He picked it up and set it on the table. "Could have started a fire," he hissed at her. Dishes with leftover food on them grew green stuff on them. An inch of dust covered everything. A dead plant stood on a filthy table by the window. Clothing and a blanket were scattered on the floor.

Mary's dress was filthy, her face and hands smudged with grime. Anthony remembered when she took pride in her thick locks of reddish-brown hair. Now it was dull and knotted. Chunks of it had been pulled out, strands of it curling around her fingers. Her eyes lifelessly stared into space. She didn't move when he talked to her. "Do you even know I'm here, Mary?"

Anthony found his way into the kitchen. It was worse. Everywhere dirty dishes were piled up. A pot of water stood on the stove with dead bugs floating in it. He shook his head in disbelief. A spider web hung from the corner of the ceiling like a curtain. He found a cloth and dipped it in stagnant water and took it into the other room. Mary didn't move when he wiped the dirt from her face. He looked at the cloth, screwed up his face, and threw it into the corner. His knees cracked when he knelt down in front of her. "Mary, I'm going to take you to our house, okay? We'll look after you."

Her face remained blank, her eyes vacant. "Die. Just let me die."

"No, can't do that, Mary." He lifted her up and helped her out of the house. Neighbours watched as he coaxed her up into his buggy. He placed a blanket on her lap, shrugged at his audience, and drove home.

Hours later, Gert and Anthony paced their parlour floor. "What is taking so long?" Gert asked as her husband stroked his chin. Gert sat down, then jumped up again and continued to pace.

"It shouldn't be too much longer," Anthony told her, "hopefully…"

He stopped in mid sentence when footsteps came down the stairs. The doctor walked around the corner, bag in hand, and glanced uneasily at Gert. He faced Anthony, avoiding Gert's eyes. "It isn't good," he told them softly. "There isn't much I can do except keep her sedated." Gert sank into her chair. "Which is fine for awhile," he continued, "but not in the long term."

Gert and Anthony looked at each other then back at the doctor. "What can be done for her?" Gert asked as she frowned at the doctor.

"I think you need to send her to Kingston. To an asylum." The doctor looked at her over his glasses. "Mrs. Paterson; she needs professional care around the clock."

"We can look after her," Gert said, hopefully.

"I don't think that's wise. You won't be able to provide the care she needs, or the medication. It'll only wear you both down. I don't need you two sick too."

The doctor knelt down in front of Gert. "I think this will be the best for everyone."

Gert nodded slowly. Anthony sighed in relief.

Pakwis sounded like an idiot when he babbled, but he didn't care, he had told his wife. "At my age, I never thought I'd father a child." White Mouse watched his every move as he waved a brightly coloured gourd rattle in front of her. "Does she need feeding?" he asked as he smiled down at his daughter.

"No. Again I tell you. Let her be, you're spoiling her too much," Little Blossom scolded him but knew it wouldn't do any good. "But if you want, you can change her bottom."

He looked at her in mock horror and backed away with hands up in surrender. "I'll leave that up to you." Pakwis kissed her, then his daughter and left the lodge.

Little Blossom emerged moments later carrying White Mouse and laid her in a tiny hammock beside her husband. The gentle breeze swung the branches enough to amuse the child, lulling her to sleep within minutes. Little Blossom sat beside her husband on a fat log and exchanged smiles with him. Ever since the baby came he seemed to be more like his old self and remained very devoted to his family. He seemed content to help her whenever he could. But she couldn't be sure that he had given up on Winda. Not yet.

Spring had arrived late. The first of the wild flowers swayed in the light breeze. A carpet of trillium spread along the hillside. Buds popped out on the trees. Robins searched the ground for worms. Pakwis squinted at the sun and greeted several people as they did their chores. Little Blossom watched him take out his knife and pick up chunk of wood. After he inspected it at it from all angles he started to whittle. Shavings fell at his feet as he worked contentedly and whistled a happy tune to himself.

Sleeping Rabbit caught her attention. Little Blossom walked over to her friend. Pakwis stayed where he was and worked on his project. “What is it, Sleeping Rabbit?”

Sleeping Rabbit could hardly contain herself. “ I am with child.”

Little Blossom gave her a hug. “ I am so glad for you. Just think. Our children will grow up together. They will play and learn together.”

“I know. This is a good time for us to have one. I know Night Wind will be happy.”

“Haven’t you told him yet?”

“I will tell him tonight when he returns from fishing.”

“How do you think Lost Boy will take to a new brother or sister?”

“I think he will be a very good big brother.” Sleeping Rabbit looked dreamily across the meadow. “We are glad we have adopted him. He is such a help to Night Wind.”

“And Night Wind is a good father to him. I watched him teach Lost Boy how to load his rifle yesterday.” Little Blossom squeezed her friend’s hand. “He will be a great father to his baby.”

Someone shouted. Both women turned toward the edge of the hill behind the wigwams. A crowd was gathering. They ran over to investigate.

Pakwis joined them part way. “What happened?”

“I do not know. It looks serious,” Sleeping Rabbit’s voice squeaked.

Little Blossom hung unto Pakwis’s sleeve as they edged passed several people. Lost Boy lay on the ground soaking wet. Sleeping Rabbit screamed when she saw his lifeless body. Night Wind stood beside him, his clothes as wet as Lost Boy’s. He brushed back his long hair with a shaky hand. Sad eyes watched his wife.

“He slipped,” he told everyone in a choked voice, “on a rock. I couldn’t get to him in time.” Night Wind sank to his knees and chanted his death song.

Night Wind hadn't eaten since the death of his son. He sat outside his wigwam while Sleeping Rabbit and Little Blossom prepared Lost Boy's body. They'd wash him all over then dress him in his finest clothes. The last thing Sleeping Rabbit would do was put an eagle feather in his hair.

When the body was ready, Night Wind, Pakwis and two more men carried Lost Boy up the hill where a pit had been dug. The shaman leading the way, chanting a special verse. Carefully, they laid the body into the hole. Sleeping Rabbit set food on top of the corpse. Night Wind gave Lost Boy his favourite bow and arrow. The shaman said a prayer.

Night Wind couldn't move, even after everyone else had gone back down the hill. He stood by the grave and was barely aware that Little Blossom had led Sleeping Rabbit away. His wife wouldn't let him comfort her. Night Wind knew that she blamed him for Lost Boy's death. If only he had gotten to his son sooner.

He had seen Lost Boy up on the rocks, jumping from one to another. Then he heard the scream. He and several others rushed to where Lost Boy fell into the raging river, leaving their fishing poles dangling in the water with no one to pull in any fish they might have caught.

Night Wind had ran along the shore, finally he was able to grab hold of Lost Boy after he got tangled up in some bushes. They pulled Lost Boy onto shore. He was already dead.

16

The cabin that Dusty had thrown up behind his old house was drafty and it leaked. "He sure didn't do a good job building this place, did he?" Grant complained as another drip of water splashed on his head.

He sat up on the only bed that had been his for over two weeks while he recuperated and healed. The bump on his head where Dusty hit him had receded, his headache gone. His hands had been unwrapped earlier that day and checked; the pink skin grew itchy when exposed to air. Winda smeared a poultice on them to ease the sensation to scratch at them. She re-wrapped his hands so that he could move his fingers. They could be scarred for the rest of his life.

"Your face isn't as burned as we first thought," she told him. After she carefully cleaned the soot off, they found only superficial burns. Winda smeared his chest with the same medicine. His legs were next.

Bright sunlight peeked in through the open door. Finally the rain had stopped. Birds were singing outside. Grant thanked Winda. "You're a wonder, you know."

Lucas kept busy by packing up Dusty's supplies that were stored in the cabin. "Sam can use some of this," he told them. "Do you think you can start travelling tomorrow?"

Grant assured him that he could. "I've got my legs back now. My fingers work and my head is as good as new, almost. Yeah, I can travel."

"Good. I think we should leave in the morning."

After Lucas packed both horses the next day, they joined Winda at Jeb's grave. Lucas had buried him next to the one they all thought Kate was in. He had carved a small inscription on her cross as well, both victims of Dusty's wrath. Although Kate died in a tornado, Grant knew his brother blamed Dusty for everything.

Both men stopped behind Winda to give her a bit of privacy as she said goodbye to Jeb. She held her arms high in the air as tears ran unchecked down her face. The brothers said their own payers quietly as they watched. She finished and wiped her face. "Good bye Jeb," she told the crude wooden cross. The first of the spring wildflowers lay on both graves. Lucas said he was grateful that Winda also acknowledged Kate and told her so.

"Not her fault," Winda told him as she backed away.

Sombrely they lead the horses along the road toward town. No one spoke until they reached the crooked bridge. "Well I can surely arrest Dusty for murder now," Grant told Winda as he tried to put her at ease. Jeb's death had hit her hard. She hardly laughed or spoke to either one of them and cried a lot. He had watched her prepare special teas for him and make up a poultice so his skin wouldn't crawl and drive him insane. He had tried to joke and tease her to cheer her up but nothing worked. She mourns for her good friend, it would take time.

Grant saw that Lucas tried even harder and helped her whenever he could. When she broke down he held her and let her tears soak through his shirt. Now Lucas walked beside her across the plank, holding her hand. She clung to him tightly.

"I'm going with you to hunt him down," Lucas told Grant. "I'd love to put a bullet right between his eyes."

"Can't, I'm supposed to bring him in alive." Grant looked into his brother's grief-stricken eyes. "Okay, dead or alive. But I don't want you hung for murder either."

Lucas just grinned at him.

They headed south now. Dusty had provided the boys with a blanket to keep them warm. The snow was all gone but the nights were still cold. The days grew longer, which meant they travelled longer each day and further from town.

They had abandoned the wagon along the trail days ago. Both boys sat on one of the horses while the other one carried their supplies Dusty had thrown into the buckboard before he collected his family. Dusty led the horses through thick brush. Carrie followed behind them on blistered feet. Both boys had been quiet since their father kidnapped them from their new home.

"Please, Dusty. Let us stop and rest a bit," pleaded Carrie. She was tired, swatted at the mosquitoes, and had puffed up from all the bites. Her skin was red and blotchy. Both boys looked exhausted.

Dusty stopped and looked at her and then up at the boys. "Just up ahead. Not far. We'll stop." He nodded to the boys and pulled the horses after him. They made their way through the woods creating their own trail. Dusty lifted the boys down when they stopped beside a wide stream. "We'll stay here for the night."

Carrie gathered wood for a fire Sombrely, the boys helped her.

Dusty headed into the trees to set snares, hoping to catch at least one rabbit. Carrie knew he would stay close to their camp.

"I don't like him anymore," Adam admitted when his father was out of earshot.

"Me neither," agreed Johnny, "he's mean."

Carrie smiled sadly at them. "We have to do as he says. I don't know what he'll do if one of us makes him mad." She looked over at the horses. No chance of escape. As usual Dusty had them hobbled. He would catch her if she were to set a horse free. She was certain that he was watching her. He had thought this all out, to the last detail. Johnny filled the canteens while Carrie put a pot of water on the fire. She sat against an elm tree to wait for the water to boil. "I should have shot him in the heart," Johnny confessed. "Next time, I won't miss."

"Yeah," teased Adam, "if you stop shaking long enough."

"We were all shaking," Carrie said. She glimpsed Dusty through the trees as he bent down and laid out a wire. How many snares was he going to set?

"You were shaking too?" Adam asked. "I wasn't."

"Yes, you were," Johnny corrected. "You grabbed my arm. Maybe you made me miss."

"It doesn't matter." She turned to Johnny. "You were brave, Johnny. I thank you for trying to help me." She gave him a loving smile. "But think of how you would feel if you had killed him."

Johnny's big green eyes widened. "I don't think I could kill a real person." He shook his head. "They would put me in jail, wouldn't they?"

"It depends on the situation." Carrie poured them each a tea and wondered how one comforted and stressed the point all at once. Rustling in the woods made Carrie sit up straight. She had the same eerie feeling that she was being watched as she did at the cabin in the woods. Her eyes narrowed as she studied the undergrowth around them.

New buds were springing up through the dead leaves that littered the forest floor. The trees were filling in with fresh new leaves or flower buds. The shadows were stretching longer as the sun dipped down behind a huge spruce on the other side of the horses.

Carrie got up and unpacked the bedding for the night. They would sleep in the open. It won't rain tonight.

Adam threw more sticks on the fire while Johnny stood poking at it with a long thin branch. "Is my dad going to kill me for shooting him?" The worried look on his face led Carrie to put her arms around them both. They were still frightened to death of their father.

"No, Johnny. You only grazed him on the arm. He won't kill you for that." Deep down, though, Carrie still worried. *What was Dusty capable of doing?*

A single lantern glowed through the window in Jeb's cabin. Lucas was attacked by Squirrel when he opened the door. The dog jumped up and licked him all over. His tail banging on the man's legs as he wiggled happily. Grant couldn't pet him, his hands were still bandaged. Winda greeted the big dog then tried to get him to settle down. "Wow. This is some greeting."

Sam hugged Winda for a long time after she told him about Jeb's death. They both sobbed and rocked as they stood in the middle of the floor. He was grateful that both of the men seemed just as affected by his grandfather's death. Especially Lucas. He liked this man a lot.

Lucas brought in some food, lamp oil and several other items that Sam might need. Sam couldn't contain himself and gave the generous man a hug. "Thank you, Lucas. I really need some of these things."

"You're welcome, son." Lucas had called him that several times now. It just seemed so natural.

He didn't call Johnny or Adam that. I must be special to him. Or, was he being extra nice to me because of Winda? Sam wondered.

Grant was good to him too, but he didn't know him that much yet. So for now he was kept at arms' length.

"Dusty, he's got Carrie and the boys," Sam told them when he found his voice through the tears and clogged throat. He had to work to clear the phlegm so he could talk. "He just took them. I didn't know what to do, so I just waited for you to come home."

After wiping her eyes, Winda told Sam, "You did the right thing, Sam. Now we know what happened and," she squeezed his arm affectionately, "that you are safe."

"What now?" he asked her. He watched the men. Both of them seemed tired and ready to give up.

"We're going to find them. We'll bring them home, Sam," Lucas said.

"I should have stopped him, Lucas. But I hid so he wouldn't see me, instead."

"No, Sam. You couldn't have stopped him," his hero spoke softly to him. "You did the right thing."

"We'll get Dusty." Grant looked worried. "He would have just taken you too, Sam." He walked over and stood beside the youth. "Right now, we need a good meal. Do you think you can help Winda make us something to eat?" He looked imploringly at her.

"Come on, Sam. Let's see what Lucas bagged for us for supper." She led Sam over to the sacks that were discarded in a pile on the floor.

"I can go with you, can't I, Winda? To help find them?" Eagerly Sam looked from one to the other.

Grant shook his head no, but Lucas spoke up. "Yes, Sam. You can come with us." He faced Grant. "Would you want to be left alone at a time like this?"

Grant eventually nodded. "We also need a good night's sleep. It's too late to start out now. We'll leave first thing in the morning." He sat at the table.

"We will eat big tonight," Winda said as she headed over to the stove. "Once we are on the trail our meals will be light."

Lucas picked up a small pistol from a table in the sitting area and frowned at it. "What is this, Sam?"

Sam turned to look. "Oh, that's Carrie's. She hid it in her bedding. When I got home, after, after…" he couldn't say kidnapping. "It was on her bed. I think someone shot it."

"Why do you say that?" Winda asked.

"There was blood over by the door. I cleaned it up though." He knew that Winda wanted the house clean and neat and tried hard to keep it that way for her.

Lucas set the pistol back down and gave Grant a worried look.

Two white men, an Indian lady, and a teenage black boy followed a wagon trail through thick wilderness. A big black dog followed along when not chasing squirrels. Sam had given them general directions as to where Dusty had headed. Lucas had seen their tracks as the wagon left the trail and headed into the woods. Now they followed, each of them on their own horse. Grant hung onto the reins with his left hand which wasn't wrapped as much as his right one was, he could use his fingers to hold on to them. Sam and Winda also lead their pack horses, leaving the two men free to scout around and keep their weapons handy.

The trail went cold. After a two week head-start, the rain had washed away tracks, and the new spring growth covered any sign of where they went. Winda bent down and studied the dirt in her fingers. The men had let her take the lead. She was a far better tracker than either of them.

Lucas walked back from a small clearing. "There's a wagon up ahead, in the bushes."

"It's Dusty's all right," Grant told them when they arrived. "It's the same one we took the rifles to General Walton in." He pointed to scratches on the side. "I recognize these markings."

Sam came up to them leading the horses. "They took the horses though, didn't they? Does that mean they can go faster now?"

Grant nodded. "That's possible." He looked into the dense undergrowth. "They'll be able to get through the woods better now." Winda picked up a horse's trail. They all followed her lead.

Days later, Squirrel gave a low bark and waited for Sam to catch up to him. The boy jumped down from his horse and went after him. They walked into an old campsite. The rest following close behind. Winda inspected the fire pit. Lucas and Grant inspected the perimeter.

"Yep, they were here all right." Lucas handed a small sock to Winda.

"That is Adam's," she said. "His favourite colour is blue."

They stayed there that night and tried to pick up the trail the next morning. It lead straight to the stream and disappeared. Lucas waited while Winda kept looking upstream then down, trying to make up her mind. "I don't know which way they went. We need to find the place where they came back out of the water."

All four of them studied the stream, checking up and down. "Which way would Dusty go?" asked Lucas.

"Where does this stream end up?" Grant didn't know this part of the country like his brother and Winda did.

"Don't know," Lucas answered him, "it could be one of those unnamed ones."

Winda shook her head too. "I do not know this stream."

"Maybe we should just split up. Two go upstream and two go downstream," Grant said, as if he wasn't sold on the idea himself. He looked at his brother who shrugged his shoulders. "I know it could be more dangerous but it might be quicker."

"We can't waste too much time," Lucas told them. "There's no telling what will happen to Carrie and the boys."

Winda walked back to the horses and separated the bundles so that each team had the supplies they needed.

"Okay then," Grant said, "me and Sam will head downstream. You two go upstream. If we don't find anything meet back here in what, three days?"

"Better make that five," Lucas contradicted, "and if one team isn't back, that's the way the rest of us will go too."

Grant nodded. "Sounds good."

Sam was a little apprehensive, going with a man that he hardly knew into the middle of nowhere. He wanted to go with Lucas instead. He also realized that Winda and Lucas wanted to be together. They couldn't keep their eyes off each other. He thought that Lucas was a good man for Winda who obviously loved him. He had noticed though, that Lucas and Grant thought and acted a lot alike. They had similar mannerisms too. As he followed Grant down through the stream he started comparing the two men.

Grant's hair was darker than Lucas's. He was also heavier set and a bit shorter than his younger brother. He had hazel eyes while Lucas had green ones. Lucas had a drawn out face which looked better when he grew his sandy coloured beard. Grant, though, seemed the stronger of the two, like a large rooted tree. Lucas looked like he would topple over in a strong wind. Sam noticed that they were both good men and decided to like Grant. They seemed honest and best of all, genuinely cared for him and other people. They were kind and generous but took no guff from anybody. Best of all, they weren't like Dusty.

Grant stopped his horse just above a small water fall. He had checked for tracks or other signs on one side of the stream while Sam crossed over to the other side. Squirrel bounded around on shore. Neither one had found anything for five days. Sam followed his new friend out of the water just above the falls.

"With all the new growth shooting up, it can hide tracks pretty quick," Grant told the teenager that evening while sitting around the campfire. He had been teaching Sam about the wilderness every day. *Just like Lucas would do.*

Sam nodded. "Just grow right over it then we can't see it anymore."

"That's why it's so hard to track this time of year, or after a rain. Because they get washed away too."

"So what do we do now?" Sam patted Squirrel who lay beside him.

"I think that tomorrow, we'll check down below the falls. Maybe another day or two and see. Then if we don't find anything, we'll go back and join up with Lucas and Winda again. What do you think?"

Sam agreed, surprised this older man asked for his opinion.

Lucas and Winda didn't have any luck either. "It's like they just vanished," Winda said as Lucas picked at a stone in his horse's hoof with a knife. He was bent over with the hoof against his lap, digging. Finally, the offending stone flew out. He dropped the leg and patted the horse's rump. Winda put her arms around his neck and kissed him.

"Is this the only way I can get you all alone? I'm all for it," he said.

"You mean all alone in the middle of nowhere or out man-hunting."

"Well, man-hunting, of course. It adds a touch of danger to it, don't you think?"

"Yes. Not to mention the mystery of it as well."

Lucas looked down at his boots, digging a hole in the dirt with his toe.

Winda knew by this action that something was bothering him. "I know that look, Lookas. What is on your mind?"

"I was thinking." He looked tense. "But only if you want to, okay?" She watched him closely, getting nervous. Turning toward the hills in the north, he said, "Pakwis is camped about four days north of here. Maybe we can ask him to help us find Dusty."

Winda mulled this over in her mind. *Do I really want to see him again? Or, for that matter, the rest of the village?* Sleeping Rabbit had been her only friend. Out loud, she said, "What if he wants me back?"

Lucas held her trembling body to him. "Then I will do whatever it takes to have you as my wife, Winda." He frowned. "Even if I have to kill him."

"Dusty, whose place is this?" Carrie asked late one morning as he led them over a hill and onto a homestead. Cattle roamed the meadow below, chomping on new grass. They passed the barn and scattered chickens as they rode by. She noticed goats, pigs, and a couple of sheep in a field beside it. Beyond the barnyard stood a low, one-story clapboard house with a thatch roof.

"A friend," Dusty finally answered, pulling tight on the reins as he led them up to the house. He yelled at the door. No one answered. He flashed a brooding look at Carrie. "Wait here, I'll be right back." He pulled out his pistol and crept inside.

"I'm hungry," Adam complained from on top of his horse.

"Shh," Carrie warned him, "wait till we see if anyone is home."

Just minutes later, Dusty held the door open and motioned for them all to go inside. Carrie helped the boys off their horse and reluctantly obeyed. "No one is home," he told her as they filed past him. He shoved Carrie toward the kitchen. "Go ahead, make something to eat."

"Dusty, this isn't right. You don't just walk into someone's house and—" *Slap!* A sharp sting on her face shocked her still.

Johnny attacked his father. His fists swinging, his feet kicking at Dusty's shins. Dusty picked him up by the hair with big hands and pushed the boy, screaming, into another room. "That's the last time you attack me," he yelled at his son. They entered a bedroom. Dusty shoved Johnny onto the bed then slammed the door shut. Carrie pictured his belt leaving his waist with a loud snap. Johnny screamed. There was a ruckus as if Johnny was trying to run. Carrie heard the belt cracking several times.

She pounded at the door, crying. "Dusty, don't. Dusty. He's just a little boy. Dusty!"

Finally, the snapping of the belt stopped. Dusty stomped out of the room, pushed Carrie aside, and then went outside, swearing under his breath. Carrie ran in to Johnny who lay on the bed face down crying into the pillow. Carrie lifted his torn, bloody shirt. Tears ran down her face. "I'm so sorry, Johnny. I'm so sorry."

Mechanically, she managed to fill a bowl of water and tend to his wounds. She found some salve in a cupboard and gently smoothed over his broken skin on his back. "I never thought he'd do this to his own kids," she whimpered, "I didn't think he'd sink this low."

"I love you, Carrie," Johnny told her in a small voice.

"I love you to, Johnny." She saw Adam shaking in the corner of the room.

"Will you be my mom?" Johnny shifted his weight so he could look up at her. "I don't want him to be my dad anymore."

"I will gladly be your mom. But unfortunately he is your dad and nobody can do anything about that."

Adam ran to her and grabbed her tight. "I want you to be my mom too," he cried so hard that Carrie's blouse was soaked in no time.

Carrie glanced out the window just as Dusty walked by.

17

Johnny fell into a light, disturbed sleep. Carrie made a quick lunch with whatever she could find. She woke him up when it was ready and helped him stagger to the table. The brothers sat across from each other in silence. Carrie sat down with them and said a prayer. They ate quietly.

Dusty banged the door against the wall and stomped in. Everyone jumped but ignored him. "Why didn't you tell me it was ready?"

Carrie remained straight-faced. "If you can't tell when a meal is ready when you are only ten feet away, then I'm not going to tell you."

He looked at her as if stunned. Then he watched Johnny, who kept his head down. Adam shovelled his food into his mouth chewing fast.

"Careful, Adam," soothed Carrie, "or you'll choke."

He swallowed hard then slowed down without a word or eye contact with anyone. Dusty filled his plate high and sat at the table across from Carrie and in between the boys. They ate in silence. Johnny asked if he could be relieved after just a few bites. Dusty looked at his plate and told him, "No."

"Yes, Johnny, you may be excused," Carrie told him and watched Dusty like a hawk. Johnny quickly left and returned into the bedroom.

Adam asked too, after a few minutes. Dusty saw the empty plate and let him go. Carrie cleaned the table and did up the dishes. Dusty tried to engage her in conversation. *Just like nothing ever happened. Like he always does.* Seething, Carrie ignored him completely. He went back outside. Carrie hugged her stomach and tried not to get sick.

She had just finished wiping her hands when a wagon pulled up outside, loaded with supplies, and stopped in front of the house. She stepped out just as a middle-aged man and young girl jumped down.

"Hey! Dusty. What are you doing way out here?" The man didn't seem happy seeing her husband; actually, he seemed a bit hostile.

"We need a place to stay for awhile." Dusty said. "I hope it's okay, Pete."

Pete looked from Dusty to Carrie then back at Dusty. "What have you gotten into, Dusty? Where's Kate?"

"She's dead. Killed in a tornado last summer." Dusty smiled as if trying to calm the other man down. Pete just stood there silently and watched Dusty with a scowl on his face.

Carrie looked at Pete with a sense of familiarity. *Do I know this man? I'm sure I've seen him someplace before.* Dusty gestured at the young girl. "I see you haven't re-married yet, Pete. This your little girl?"

"No, I haven't." He turned to his daughter. "This is Sophie."

"Hi Sophie." Dusty extended his hand. The timid girl turned and ran past Carrie and into the house. Dusty laughed it off. Carrie followed her, still feeling disgusted with her husband.

Pete lifted a huge sack from the back of the wagon and headed toward the barn. Dusty picked up another one and followed him. After dumping his load, Pete turned on the big man. "What is going on, Dusty? Why is Carrie here? You weren't supposed bring her out here for heaven's sakes."

"The boys are here too." Dusty laughed with a nervous tilt. "They're in the house."

Pete studied Dusty closely, "I thought we had an arrangement. I was never going to see either you or Carrie again."

Dusty scowled. "I know. I know. I had no where else to go."

"What do you mean? There's always a choice."

"I," Dusty stammered, "had to get away."

"What do you mean? Someone after you, Dusty?"

"You know the guns. They're closing in." Dusty looked around nervously. "So I brought my family here. No one will find us way out here, Pete."

Pete could almost hit this man. He knew Dusty was lying. There was more to this than what he was telling him.

Several days later, Carrie sat in the shade watching Sophie chase Adam around a big tree. Johnny sat quietly beside her. The fourteen-year-old girl had taken to the boys like a big sister. She was always fussing over them. Carrie felt sorry for her, being stuck way out here by herself. The girl was tall and lanky, just starting to fill out. Her long, wavy blond hair was tied back in a blue ribbon. Carrie noticed the girl had long, delicate fingers, and her bright, blue eyes were quick to smile. *She's going to be a beautiful woman.* Carrie guaranteed that. She liked the spirited young lady.

Sophie was also starved for female company. She had asked Carrie all kinds of questions that her mother should be helping her with. At first she felt uncomfortable telling these things to a stranger, but in to time at all she started to feel more at ease about it.

Johnny's back was healing. Carrie put salve on the long, red scars every night before he went to bed. He didn't seem as stiff either when he moved. He went out of his way to avoid his father. Adam, too, gave Dusty a wide berth. Carrie ignored him when she could get away with it.

Dusty was out in the fields helping Pete plant a late crop of wheat. Carrie walked around the side of the house to check their progress. The men were in a back field now, ploughing. Dusty pulled the horse while Pete guided the single blade back and forth along neat rows. She watched her husband bend down and then throw a large rock off the field, dumping it along the tree-line. Pete stopped, lifted his hat to wipe the back of his sweaty neck. That single movement gave Carrie a flash of recognition.

Her hand flew to her throat. *That's the preacher. The one who married us.* No wonder he tried to avoid her and seemed nervous all the time. *Now I know why I had the feeling of seeing him before.* Pete had grown a moustache since then and put on some weight. His hair was thinner, but it was him, she was sure of it.

They were back ploughing again. *Is he even a preacher at all? Who would he even preach to way out here? Is he retired? He sure doesn't act like one, that's for sure, far from it.* She walked back to where the kids were still playing and called Sophie over. "Is your father some kind of a preacher or something?"

"No," the young girl laughed. "He's just a farmer."

"Does he go away a lot?"

"No. Well, he didn't until he met Dusty, and a man they called Ivan. They don't know I saw them talking. Then he left." She looked at the older woman uncertainly.

"It's okay, Sophie, I'm just trying to find out where Dusty has been."

"He went away a couple of times last year for a long time."

"He leaves you way out here by yourself?"

"No. I went to my grandmother's in Detroit, but she's dead now." Sophie started to fidget with her skirt. "Are you mad at my dad?"

"No, Sophie. I'm just trying to find out what my husband has been up to, that's all." She hated lying to her.

Johnny called Sophie, who ran back to chase him. The young girl watched Carrie closely for the rest of the day as if wondering if she somehow had betrayed her father. Carrie kept smiling to reassure her. She made no more move to reveal her suspicions.

The bed was empty and cold beside Lucas when he woke up the next morning. He jumped up, naked, and looked around, wiping sleep from his eyes. Splashing in the nearby lake told him where Winda was. He walked down to join her and stopped at the edge and watched her. The water sparkled around her from the morning sunlight, giving her an angelic look. He waded toward her slowly while she was bent over at the waist, washing her long silky hair. He was about to scare her when she flipped her hair back, splashing his face, laughing.

"Will you wash my back for me?" Lucas tried to feign innocence.

"No," she teased, "but I will do this." Her hand slid down his hairy chest and in between his legs. He moaned and pulled her closer pressing his lips to hers. He wouldn't have heard a loon's lonely call from the centre of the lake, or see a moose charging through their camp. He made love to her slow and gentle; savouring what might be their last time together.

When they'd finished, Lucas took her hand and walked along the beach just to be near her. They dried each other off then got dressed. Winda pulled out her comb and sat on a rock. Lucas ran over to her, took the comb, and pulled it though her lavender scented hair. "I love the way your hair smells. Please, don't ever change that."

Later, when they were sipping tea, Lucas asked, "Are you sure you want to face him again?"

"I must," she told him, hesitantly. "I have to find out what he will do with me." She looked up at him. "Or what he will do to you."

Lucas said nothing. For the last few days he worried that he might have to challenge his friend for her; but at the same time, he didn't want to jeopardize that either. But if he had to he would.

When they rode side by side later, Lucas listened to frogs croaking at them as they passed the marsh. Twin Hills stood high in the distance. Maple, birch, hemlock, elm and oak were all in full leaf now. Winda's hands were sweaty when he gave them a squeeze. He half expected her to turn and run the other way. They rounded the marsh turning westward. Winda stared straight ahead.

Three riders raced out to meet them. Night Wind and two warriors that Lucas didn't know stopped in front of them. Night Wind's eyes widened when he recognized Winda. "Winda. You are truly alive."

"Hello, Night Wind. We have come to speak to Pakwis."

The warrior smiled at her knowingly. He extended his hand to Lucas in the white man's way of greeting.

Lucas accepted it, smiling. "Hello Night Wind. You look well. Everything must be good for you."

"Yes it is." He watched the white man, closely. "Sleeping Rabbit is my wife now." He paused as if to see the effect in Lucas's eyes.

"Good for you. You finally caught her, did you?" Lucas laughed. Then he leaned over in his saddle and told the warrior, "We are just good friends. I was never your rival, Night Wind."

Night Wind considered this then nodded. "We are having a child this fall." He smiled widely.

"Congratulations," Lucas told him sincerely. "I wish you all the happiness."

Night Wind sobered. "Lost Boy is dead."

Lucas felt like he was hit in the chest with a rock. "How? He was so young."

"Drowned. Fishing accident."

They rode slowly into the village, deep in conversation. "Oh," remembered Night Wind, "Pakwis is a father." Night Wind said as if he wanted to lighten things up and present their guests in a good mood. "He and Little Blossom have a little girl named White Mouse."

Winda rode quietly beside them. Looking around as if remembering what each person looked like and how each one of them had treated her before.

Grant was at his wit's end. "I guess we should head on back the other way." He was walking his horse along the clay bank below the waterfalls. He had long discarded the bandages that impeded him from using his hands. They were blotchy white and pink but he didn't care. They no longer itched and drove him nuts.

Sam had told him that his face was also scarred from the fire. "Not that bad, just a little around your left eye." He was on the other side of the stream checking the ground for clues as well. "Over here," he yelled and waved Grant over. The young boy picked up something red. Grant jumped on his horse, splashed across to the other side, and slid off in front of Sam. "I think this is Carrie's." Excitedly, he waved the ribbon in front of the older man. "She used this to tie her hair back. I've seen her."

" Great job, Sam," praised Grant. "You have good eyes."

Sam handed him the ribbon. Grant closed his eyes and pressed it against his cheek. *Hang on, Carrie, I'm coming. I'll get you away from Dusty, I promise.* Sam coughed, Grant jumped. The boy was still beaming from the praise he gave him. Grant blushed at being caught fantasizing. "Now, do we keep following the stream or head inland?" Grant bent down and searched the area for more clues. "See here," he pointed, "they went down this way."

Sam followed Grant down the trail through the brush, across open land then topped a small hill. The older man put his hand out to stop Sam. "Look down there at that farm. Do you see anyone you know, Sam? Maybe we should sneak…Oh no."

Squirrel had bounded down the hill toward the boys. They squealed in delight when the dog jumped up, licking them all over. Sam couldn't catch him in time. "Squirrel," called Grant, who ran after the big black dog. He didn't know what they were getting into yet. Sam gathered up the reins and followed him with the horses, hanging his head as if he was feeling ashamed he couldn't keep his dog back.

Carrie rushed out of the house, only to be attacked by Squirrel. She too laughed and hugged the happy dog. Grant was only a few yards away, smiling at Carrie as he approached her.

Sophie stopped beside Carrie after Squirrel ran back over to the boys. She was looking scared, as if fearing the dog to be rabid. "I'll go get the gun!"

Carrie grabbed her sleeve. "No, we know this dog. He is our dog, Sophie." Sophie relaxed and watched the boys play with the big animal.

Grant turned to watched Sam coming down the hill. Then shots rang out. Everyone jumped for cover. Another crack of the rifle. A horse fell over dead. Sam kept going letting the other horses go, then hid behind a big barrel. Carrie pushed Sophie and the boys into the house and slammed the door. Squirrel followed them inside.

Grant ran back to one of their horses and pulled out his musket. Another shot rang out. Dust went flying at Grant's feet. *Who is shooting at us?* He skirted over to the barn and edged around the corner. Another shot. *Where did that come from?*

Sam edged up from behind the barrel. Another blast of the rifle splintered it just above Sam's head as he ducked back down. Splinters flew everywhere. Grant couldn't tell from where he was if the young man had been hit. He ran over and slid behind a wagon. "Sam. Sam, you hurt?"

"No, I'm okay," a squeaky voice answered.

"Good. Stay down."

"I ain't going no place. I'm just about to wet my pants."

Grant still didn't know where the shots were coming from. *How many are there?* Judging the distance between him and the house where he saw Squirrel follow Johnny and Adam in, he figured it wasn't that far. He could make it. *Maybe I can get inside there?* He made a dash toward the fence. Another shot. *Closer than I thought.* A sharp pain exploded in his thigh. The rifle flew away when he tripped and fell, grabbing at his leg.

Minutes later Dusty stood over him, aiming his musket at Grant's head. "I should have killed you a long time ago."

Grant withered in the dirt, watching the big man through glassy eyes.

Another man ran up. "Don't Dusty! If you do, you're next." His rifle was aimed at Dusty.

"He knows everything." Dusty's fingers wiggled on the trigger.

"Don't Dusty," repeated the man. "You don't need another charge against you. That is, if you live through my bullet."

Dusty just stood there, glaring down at Grant. After a few tense moments, he spit in the dirt beside him and slowly lowered his rifle. He stepped back. The man grabbed the weapon. Dusty stormed off toward the barn.

Sam cautiously rose up and helped the man drag Grant into the house.

Winda stood in front of Pakwis, trying hard not to shake so badly. She watched his facial expressions carefully. This day, she had deliberately worn loose clothing so she wouldn't see the lust in his eyes as they raked over her curves. *I am not going to cower in front of him anymore!* Defiantly, she held her head up high and back straight and tall. *He has aged,* she thought, *since the last time I saw him.* His hair was all white now. Deep lines etched his face. He didn't seem as self-assured as he used to. His shoulders slumped a little.

"I have thought of this day for a long time," he told her. "Now that you are truly here..." Pakwis couldn't finish. Instead, he paced inside his wigwam. "I still don't know what to do." Reaching inside his daughter's bed, he stroked the sleeping child's face, giving White Mouse a weak smile.

Pakwis faced Winda again, looking at her longingly. His eyes travelled up and down her body as if remembering every curve, and every sigh she made when he had made love to her. He cleared his throat and turned away. "It is hard for me to let you go, Winda. I do have feelings for you." He paced some more. "But," he sighed, "I think it best that you go." Sad eyes turned to face her. "You truly love Lucas?"

He had never admitted that to her before. Winda nodded, trying not to feel sorry for this man. "We are to be married." He said nothing for a while. "I love him with all my heart." She saw the anguish in his eyes.

"As I do with Little Blossom." He stepped toward her and stroked her cheek then he let his hand fall to his side. Pakwis shook his head and walked away. "I have to break this spell you have on me," he said as if scolding himself. Back at White Mouse's little bed, hc watched his daughter sleep soundly.

From where she was, Winda could see that she looked just like Little Blossom.

"How can I turn my back on her?" he said as he stroked his daughter's cheek. "Or my wife?" He glanced at the door. "If I take you back, Little Blossom would throw me out of the marriage lodge. She has the right, and to take my child away from me." Winda merely nodded, knowing this. He sighed then said, "I might never see either one of them again. I do not think I could live with that."

With self determination, or defeat; Winda couldn't tell. Pakwis faced her as if she were anyone else but her. "I owe Lucas a great deal. We will help him find this man he is looking for."

"Thank you, Pakwis."

"I think it best for all of us," he said through gritted teeth, "that you two get married as soon as possible."

" I am sure that can be arranged. Lookas will not have any problem with that."

"Tomorrow." He was begging her to do this as quickly as possible.

With both Little Blossom and Lucas between them, maybe he could stop longing for her. "Tomorrow," she repeated.

Carrie looked down at the man lying on the bed and remembered the day they'd first met in the tavern. *Another one of Dusty's friends. But why did Dusty shoot him?* From what she saw through the window, he would have killed him if it wasn't for Pete. Grant groaned in his sleep. *What happened to their relationship? Are all of Dusty's partners turning on him?* She certainly didn't blame them. *What a dangerous game you play, Dusty.* "That's it then." Sophie brought her back to reality. "All cleaned up."

"Thank you, Sophie. You're a great help."

"I didn't think I could do it," she admitted, sheepishly. "I've never done anything like this before." The young girl had helped Carrie dig out the bullet, wipe up the blood and wrap Grant's leg up in bandages. She helped to keep a cool cloth on his feverish forehead to keep his temperature down. Carrie watched her take the bloody clothes out of the room. She walked over to the corner, sat on the rocking chair and closed her eyes.

Sam had told her earlier that he saw Dusty drag her and the boys out of their cabin. She knew too, that Winda and Lucas were out somewhere looking for them. "But they went the wrong way," he told her proudly, at finding her first. Carrie pictured Jeb, sitting in his favourite chair laughing at one of his jokes. Tears ran down her face, unchecked. Jeb was dead! *Oh, Jeb, what I would give to be able to read to you again.* She would miss his questions, or remarks. They wouldn't be able to talk about happenings of man or the universe anymore. Who will engage her in such deep discussions now? She missed the kind, gentle old man.

To clear her head, Carrie stood and paced the room. Grant groaned in his sleep again. She dipped a cloth into cool water, then sat on the bed to lay it gently on his forehead. *So, this is Lucas's brother. How did he get mixed up with Dusty? How could two brothers be so different?* She liked Lucas and concluded that he was right for her friend, Winda. Their different races made no never mind to her and she was glad it didn't come between the happy couple. *I don't think Lucas sees any difference at all. He is just so in love with her.* Without realizing what she was doing, her mind wandered. Her fingers curled around Grant's hair. *He does look like Lucas.* She sighed, remembering who this man was. *Why am I helping him?* Her fingers brushed back his bangs, absentmindedly.

Suddenly, she jumped back. Grant was watching her. "I, ah. You're hair was in your eyes." Red-faced and embarrassed, Carrie tried to get up. He caught her arm and held her. "Hello pretty lady. Are you my angel?" He smiled at her as if amused.

"I, ah," she stammered, eager to get away. "You're hurt. I'm just looking after you." *How can he look so smug?*

"Please, angel, stay awhile." He took in a sharp breath when he shifted his weight. "What happened?"

"My name is Carrie." She tried to correct him. He just smiled up at her. "Dusty shot you."

"Oh yeah." He was looking deep into her green eyes. She sat there transfixed. *What is it about this man that draws me to him? Remember. He's Dusty's friend!*

"How is Sam? He okay?"

"Yes, Sam is just fine." *Those lips are so inviting.*

18

Night Wind acted friendlier toward Lucas, now that he knew for certain that he wasn't a threat to him. He had watched when the white man and Sleeping Rabbit greeted each other, then moved on. They still shared secrets and teased each other. But he saw how Lucas kept glancing at Winda. Night Wind knew what it was like to be "love-sick," as he called it.

Winda and Sleeping Rabbit had talked and giggled while he made amends with the white man. "I have made a canoe like the one you have. It is stronger and lasts a lot longer than the birch bark ones do." He showed his handiwork to Lucas who inspected it carefully.

"This is good, Night Wind. With your building skills and my directions, you made a fine canoe here." Night Wind was pleased with the praise. Their talk had become easier for the warrior who was starting to like this white man.

Sleeping Rabbit sat alone in front of her wigwam watching the door of Pakwis's lodge. Lucas and Night Wind joined her after inspecting the canoe. Lucas teased her about getting too big with her pregnancy. She teased him back as if knowing how nervous he must be waiting for Winda to emerge from Pakwis's grip.

Lucas kept glancing over at the lodge and frowning. "Where did all these people come from?" he asked, trying to keep his mind too busy to think. The village had grown a great deal since he last saw these people. There were three times as many wigwams now.

"Some more of our people have joined us. Most have been pushed out of their own lands, either by other tribes or white settlers." Night Wind looked sadly around his village. "We are becoming fewer every season. With disease, starvation and war, there are not many of us left anymore."

Lucas watched many people doing their daily chores. Kids were playing nearby, laughing like they had no care in the world. "You wouldn't know it by the looks of this village, though."

"We used to cover the whole land like the stars in the sky." Night Wind pointed out. "Now we are like the leaves falling from the trees."

Lucas looked at his friend sadly. He didn't tell him that he thought that it was just going to get worse. *How long can these people hold on until there are no more of them? More importantly, how long will they keep their freedom?* "We could go to war against the Americans. What will you're people do then?"

Night Wind stared up toward the hills. "Pakwis does not want war. But I think it will come. I do not think we will have a choice." He looked back down at Lucas. "If there is war, I will fight alongside my friend."

Lucas nodded. "Thanks, Night Wind. I hope it doesn't come to that."

Sleeping Rabbit shifted and smiled at her husband. "Your son is kicking hard today."

Night Wind bent over and laughed when the baby kicked his hand that rubbed his wife's belly.

Lucas jumped to his feet. Winda and Pakwis had emerged from his lodge. Pakwis found his wife and went over to her, giving her a tender hug and kiss. She had been pretending to be mending clothing, all the while watching the entrance of her wigwam where her husband was alone with her enemy. She stood when he approached her and looked apprehensive. Pakwis put his arm around her. "I have let her go, my wife. You need not fear."

Winda skipped up to Lucas and hugged him tightly. Then she pulled him down to sit beside her. "Sleeping Rabbit," she addressed her friend. "I have valued your friendship for a long time. Will you help me prepare for my wedding?" She looked at the bewildered man beside her. "To Lucas."

"Yes I will, my friend," Sleeping Rabbit told her.

Lucas sat there as if in a daze. *I don't have to fight Pakwis for her? I get Winda just like that?*

"I hope this is okay, Lookas?" Winda watched him nervously.

Night Wind nudged him. "Lucas."

"Oh." Lucas woke from his wandering mind. "Yes. I just don't understand how it was so easy, that's all. I thought I might have to kill him or something."

Winda smiled at him. "I think he wants to avoid that."

Lucas beamed then gave her a long, deep kiss. "That's more than okay. How long until all the arrangements are ready?" Suddenly he was eager to get it over with.

"We have to do this tomorrow. Before he changes his mind."

Lucas nodded then giggled at Night Wind. "And you will be my witness?" His new friend accepted.

Suddenly, Lucas couldn't contain himself and jumped up pulling Winda with him. He hugged her to him and swung her around, laughing.

He ignored Pakwis, still holding Little Blossom while he cringed over her head as he watched them.

Knocking on the door sent Carrie to her feet. She took several breaths to calm down before opening it. Pete entered, hat in hand, and looking sheepish. He nodded to Carrie then addressed both of them. "Dusty's gone. Took one of the horses and left last night."

Carrie looked out of the window. *It's morning! Where did the time go?* Then a rooster crowed to emphasize just that. Someone clanged dishes in the kitchen, probably Sophie preparing their breakfast.

"Glad you're doin' better, sir," Pete told Grant. "Didn't want that, ah," he stopped, as if realizing Carrie was just behind him. "I didn't want anymore killing." Grant just watched him. "I didn't know he was going to shoot you. I thought he was just trying to scare you off."

"I don't hold you responsible, Pete. And thanks for stopping him."

Pete nodded at Grant then turned back to Carrie. "You recognize me, don't you, Carrie?"

"You really aren't a preacher, are you, Pete?"

"No, I'm not. I'm sorry for what I did. I didn't know it was going to turn out this way." He watched her flinch. "I wouldn't blame you if you took a swing at me." He squinted as if expecting her angry fists on him any second. "It was Ivan that hired me. Dusty knew I wasn't a real preacher. He went ahead with it anyway."

Grant lifted himself up to sitting position. "What's going on here? What do you mean, Pete?" Carrie automatically adjusted his pillow for him.

"It means," Pete told him, "that Carrie and Dusty aren't married at all."

Grant let out a long whistle. "But why? How could you do such a thing?"

Pete watched Carrie and stepped back ,twisting his hat around in his hands. "Ivan got me out of a scrape once, a while back. I owed him. I thought it was going to be an easy job." He sniffed. "I didn't know I was supposed to marry you to Dusty until the last minute. I tried to back out of it. Ivan had me cornered." He shook his head. "If there's anything I can do, Carrie; just let me know. I know now that I owe you a great debt. I'm very sorry." He looked at the floor then walked out, softly shutting the door behind him.

Carrie's whole body built up into a rage. "Of all the..." She paced back and forth in the small room. "I've put up with Dusty's lies and abuse." She balled up her fists, tears ran down her face. "And the way he took me. And we weren't even married?" She clenched her hands so tight that her nails dug into her palms.

"We'll get him," Grant said. "Dusty won't get away with this. I'm personally going to feed that man to the wolves." She stopped and stared at him. "You have my word on it, Carrie. I will personally see to that."

He talked to her until she cooled down. Then he tried to joke with her. "Just think of it this way, now you can devote all your time just to poor old me."

Her looks threw daggers at him. Then she stomped out of the room. "Men."

"Do you have everything now, dear?" Anthony stuffed the last of the baggage into the back of the buggy. Gert did a quick check in her head and nodded. Anthony helped her up then ran around the other side and hopped up, grinning at his wife. "Giddap." The reins were snapped and the horses pulled them down the street.

As they passed the bank, Anthony waved to his clerk. Gert looked apprehensively at him. "Do you think he will be all right, running the bank while you're gone?"

"He's more than capable," Anthony told her confidently, "he's been with me for five years now. I trust him. He'll be fine." He patted Gert's gloved hand. "We need this vacation, don't you think?"

They left York and drove through the countryside. "Yes. What a lovely anniversary gift, Anthony. I have wanted to travel for along time now."

"Well, we should do something special for our thirtieth, right?"

"And I am glad to get away now too, now that Mary is settled in Kingston." Gert watched the landscape go by. Early summer flowers dotted the hill on their right. Flea bane, buttercups, and daisies grew along the trail and up the slope. On her left, Lake Ontario glistened and shimmered as they drove along the shore. "I'm glad you got a good price for Mary's house, Anthony. I didn't think we'd get that kind of money for that dump."

"Well, York is growing fast. It'll help pay Mary's bills."

"Yes," Gert agreed. "I don't think Carrie would have wanted it either. Not after what she has been through and all."

Anthony put the horses into a trot. "Using the money that Ivan left in his account still bothers me. His left eye twitched as he spoke. "Even though no one has claimed it yet. They still might, you know?"

"I know," Gert sniffed, feeling equally guilty. "We'll just have to deal with it when we have to, I guess." She squinted into the sun. "It will go a long way for Mary's upkeep at the asylum. Those places sure aren't cheap, are they?"

They drove for awhile before Gert said, "She'll be well looked after. Won't she?"

"Yes, she will, Gert. And for a long time, too. I wonder, though, how upset Carrie will be when she finds out that Ivan is dead and that we put her mother in an insane asylum."

Gert just shook her head. She didn't want to dwell on that right now. She just wanted to enjoy their trip as much as possible. "You know how long it has been since we took a trip just for the fun of it?"

"Let's see." Anthony counted it out. "At least twelve years." He whistled. "I didn't realize it was that long."

"We should travel more often," suggested Gert, "see this new country."

"Well, right now, we have to be careful, with the Americans and all. I just hope we don't end up in a full scale war."

Gert shivered but said nothing.

"I'm sure it will turn into nothing," Anthony said, soothingly.

Gert had pulled out their rain gear when it had started to sprinkle. Now she sat holding her rain hat over her ears, clutching it at her chin. She started to squirm. "These seats are getting hard already."

"And we've only just begun," Anthony laughed.

Grant woke up to a little boy staring at him. "Morning."

"Hi." Adam's eyes darted around the room as if he didn't know if he should run or not.

"And who are you, young man?"

"Adam."

"Well, Adam. Nice to meet you."

The young boy studied him. "My dad shot you, didn't he? But you're not dead."

"No. He just shot me in the leg."

"Oh."

"How old are you, Adam?"

"Seven. And Johnny is ten. He just had a birthday awhile ago."

"And when is your birthday, Adam?"

Adam forgot to feel nervous and sat on the edge of the bed, then shrugged his shoulders.

"Is there snow on the ground when you have your birthday?"

The boy nodded. "But not when Santa Claus comes."

Johnny sauntered in and plunked down behind Adam. This movement made Grant grit his teeth as he narrowly missed his injured leg. He tried not to let the pain show on his face.

"Dusty shot you, didn't he?" Johnny asked.

He had disowned his father, Grant noticed. He nodded, wondering where this was all heading.

"He hit Carrie." Johnny screwed up his face. "I hate it when he hits people. He hits her all the time." The boy looked like he was on the verge of tears.

"He hit Johnny, too," Adam put in, not wanting to be left out, "with his belt."

Grant's stomach tightened. "Are you all right, Johnny?"

Johnny nodded. "It ain't so bad now." He sniffed and wiped his nose on his sleeve. "I shot him, you know. When he brung us here. But I didn't kill him."

"You shot Dusty?" That was incredible. *And the boy still lived. So, that explains Sam finding the gun and blood in the cabin.*

"I only hit his arm," Johnny confessed. "Carrie said I don't want to kill him, 'cause I'd feel bad about it if I did. Maybe go to jail."

"That's right, Johnny. You would feel bad about it. But it will depend on what happened whether you go to jail or not."

"That's what Carrie says," Johnny said, his blond curls dancing as he nodded his head.

"You really like Carrie, don't you guys?"

"Yep," both boys answered in unison.

Sam walked in and stopped in the middle of the room. "How ya doin', Mr. Grant?" His eyes travelled up and down the bed.

"I'm fine, Sam. How have you been?"

"Just fine." He stood there, hesitating in his movements, looking nervously at Grant.

"Ah. Why don't you boys go outside and find you're dog. Okay?"

Adam slid down off the bed and ran out the door. "Okay, see ya later." Johnny jumped down and ran after his brother.

Sam didn't move.

"What's bothering you, Sam?" Grant wondered what had happened now.

"Well, I was wondering," he shuffled his feet, glancing at the floor. "How do you get a girl to like you?"

Carrie and Sophie were hanging clothes on the line to dry when Squirrel darted past them. Both women turned to follow his line of direction. Sophie inhaled and dropped her handful in the mud. "Indians!" Panicking, she ran toward the house.

"It's okay. Sophie," Carrie called to her, "they're friends of mine."

The young girl stopped and stood rooted in one spot. Her eyes were wide and unblinking.

"It's okay," Carrie repeated and gave her a quick hug. *She's shaking.*

Winda, Lucas, and four warriors faced Pete and his rifle at the edge of his corn field. Carrie ran toward them. "Pete! Pete! They're here to help us. It's okay, Pete. They're friends."

Pete turned at the sound of Carrie's voice. "What?"

She stood beside him panting. "They're friends. They are here to help us find Dusty."

Pete lowered his musket but still clung to it.

Lucas slid off his horse. Carrie noticed that he looked more Indian than white. He wore buckskins and had his long hair was tied back with feathers in it. "Hi, Carrie." He hugged her and shook Pete's stiff hand.

Winda dismounted and the two women hugged excitedly. Carrie turned to Lucas. "Dusty shot Grant in the leg." She quickly added, "He's okay. He's in the house."

Lucas nodded, looking at the house across the corn field. "Where is Dusty?"

"We don't know. He stole a horse and left about seven days ago."

Lucas and Winda took turns fussing over Squirrel. Pete visibly relaxed, letting out a huge sigh then smiling. "Come on up to the house," he invited.

They were halfway through the corn field when Sam came charging out of the house and jumped at Winda, hugging her with all his might. "Oh, Sam," she gasped. "I can't breathe."

"Sorry." He hugged Lucas tight. Lucas hugged him back just as hard.

Lucas grinned. "Glad to see you too, son."

Sam beamed and looked up at Lucas as if he were his hero.

Sophie hadn't moved from her spot between the clothes line and the house. Carrie watched as Sam ran up to her and grabbed her hand. "It's okay, Sophie. These are friends. It's Winda and Lucas." As if this alone would solve all the problems in his world.

"This is Sophie," Sam announced to the gang, proudly. She stood beside him, holding his hand.

Winda walked up to her and offered the shy, young girl her hand. Slowly, Sophie reached out and smiled. Sam was beaming behind at her. *He really likes her,* Carrie thought. She'd never noticed it before. His eyes never left the striking blond.

Lucas shook her hand next. Sophie nearly swooned over this tall, rugged, half-wild man. After he moved on, she said, "He's so handsome."

Carrie was introduced to Pakwis and Night Wind and the other two warriors. Sophie's eyes widened as they approached her. Carrie knew that she had never been this close to an Indian before. "You won't vanish," she told the young girl. They shook her hand then moved on with their imposing statures. Winda thanked all the men for their understanding.

Johnny and Adam came running up, their sleeves wet from playing in the creek behind the barn. They both jumped up at Winda and stared at the warriors. "They won't eat us either, will they, Winda?" asked Adam.

Lucas paced the small bedroom, watching his brother sleep. *Should I leave him be or wake him?*

Grant's eyes fluttered open. "Hey, little brother, you found us." He grunted and pulled himself into sitting position. "It's about time."

"How are you, Grant?" Lucas took two big steps to the bed and lifted the blanket. A clean bandage was wrapped around Grant's leg. Other than that, he looked well and healthy.

"I'll live."

"Can you walk?" Lucas was beside himself.

"Yeah, I can walk. Just need to get my strength back is all." Lucas finally relaxed. Grabbing the back of a chair, he flipped it around and sat on it kneeling on the back rest.

"You haven't decided yet, have you?" Grant asked him, smiling widely.

Lucas raised his eyebrows. "Decide what?"

"Whether you are red or white?"

Lucas laughed. "Well I guess it depends on what mood I'm in." Then seriously, he told his brother. "Me and Winda got married."

Grant's face lit up. "Congratulations, Lucas." And offered Lucas his hand.

"I've got us some help to find Dusty. Pakwis, Night Wind, and a couple of others are here."

Grant's eyebrows lifted. "The Pakwis?" Lucas nodded. "How does Winda feel about that?"

"They've come to terms." Lucas frowned. "More like an uneasy truce."

"I'm sorry I missed your wedding, Lucas. I'd have given anything to be there."

"Don't blame yourself. Pakwis forced it. More like sealing a contract to get her out of his mind, I think." Grant watched his brother's face sadden. "I really don't feel we're actually married. We had the ceremony and all, but it was so rushed, I couldn't even give her this." Lucas pulled out a gold wedding band from his pocket.

Grant whistled. "You were serious, weren't you?"

Lucas returned the ring. "Indian ceremonies are quiet different than ours, you know."

Grant said with, a devilish smile on his face. "I have an idea."

19

Pete stood in front of the small congregation on his front lawn. He felt ridiculous in his getup and a little apprehensive of all these Indians around his home. *What a farce this is! They know I can't marry them.* Winda and Carrie had been giddy all day making preparations, cleaning the house, and baking. The boys even took a bath. They sat on one chair poking each other and giggling. Sophie stood beside Sam, wringing her hands.

Pete gave her a disgusted look. "You stay away from that black boy, Sophie. What will people think?" he'd told her earlier. So far, she hadn't listened, which irritated him. These people were setting a bad example for his daughter. He'd be glad when they all left. *Then, she'll forget all about him.* He vowed, *I will see to that!* Sam looked at her adoringly, Sophie smiled sweetly at him. Pete's gut wrenched.

Carrie eyed him suspiciously. Pete didn't blame her, but hoped she would just put his deceit behind her. *What else was I supposed to do? Ivan had men holding my family hostage!* Behind her chair, stood Pakwis, Night Wind, and the other warriors. They stood stiff and tall. Menacing. One of them watched his every movement. *They don't trust me either. Maybe they think I helped Dusty escape? If they only knew. I would have rather put a bullet between his eyes.* He knew Grant hated him for what he had put Carrie through, that was obvious. *He's pretty ungrateful that I saved his life. Don't look down your nose at me, Grant, you're no better.* Then there was Lucas, who stood anxiously in front of him. This man scared him. Wild. He lived with savages. *How can you trust a man like that?* Winda stepped out of the house and walked toward them, her eyes on the wild man only. She was radiant. Pete didn't know how to take her yet. Aside from being a savage, she treated him just like she treated everyone else. *Should I trust her?* Winda and Lucas faced each other, holding hands. Pete started to sweat profusely. *Why am I doing this again?* "Dearly beloved. We are gathered here today.." Pete said all the right words. Blessed the couple then sank into the background.

Lucas slipped the gold ring on Winda's finger and kissed her passionately. Cheers rang out. Kisses and hugs spread all around freely for the happy couple. It made Pete sick.

Winda kept admiring her ring. "No one had ever given me such a valuable gift before." She hugged her best friend. "Someday you will be just as happy as I am today, Carrie."

Carrie just nodded as if not trusting her own voice. Like she didn't believe it would happen to her. Pete noticed Grant watching her.

Pete shook his head and walked away from the house. He stopped by the well and watched Pakwis walk toward the hill, kicking the big black dog as he went.

Night Wind was an excellent tracker. Even better than Winda. She was more than happy to let him lead. They followed Dusty's trail right back to Blackman Falls.

"He's restocked his supplies," Lucas told his posse after he'd checked several shops. "Spent a few nights in the tavern."

Winda knew he was wishing his brother was there with them. She assured him that Grant was getting better and all he needed was rest. She looked back toward Jeb's cabin, half expecting the old man to walk out of the door. Then she noticed people going out of their way to avoid this group. Too many warriors sat on their ponies were in the middle of their town. But some of them recognized Winda and Lucas and greeted them, albeit a little warily.

One young man walked right up to Lucas. "You going after Dusty?"

"Yes, we are, sir." Lucas jumped back up on his horse.

"Hope you get him mighty quick. After what he done to Jeb."

"We'll get him." Lucas waved his hand at the man as they rode out of town.

They followed Night Wind eastward through thick woods. Lucas swatted at mosquitoes. Winda handed him a jar of bear grease to spread on his hands and face. He smiled a thank you at her and said that he was glad to be in the shade. It was hot and humid today. He kept his jacket on because of the bugs.

Night Wind picked up the pace. Lucas galloped up to discuss strategy with him.

Pakwis rode up beside Winda. "You have found a good man," he told her as he watched her husband's back.

"Yes, I have," she answered, wondering what was really on his mind.

"I hope you can forgive me. I should have just adopted you as my daughter. Not taken you as my second wife."

She rode silently, watching the men in front of her.

"I did, uh, do, care for you, you know. More than I did Lanick." He watched the ground as he passed over it. "I think she knew it too. I tried not to have favourites, but, she made it very difficult."

Why is he telling me these things now? Winda knew Lanick would argue with him over the tiniest of things. She had gone out of her way to upset him.

"Are you happy with Little Blossom?" She tried to get his mind off her.

"Yes. Very happy. And with my daughter, White Mouse." Pakwis smiled. His eyes glazed over as if seeing them in his mind. "I don't want to upset this." He looked at her. "But when I saw you again. All the old feelings came rushing back at me."

Winda didn't believe him. Lucas had told her how Pakwis acted when he picked up her hair pin.

He checked to see how far Lucas was from them. " You and Lucas together. I know you were not meant for me."

She guided her horse around a tree saying nothing.

"You have changed, Winda." Pakwis went on when they rejoined. "So have I, I guess," he paused. "I do hope that we can be friends. You and Lucas."

Lucas and Night Wind were laughing together. "Because I respect your husband too much, Winda." He kicked his horse into a gallop until he caught up to the men in front.

Winda rode silently on. *Did Pakwis just admit he was in love with me?* She checked behind her. The other two warriors rode a few feet away locked in their own conversation. *Did they hear any of that? What do I tell Lucas?*

Gert and Anthony pulled their buggy up in front of a swanky new hotel in Berlin. He jumped down and surveyed his surroundings. "This is quite the bustling place." Berlin was growing fast. New construction was taking place in several areas. People were rushing around everywhere. Anthony helped Gert down and led her into the hotel to secure a room.

A bus boy took them up to their room on the second floor and carried the baggage in for them. Anthony tipped him then watched Gert as she walked around the room, touching the gold-gilded mirror, the red oak furniture, and the luxurious bedding. "This is a nice room, isn't it, Anthony?"

"Yes it is." Anthony put his arm around his wife's ample girth. Together they walked to the window and stood watching the activity out on the street. "Sure is a busy town."

"I heard that someone found silver around here someplace," Gert told him. "That must be why there are so many people."

"Let's go for a walk," Anthony suggested.

"Okay. I saw a nice hat shop I want to check out," Gert said excitedly.

They walked down the street checking the shops and marvelling at all the new gadgets and inventions they saw. "Look at this." Anthony pointed out a beautiful gold necklace in the jewelry store window. Gert gasped when she saw it. Anthony ducked inside and bought it for her. Thanking old man Zuker for the money as he paid the clerk. He watched through the window as Gert's eyes glazed over when the clerk lifted it from its case and handed it to him. She stood there like a statue in front of the store until he re-emerged. Anthony came back beaming and feeling smug as he lifted it over her head. After he fastened it, he kissed his beloved wife. They walked down the street holding hands.

"Thank you, Anthony," Gert said. "This is a most precious gift."

"Happy anniversary, dear." Anthony gave her a squeeze.

Grant sat on a crude bench outside playing with Squirrel. He found a stick that he threw over and over so the dog could chase it and bring it back to him. Beside him, leaning against the house, was a cane that Pete had made for him before Lucas and the rest left to find Dusty. He kept checking the edge of the woods for them to return.

Carrie walked up with a basket of folded clothes she'd just taken off the line. "They'll find him," she told him heatedly. "But it seems to be taking so long."

Grant smiled up at her, devilishly. "Miss him, do ya?" She glared at him. He wanted to become a bug and crawl into the woodwork.

"I would love to see that man hung," Carrie told him with such conviction that it made him squint. "To think of what he put me through. And he's not even my husband. How did he think he would get away with all the stuff he's done?"

Grant blinked her. "I don't think he's all there. I don't know how anyone could do the things he's done either."

Carrie sighed and put the basket down on the ground in front of her. "I just hope this is all over with soon. I'm tired of it all."

"Well, he's supposed to have a stash of rifles hidden someplace. I think he's the only one who knows where they are." Carrie's eyes narrowed. Grant ignored her. "I was trying to get him to show me, but he wouldn't bite."

Carrie stood silently beside him for a few minutes. Finally she told him. "I saw him and Ivan take crates out of the warehouse in Blackman Falls. Maybe that's where they are."

Grant was flabbergasted. *She must have been the third man! How did I miss that?* He pictured the wagon in front of the big doors of the warehouse just before he jumped into the back of it as Ivan slowed down for the corner. *How can I be so stupid? It would be just like him to hide them right in front of our noses.*

Grant pulled himself up and leaned on his cane then he pecked Carrie on the cheek. "Thanks, Carrie, I'll look into that as soon as I can."

Carrie blushed and looked away. He watched as conflicting emotions wrestled across her face. "I'm not like Dusty," he told her. "I'd never hit you." When she looked back at him, he smiled at her, hopefully.

She stood frozen to the ground, wide eyed. He kissed his angel on the lips, softly and gently. She responded, reluctantly at first. Giggles came from behind them. The kiss broke. Adam and Johnny were crouched down a few feet away. Carrie giggled and whispered to Grant. "I feel like a school girl who'd just got caught being sinful."

The boys jumped up. "We saw you kissing. We saw you kissing."

She chased after them, caught then tickled them all over. Squeals of delight floated back to Grant. He sat back down to watch.

Pete walked out of the barn, heading toward the house. He stopped and watched Carrie chase the boys then nodded to Grant. "I wish I could have stopped that wedding I did," he confessed, sincerely.

Grant just scowled at him, but Pete continued anyway. "Ivan threatened my family. I owed him a huge debt."

"And there was no other way?" hissed Grant. He wanted to strangle the man.

"He had my wife and daughter as hostages. What was I supposed to do?" Pete started yelling back at him, then lowered his voice so Carrie wouldn't hear him. "I paid it all back though. I don't owe anybody anything, anymore." He shook his head. "Just about turned into another Dusty."

"That doesn't excuse what you did to Carrie, though, does it?" Grant didn't think he could ever forgive this man. "For sending her into hell."

Pete looked at him with sad eyes. "I wish I could just undo it, like it never happened." He continued on into the house.

Grant undid his balled up fists.

Lucas had never seen so many people in one place before. He wondered at all the different races and colours that he saw.

"Lucas, who are those people?" Winda pointed out a small group of small, slanty-eyed men who stood in front of a laundry shop. They wore their hair long and braided much like the Indians did. But they looked so different.

"They're Chinese," he told her. "From the other side of the world."

"The world must be very big."

"Yes, it is. It would have taken these people several years to get here."

They rode down the main street of Berlin. Lucas heard several strange languages as they passed the various shops and businesses. He too was fascinated seeing all the different immigrants in this small city.

Pakwis and Night Wind had wisely camped a few miles out of town. "Too many warriors in there might start a war. We would be just asking for trouble," Pakwis pointed out.

Night Wind had frowned as he watched all the new people in his land converge into a white man's city. "There are more of them than the black flies in the spring."

Lucas wondered how so many immigrants moving into this country was going to affect his friends in the long run. *No wonder Night Wind feels bitter. He's feeling squeezed out of his homeland.* Slowly this land is being gobbled up by settlers, pioneers and a whole host of others. Towns were starting up all over the place. He could see it in his mind. *The white man pushing the Indians further and further into uninhabitable lands.* They dismounted and tied up their horses. Winda followed Lucas down the street between tall buildings. She waited in front of a tavern while he ducked inside to search for Dusty. Several minutes later, Lucas emerged and stopped behind a drunken white man who had staggered up to Winda.

"Hey! Squaw." The drunk teetered on his feet. "You lookin' for a real man?" The foul smelling man slobbered onto his jacket.

Not seeing Lucas, Winda backed away. "No, I'm just waiting for my husband." "Husband? You mean that half-breed?"

Winda tried walking away. He grabbed her arm. "What's that half-breed got that I ain't got?" He tried pulling her. Several people stopped to watch. Winda twisted free and whipped out her knife. The drunk staggered backward, hands in the air. "Okay! I didn't mean any harm. Just put the knife away."

"Get back," she told him through clenched teeth. The man yelped and backed up into Lucas, who stood, arms folded, glaring at him. The man screamed and ran into the crowd.

"You all right?" Lucas asked while leading her off the street.

She nodded. "Just shook up a little."

Lucas kissed her. He stepped back and furrowed a brow as he watched the crowd disperse. *That's all we need, to announce to Dusty that we are here.*

"Come on." He led her across the street and down the other side. They dodged crowds and new construction. He witnessed the awe on Winda's face as she studied the new tools these people had. They were always making new and better things. And the Indians had no clue as to how all of these inventions were going to change their lives. Lucas squeezed Winda's arm and smiled as she marvelled at all the different clothing styles and fabrics people wore.

"How can so many tongues understand each other?" She asked him.

He shrugged. "Just like the different Indian tribes; by gestures and sign language." A young Indian boy stepped out of the shadows. Ottawa, Lucas thought by the way he was dressed. His hand was held out to them, begging for money. Lucas flipped him a coin. The boy smiled and ducked back into the corner.

Winda looked back at him. "I wonder where his parents are?"

"Don't know," Lucas answered as they continued on their way. *Probably laying around drunk someplace. More and more of the Indians were being misplaced. Now the white man's influence on them is only making things worse.* They crossed the street again at the far end of the city and headed back up the other side toward their horses. Winda stopped Lucas in mid-step. "Look over there." She pointed through the crowd. A big bald man stood half in the shadows watching an older couple looking in a store window.

As they sauntered down the street, the big man followed them, unseen.

"It's him," confirmed Lucas. "What does Dusty want with those people?"

The following day, Anthony hitched up the team to the buggy and drove out of Berlin. "Thank you so much for the necklace, Anthony," purred Gert, as she fingered it at her throat.

"You're quiet welcome. And thank you for my new beaver hat, it fits perfectly." He didn't wear it today, it was for special occasions.

"It's the best anniversary gift I've ever gotten." Gert pecked him on the cheek.

Several minutes out of town, Dusty caught up with them on his horse. With gun in hand, he ordered them to turn into the nearby woods. Anthony couldn't believe they were being held up by Carrie's husband. Anthony started sweating, his face heating up. He was at a loss for words. Dusty made them crash through the trees until the growth became too thick to continue. Gert and Anthony were ordered down and stood in front of Dusty, shaking.

"What are you doing here?" he demanded, glaring at them and waving his pistol around. His horse shied away from him. "You meddling' again, ain't ya?"

"We're only on vacation, Dusty." Gert's voice was squeaky. "It's none of your concern." She put on a brave front but clung desperately to her husband.

"What do you want?" asked Anthony, while trying to figure a way out of this.

"I don't want you here, that's for sure." Dusty paced back and forth as if deciding what to do next. When he stopped, he reached for a rope from his horse and tied Anthony's hands behind his back. After cutting the end of the rope off with his knife, he pulled Gert over and did the same to her.

Baggage, gifts and supplies were thrown from their buggy. Dusty rifled through everything and took whatever he wanted, sneering at the couple. He staggered over and glared at each of them, inches away from their faces then forced them down on their knees. Suddenly, his big hand ripped Gert's new necklace from her neck, sending her backward choking and gasping. Her neck bled from where the chain grazed her skin.

"Think you have it all, don't you?" He slapped her, sending her to the ground.

"Stop that, you brute. Stop," Anthony pleaded. He was shaking so bad that his teeth chattered. Dusty raised a hand.

"Dusty," a voice yelled from behind the trees.

Dusty grabbed Anthony, pulling the smaller man up and holding him in front as a shield. The gun waved in all directions, not knowing where the call had come from. "Who's there?" Wide-eyed, he searched through the trees.

"Dusty." Another call came from behind him this time. He whirled Anthony around and faced toward that call. Then a holler came from a different direction. Dusty, anxious now, kept whipping Anthony around in front of him, making him dizzy.

The voices were closing in on him, louder and more frightening. Dusty couldn't take cover. He didn't know which way to face, so he just fired into the woods. "Go away."

He let Anthony drop at his knees. Another yell came from his left. He shot in that direction. Re-loading as quickly as possible. Then, a shout from behind him. He shot through the trees blindly.

Anthony stayed on his knees, arms over his head afraid to move. Dusty's tormentors continued until Dusty ran out of ammunition and waved the pistol around in fear. Anthony scrambled over to his wife.

Dusty ran to his horse for more ammunition. Winda walked out beside it. "What?" Dusty stopped short and wiped his eyes. "How did you get here?" His eyes darted around as he searched through the trees then whipped the pistol at her, narrowly missing her head.

He lunged at her. "Dusty!" an angry call from his right, stopped him in mid step. A half-breed walked out, pointing his rifle at Dusty's chest. Dusty looked around while backing up. "You won't get away this time," warned the half-breed.

Anthony fanned Gert with his hand; she looked like she was going to swoon.

Four warriors stepped into the tiny clearing, each one holding a weapon on the big, bald man in the centre. Finally, Dusty put his hands up. An Indian walked up behind him and tied his hands securely behind his back. Anthony was still shaking when the half-breed and the beautiful Indian lady untied them.

20

"You are Carrie's aunt?" Winda sat beside the plump woman at their campfire, coffee in hand. Dusty sat tied to a tree a few yards away, guarded by the two warriors Pakwis had brought with him.

"Yes, I am, dear," laughed Gert. "We were so worried about her. But you tell us that she is fine. That makes me so glad, you know." She smiled at the pretty Indian lady. "We can't wait to see her."

"She has told me so much about you." Winda took another sip.

"What's going to happen to him?" Anthony nodded toward their prisoner.

"We're going to deliver him to my brother," Lucas said. "Then take him to be tried for murder, smuggling, and even treason; and any thing else we can get him on."

"Murder?" Gert asked, as she rubbed her sore neck.

Anthony watched Dusty glaring at the bunch of them and shifted a few inches away from him.

"He has more guns hidden somewhere," Lucas sighed. "I don't think he's willing to tell us where they are, though."

Pakwis and Night Wind carried a deer carcass into camp. Winda went over to help butcher it. Gert turned green when she saw its intestines fall out. Lucas moved to block her view. Anthony nodded a thanks to him. The last thing he wanted was his wife getting sick.

"I know that Dusty didn't treat Carrie right. He's a mean one." Anthony looked helplessly at Lucas. "We know he and Ivan were up to no good, but didn't know what it was. We guessed, of course, but had no proof." Anthony took a sip of coffee. His insides were still shaking from his ordeal. "Did you know Ivan?" "He's dead now."

"I didn't." Lucas did a quick check on Dusty. "Grant did."

"Who's Grant?" Gert wanted to know.

"My brother, Grant Sievers." Lucas leaned in and whispered so Dusty wouldn't hear. "He's investigating Dusty and Ivan and this whole outfit. He's laid up right now. That's why we were out chasing him."

Anthony looked at the wild man across the flames. He knew who Grant was. The major that he dealt with at the bank. *If it is him? How can two brothers be so different, then? If Grant wears a uniform and presents himself immaculately? Lucas wears buckskins and runs around with Indians?*

Night Wind stuck a couple of sticks into the ground over the fire, each with a roast speared onto it. Instinctively, Anthony cowered from the imposing warrior. *How can Lucas not be intimidated by these wild, unpredictable creatures?* Then, he watched him. Lucas fit right in with them. He seemed just as dangerous as his friends. Anthony had heard horror stories of what these people did. That they killed and scalped, even women and children. He also heard of cannibalism, and hoped that none of these men had ever done such a horrible thing. *But at the same time, what have we done to them?* He knew of the raids on unsuspecting villages. Of women and children being dragged behind horses until their screams stopped. *How can men be so cruel to each other?* Winda sat down again and smiled at Gert. "This should be ready about sundown."

Anthony wondered about the beauty sitting next to him. *She seemed better mannered and more intelligent than most white people he knew. Just like Carrie said in her letter.* Lucas gave Winda a loving pat on her arm. He surely doesn't care if anyone objects to their relationship. In fact, Anthony thought, he'd be the type that would flaunt it, just to get a rise out of some people. He knew too, that Gert liked Winda, who put them at ease with these savages among them. Pakwis joined them. Anthony sensed tension between him and Lucas. Then he saw the chief look at Winda, longingly.

The leaves on the trees had turned brilliant colours again. Most of the summer flowers had withered and died. Pete was bringing in the last of his harvest. Carrie, Sam, Sophie, and Grant all helped him as much as possible.

"Thank you," Pete told them. "Everything is in on time this year." Meaning before winter hit. "Now I have time to fix things around this place." They were all out in the field when a black buggy pulled down the lane. Carrie saw Winda, Lucas, and the four warriors close behind it. Then she saw the horror of her dreams, Dusty sat tied to his horse. The warriors surrounded him, weapons drawn, not taking any chances. Yet, he still remained defiant and glared at everyone that dared look at him. Carrie shivered as she watched them pull up in front of the house. Sam ran past her calling to Winda. Grant led her down between the rows of carrots. "He won't ever hurt you again, Carrie," he promised her again. "I'll see to that." She smiled at him then walked over to the hunting party. It took her a few minutes to realize that the people in the buggy were her aunt and uncle. Squeals of delight escaped her when she hugged them. "You found me. I didn't think you'd come all the way out here."

"We just wanted to see how you were doing for ourselves." Gert hugged her niece tight. "We were worried about how Dusty was treating you. Especially after we got your letter."

Carrie sobered as she thought about that letter. She hugged her uncle.

"Well, look at you," Anthony said. "You have become quite the pretty young lady."

"Well," Gert said as she held Carrie's arm. "You aren't the shy, frightened little girl anymore."

Carrie smiled. "There's so much to tell you. I don't know where to begin." She looked over to see Grant watching her and blushed.

Carrie's smile faded when she watched the Indians drag Dusty to a tree in the yard and tie him securely to it. "So, you actually got him?" She wanted to confront him, to punch and slap him for once. Then she reluctantly turned away. *I will not lower myself to his level! Maybe one of these men will kill him for me.*

Lucas hugged her. "We caught him terrorizing your aunt and uncle."

"He was robbing us," Gert's voice shook. "I think he would have killed us."

Anthony put his arm around his wife's ample waist. "He won't do that now, will he? Thanks to your friends, Carrie."

Winda walked up to the group after greeting the boys. Carrie gave her a big hug. "I'm so glad you're all back."

"Me too. I need to rest." Winda went over and sat on the porch steps. " I am not feeling all that well."

"What's wrong?" Carrie looked over at Lucas, who had joined the rest of the men a few yards away. "Anything I can do? Should I get—?"

"Slow down, girl," Winda laughed. "I'm I am fine. Just having a baby, is all."

Carrie's head snapped back. "A baby? Why Winda, congratulations." She bent down and gave her friend a tearful hug. "I'm so happy for you." Everyone heard her. Lucas beamed when all the men slapped him on the back. Winda smiled at them all. Carrie caught Pakwis masking his sad eyes.

"I'm happy for you, Lucas," Grant grinned. "You'll make a great dad."

"Thanks, brother. How's that leg coming along?"

"Fine. Just hurts when it rains." Grant glanced over at Carrie. "Carrie is a good nurse."

The brothers found themselves alone after everyone had drifted apart. "I've noticed you watching her." Lucas nodded in Carrie's direction. "Anything you want to tell me?"

"I'm hoping." Grant shook his head. "I think it'll take some doing though. She knows I helped Dusty with the guns. I don't think she trusts me yet."

"You want me to talk to her?"

"No, I will." Grant watched the women fuss over the boys. Gert told them something that made Sophie laugh. The young girl was coming out of her shell. "I'm going to tell everyone who I am tonight."

Lucas nodded. "I think that would be a good idea."

Grant looked over at Anthony. Anthony had recognized him when he jumped out of the buggy, even though Grant was out of uniform and knew he looked scruffy. Usually he'd be neat and polished. When he'd shook his head slightly at the banker, asking for secrecy, Anthony had nodded. Anthony whispered, "I feel more at ease knowing that you are here." Grant knew that Pete didn't want Dusty inside his house, to everyone's relief. They tied him up inside the barn, out of the wind and rain that blew in that evening. Pakwis assigned his two warriors first watch as the rest went inside the house. Winda took the warriors out a hearty meal and threw Dusty a piece of bread. Grant had heard Pakwis instruct his men. They were to wait, arrows drawn, until Dusty was done eating before they ate their own supper. They were not to untie him. After everyone was full, the men pulled out pipes for a leisurely smoke while the women did up the dishes. When everything settled down, Grant got everyone's attention. He looked around the crowded room. "I just want to let everyone know what's going on here. I am Major Grant Sievers of the Twelfth Militia."

"I knew it." Pete pounded the table. "You sure think your better than anyone. Ordering us around."

Grant ignored Pete. He watched as Carrie inhaled, her face turning white. Loudly, he continued. "I intend to deliver Dusty Blackman to Greenstown for General Brooks." He faced Carrie. "I have never been a friend of his. And," he turned to Winda, "I know that I have acted like an ass at times." Some people chuckled. "I'd apologize to you again, but I don't want to be poisoned." A twinkle sparkled in his eyes at their private little joke.

"When are you going?" Lucas asked.

"As soon as possible, and I'm asking for your help, little brother." Grant turned to Pakwis and Night Wind. "I'm very grateful for your help, Chief, Night Wind." He shook both their hands. "I think we can take it from here. I know you must be anxious to get back to your own families." Pakwis nodded and told them they would leave in the morning. Grant noticed the look he gave Winda. *Damn that man!* He's still not over her, and he vowed to keep a close eye on him for his brother. "I've met your uncle before," Grant told Carrie, "I've been to his bank." Carrie gave Anthony an astonished look.

"Yes," he told her, "we have done some business together. He is a major. I can vouch for that."

"He is," Winda confirmed. "I have known for a while." Lucas just nodded at her, smiling.

"All of you knew? Why didn't anyone tell me?" Carrie jumped up, glaring at Grant. "You told everyone but me. And you expect me to trust you?"

"Hold on, Carrie." Grant moved to block her from running out on him. "I had to do business with your uncle, and Winda was told only out of necessity. I had to keep my cover until I had Dusty in custody, at least." He kept pleading with her. "If he knew who I was, he wouldn't have let me go on that gun run with him. I was able to find out where General Walton was hiding out. Along with other information." Carrie settled down and sat back in her chair.

"By the way," he added softly, "it was Jeb who confirmed to us about Dusty's involvement." Everyone looked at him with stunned expressions on their faces. "He sent a letter to General Brooks. I was following up on the lead, even though I was already in Blackman Falls. He didn't know who I was either. It shaved off a couple of weeks worth of investigating."

"We never knew." Winda's eyes misted over.

The warriors were up early the next morning, and were given food and supplies for their journey home. All the men shook hands. Night Wind hung back and let his Chief say his goodbyes first. Pakwis walked up to Winda and gave her a quick hug. He didn't say a word, but simply turned and jumped up onto his horse. He smiled and nodded to Carrie and her aunt.

"Thanks again, Chief." Lucas shook Pakwis's hand.

"We are now even, my friend." Pakwis held his head high. "You will always be welcome at my fire." Lucas watched as he galloped down the lane.

Night Wind stopped his horse in front of Lucas. "I truly see that you and Sleeping Rabbit are just good friends. I also welcome you at my fire, Lucas." With that, he rode over to Winda, bent down and kissed her cheek loudly, smiling affectionately at her. "We have always been friends, you and I. Sleeping Rabbit cherishes your friendship. I hope that you and Lucas will visit us sometime."

"Bye, Night Wind. Thanks for your help." Winda hugged him.

Night Wind caught up to Pakwis.

"I have a funny feeling," Pakwis told him. He looked behind them before he said, "Remember when Stealth Man talked us into raiding that military camp, and all we got were two horses? The one he got killed in?"

"Yes." Night Wind started to feel uneasy.

"I think it was Major Grant, Lucas's brother that we attacked."

Night Wind checked behind them, afraid that the wind carried his chief's words that way. "Why do you think that?"

"I saw him that day, and I heard his name being called. I'm I am sure it was him."

"Well, I am not going to tell him." Night Wind picked up the pace. "Or Lucas, either." They rode in silence for awhile, nervously checking behind them every few yards.

"I wonder," Pakwis said, "if Major Grant knew it."

Grant stood beside his brother, watching the Indians ride away. "You have made good friends there, Lucas."

"Yes, I know. I just wonder what's going to become of them with all the settlers moving in on their territory."

Grant nudged his brother when he saw Johnny sneak into the barn. They edged over to see into doorway. Johnny walked right up to his father. Dusty watched the boy through slitted eyes as if pretending to be asleep. He was tied to a pole that supported the roof, hands behind his back, knees up.

"You hurt Carrie," Johnny spat at him, "and you hurt me too."

"Come to see your pa, eh, Johnny?" Dusty smiled. "How bout you untie me. I'll buy you your own horse."

Johnny gave him a hard kick right in his privates. Dusty grunted on the intake of breath and squirmed in the dirt, eyes watering. Johnny just laughed at him. "See how you like it." He spit before turning and marching out. Pete walked by, taking a plate of food out to Dusty. He made a wide berth around Lucas and Grant, probably afraid of also being arrested for his role in the mock wedding he'd performed on Carrie and Dusty. He was watching the Sievers brothers and didn't see the young boy come out of the barn.

Grant knew Pete was wary of him, but hadn't decided what he wanted to do about it yet. "They used to be friends, you know," he said to Lucas, watching Pete through the open barn doors. Pete dropped the plate at the prisoner's feet, keeping his gun trained on Dusty as he undid his binds. "He's not taking any chances now, is he?"

They turned around and watched Johnny go back into the house. "That kid has guts," Lucas said.

"I just hope he doesn't develop a temper like his dad has."

Both men decided they better get moving and turned toward the barn for the horses. A gun exploded from inside. Lucas and Grant pulled out their pistols and ran behind the door. Grant poked his head around the corner. Dusty held Pete's gun and stood pointing it at his old friend's head. Pete backed into the shadows, shaking. Grant fired over Dusty's head. "Drop it, Dusty," ordered Grant. "You have nowhere to go."

Dusty waved the gun in their direction. Pete jumped him, knocking the gun to the ground. Lucas and Grant rushed inside and helped to secure the prisoner. As Grant tied Dusty's hands, the big, bald man spit in his face.

"I'll see you in hell, Dusty," Grant leered at him.

The three of them secured Dusty to the pole again. Then the brothers headed for their horses.

Lucas had finished loading his horse and led him out into the yard to wait for Grant.

"Lucas, I want to go with you," Sam announced as he walked up to him.

"This is very dangerous work, Sam."

"I know. But, I know how to use a gun. Winda taught me," the young man pleaded, looking Lucas right in the eyes.

"It's different if you have to shoot a man, Sam."

Sam looked toward the woods, digging the dirt with the toe of his shoe. "I've never been anywhere before now. I don't want to go home yet."

Lucas understood. Jeb's memory was still fresh in Sam's mind. "Let me talk to Grant then. It's his call."

"Thank you, Lucas."

Grant lead his horse out and went back to get Dusty's mount. Lucas caught up to him half way back to the barn. "Sam wants to come with us."

Grant looked at the youth standing in the middle of the yard. "I don't know. It could get too dangerous."

That's what I told him. But it will give us another gun. And Squirrel could help us."

"I'd hate to be responsible if anything goes wrong."

"I'll be responsible for him," Lucas said. "I think we could use another hand. Even if he is green."

Grant paused as he muddled this through his mind. "Okay, we'll both be responsible for him then."

"I'll go get him a horse." Lucas waved to Sam, who came running. "You're going to prove what kind of a man you are, son."

Grinning, Sam saddled his own horse then ran over to say goodbye to Winda and Sophie. The brothers pushed Dusty onto an old, slow horse, and tied him down. Sam was shaking the boys' hands when Lucas kissed his wife before jumping onto his own horse.

"I'll be back, Sophie," Sam promised the giddy girl.

"You be careful, Sam, you hear?" she ordered.

Carrie got a peck on the cheek from Sam, then Winda another hug. "See ya in a couple of weeks. Don't worry about me. I'll be fine."

Lucas bent down for another kiss. Winda gave him worried look. "Please come back to me, my love. Be safe."

"I will. You look after yourself, and the baby." He teased the boys and said goodbye to Carrie.

Grant told everyone goodbye except one person. He walked up to Carrie and offered his hand.

Lucas grinned as Grant approached Carrie. She reached out to shake his hand, but he grabbed it instead, pulling her to him. "I know I haven't been forthcoming to you. I hope you understand and forgive me, Carrie." He kissed her quickly, before she could pull away. "Please say you will wait for me at Jeb's."

"I will wait," she said, weakly.

Dusty sat on his horse throwing daggers at them then he looked away as if he'd realized his farce was over. He had no more claim on Carrie. But Lucas knew that he still vowed to kill Grant.

Pete was in a better mood since the men had gone; each for a different reason. Dusty was obvious, he was trouble, and he hated the man for bringing Carrie and the law to his farm. Lucas still frightened him. Then, there was Sam. Finally, he's out of Sophie's life, and would stay out if he could help it. He didn't know what Grant had planned for him but feared the worse. He could still be charged for fraud and smuggling. He liked Anthony, though. When they were alone, he brought out a bottle of rum. They sat on the front porch and watched Adam and Johnny play on a swing that Grant hung in a tree. The women were inside baking apple pies.

"I'm sorry about Mary," Gert told Carrie. "We had no choice. She was just too far gone. The doctor wouldn't hear of us looking after her. She needs too much care." Gert looked guilty for sending her sister away. She kept twisting the cuff on her sleeve.

"I understand, Aunt Gert." Mixed emotions fluttered through Carrie. Mary had never been a strong person. At that moment, she realized that she had missed her aunt a lot more than her own mother, and felt ashamed for it. "Did you know that Ivan wasn't my father?"

"Not until just before we found out he was dead."

"Do you know who my real father is?"

"No. All I know is that he died. Your mother was sent to Kingston where unwed mothers go. She was supposed to have the baby then give it up for adoption. Then she met Ivan."

Winda handed them each a cup of tea and joined them at the table. "The last of the pies are in. She inhaled deeply. "I love the smell of pies cooking." After a sip of tea she faced Carrie. "It seems neither of us know where our fathers are. At least you know your mother."

Gert put her hands, one on each woman's hands in a friendly gesture then turned to Winda. "Are you going to look for your parents, dear?"

Winda shook her head. "No. I am sure they are not alive anymore. They died from smallpox about six years ago. I think if they were alive, I would have heard something by now. Besides, I was raised Ojibwa. I was captured by them when I was little. I am actually Cree. I do not remember my own language or beliefs anymore." Winda chuckled. "Now I think I am turning white."

"Well," Carrie told her. "You arc bctter than a lot of white people. You just be yourself, Winda."

"Thank you."

Sophie sat quietly as if remembering her own mother who had only died a couple of years ago. Carrie knew just how much the young girl missed her.

The boys were put to bed early that night to be woken up before dawn next morning. "Are we going home today?" Adam asked after Carrie shook him awake.

Johnny yawned, "Yes, Adam. That's why we're are up when it's still dark outside."

After a pancake breakfast with lots of syrup, the buggy was loaded with supplies. Anthony gave Pete advice on investing while they saddled horses for those riding. Both boys were lifted on one horse while Winda and Carrie rode on their own horses. Gert and Anthony sat in the buggy on new pillows to cushion their bottoms. The journey home began.

21

Little Blossom ran down the hill to meet the warriors riding toward the village. Pakwis jumped down from his horse when she was near. He lifted her and held her tight, kissing her hungrily. "Little Blossom, I have missed you so much."

"I have missed you too, my husband. I am so glad you are home."

Pakwis could see it in her eyes. She was looking for signs of guilt, of betrayal. Hoping that Lucas had been able to keep him away from Winda.

"I have some sad news," she finally said. "Sleeping Rabbit lost her baby. She is not well."

Pakwis watched Night Wind enter his wigwam with a sinking heart. "Where is my daughter? She is well?"

"She is fine. Growing up fast. And ready to be fed." Little Blossom took his hand and led her husband toward their own lodge. "Come, Pakwis, I will fix you something to eat."

White Mouse had grown significantly since he left a few months ago. He played with her while Little Blossom fixed a meal for him. His daughter laughed at him while he made faces at her, her chubby little hands and legs waving wildly in mid air.

Little Blossom handed Pakwis a hunk of bannock filled with berries. "Six families left since you went away, moving further west. Three elders died, probably of old age. One boy broke his arm, and one man was killed while out hunting."

Pakwis told her he would visit the families of the dead and injured tomorrow. Today he just wanted to rest and be with his own family. He knew the people that moved on and wished them well. "Sometimes I wonder if we should move further west." He tore off a piece of the bread with his teeth and chewed. He noticed the slight smile before she turned back to her chore. If they moved further west then Winda would be out of his reach. He changed the subject. "Tell me about Sleeping Rabbit."

"Shortly after you left, she started getting pains. She had no energy. The shaman tried to save the baby. He prayed over them but, his powers were not enough. She lost it anyway." She spooned stew into a bowl and handed it to Pakwis. "He buried it someplace." White Mouse was put to her mother's breast to feed. "Sleeping Rabbit is getting weaker and weaker." She sighed, "I think she is giving up this world. I was hoping Night Wind's return will help her spirits get well again."

Pakwis nodded between bites. "Maybe I should send for a better shaman."

Night Wind had entered a dark lodge. The smell of sickness almost over-powering him. After lighting a small fire in the pit, he looked toward their bed where his wife lay motionless. He knelt down beside her. "Hello my husband," a weak voice rasped. "I lost our baby. Our son is gone, our baby is gone."

Night Wind closed his eyes at the mention of Lost Boy. His heart still missed his son. He also grieved for the baby he never saw. He opened his tear-filled eyes. "Sleeping Rabbit. I'm home now. I will help you get better," his voice quavered. "I am sorry about the baby, Sleeping Rabbit. You have to get better now."

He held her limp hand gently and kissed her cheek. "We can have other children." The tears pooled in his eyes. *She's not fighting to stay alive!* "Sleeping Rabbit. I need you. Do not give up. Please." He held her close to him, swaying back and forth in agony and desperation. "I love you, Sleeping Rabbit."

Softly, she replied. "So sorry."

He felt her life slip away from her body and held her for along time. Exhausted, he slowly laid her head down and closed her eyelids. His body sagged to the floor where he sat and cried.

"We should be in Greenstown in about three days," Grant told Lucas and Sam.

Sam nodded; he would breathe easier after depositing their prisoner. They were leading the horses down a steep hill, pulling Dusty's horse while he still rode tied up. Sam could feel the steely glare on his back; the hairs on the back of his neck were scratchy. Dusty had said very little during the trip which was just fine with all of them.

"Good," Lucas acknowledged. He puffed out his breath and watched the vapours float into the air. "It's going to be another cold night."

"Starting to snow," Sam informed them.

"Already? It's too early to snow," exclaimed Lucas, even though he should have known it wasn't. Light flakes floated down and landed on his nose. "Well I'll be!" The trees were still full of colour. Sam chuckled.

They found a nice small clearing in a stand of cedars at the bottom of the hill. "I think we should camp here tonight. What do you think, Sam?" Grant asked.

"Fine with me. I'd like to turn in early tonight." It still surprised him when these big men asked for his opinion on important matters, which they both did often. It made him feel grown up. Grant and Lucas helped Dusty down while he gathered firewood. Squirrel chased a black squirrel up a tree. He circled it barking until Sam scolded him. They had a quick meal and bedded down early.

Sam lay shivering with his blanket over his head, wide awake. The wind had picked up. The snow turned into freezing rain which pelted down on them. He peeked into the darkness. The fire was out. He could make out Dusty sitting against the tree, head down, snoring. Grant and Lucas were both sleeping soundly in their bedrolls. Sam shut his eyes, hoping to get in a few hours of sleep before daybreak. An hour later he heard a movement and peeked over the edge of the blanket. Dusty was getting up. Somehow, he had freed himself. Sam watched as the big man headed toward Lucas, lifting a large rock high over his head with both hands.

Sam jumped up, pulled out his pistol and aimed it at the big man, trying to hold it steady. "Stop."

Dusty froze. "You ain't going to shoot your pa, now are you?"

"You ain't my pa. You killed my pa."

"Well now, you don't know everything now do ya." Dusty lowered his arms. "How do you think you got blue eyes, my boy?" He slowly walked toward Sam. The rock was thrown, missing Sam by mere inches. The gun went flying.

Sam fell backwards. Lucas and Grant jumped up. Dusty dove at Sam. Squirrel knocked Dusty down on the wet ground. His teeth snapping at his arms and legs. Dusty kicked at the dog and missed. Squirrel aimed for his throat but got a shoulder instead.

Sam crawled out of the way. Squirrel's big jaw clamped down on Dusty's arm. He screamed. He tried beating the beast off him, but Squirrel was all over him.

Behind them, Lucas rushed to stop the dog. Grant grabbed his brother and held him back. Sam knew he wouldn't help Dusty. Not after he'd tried to kill him. Especially not after he'd raped Carrie over and over. And not after all the abuse and heartache this man had caused.

Dusty had somehow gotten to his feet and started to run but slipped on he wet grass. The dog knocked him down and tore at his side. Dusty swatted at Squirrel with little effect. He screamed as the dog sunk his teeth into his arm and shook his head violently. Blood gushed out splattering Squirrel. Sam just stood there, blinking through the rain, and watched his dog tear the man to pieces. Finally Dusty's screams stopped. He lay on the wet ground soaked in blood. Sam grabbed Squirrel and held him back.

"He ain't my pa, is he?" Sam wanted desperately to believe that.

"No, he isn't, Sam," Lucas told him. "He just wanted to mess with your head so he could attack you, that's all."

God, I hope your right, Sam thought.

Sam looked down as blood slowly spread out from under Dusty. Only to be washed away from the rain.

"He's not going to make it." Dusty was still, eyes bulging out. Lucas bent down to feel for a pulse. "He's gone."

Grant stood there, smiling.

Greenstown had doubled in size since Grant had last been there. They hitched the horses up in front of the militia office and went inside, stomping mud from their boots. All three took off their dripping hats and stood in the office as water dripped from their raincoats and puddling on the floor.

"Major Sievers." General Brooks rounded his desk and grabbed Grant's hand, pumping it up and down enthusiastically. "Glad to see you're back."

"We got him, General. Dusty Blackman. But I'm afraid he won't be standing trial." The general lifted an eyebrow. Grant pointed out of the window. Dusty's body lay draped over a horse. "He was attacked by an animal a couple of days ago."

General Brooks went outside to inspect the body. Grant was confident that the wounds would tell the general that he was telling him the truth, and that the description the general had of the man would confirm that it was indeed Dusty Blackman.

When he returned, General Brooks asked, "What kind of animal did all that?"

"Squirrel," both Grant and Lucas answered at once. Grant glanced over at Sam, who seemed tongue-tied in front of such an imposing figure as this general. He knew Sam had never been this close to anyone with such authority before.

"A squirrel?" A disapproving look studied the men in his office. "And who are you?" demanded Brooks as he faced Lucas.

"I'm Lucas, sir. Grant's brother. And this is my son, Sam." Devilish eyes watched the general's surprised look.

Grant snickered beside him. Sam's mouth dropped open.

General Brooks watched the man who dressed like an Indian, but had a black son. "So you have a black wife?"

"No, I have an Indian wife." Lucas smirked.

Grant almost burst out laughing at the general's confusion.

Sam stood taller and finally closed his mouth. "Well, you did tell me that your family was different," the general said to Grant.

General Brooks looked down. "That's the biggest dog I've ever seen. He friendly?"

Squirrel was sitting beside Sam. "Ah, this here is Squirrel," Sam told him in a high-pitched voice.

"Dusty tried to escape. He attacked Sam here and the dog stopped him," Grant informed his superior. "We couldn't stop it in time."

General Brooks went to the door and called his sergeant. "Take the body down to the doc's. Tell him to do an autopsy for cause of death."

When he returned, he addressed both brothers. "I suggest you stay in town until I get the results back." Taken aback, the brothers nodded their heads in unison and went down the street to find a room for the night.

"He thinks we killed Dusty, doesn't he?" Lucas said after they were standing in their room. "I'm not a murderer." He looked over at his brother. "Does it count when you're hungry?"

Grant tossed his gear into the corner. "What are you talking about?"

"Well," Lucas plopped down on a wooden chair, nearly tipping it over. "When I was with Pakwis. We stole some cattle. Killed four men."

"For food?" Sam asked.

"Yep."

Lucas didn't get an answer. Instead Grant said, "He just wants to make sure we didn't shoot Dusty first."

They weren't summoned to the general's office until the following afternoon. Sam decided to wait outside for them to watch the militia men parade in the field across the street.

Both brothers stood with their hats in their hands and waited for agonizing minutes for the general to finish up his paperwork. When he finished, he took off his glasses, reached for a cigar and lit it. After savouring a couple of puffs, he addressed the men. "I got a dispatch this morning. Seems that General Walton died, lead poisoning." He paused and squinted at them then checked a paper on his desk. "It seems the cause of death of Mr. Blackman is 'mauled by a bear."

Grant and Lucas let out a sigh of relief. "A bear?" Grant asked. "But it was a dog."

"Yep." The general ignored him. "He escaped and got tangled up with a bear. Right?"

"Yes, sir." Grant saluted.

"That way, there will be no hearing." General Brooks pulled out two more cigars and handed them out. "Looks like we've avoided a full-out war here. We've confiscated hundreds of guns and ammunition. All the smugglers are accounted for, as far as we know. They've captured the ship in Montreal that was bringing the guns in. The whole crew has been arrested."

"So tell me." He faced Lucas. "How is it you have an Indian wife and a black son?"

Sam leaned against the building outside the general's office watching the men do their daily routine. Squirrel lay at his feet with his head on his paws and let out a loud yawn. Sam especially liked watching them drill on the field across from him. Back and forth they marched in perfect unison, in the slush. It had finally stopped raining. The sun competed with the clouds overhead.

Down further, some men were target shooting. Sam wished that he could join them and practise what Winda had taught him. But, he told himself, he wasn't cut out to be an army man. He also thought he was too young. Although some looked a lot younger than he was. *I'm only seventeen.*

"Hey, you lookin' for a job, n——?" Two boys his age approached him, nudging each other. When they got too close, Squirrel stood up growling. They stopped. "Bet you ain't so tough when your dog ain't around," one dared.

"Squirrel, stop." The dog sat back down and quieted, but kept a close eye on the intruders. "What y'all want?" Sam was going to play the 'dumb n——' some people just expected him to be. They just automatically see a black man and expect him to act like a fool.

"You named your dog Squirrel?" they laughed.

"Ya, you got a problem with that?"

"That's a dumb name."

"What would you call him, then?" Sam was getting braver.

"Well now. How about Chicken? Ya, I like that one."

"He don't like Chicken," taunted Sam.

"What about you? You come to Chicken?"

"Naw. That ain't my name neither."

The boys started losing patience with this n——. Sam saw it on their faces. "You come anyway, or we'll beat you up."

"Why that?"

"Because, we don't like n——."

"Well now, Squirrel here don't like stupid fools either. And when he sees one, well, I can't hold him back. See?"

The boys looked from Sam to the dog and back to Sam.

"Let's go." One pushed the other one back. "You just wait when your dog's not around," he threatened as they turned and ran.

Sam continued his vigil in front of the office. He watched a wagon pull up to the general store a couple of buildings down. Two uniformed men jumped down and went inside. He sprinted over and watched through the window then ran back inside the office. "Grant, I saw one."

"Saw one what, Sam?" Grant stubbed out his cigar.

"One of Dusty's friends. I saw them talking in the tavern. They had a meeting. Just like you did." *Whoops.* Sam knew he'd slipped.

"What do you mean, just like I did?" Grant narrowed his eyes.

"That's where he met all the other men that helped him with the guns. He's here. In the store."

All three men rushed out into the slushy street and brought back the two officers. "Which one did you see?" General Brooks asked the shaking youth.

"That one," Sam pointed.

"And this one?" The general indicated the other man who stood there looking dumbfounded.

"No, never seen him before."

Brooks clasped his hands behind his back and walked around the two men eyeing them with contempt. On his third round he stopped behind the first man Sam had pointed to. "What have you got to say for yourself Lieutenant Baker?

The lieutenant swallowed then pulled on his collar, mumbling under his breath.

General Brooks walked around and stood in front of Baker. "Sorry. Did you just tell me that you were working for Dusty Blackman? That you committed treason by going against your country?"

Baker's face reddened. The other man looked at him in astonishment then took a step sideways, away from his companion. "You've defiled your uniform, sir."

"Sergeant," yelled the general. "Take Lieutenant Baker into custody."

The sergeant pulled his gun out and led Lieutenant Baker away. The other man was let go after being questioned.

"Well. I hope that was the last one," sighed the general.

Lucas turned to Sam "Good job, son."

Lucas wanted to get back to Jeb's before the heavy snows came. He sensed that Grant just wanted to get away. "What are you going to do now?" Lucas asked him.

"I've officially resigned my commission. General Brooks let me go in good standing." Grant chuckled. "He even pleaded for me to stay on, bribing me with a promotion."

Lucas watched his brother as they rode side by side. "I mean, what are your plans now?"

"Oh." Grant smiled slyly at him. "I think I might just settle down with a certain little red-head."

Lucas was expecting this and hoped his brother's dreams would come true. He liked Carrie a lot, and would be happy to have her as a sister-in-law. He also knew that she had her reservations when it came to Grant. *Will he be able to convince her?* Everyone could see that he was head over heals over her. "Have you asked her yet?"

"No. But, I'm going to when we get back."

They watched Sam and Squirrel just ahead of them. "Who knew that Sam was spying for Jeb, " Grant said. "I don't know how to take that. The boy spying on me." He urged his horse to go a little faster. "But that's how Jeb knew for sure about Dusty's involvement in the smuggling ring. And he gave them names."

Lucas nodded. "And then he did the right thing and informed the authorities." He sensed his brother was a little perturbed with Sam, who he considered his son now. "Which was a big help in your investigation. Right?"

"Ya, sure was." Then Grant looked at his brother and grinned. "It's just a little discerning to find out you've been spied on when you're doing the spying."

Lucas punched Grant's arm. "All in a days work, big brother."

After riding in silence for a few miles. Grant asked Lucas, " What are your plans?"

"I don't know. All I know is that Winda won't leave Sam behind. Neither will I."

Lucas watched Sam and his dog. Squirrel seemed to be a little listless. *He's slowing down. Poor old dog.*

"So, you really have adopted him, then?"

"Yeah," Lucas laughed. "I've adopted him all right. I feel like the dad he's never had. I can't believe Dusty told him he was his father. Do you believe that?"

"I think he just wanted to mess with the kid, is all," Grant told him seriously. "He is a good kid."

Lucas wasn't too sure about those accusations. "What about Adam and Johnny?" Grant was silent for so long that Lucas was about to repeat the question.

"Carrie won't give them up," said Grant. "Maybe they'll forget about their real dad. They're young enough."

"Johnny did try to shoot him," reminded Lucas. "Neither of them liked Dusty. Even feared him. That's no way for kids to live."

"No. And Carrie has been so good to them, even though they aren'thers either. And as far as I know, they don't have anywhere else to go."

"So," continued Lucas, "like me, seems you have to take the whole package."

"Looks like, little brother."

"Looks like, big brother."

Carrie opened the cabin door and walked inside. The first thing she saw was the pistol on one of the small tables. Quickly, she snatched it up and stuffed it under her pillow on her bed. She didn't want to look at it right now. Nor did she want Johnny to see it. *It'll only bring back bad memories for him.*

Winda followed Carrie inside and looked around as if expecting Jeb to greet her. She stopped in centre of the room and looked sadly at her friend. Carrie, seeing that she looked lost, hugged her. "I miss him too."

Both women took deep breaths and wiped their eyes. Then the boys ran in, jumped on their own bed, and started playing with their wooden toys that Jeb and Lucas had made for them.

Gert and Anthony followed. Anthony dropped his load of bags on the floor and looked around the cabin. "It's quite the charming little place, isn't it?"

Gert laughed at him. "Yes it is. I love it. It's small, but quite practical."

Carrie took her by the arm and led her around. "This is the main kitchen, the grand dining room, the golden parlour, the master suite and oh, the north wing is behind that wall." Everyone laughed at her grandeur performance.

"Oh!" Gert walked over to Carrie's bed, tears filling her eyes. "You still have the quilt."

Winda spoke up. "She rescued it from a tornado."

"Tornado?" Gert looked astounded at her niece. "Tell me all the details. I want to know everything."

"I'll make us some tea," volunteered Winda. "I know I could use some."

"Yes," agreed Anthony. "We can unload the buggy later. I want to hear this too."

"C'mon Squirrel, get up," cried Sam. His dog had just laid down on the trail and refused to move. Sam tried to lift him but the animal was just too heavy. Tears ran down the boy's face, soaking his coat.

Squirrel looked up at him with big, sad brown eyes, as if he was saying sorry he had to go. He thumped his tail, put his head down, and stopped breathing. Sam cradled Squirrel's head in his lap.

Lucas and Grant watched, swallowing hard and trying not to break down too. "He was just too old, Sam." Lucas rubbed the boy's head. "He had a good, full life. He was lucky to have you as his friend."

"We'll bury him." Grant said then dug a shallow hole. It took both men to carry the dog and lay him in it. They covered him up and Grant said a short prayer over the grave.

Lucas put his arm around the boy. "We are all going to miss him."

Sam stood at the grave, head down. "He was my best friend."

"I know, Sam." Lucas looked up at the heavy clouds rolling in. "We have to go, Sam, there's a storm coming." Gently, he pulled Sam away and helped him up on his horse.

Sam wiped his face on his sleeve then looked at Lucas with sad, blue eyes. "Am I really your son now?"

"Yes, Sam. If that's what you want."

Sam reached down and hugged him. "I really need a dad right now."

Lucas held on to him. "I need you too, Sam."

Sam smiled through his tears at him and kicked his horse into a slow walk. A few yards down the trail, he turned and looked back. "Good bye, Squirrel."

Lucas and Grant rode behind him. "Too bad," Grant said.

22

1803. Lucas just wanted to go to his room at the boarding house, have a hot meal and a good night's sleep. He was cold, tired and miserable. It was late and dark, just like his mood. Then he remembered, "*Oh ya! I'm married now.*

He watched Grant head in that direction while he took Sam home and to find his wife. When they arrived, Winda was the only one there.

"Where is everyone?" Sam asked.

To Lucas, the cabin seemed too empty and lonely. There was no sign of the boys. Carrie's pretty quilt was missing. Her aunt and uncle had left. Everything was back to the way it was before Carrie had moved in with them, he was sure.

Winda ran up to him, hugged and kissed him hungrily. He looked down at her swollen belly and patted it. "Hello, little one."

Winda smiled at him, "I missed you so much, Lookas." He hugged her tight, a sense of foreboding running through his veins. When she pulled away, tears were in her eyes. "Carrie went back with her aunt and uncle. Took the boys with her."

"What?" Lucas couldn't believe what he was hearing. "Why? I thought she was going to wait for Grant?"

"I think she is uncertain of her feelings. You know, too soon after Dusty."

A slow whistle escaped from Lucas. "This is really going to upset Grant."

Winda looked around then asked Sam, "Are you not going to let Squirrel inside?"

The boy looked at her through hazy eyes. "He's dead, Winda."

Her hand flew to her mouth. "How?"

Sam told her. "He just laid down and died."

"I am so sorry, Sam." They stood in the middle of the room, hugging each other.

It was just like when Jeb died, Lucas thought as he watched them. "He was just too old." Lucas also grieved for the big, black dog.

Sam pulled away and wiped his eyes on his sleeve. "Can we eat? I'm starving."

Winda smiled through her tears and went to fix supper. Sam headed for the other side of the room.

"Look at this, Dad," Sam said a moment later.

Shocked at the new name Sam afforded him, Lucas stammered with delight. "Yes, son?"

Winda looked surprised and smiled. "I am glad," she said to Lucas. "He has already taken to calling me Ma."

Sam held out Carrie's little pistol. "It was stuck in that crack." He pointed to the corner where Carrie's bed had been. The three stood silently looking at it. Each one with their own memories floating by. Most of them were of Dusty and his brutal ways. Sam tucked it back where he'd found it then walked closer to them.

"Let's eat," Winda whispered.

"Yes. I'm starving, too." Lucas put his arms around his family and turned them toward the kitchen. "Did you cook up a horse? I know I could eat one?"

After their huge meal, Lucas sat drinking his coffee and told his wife. "By the way, Dusty is dead."

Winda just smiled.

Everyone woke up with a start the following morning from someone banging on the door. Sam jumped out of bed, wiping sleep from his eyes. Winda plodded into the kitchen and lit the stove.

"Morning, Grant." Sam squinted into the sun as he held the door open for his new uncle.

"Morning to you," laughed Grant as the young man yawned hugely. "You don't even have your eyes open yet, do you Sam?" A ruffle of the black wavy hair sent the boy back to get dressed.

Winda was putting coffee on while Lucas struggled into his pants. "Hi, Grant," Winda greeted him. Grant rewarded her with a big kiss on the cheek.

"She's gone," Lucas said as he joined them.

Grant's good humour soured when he saw that Carrie wasn't there. He scowled. "I don't understand it. I thought we had something between us?" He paced back and forth, pushing his hair back out of his eyes.

"Grant, sit down before you wear a hole in the floor," ordered Lucas

"Yes, you are making me dizzy," added his wife.

Sam, fully dressed now, slid into a chair and waited for his breakfast. Winda served the rest of them then sat down.

Grant looked sheepishly at her, fearing he'd make her sick, so he plumped down on the nearest chair. Winda put a cup of coffee in front of him, then a plate of bacon and eggs. He took a couple of bites then set his fork down. "What's got into her?" Pleading eyes asked Winda to give him an answer he could accept.

"I think she just got overwhelmed. Everything happening too fast for her." Winda leaned in closer and put her hand over his. "She does care for you, you know? A lot. I have seen the way she watches you. But do not forget, she doesn't really know who you are, either. Does she?"

"She probably needs to get over being tossed around by Dusty," added Lucas. "I can't imagine the stuff he put her through." He'd finished his eggs.

"A lot," Winda told them. "He kept her isolated for a long time. Left her in a cabin in the middle of nowhere for weeks at a time. Then he left her in the tavern in a strange town, not knowing anybody. He actually took her to meet his fist wife, if that's what you want to call her? And," she sighed, "don't forget the belittling and hitting he did to her."

"That's a lot to get over isn't it?" Sam asked. He shivered, picturing the beatings. He remembered seeing bruises on Carrie before. He picked up a piece of bacon and chewed on it.

"Yes, it is," Lucas told him quietly. "I think she just needs a little time, Grant."

Winda picked up the empty plates and poured a round of coffee. "It has been so lonely here with her and the boys gone. So quiet."

Grant sat back in his chair. "Well. I don't intend on giving up on her." He looked at his brother. "But first, I think we should see to Dusty's property."

"You mean to see if he left a will?" Lucas nodded. "We don't even know what he has."

"What about this place?" Sam asked, indicating the cabin.

"We have to find that out too," Lucas told him. "We don't know if Jeb owned it or if Dusty did."

Sam looked around at the familiar surroundings. It was the only home he'd ever known. After a few minutes he told everyone. "That's okay if I have to move. As long as I can go with you two."

Lucas squeezed his arm. "You can always go with us, Sam. You're part of this family now. Don't ever forget that."

Pakwis threw back the flap on his wigwam and stepped out into the morning rain of early spring. He frowned as he headed over to the shaman's dwelling and scratched on the door.

"Enter," the shaman said from inside.

Pakwis stepped into the wigwam. The shaman was sitting at his fire smoking a pipe. He waved an arm, inviting Pakwis to join him. Pakwis sat down and crossed his legs at the ankle, knees up. Protocol dictated that he waited for the shaman to speak first. The shaman re-filled his pipe, made sure it was lit by sucking on it, then offered it to Pakwis. Pakwis inhaled the tobacco, blowing the smoke up toward the smoke hole in the wigwam. He then handed the pipe back.

After the shaman smoked for a bit he set the pipe aside. "You look troubled, my chief."

"I am worried about Night Wind. His heart has not healed from losing Sleeping Rabbit, or his children."

"He needs time. Some people take longer than others for their grief to become bearable."

"It has been since before the snow came. All he does is sit in his wigwam and mourn for her. He has not been out hunting or fishing. I have been doing that for him but he eats very little. It is time for him to do these things for himself. He needs a purpose."

The shaman's rheumy eyes studied Pakwis. "You have fed him all winter. Now that game should be more abundant you do not want to anymore?"

"It is not that. I fear for him. I am a afraid that he has lost the will to live."

"What if he has?"

Pakwis narrowed his eyes. "I do not want to lose my best friend."

"Aw," the shaman smiled. "You are greedy for your friend."

Pakwis just sat there, well aware how this shaman liked to turn things around so that a person looked at things in a different way. He nodded. "I do not want Night Wind to die."

"Maybe he wants to join Sleeping Rabbit."

"He is young. He could live for many summers yet. Maybe he will find love again. I wish this for my friend."

They sat there in silence for quite awhile. Finally the shaman said, "I will pray for your friend. I too believe that he is too young to die."

Anthony locked the front door to his bank and pocketed the key. It was late. He looked hungry and tired and probably just wanted to get home. He turned and watched a regiment of British soldiers marching down the street.

Grant walked up and stopped beside him. "Mr. Paterson."

Anthony jumped. "Well, hello, Major."

"I'm not in the militia anymore, Mr. Paterson. Please, just call me Grant." He wondered where the soldiers were headed.

"Okay, then. Grant. I take it you are here for Carrie?" The banker started to sweat as they walked toward his house. Grant fell in step with him.

"Yes," the tall man told him. " I want to know if I even have a chance with her at all."

"Oh. I think you do, Ma-, ah, Grant. Yes, very much so." Anthony said. "Come, her and the boys are at our house."

Grant followed Carrie's uncle down the busy street. He watched as people rushed about doing their daily business. Grant, however, was trying to enjoy the bright sunny spring day. He had noticed the first blooming wildflowers when he rode into York earlier.

"Please, join us for supper tonight, Grant. I'm sure the boys will be delighted to see you."

"Thank you. I will." Grant squinted at Anthony. *Why is he so nervous?* The banker was fidgeting with his shirt collar as they walked.

Anthony led him to a two-story, yellow brick house with a big front porch and a huge maple tree in the front yard that was starting to bud. The front door swung open, Johnny dashed out and jumped up on Grant.

"I knew you would come. I told Adam, but he didn't believe me." Long, skinny arms hugged him, the boy squirmed excitedly. *My, he has grown! I didn't realize I would miss them so much!* He set the boy down. "Hi there, soldier. Where's your brother?"

Johnny grabbed his hand and pulled him into the house, yelling for Adam. Adam slid down the polished banister from the second floor. He smiled triumphantly at Grant when he landed on his feet at the bottom. "Hi, Adam," Grant laughed. "How are you?"

Adam hugged him. "You came back."

Both boys left giggling after Anthony told them to wash up for supper.

Gert rushed into the front hall after hearing a commotion, she spotted Grant. "Well, hello, Major. Glad to see you."

He kissed her plump cheek. "Hello, Mrs. Paterson. Please, just call me Grant. I'm not in the militia anymore." Then he told both of them. "I retired after my last assignment." He told them of Dusty's death and how Squirrel had just laid down and died.

"So, everything is done with all that, now?" Gert asked.

"Yes, everything." Nobody wanted to mention Dusty's name again.

Gert leaned toward Grant and whispered, "She's out back. In the garden." And pushed him toward the back door. "Supper will be ready shortly. Don't forget."

Grant stopped with his hand on the doorknob and looked back. He saw Anthony put his arms around his wife. "You really like him, don't you?"

She blushed. "Yes, I do. I think he's just what Carrie needs. I've seen how they watch each other. Although Carrie tries to hide it."

Anthony smiled at her. "Always the romantic, aren't you?"

Grant grinned as he opened the door. He found Carrie, bent over in the garden planting seeds. He watched her bum swinging in mid air as she dug into the dirt. He let out a low, suggestive whistle.

Carrie jumped up, too quickly, got dizzy and staggered. Grant caught her in his arms and steadied her. When she could focus again, she threw her arms around his neck and plastered him with kisses. "Oh, Grant."

He led her to a nearby bench. "I'm glad to see you too, Carrie." He sat down beside her. She must of realized what she just did because she blushed.

That evening, Gert and Anthony sat drinking wine at their dining table to give the young couple in the other room some privacy. "Maybe having him in the family won't be such a bad idea, Gert," Anthony whispered. "If we do get arrested for stealing Ivan's money, well, maybe he could lessen the charge, or something."

Gert's head bobbed. "That's the only thing I worry about. I'm almost ashamed we took it. What were we supposed to do? We don't have that kind of money."

"Not after the trip we took."They'd spent half of what Anthony had saved in his so called charity fund. He'd have to rebuild it. "Technically," Anthony rubbed his chin. "It is Mary's money now. That's if the smugglers don't come for it. How could they prove it was theirs?" Anthony tried to reassure himself as well as Gert. "How could they? Usually people like that don't keep records, you know, a bill of sale or anything."

"Yes, but I think I'd feel better if we didn't do it on the sly like we did." She looked toward the other room. "I really like Grant."

They talked quietly, while half listening to Carrie and Grant in the parlour.

Carrie sat on the settee against the wall watching Grant pace back and forth in front of her. "I just don't know, Grant." She was saying, "I still feel married to Dusty, as weird as that sounds."

Grant stopped and sat down beside her, taking her hands into his. "All I can tell you right now is that I love you, Carrie. Will you at least consider being my wife?" Still she hesitated. His hands flew up in desperation. At the sudden movement, Carrie's eyes widened. She recoiled into the settee and started shaking, her eyelids flickering.

Quickly, he lowered his arms and pulled her to him, holding her tight. He rocked her and kissed her forehead. "I'm so sorry, Carrie. I didn't mean to scare you," he soothed. "That's the last thing I want to do, is to hurt you. Please forgive me. I will never hit you."

She pulled back, tears in her eyes and studied his face. He looked so miserable and full of anguish that she smiled weakly at him. "I know that, Grant. I know that." But she shook. "That's what I mean. It's going to take some time to get over…him."

"I know that, sweetheart, I know." Grant kissed her softly, wiping the tears tenderly from her cheeks. "I want to protect you from going through that kind of stuff ever again."

So, what is holding me back? Carrie wondered. *Why do I feel torn so? What is it about this man that draws me?* She watched his hazel eyes that tugged at her heart. His lips looked soft and warm and inviting. She loved the way his long hair hung over his eyes and touched the top of his collar. She loved the smell of him. She leaned into him to inhale his scent. Grant's arms enfolded her. *It just seems so natural being here.* And yes, she did feel completely safe with him.

"I didn't mean to leave you in the dark about my true identity, Carrie. Please believe that ."

"Mmm." Her eyes had closed. *Am I dreaming? Is he really here? For me? Why do I feel numb?*

Carrie sat up and watched his gorgeous eyes hunger for her only. "I already do, Grant." She loved saying his name. "I love you."

"Yes," came a cheer from the dining room. "Well," Grant laughed, "at least they're happy about it."

Carrie's face turned hot. "I know they all like you too, Grant."

"Well, at least I don't have to convince them."

He looked seriously at her. "Do you really mean it Carrie? Please say it again."

She looked into his handsome face and told him again. "I do love you, Grant. I will marry you."

Lucas sat in the lawyer's office holding Winda's hand. Sam fidgeted in his seat on the other side of him. They had dressed up for the occasion. Winda wore a light blue dress and a matching bonnet. Sam had on new trousers and a green shirt. Lucas had changed out of his buckskins and was in his grey shirt and darker grey pants. The lawyer shuffled papers around on the desk before looking up and peering at them through wire-rimmed glasses. "This is very unorthodox, Mr. Sievers."

"It's what we all want," Lucas said, his voice had a finality to it. He had made up his mind. And if this lawyer was unwilling to do as they asked he'd go somewhere else.

The lawyer frowned then looked over at Sam. "But to adopt a black boy?"

Anger seethed inside Lucas. "He's part white. Can't you tell by the light colour of his skin, his wavy hair, or from his blue eyes? His father was Dusty Blackman. He's dead." Lucas produced Dusty's death certificate he'd gotten through General Brooks. "Sam's mother died years ago." He handed over the document.

After the lawyer studied it he set it down on his desk then glanced up at Winda. "You are married to this man?"

"Yes," she beamed at Lucas.

Still hesitant, the lawyer addressed Sam. "You're almost old enough to be on your own. You don't need to be adopted at your age."

Sam stared at the man across the desk from him. "My grandpa raised me. He is dead," Sam's bottom lip quivered. He pulled himself together then said, "I've never had a ma and pa. I want Winda and Lucas to be my ma and pa."

After studying the three in front of him for a bit the lawyer finally nodded. "Okay. I'll start proceedings right away, Mr. Sievers." He stood and walked around the desk.

Lucas left his chair and shook the outstretched hand. "Thank you."

The three of them left the office and stood outside on the raised wooden sidewalk. Both Winda and Sam were smiling. "I think this calls for a celebration," Lucas said, and ruffled Sam's hair.

"What do you want to do?" Winda asked as she slid her arm into Lucas's.

He headed toward the restaurant down the street. Winda pulled back when they were close. "I do not think they'll let me or Sam in there."

"I was in there before," Sam said. "Sally don't care as long as you can pay real dollars for a meal."

Lucas grinned at Sam. He had been in that restaurant several times when he first moved into Blackman Falls and had flirted with Sally. But unlike Hazel in the boarding house, it was all in fun with Sally. Sally was happily married to the cook. Lucas put his arm around Winda. "She will see what a fine lady you are and serve you. If not, I will never go in there again."

Winda eyed the restaurant for a bit before nodding. "Only one way to find out."

Feeling a bit apprehensive, Lucas led his family through the door. Several people looked up at them. One man jumped up, knocking his chair over. "We don't want that squaw in here. Or that darky."

Lucas stood in front of Winda, his fists clenched at his sides. "It's not up to you. Is it?"

Sally stormed over, stopped beside the gruff looking man and gave him a withering look. "He's right," she said. "I've known Sam since he was a sprout. And his grandpa, Jeb Horne, was the one who really built this here town."

The man pointed to Winda. "That squaw don't belong in here."

Sally jabbed a finger at the man's chest. "You leave her be. She ain't dressed like the squaw you keep up in your cabin. She's as fine a lady as your wife. And if you cause trouble for these people, I will make sure your wife finds out about your squaw."

The man glanced around the room then sat back down in his seat.

Sally smiled at Winda and said, "Right this way."

Grant didn't think it proper that he stayed at Anthony's house, but Gert wouldn't have it any other way. She'd prepared the small room at the end of the hall for him. It was as if the Patersons were pushing him and Carrie together. As he sat in the dining room eating breakfast with them he saw the logic in it as he watched the boys. If he was to marry Carrie, he'd have to get to know Johnny and Adam better.

He pointed his fork at them. "What about schooling?"

"I'm teaching them to read," Carrie said. "And Uncle Anthony is teaching them their numbers."

"Good," Grant said. "I'll show them how to handle a rifle."

Johnny's eyes widened. "I don't want to shoot a person again."

"No," Grant said. "But you do need to learn how to hunt. And to defend yourself." Most ten year olds knew that already. At least that was his opinion.

Seven year old Adam set down his fork. "I can hunt with my slingshot."

"Uncle Anthony doesn't have a gun," Johnny said.

Grant conceded. "He doesn't live in the wilderness either."

"Are we going to live in the wilderness?" Adam asked.

Grant looked over at Carrie. "We haven't decided where we're going to live yet. But as you can guess, I'm not one for city living."

While Grant took the boys out of York to show them how to use a rifle, Carrie went with Gert to the dressmaker's house. "Now don't you worry about paying for your wedding gown," Gert said, as they waited for someone to answer the knock on the door. "It's our gift to you."

"Thanks, Aunt Gert. You've done so much for us all ready." She could hardly wait to pick out the material and hoped that her aunt would let her have her dress made out of satin.

The door opened and the lady stepped aside when she saw Gert. "Mrs. Paterson. How nice to see you again so soon."

They went inside and stood in the vestibule. Gert undid her bonnet, slipped it off her head then held it in her hand. "I'd like to commission you to make a wedding dress for my niece." She indicated Carrie.

The dressmaker looked at Carrie as if sizing her for a dress. "Of course. When is the wedding?"

"In two months," Carrie said.

"Oh?" The lady raised her eyebrows. "In a rush, are we?"

Carrie lifted her chin. "I'm not in the family way. It's just that—-"

"They have to get back out west," Gert came to the rescue. "Her finance` has business out there."

"My apologies," the dressmaker said. Although Carrie could see that she didn't believe them.

"I can pay you extra," Gert said, "to get one made in time."

The dressmaker's face brightened. She waved her arm toward the parlour. "Please. Come in and I'll show you some bolts of fabric."

Anthony hated hospitals. But it didn't stop him from visiting his clients in there. He held a handkerchief to his nose as he walked down the hall. The smell of cleaners, drugs and sickness turned his stomach. He shoved the handkerchief into his pocket before turning into the room he sought; fighting back nauseousness. The practised smile was on his face, not too cheerful but friendly. He went up to the bed and studied the man laying there under a crisp white sheet. His head was wrapped in a bandage, his arms showed bruises, one was in a cast. His eyes were red as if they'd been bleeding. He was hardly coherent. Mr. Grayson had been a client of Anthony's for the last four years.

"Mr. Paterson," the man said. A horse had kicked him in the chest before he was run over by a wagon. Causing internal bleeding and damaging organs beyond repair. The doctor had given him less than a week to live.

Anthony didn't care about the details. He was there to finalize his deal. "I have the papers drawn up." He lifted his briefcase. Mr. Grayson nodded. Anthony set the briefcase on a chair and opened it. He produced a sheet of paper. Then he opened up a jar of ink and dipped a pen into it. "Just sign on the bottom." He handed the paper and pen over.

Mr. Grayson tried to read the paper but his eyes wouldn't focus. He sighed in frustration then signed the paper, dropping his arms on the bed when he was done.

Anthony glanced at the scribbled signature then shoved the paper into his briefcase. "Thank you, Mr. Grayson. The charities you have chosen will be grateful for your donation."

Mr. Grayson had closed his eyes as if that little act had made him exhausted. He just waved a hand weakly as Anthony picked up his briefcase and headed out of the room, smiling.

23

Three weeks later, Winda rubbed her swollen belly and wondered if she was having a boy or a girl. It was the first time she felt the baby kick. She stood in front of the stove waiting for the water to boil for her tea. Lucas had gone to the town hall to see if he could find what Dusty had owned. Maybe get copies of the deeds. Sam had gone fishing with two of his friends. Winda picked up the boiling kettle and poured the water into her cup. She set the kettle back down and turned off the stove. Someone knocked on the door.

The man tipped his hat when she opened it. "Ma'am." He handed her a envelope then went on his way. Winda shut the door then walked over and picked up her cup, studying the envelope in her other hand. It was the first one she'd received that was addressed to her. Lucas had taught her to recognize her name. He had been teaching her and Sam how to read. She knew she didn't know all the letters yet, so she set the envelope on the table then sank down on one of the big chairs to savour her tea.

Lucas came home an hour later. Winda left her chair and showed him the envelope. He opened it and squinted as he read the letter. A smile graced his handsome face. "Well, I'll be." He looked up at his wife. "This is from Anthony. He says that Grant is winning Carrie over. According to Anthony, Grant wants to get married near the end of June."

Winda squealed then kissed Lucas. "That's great. We need to pack."

Lucas set the paper on the table and frowned. "Are you sure you want to go in your condition?"

"Why not? I am only pregnant. I am not sick. Ojibwa women work right up until they go into labour."

Lucas took her into his arms. "I just don't want anything to happen to you."

"I know. But I will be fine, Lookas." She snuggled into him, his arms tightened around her.

Sam ran in, slamming the door behind him. "I caught five fish," he said, excitedly. He lifted up the string of fish to show them.

Winda left the secure arms of her husband and took the fish from Sam. "I will clean these for supper."

Lucas gave Sam's shoulders a squeeze. "Good for you, son."

Sam left his fishing pole leaning against the wall by the door and ran back outside. Winda set the fish on the counter by the wash basin and took out a knife. She unhooked the fish from the string and began to clean them.

Lucas walked up to her and leaned on the stove. "The clerk at the town hall is going to give me copies of Dusty's properties. As it turns out, he owned the tavern, the saw mill, his farm and this cabin."

Night Wind sat on his horse and waited for Pakwis to catch up. They were down in a valley stalking a moose. The two of them had been trailing it since the sun had risen over the treetops. It had been a long time since he'd been out hunting. Night Wind saw the new growth on the trees and the shoots coming out of the ground. The world was warming up, the sun stayed out longer each day. It made him feel glad that he was alive. He thought about the recent events that made him want to live again. Yesterday, Pakwis had sat by his fire. Night Wind told him about the vision he'd had.

For the fifth night in a row he had heard strange noises outside his wigwam. At first he didn't care, his heart was still too heavy. But the noises got louder and more persistent with each night. Anger slowly replaced the heartache. Night Wind had stormed out of his wigwam, spear in hand, ready to kill the beast who wouldn't leave him alone. Instead, he saw the image of his wife in the shadows. The noises had suddenly stopped as he stood there unable to comprehend what he was seeing.

Sleeping Rabbit smiled at him. "My husband. I do not wish for you to join me. Your journey has yet to begin. Live my husband. You are still needed."

Slowly, her image had faded away. Night Wind stayed where he was for several minutes, trying to make sense of what he had just witnessed. Then he wiped his eyes and returned to his wigwam. He opened his flap to see the shaman standing by his fire. Night Wind walked up to him. "That was your trick. Wasn't it?"

The shaman faced the warrior. "What trick? I just got here."

"Why? In the middle of the night, do you visit me?"

"If you decide to die, then Pakwis will lose the will to live. His wife and child will starve."

"No they will not. Little Blossom will find a new man to provide for her."

The shaman shrugged. "Maybe she will. Maybe she will not."

The warrior had stood by his fire and watched the shaman leave. He didn't move for several minutes later.

Night Wind turned his horse to face the trail behind him. Pakwis rode up the small incline and stopped beside Night Wind. "I think that moose has turned back toward the village."

Lucas steered the wagon onto a wider trail and smiled at his wife. Winda sat beside him looking at the wildflowers. Sam was riding beside them on his new horse. Except for the colour of his skin he looked like any other cowboy with his six-shooter and hat. He'd been officially adopted. And Lucas couldn't have been prouder. He had come to love Sam as his own. And Sam returned that love tenfold.

Lucas pointed. "Let's camp on that rise over there."

Sam kicked his horse and it galloped to the top of the rise. He was standing by a small fire he'd started when Lucas stopped the wagon and jumped down. "You're going to make a fine cowboy, son."

Sam just beamed at him as he headed to the back of the wagon for supplies. Lucas helped Winda down and gave her a kiss. "How are you doing?"

She smiled and shook her head. "You ask me that every day. I am fine, Lookas."

Sam walked up with the coffee pot and a sack. He set them by the fire as Lucas grabbed his rifle. "You stay here with your ma," he told Sam. "I'll see what I can get us for supper."

Sam nodded and tended to his fire. Winda filled the coffee pot with water from the barrel on the side of the wagon.

Lucas loaded his rifle then headed into a small thicket. It took him a while to find any decent tracks. He wanted something other than rabbit or wild turkey for a change. The deer tracks led down into a gully. Lucas followed them until he came to a clearing. But he stayed hidden in the trees. Someone else was cutting up his deer. An arrow stuck out of the dead animal's throat.

Three Mohawk warriors had a small fire going. One was cutting up the deer while the other two were drinking from a brown bottle. They must have gotten moonshine from somewhere. Lucas slowly backed up until he was far enough away, then he turned and ran back to his wagon.

Sam stood when he saw him. Lucas glanced behind him then said, "Put that fire out. We're leaving."

"What is it?" Winda asked as she gathered their belongings.

"Mohawk warriors. Drunk. Three of them."

Gert sat on her front porch sipping tea with her best friend, Dorothy; and watched a blue jay in the maple tree. "Carrie is at the dressmaker's right now, trying on her dress. It's almost done. Then I'm going to have a dress made."

"I bet she's getting excited." Dorothy picked up a lemon tart and bit into it.

"If you ask me, I think Grant is more excited than she is."

Dorothy fanned herself. "Well, if she doesn't want Grant Sievers, you can send him over to me."

Gert laughed and swatted Dorothy on the arm. "If only we were thirty years younger."

"You hear from his brother yet?"

"Yes. Anthony got a letter the other day saying they were half way here. So, by now they would be a lot closer. I can't wait to see Grant's face when Lucas shows up. I just hope they get here in time for the wedding." Gert picked up her second lemon tart and took a bite. After she swallowed she said, "It said in the letter that they've adopted Sam. The coloured boy I was telling you about."

Dorothy shook her head. "It will take a strong man to hold a family like that together."

"Oh, Lucas could do it. He's the wild brother. Used to live with Indians. I've met some of them." She smiled at Dorothy. "His wife, Winda, is the most beautiful Indian woman I've ever seen. And she can speak perfect English. Lucas has been teaching her."

"You like her. Don't you?"

"Yes. She's smart. Smarter than most white folk I've met. She helped Anthony and I after Dusty held us up that time. Made us feel at ease amongst those warriors. But it was those warriors and Lucas who caught Dusty. I'm glad he's dead."

"Likewise with Ivan."

Gert frowned as she thought about the money she and Anthony had taken out of the bank that Ivan had deposited. All of it had gone to the asylum in Kingston. She wondered how Mary was doing; missing her sister.

Carrie stood in front of a full length mirror in her wedding gown feeling like a princess. Aunt Gert had spared no expense and had let Carrie choose what she wanted. The dressmaker carefully set a lace veil on Carrie's head. Her hair would be put up on her big day. Today it was down and hung around her shoulders. Carrie thought about her fake wedding to Dusty. She had borrowed a dress that had been too big for her, it continuously fell off her shoulder and she kept tripping on it. Carrie closed her eyes and forced Dusty from her mind, telling herself that Grant was a better man and that she loved him.

After taking a deep breath she opened her eyes. The dressmaker was smiling as she adjusted the veil. Then she stood back to survey her creation. "Just beautiful."

Carrie focused on the mirror and noticed the glow in her cheeks. Was it true love this time, or because her fantasy was about to become a reality?

Now that the dress was completed, Carrie's dream of a formal wedding was about to take place. The dress had been made exactly how she'd described it. The dressmaker had made sketches, allowing Carrie to make changes until she was satisfied. She ran her hands down her sides, touching the several layers of satin of her ivory gown. It wasn't fancy, but it was elegant. The skirt was plain with a row of six satin bows running down the back. Hand-stitched lace covered the bodice over the silk. Twenty tiny pearl buttons ran from her waist to her neck. A row of buttons ran up to her elbow on each laced sleeve. Carrie knew she'd be cool in this dress no matter how hot the weather.

Her veil reached down to her tiny waist. It was made of the same lace pattern on her dress with scalloped edging. Carrie flicked her eyes over to the dressmaker. "Yes. It's beautiful."

Grant had moved out of the Paterson's house and stayed in a hotel three blocks away from Anthony's bank. It was to protect Carrie's reputation. Not everyone in York knew about Dusty and how he'd used Carrie. And Grant hoped to keep the gossip-mongers at bay by visiting her during the day and taking his leave early in the evenings.

He still taught the boys how to care for various weapons, like a musket and a pistol. Johnny had killed his first squirrel. And Adam had hit the target Grant had made, once. The boys were getting used to handling the weapons, more at ease with them.

Last week, Grant had taken the boys to a tailor's to get outfitted for the wedding. He didn't know much about boy's fashion so he ordered miniature outfits to match his. They would be dressed in linen shirts with ruffles down the front and breeches that stopped just below the knee, worn over long stockings. All three of them had been measured for greatcoats that would be made out of velvet. The boys would wear leather shoes. He'd have on new Hessian boots.

After they'd left the tailor's, Grant had taken the boys for ice cream. Johnny finished his bowl and set down his spoon. He smiled at Grant and said, "Dusty never did things like this with us."

Pakwis rode his horse up the hill then stopped between Night Wind and a scout. The scout had seen a Mohawk hunting party on Ojibwa land. The three of them left the horses then crawled up the remaining few yards to the top of the hill, keeping out of sight behind trees and large boulders. "Down there by the river," the scout pointed.

The Mohawks were on the other side of the river below a small waterfall. Five of them were eating as they sat around a small fire. Their horses were behind them being guarded by three youths. "I see two more in the trees to their left," Night Wind said.

"I do not see any canoes," Pakwis said.

"They came by horse," the scout said. "They did not bring a canoe this time."

Pakwis studied the camp below them for some time before they backed out of their hiding place. They gathered their horses and led them down the hill where they met up with the rest of their men. Pakwis said, "I think we should surround them. Half of us can cross the river over there," he indicated a spot where the river was wide and shallow, "while the rest of us will go down that way and cross over behind them."

Night Wind led the first group across the river on foot. After they were out of sight in the trees on the other side, Pakwis left two warriors to guard the horses before leading the rest of the men through the woods. Silently they made their way past the Mohawk then crossed the river downstream, well out of their sight. They were sneaking up to the camp when Pakwis saw a guard standing behind a tree looking out toward the river. Pakwis gestured to one of his men who nodded then crouched down as he made his way toward the guard. Minutes later, all Pakwis heard was a grunt. Then the Ojibwa warrior appeared and waved them onward.

When they were close to the camp, three warriors fanned out to sneak up behind the horses. The youths who were guarding them all had their throats slit before a call of alarm could be given. The Ojibwa inched closer to the fire. Pakwis couldn't see any of Night Wind's men. He went on faith and trust as they came to the clearing and squatted behind the trees.

There were nine Mohawk now as more had joined the ones at the fire. Pakwis was going to wait, to give Night Wind time to get situated. Then their numbers would be more evenly matched. Pakwis had four men with him. Night Wind had three. They'd been spotted. One of the Mohawk let out a war whoop as he charged at the Ojibwa. Pakwis and his warriors attacked, swinging clubs. This would be a hand-to-hand battle.

Pakwis attacked a man half his age, punching him in the face. The man staggered back a few steps then charged Pakwis with a knife in his hand. Pakwis jumped backward as the man sliced the air. The Mohawk grinned and stepped closer as one of his companions joined him. Pakwis glanced around and noticed that two of his men lay dead on the ground. There was no sign of Night Wind. He crouched and tried to keep both of his assailants within view. The one with the knife charged, slicing Pakwis across the arm. The second man jabbed Pakwis in the side with his knife. Pakwis felt his side then brought up his hand. Blood dripped from it He staggered sideways then fell to his knees.

Then he saw Night Wind rush toward the Mohawks with his club held high.

Grant beamed as Carrie walked down the aisle of the same church that she had married Dusty in. This time though, she was happy and giddy. She wore a beautiful, satin and lace gown that fit perfectly. Her hair was done up with pearls in it that matched her necklace and earrings that Grant had given her as a wedding gift. She smiled broadly through happy tears as her uncle led her down the aisle toward him.

Grant stood transfixed, waiting for her. He had on a navy suit fashioned in the latest style. Adam stood beside him bobbing up and down, excitedly. Johnny stood next to him, fidgeting in his new clothes.

He could hear Gert, sitting in the front seat with her best friend, Dorothy. "This is how it should be."

Dorothy wiped her eyes. "She's so beautiful, Gert. Look how happy she is." She sniffled. "Nothing like the last time."

"I know she will be very happy this time too, Dorothy," Gert beamed. "And this time we have our own reverend too. We know this wedding will be legal."

Carrie stopped beside him. Everyone in the packed church bowed in prayer. Reverend Bates blessed the couple. Adam and Johnny handed out the rings for Carrie and Grant to slide onto each other's hands. Cheers erupted when they kissed as man and wife.

"I love you, Carrie," Grant kissed her again.

She squeezed his hand and smiled, her eyes sparkling.

Grant grinned as Johnny tugged on Carrie's dress.

Carrie looked down. Johnny was smirking up at her. "Don't I count, Carrie?"

Immediately, she bent down and smacked him on the lips. "You are very handsome today, Johnny." Turning to Adam, she did the same. "You both did such a good job , looking after our rings. That was a big responsibility. I'm proud of both of you."

They both beamed under the praise. "Can I take my topcoat off now? It's too hot," complained Adam.

Carrie laughed. "You both can if you want."

Their topcoats flew off before they were engulfed in the well-wishers.

Anthony pulled Grant aside. "I am glad you finally talked her into it. I know you'll be good for her, Grant. You don't know what a relief it is to finally see her truly in love and so happy."

"I'll do my best to keep it that way, Anthony. Don't worry about that."

"Gert was afraid that she'd fall for someone like, like, well, you know." Anthony patted Grant's shoulder.

"Yes, I know. I was afraid of that too."

Grant walked over and kissed Gert's cheek. "Welcome to the family, Grant," she told him. "I hope you two will be as happy as we have been in our marriage."

"Thank you. This means a lot to me."

Only one thing would have made this day perfect. Grant looked through the crowd. Not seeing what he was hoping to find, his heart sank.

Minutes later a tap on Grant's shoulder made him turn around to face yet another well-wisher, except this one was different. Lucas stood beaming about as much as the groom. "Lucas! You're here." Grant gave his brother a big hug.

"I wouldn't miss this for the world, brother." Lucas patted Grant's back.

"I'm so glad you came. How did you know? It all happened so fast. Then that means you missed the letter I sent you."

"Slow down, Grant," Lucas laughed. "We came as soon as we got word. Carrie's uncle sent us a special post."

"I didn't think you'd have enough time to get here after she finally said yes. I wanted to get married as soon as possible in case she fled again." Grant's eyes narrowed. "You still wouldn't have enough time. Would you?"

Lucas threw up his hands. "You're right. It still would have taken another couple weeks, at least. I've been in touch with Carrie's uncle. When Anthony told me that you were winning Carrie over, well it was obvious. So we packed up and started this way. We were already half way here when we got the message saying when the wedding was."

"Well, I'm just glad you're here." Grant shook his head and laughed. "What do you mean us?"

Lucas pointed to the pew behind a small crowd. Winda sat smiling up at them. "Oh." Grant rushed over and Winda stood. "Wow. You're huge. I'm sorry Winda."

She laughed and kissed Grant. "It is all right, I have gained so much. I can hardly waddle anymore."

A screech from behind erupted as Carrie rushed over and hugged Winda and Lucas. "Now this is perfect, isn't it?" she cried. "I was hoping you'd make it."

Grant looked at her. "You knew?"

Carrie kissed him. "Yep. You're not the only one with secrets, my husband."

"Uncle Lucas." Adam threw himself around the man's waist. "Glad you came. I missed you."

Lucas hugged Adam then Johnny when he ran up to them.

Johnny had gone up to Winda first. "Is there only one in there?" he asked, pointing to the huge belly.

"Yes, as far as I can tell right now, Johnny." But when she straightened she said, "I feel too many kicks from just one child."

Carrie turned to find Sam next to her. "Oh, Sam." She hugged him. "Now we are all together."

"Congratulations, Carrie." His hug was long and tight. "Lucas and Grant are a lot alike, you know?" he informed her. "They are both good men."

"Thank you, Sam." She looked at him as if wondering what brought that on. "You are wise beyond your years, you know?" Sam beamed at her.

Grant put his arm around the young black man. "Thanks for coming, Sam. I have something for you. It's back at the house, though."

Anthony squeezed into the small crowd. "You are all coming back to the house. We have a banquet waiting."

Grant noticed that most of the guests had dissipated.

Gert stepped up to give everyone hugs and kisses. "I'm so glad you all made it." She gave Winda an extra pat on the belly. "You take care of yourself now, Winda. I lost all three of my babies. All stillborn." Gert turned away. Grant figured she was trying not to dwell on her loss and make herself depressed. "That was a long time ago," he heard Gert say.

"Let's go and eat!" Anthony interrupted. "I'm starving." To Lucas, he asked, "You're staying at our place. Right?"

After a festive wedding banquet, everyone sat around in Anthony's parlour with various drinks in their hands. Adam and Johnny had gladly gone to bed after such an exciting and busy day. They were both exhausted and it was getting late. Lucas knew that Sam was waiting for his surprise from Grant, who reached into a drawer in the sideboard and pulled out an envelope. "This is your reward for helping us bring Dusty in, Sam," Grant said.

Sam opened the envelope and peeked inside, his eyes widened. "This is more money than I could even imagine having all at once. In my whole lifetime, even." He looked at Grant. "Uncle Grant, this is, this is," he stuttered. "Thank you." Sam flopped back in his chair, tears in his eyes. Clutching the envelope to his chest. "I can't even count that high."

"I didn't know there was a reward," Lucas whispered to his brother.

"There wasn't. I just thought he should have gotten something."

"Thanks, Grant. For thinking of him."

"You make sure that is put in a safe place," coaxed Winda, who then laughed. "Well. I know this banker, see."

Everyone laughed at her reference to Anthony, who cleared his throat. "Yes, good idea. You should put it into safe keeping for awhile, earn some interest on it."

Lucas looked at his brother. "How much is in there?"

"Three-hundred dollars."

Everyone froze, astonished at such a high amount.

"Ya," Lucas choked. "You better put it into the bank. Then when you are old enough, it will give you a good start in life, Sam."

"I will, Dad." Sam was still in shock. "I want to buy a store or something like that."

"Good for you, Sam," encouraged Winda. "But right now, I think you should turn in, okay?" He handed the envelope to Lucas and watched when his dad put it into his pocket, as if he still couldn't comprehend having that much money.

Sam nodded and went upstairs to climb in with the other boys in one big bed. "Good night," he called back to everyone. Then he stopped halfway up the stairs. "I love my new family."

Gert yawned and told everyone she was turning in. Anthony followed close behind. Lucas had told Winda that he wanted to talk to Grant, so she went upstairs to help Carrie out of her wedding dress before they went to bed.

"Dusty did have a will drawn up, Grant." Lucas poured another shot of rum into his glass. "Everything is to be divided among the boys." He turned to face his brother. "All three of them."

Grant clutched at his chest, spilling his drink. "All three of them? You mean Sam too?"

"Yep! Seems Dusty was telling him the truth. For once."

"Well, I'll be." Grant let out a whistle. "I doubted that Sam's mother would have gone to him willingly. Why didn't Dusty say anything before that time on the trail?"

"I don't know. Maybe it's why he didn't make Sam a slave, and just let him be, instead." Lucas sat down in an overstuffed chair. "Even though, by law, he would be free now anyway."

"But this all happened long before the slaves were freed. Is that what Jeb had over him?" Grant refilled his glass and sat next to Lucas.

"Another thing. Beings the boys have to be twenty-five and married to get their shares, they need a legal guardian to look after their affairs."

"Well, isn't Carrie their legal guardian? Adam's and Johnny's, I mean."

"Sort of. No, not legal. She's not their real mother. And anything she owns becomes yours too, now." Lucas shook his head. "It doesn't seem fair does it?"

"Then they lose everything?" Grant shook his head.

"Not necessary. You will need to adopt the boys, as we have legally adopted Sam." He gave a short chuckle. "Before I even found out about this." He lifted his glass. "Then two thirds of his holdings would go into your name until the boys come of age."

"By why do they have to be married? This is unusual, isn't it?"

"I wondered about that too. But it is in the will and we can't dispute it." Lucas yawned. "Maybe it has to do with Dusty's aversion to women."

"What all does Dusty own, anyway?" Grant's eyes lit up.

Lucas watched his brother. *Seems to me, he's getting a little greedy here.* "Well, we know about the cabin. He also owned his farm, the sawmill, and the tavern." Lucas stood and headed upstairs. "We will have to see who can get what, when they turn of age." He went up to bed, leaving Grant in the dark to ponder it all over.

Carrie waited in bed upstairs for her new husband. She knew that he was downstairs talking to Lucas, discussing family matters. *This is our wedding night. And he spends it with his brother?* She had put on a sexy gown for this occasion. Lucas softly closed his bedroom door a half hour ago. *What's taking Grant so long? Doesn't he want me? Does he want me?* The last question frightened her. *What if he was like Dusty?* She scolded herself. "Don't let Dusty ruin this for you too." *Even from his grave, he haunts me.*

Grant entered the room silently. "Carrie, you awake?"

Her eyelids fluttered open. "What?"

He slid into bed beside her and kissed her. She smiled tiredly at him.

"Sorry I took so long. I didn't realize it was so late." He snuggled closer and slid his hand under the covers to rub her breasts. She froze, her body stiffening.

Grant recoiled. "What the?" He watched her frightened eyes. "Carrie." He tried again more gently. "I will never hurt you."

. I know that, Grant." She couldn't bring herself

Grant took his time with her. He talked to her and caressed her until she felt new sensations flutter through her body. She knew she didn't respond to him as he had hoped she would. His hand slipped between her legs and rubbed her there. She just lay there, unable to return the passion.

"Please, Carrie. I need you." Grant finally climbed on top of his wife and made love to her. She stiffened slightly. But she tried to hide it. He was gentle and lasted longer than Dusty ever had. Still Carrie couldn't respond to his touch. She knew she had disappointed him, even though he held her after he was done.

"I love you, Carrie." Grant hugged her and let her cry herself to sleep.

The next morning, Carrie woke up in an empty room stretching and yawning. The more she thought about the night before, the more disgusted she was of herself. Grant had tried to get her to enjoy making love with him. She realized that there was a difference between making love and having sex. With Dusty it was just sex. Raw and brutal. Grant was trying to make love to her.

She liked the feeling that Grant sent throughout her whole body. It scared her. She didn't know what to do with the new sensations that made her feel good. She was use to being taken roughly. But Grant wanted to please her. She had let him down; she saw it in his face last night. He was disappointed in her. *I have to try. I just have to relax and enjoy it.*

Grant entered the room carrying a tray. He set in on a table and handed her a plate and fork. She scurried to sit up. "Thank you, Grant. I certainly didn't expect this."

The smile he gave her didn't reach his eyes. "You're welcome, Mrs. Sievers." He sat on the side of the bed and watched her eat her breakfast. When she was done, he took her plate and set it aside.

He presented her with a bouquet of wild flowers, some with the roots still attached. "These are from Adam and Johnny," he laughed.

"They're lovely." She started to get up. Grant eased her back down. "We are spending our wedding day right here. Everyone else has gone out for the day. We have the house to ourselves."

The full meaning of what he just said slowly sank into her head. She knew exactly what he had in mind. Her mouth formed an *O*. He didn't give her time to react.

Grant undressed quickly and jumped into bed. He kissed her deeply and stayed there for what seemed like hours just stroking her. He watched her reactions as new sensations took over her body. Carrie knew when her mind gave in to him. Finally she was responding to him. Her hands were all over him. "Oh Carrie, that's right, keep going. You got it."

Tears welled up in his eyes. "You're mine now, Carrie."